THE SOLDIER SPIES

ALSO BY W.E.B. GRIFFIN

HONOR BOUND
HONOR BOUND
BLOOD AND HONOR

BROTHERHOOD OF WAR
BOOK I: THE LIEUTENANTS
BOOK II: THE CAPTAINS
BOOK III: THE MAJORS
BOOK IV: THE COLONELS
BOOK V: THE BERETS
BOOK VI: THE GENERALS
BOOK VII: THE NEW BREED
BOOK VIII: THE AVIATORS

THE CORPS
BOOK I: SEMPER FI
BOOK II: CALL TO ARMS
BOOK III: COUNTERATTACK
BOOK IV: BATTLEGROUND
BOOK V: LINE OF FIRE
BOOK VI: CLOSE COMBAT
BOOK VII: BEHIND THE LINES
BOOK VIII: IN DANGER'S PATH

BADGE OF HONOR
BOOK I: MEN IN BLUE
BOOK II: SPECIAL OPERATIONS
BOOK III: THE VICTIM
BOOK IV: THE WITNESS
BOOK V: THE ASSASSIN
BOOK VI: THE MURDERERS
BOOK VII: THE INVESTIGATORS

MEN AT WAR
BOOK I: THE LAST HEROES
BOOK II: THE SECRET WARRIORS

W.E.B. GRIFFIN

THE SOLDIER SPIES

ORIGINALLY PUBLISHED UNDER THE PSEUDONYM
ALEX BALDWIN

G. P. PUTNAM'S SONS
NEW YORK

This novel is a work of fiction. Names, characters, places,
and incidents are either the product of the author's
imagination or are used fictitiously. Any
resemblance to actual events or
locales or persons, living or dead,
is entirely coincidental.

G. P. Putnam's Sons
Publishers Since 1838
a member of
Penguin Putnam Inc.
375 Hudson Street
New York, NY 10014

Library of Congress Cataloging-in-Publication Data
Griffin, W.E.B.
The soldier spies / by W.E.B. Griffin.
p.   cm.
"Originally published under the pseudonym Alex Baldwin."
ISBN 0-399-14494-3 (acid-free paper)
1. World War, 1939-1945—Secret Service—United States—
Fiction.   2. United States. Office of Strategic Services—
Fiction.   I. Title.
PS3557.R489137S55   1999   98-33260 CIP
813'.54—dc21

Printed in the United States of America

1   3   5   7   9   10   8   6   4   2

This book is printed on acid-free paper. ∞

BOOK DESIGN BY JENNIFER ANN DADDIO

*For Lieutenant Aaron Bank, Infantry, AUS, detailed OSS
(later, Colonel, Special Forces)
and
Lieutenant William E. Colby, Infantry, AUS, detailed OSS
(later, Ambassador and Director, CIA)*

*They set the standards, as Jedburgh Team Leaders
operating in German-occupied France and Norway, for
valor, wisdom, patriotism, and personal integrity
that thousands who followed in their steps
in the OSS and CIA tried to emulate.*

THE SOLDIER SPIES

I

[ONE]
Marburg an der Lahn, Germany
8 November 1942

On the night of November 7, Obersturmführer-SS-SD Wilhelm Peis, a tall, pale, blond man of twenty-eight, who was the senior Sicherheitsdienst (SS Security Service) officer in Marburg an der Lahn, received the following message by Teletype from Berlin:

YOU WILL PLEASE TAKE ALL NECESSARY STEPS TO ENSURE THE SECU-
RITY OF REICHSMINISTER ALBERT SPEER AND A PERSONAL STAFF OF
FOUR WHO WILL MAKE AN UNPUBLICIZED VISIT TO THE FULMAR ELEK-
TRISCHES WERK AT MARBURG 8 NOVEMBER. THE REICHSMINISTER WILL
ARRIVE BY PRIVATE TRAIN AT 10:15 AND DEPART IN THE SAME MANNER
AT APPROXIMATELY 15:45.

The message from Berlin seemed more or less routine to Peis, and he at first treated it as such until early in the morning of the eighth when Gauleiter Karl-Heinz Schroeder—in a state somewhere between chagrin and panic—burst into Peis's sleeping quarters (Peis was not in fact asleep) and pointedly reminded him that not only had Speer taken the place of Dr. Fritz Todt as head of the Todt Organization—in charge of all industrial production, military and civilian—which made him one of the most powerful men in Germany, but that he was a *personal* friend, perhaps the *closest* personal friend—of the Führer himself.

The intensity of Schroeder's concern impelled Peis to double his efforts on behalf of welcoming the Reichsminister, and he rounded up half a dozen Mercedes, Horch, and Opel Admiral automobiles to carry Speer from the railroad station to the Fulmar Electric Plant—or wherever else he might wish to go. He canceled all leave for the police and the SD. And he dressed in a new uniform.

By this time Peis was less motivated by the concerns of the Gauleiter than by more pressing and personal concerns of his own:

The Reichsminister would certainly be accompanied by a senior SS officer—at least an Obersturmbannführer (Lieutenant Colonel) and possibly even an Oberführer (Senior Colonel). If this officer found fault with his security arrangements for Reichsminister Speer, Peis could start packing his bags with his warmest clothes. There was always a shortage of Obersturmführers on the Eastern Front, and a long list of SS officers already there who had earned a sweet sinecure like the SS-SD detachment in Marburg an der Lahn. Peis had long before decided that it was far better to be a big fish in a little pond than the other way around.

Peis set up his security arrangements at about seven in the morning, soon after Schroeder had left him; he personally checked his arrangements twice; and he was at the Hauptbahnhof forty-five minutes before the scheduled arrival of the private train.

The train itself, though it rolled into the station on schedule to the minute, was otherwise a disappointment. To start with, it wasn't actually a train. It was one car, self-propelled—not much more than a streetcar. And there were no senior SS officers to be impressed with the way Peis had handled his responsibilities. Only Reichsminister Speer and three others—all civilians, one a woman—stepped out of the car.

And even Speer himself wasn't in uniform. He was wearing a business suit and looked like any other civilian.

After the Reichsminister and his party reached the platform, Karl-Heinz Schroeder, wearing his best party uniform, marched up and gave a stiff-armed Nazi salute, then launched into his welcoming speech. Speer made a vague gesture with his hand in reply to the salute and cut Schroeder off at about word five.

"Very good of you to say so, Herr Gauleiter," Speer said, and then went quickly on. "I had hoped that Professor Dyer would be able to meet us."

From the look on Schroeder's face, it was obvious to Peis that Schroeder had never heard of Professor Dyer.

Peis had.

Unless there were two Professor Dyers, which was highly unlikely, Reichsminister Speer desired the company of a man who had one foot in a *Konzentrationslager* (concentration camp) and the other on a banana peel.

"Forgive me, Herr Reichsminister," Schroeder said. "Professor Dyer?"

And then, Peis thought, Schroeder finally put his brain in gear. "Perhaps Obersturmführer Peis can help you. Peis!"

Peis marched over and saluted.

Speer smiled at Peis. "There was supposed to have been a message sent—" he began.

"I sent it, Herr Speer," the woman said.

Speer nodded.

"—requesting Professor Friedrich Dyer to meet with me."

"I have received no such message, Herr Reichsminister," Peis said. "But I think I know where he can be found."

"And could you bring him?" Speer asked.

"If I may be so bold as to suggest, Herr Reichsminister?" Peis said.

"Of course," Speer replied.

"While you and your party accompany the Gauleiter, I'll see if I can find Professor Dyer for you and take him to the Fulmar plant."

"Good man!" Speer smiled and clutched Peis's arm. "It's quite important. I can't imagine what happened to the telegram."

"I'll do my best, Herr Reichsminister," Peis said.

Peis hurried to the stationmaster's office and grabbed the telephone. He dialed the number from memory.

Gisella Dyer, the daughter (and the only reason Professor Dyer was not making gravel from boulders in a KZ somewhere), answered the phone on the third ring.

"How are you, Gisella?" Peis asked.

"Very well, thank you, Herr Sturmbannführer," she said, warily. Peis understood her lack of enthusiasm. But she wasn't the reason for his call today.

"Do you know where I can find your father?" he asked.

He heard her suck in her breath, and it was a moment before she spoke again. She was carefully considering her reply. Peis knew that she would have preferred that Peis direct his attentions toward her not because she liked him (she despised him), but because as long as Peis liked her, her father stayed out of the KZ.

"He's at the university," she said finally, with a slight tremor in her voice. "Is there something wrong, Herr Sturmbannführer?"

"Where exactly at the university?"

Gisella Dyer considered that, too, before she replied.

"In his office, I imagine," she said. "He doesn't have another class until four this afternoon." She paused, then asked again, "Is there something wrong?"

"Official business, Gisella," Peis said, and hung up.

It would be useful for Gisella to worry a little, Peis thought. She tended to be arrogant, to forget her position. Periodically, it was necessary to cut her down to size.

Peis found Professor Friedrich Dyer where his daughter had said he would be, in his book-and-paper-cluttered room in one of the ancient buildings in the center of the university campus. He was a tall, thin, sharp-featured man; and he looked cold, even though he was well covered. He wore a thick, tightly buttoned cardigan under his many-times-patched tweed jacket and a woolen shawl over his shoulders. The ancient buildings were impossible to heat, even when there was fuel.

Professor Dyer looked at Peis with chilling contempt, but he said nothing and offered no greeting.

"Heil Hitler!" Peis said, more because he knew Dyer hated the salute than out of any Nazi zeal of his own.

"Heil Hitler, Herr Peis," the professor said.

"I wasn't aware you are acquainted with Reichsminister Albert Speer, Professor," Peis said.

"I gather he's here," Dyer said.

The professor was not surprised, and this surprised Peis.

"You were supposed to meet him at the station," Peis said.

"No," the dignified academic said simply. "The telegram said only that the Reichsminister would be here and wanted to see me."

"What about?"

"I really have no idea," Professor Dyer said.

Is that the truth? Peis wondered. *Or is the professor taking advantage of his association with the head of the Todt Organization and trying to impress me?*

"He is at the Fulmar Electric Plant," Peis said. "I am here to take you to him."

Professor Dyer nodded, then rose and with difficulty put his tweed-and-sweater-thick arms into the sleeves of an old, fur-collared overcoat. When he had finished struggling into it, the two top buttons would not fasten. He shrugged helplessly, set an old and shaggy fur cap on his head, and indicated that he was ready to go.

The university was in the center of Marburg atop the hill, and the Fulmar Elektrisches Werk was about ten minutes north of town. It was an almost new, sprawling, windowless, oblong building with camouflage netting strung across it. The netting was intended to blend the plant into the steep hills around Marburg to make it invisible from the air.

The plant had no guards now, but that was to change, Peis knew, as of the first of December. (The coming change sparked considerable curiosity in Peis: What were they going to make in there that required all that security?) The local SS-SD office (that is to say, Peis) had been ordered to dig up before December enough "cleared" civilians to handle the security job. If he could not provide enough "cleared" civilians, the police would have to provide the guard force, at the expense of whatever else they were supposed to be doing.

Meanwhile, a substantial guardhouse had been built. And a nearly completed eight-foot fence, topped with barbed wire, surrounded the plant property. At hundred-yard intervals there were guard towers, with floodlights to illuminate the fence.

Peis found Reichsminister Albert Speer and his party by driving around until he discovered the little convoy of "borrowed" automobiles.

Speer was inside a work bay. The bay was half full of milling machines and lathes, and there were provisions for more. As soon as he saw Peis and Professor Dyer, Speer walked over to them. He was smiling, and his hand was extended.

"Professor Doktor Dyer?" Speer asked.

"Herr Speer?" Dyer replied, making a bow of his head and offering his hand.

"I'm very pleased to meet you," Speer said. "I've been reading with great interest your paper on the malleability of tungsten carbide."

"Which paper?" Dyer asked, on the edge of rudeness. "There have been several."

"The one you delivered at Dresden," Speer answered, seemingly ignoring Dyer's tone.

"That was the last," Dyer said.

Speer looked at Peis the way he would look at a servant.

"We will be an hour," Speer said, dismissing him, "perhaps a little longer. Could I impose further on your kindness and ask you to arrange for Professor Dyer to be returned afterward to wherever he wishes?"

"It will be my pleasure, Herr Reichsminister," Peis said.

"You are very kind," Speer said.

"I am at your service, Herr Reichsminister," Peis said.

Since there was time before he had to retrieve his car, Peis walked the new fence surrounding the plant. The professional cop in him liked what he saw. In his judgment, whoever had set up the fence knew what he was doing. It would be difficult for any undesirable to get into the plant area. Or to get out of it.

He noticed too, on his journey of inspection, that the fence enclosed an open area large enough to build laborer barracks. He had heard that the Todt Organization was recruiting laborers from France, Belgium, the Netherlands—and even from the East—to work in German industry. They could not, of course, be permitted to roam freely around Germany.

After his tour, he settled into his Mercedes-Benz and started the engine. It was a waste of fuel, but he wanted the engine running anyway, partly because he intended to turn on the radios (unless the engine was running, the radios quickly drained the battery), but primarily because it was cold: Whatever the virtues of the Mercedes' diesel engine, it was a sonofabitch to start when it was cold. He did not want Reichsminister Speer to remember him as the SS officer whose car couldn't be made to run. Peis himself didn't mind some additional warmth either.

Over the shortwave radio, Peis checked in with both his headquarters and the detachment guarding the Reichminister's railcar at the Bahnhof. He then tuned in Radio Frankfurt on the civilian band radio.

The news was that the Wehrmacht in Russia continued to adjust its lines and inflict heavy casualties upon the enemy. But then there was a surprise:

In blatant violation of international law, at four that morning, United States naval, air, and ground forces had started shelling and bombing French North Africa. Later, an American invasion force was sent ashore on both Atlantic and Mediterranean beaches. Terrible casualties were inflicted upon innocent, neutral civilians, etc., etc., etc.

The invasion was obviously successful, Peis concluded. Otherwise, the announcer would have gleefully proclaimed that it had been thrown back into the sea.

Why didn't the Americans mind their own damned business? Peis wondered. Germany had no real quarrel with America. What the hell did they want with French North Africa, anyhow? There was nothing there but sand and Arabs riding around on camels.

And then he remembered that he actually knew somebody in French North Africa, a policeman like himself: Obersturmbannführer SS-SD (Lieutenant Colonel) Johann Müller, who had been raised on a farm in Kolbe not three miles from where Peis sat, was on the staff of the Franco-German Armistice Commission for Morocco.

Müller, who came home to see his mother from time to time, had once been a simple *Wachtmann* (Patrolman) on the Kreis Marburg police. But he had been smart enough to join the Nazi Party early on, and he had been transferred to Berlin and commissioned in the SS-SD. And now he was a big shot.

Who just might, Peis thought, *spend the rest of the war in an American POW cage. But better that,* Peis decided, *than the Eastern Front.*

It was an hour and a half before he saw Professor Friedrich Dyer walking toward the car.

"You won't mind, Professor, if I see the Reichsminister safely onto his train?" Peis said when Dyer had gotten into the car.

"We all must do our duty," Dyer said dryly.

Peis discreetly followed the Reichsminister's convoy to the Hauptbahnhof.

On the way from the Hauptbahnhof to the university, Peis asked, as casually as he could, "What did Reichsminister Speer want with you?"

There was no reply for a moment, as Dyer considered his response.

"We spoke of the molecular structure of tungsten carbon alloys," Dyer finally said. "Specifically, the effect of high temperatures on their dimensions, and the difficulties encountered in their machining."

Peis had no idea what that meant, and he suspected that Dyer, aware of that, was rubbing his ignorance in his face. Yesterday, the professor would not have dared antagonize him. But they both knew that things had changed.

"I have no idea what that means," Peis admitted. And then he changed the subject before Dyer had a chance to reply: "Radio Frankfurt just said the Americans have invaded North Africa."

"Really?"

"You're an educated man, Professor," Peis said. "Why would the Americans want North Africa?"

"No telling," Professor Dyer said. And then he added, "You must remember, Herr Obersturmführer, that the Americans are crazy."

"Why do you say that?"

"Well, for one thing, they believe they can win this war," Dyer said. "Wouldn't you say that makes them crazy?"

Peis's face tightened as he realized that the professor had mocked him again. And his anger grew as he realized that there was absolutely nothing he could do about it.

Peis did manage a parting shot, however. As the professor was about to slip out of the car, Peis stopped him with his hand and gave him a knowing, confidential look. "Do please give my very best regards to Fräulein Dyer," he said through his very best smile.

Professor Dyer had no reply to make to that.

[TWO]
Ksar es Souk, Morocco
0700 Hours
9 November 1942

The palace of the Pasha of Ksar es Souk was pentagonal. It was half a millennium older than the nearly completed world's largest office building, the Pentagon, in Washington, D.C., and bore little resemblance to it. But it was unarguably five-sided, and it pleased the somewhat droll sense of humor of Eric Fulmar to think of the palace as "The Desert Pentagon."

There were five observation towers at each angle of the Desert Pentagon. Over the centuries, lookouts had reported from these the approach of camel caravans, tribes of nomads, armies of hostile sheikhs and pashas—and in more recent times, patrols and detachments of the French Foreign Legion and the German Wehrmacht.

Today, there was nothing in sight on the desert in any direction, and it was possible to see a little over seven miles.

Eric Fulmar, who was tall, blond, and rather good-looking, sat in the northwest tower of the Desert Pentagon holding a small cup of black coffee. Except for olive-drab trousers and parachutist's boots, he wore Berber attire, robes and a burnoose. The cords around his waist, as well as those holding the burnoose to his head, were embroidered in gold, the identification of a nobleman.

Depending on whether his dossier was read in Washington, D.C., or in

Berlin, Germany, he was 2nd Lieutenant FULMAR, Eric, Infantry, Army of the United States, or Eric von Fulmar, Baron Kolbe.

The chair he sat in was at least two hundred years old. He had tipped it back and was balancing on its rear legs. His feet rested on the railing of the tower. Beside him on the stone floor was a graceful silver coffeepot with a long, curving spout. Beside it was a bottle of Courvoisier cognac. His coffee was liberally braced with the cognac.

Next to the coffeepot was a pair of Ernst Leitz, Wetzlar, 8-power binoculars resting on a leather case. And next to that was a Thompson .45-caliber ACP machine-pistol—which is to say, a Thompson equipped with a pair of handgrips, rather than a forearm and a stock. The Thompson had a fifty-round drum magazine.

Fulmar leaned over and picked up the Ernst Leitz binoculars and carefully studied the horizon in the direction of Ourzazate. He was hoping to see the cloud of dust an automobile would raise.

When he saw nothing, he put the binoculars down, then leaned to the other side of the chair, where he'd placed a Zenith battery-powered portable radio. He turned it on, and a torrent of Arabic flowed out.

Fulmar listened a moment, then smiled and started to chuckle.

It was an American broadcast, probably from Gibraltar, a message from Franklin Delano Roosevelt, President of the United States, to the Arabic-speaking population of Morocco.

"Behold, the lionhearted American warriors have arrived," the announcer solemnly proclaimed. "Speak with our fighting men and you will find them pleasing to the eye and gladdening to the heart."

"You bet your ass," Fulmar said, chuckling.

"Look in their eyes and smiling faces," the announcer continued, "for they are holy warriors happy in their sacred work. If you see our German or Italian enemies marching against us, kill them with guns or knives or stones—or any other weapon that you have set your hands upon."

"Like a camel turd, for example," Fulmar offered helpfully.

"The day of freedom has come!" the announcer dramatically concluded.

"Not quite," Fulmar replied. "Almost, but not quite."

He was thinking of his own freedom. Second Lieutenant Fulmar was at the moment the bait in a trap. Well, there again, not quite. Some very responsible people considered it likely that the bait—whether through cowardice, enlightened self-interest, or simply ineptitude—would, so to speak, stand up in the trap and wave the sniffing rat away. The bait himself kind of liked that idea.

That, of course, hadn't been the way they had explained the job to him. In several little pep talks they'd assured him they were *totally* confident that he could carry this "responsibility" off. But Fulmar's lifelong experience with those in authority had taught him otherwise.

Fulmar had his current situation pretty well figured out. It was kind of like a chess game. From the time he had received his first chess set, a Christmas gift from his mother's employer when he was ten, he had been fascinated with the game—and intrigued by the ways it paralleled life. In life, for instance, just as in chess, pawns were cheerfully sacrificed when it seemed that would benefit the more powerful pieces.

In this game, he was a white pawn. And he was being used as bait in the capture of two of the enemy's pieces, whom Fulmar thought of as a bishop and a knight. The problem was that the black bishop and knight were accompanied by a number of other pawns both black and white.

If the game went as planned (here Life and Chess differed), the bishop and the knight would change sides. And the white pawn wearing the second lieutenant's gold bar would be promoted to knight. If something went wrong, the second lieutenant pawn and the black pawns (who didn't even know they were in play) would be swept from the board (or—according to the rules of *this* game—shot) and the remaining players would continue the game.

The bishop was a man named Helmut von Heurten-Mitnitz, a Pomeranian aristocrat presently serving as the senior officer of the Franco-German Armistice Commission for Morocco. His knight was Obersturmbannführer SS-SD Johann Müller, presently serving as the Security Adviser to the Franco-German Armistice Commission.

Helmut von Heurten-Mitnitz, who had been educated at Harvard and had once been the German Consul General in New Orleans, had not long before established contact with Robert Murphy, the American Consul General for Morocco.

Von Heurten-Mitnitz informed Murphy then that he was convinced Germany was in the hands of a madman and that the only salvation he saw for Germany was its quick defeat by the Western Powers. He was therefore prepared, he said, to do whatever was necessary to see that Germany lost the war as quickly as possible.

The German diplomat went on to tell Murphy that Obersturmbann-führer Müller, for his own reasons, had come to the same conclusion and was similarly offering his services: Through his own "official" sources, Müller had come into knowledge of the atrocities committed by the SS "Special Squads" on the Eastern Front and of the extermination camps operated at several locations by the SS. Müller was a professional policeman, and he was shocked by what the SS was doing (it was not only inhuman, it was unprofessional).

Also, Müller understood that his one great ambition in life—to retire to the Hessian farm where he had been born—would not be possible if he were tried as a war criminal and hanged.

This being not only the real world, but also the real world at war, Helmut von Heurten-Mitnitz's noble offer could not be accepted at face value. His intentions had to be tested. He was offered a choice: He could do a job for the Americans, at genuine risk to himself; or he could choose to satisfy other needs.

Enter the pawns:

There were in French Morocco a number of French officers, Army, Service de l'aire, and Navy, who did not regard it as their duty to obey the terms of the Franco-German Armistice. Rather, they saw it as their duty as officers to continue the fight against Germany. These officers had provided considerable information and other assistance to curious Americans. And they were fully aware that what they were doing was considered treason.

Helmut von Heurten-Mitnitz's controller told him that he would be expected to round up twenty "treasonous" French officers whom the Americans wished to protect from French forces loyal to Vichy, and from the Germans themselves, and take them to the palace of the Pasha of Ksar es Souk, where they would be turned over to an American officer.

The American officer was to be parachuted into Morocco shortly before the invasion began. As soon as possible *after* the ships of the American force appeared off the Moroccan coast, he would contact Helmut von Heurten-Mitnitz to furnish the names of the twenty officers.

Finally, Helmut von Heurten-Mitnitz was informed that the American officer's name was Second Lieutenant Eric Fulmar. Von Heurten-Mitnitz would not fail to take note of this. A U.S. Army second lieutenant, even one assigned to the Office of Strategic Services, was small potatoes. But Second Lieutenant Fulmar, Infantry, United States Army, held dual citizenship. His father, the Baron von Fulmar, was not only highly placed in the Nazi Party, but was General Director of Fulmar Elektrische G.m.b.H.

For months Eric Fulmar had been a thorn in the side of his father and of many highly placed Party officials. When the war began, Eric had been a student of electrical engineering at the University of Marburg an der Lahn. But he had not remained in Germany to accept his duty to don a uniform to fight for the Fatherland. Young Fulmar's departure was of course seen as a mighty thumbing of his nose at the Thousand-Year Reich. In other words, he was a messy embarrassment to his father and the Party.

Worse yet, he had not dignified his desertion by going to the United States. That could have been more or less explained. But he had gone to Morocco, of all places, as the guest of his classmate, Sidi Hassan el Ferruch, Pasha of Ksar es Souk.

Once there, he promptly made matters even worse by entering into the profitable business of smuggling gold, currency, and precious gems out of France through Morocco. His American passport and a diplomatic passport issued to him by the Pasha of Ksar es Souk saved him from arrest and prosecution.

When Helmut von Heurten-Mitnitz was named to the Franco-German Armistice Commission, one of his missions had been to see that young Fulmar was returned to Germany. His best efforts (really those of Obersturmbannführer Müller) had been to no avail. And when the Americans entered the war—when he could have been arrested without offending American neutrality—Eric von Fulmar had simply disappeared.

In the American vernacular, then, Helmut von Heurten-Mitnitz and Obersturmbannführer Müller were now offered the choice of putting up or shutting up.

The easiest thing for them would be to round up the twenty French officers and Baron Eric Fulmar and accept the congratulations of their superiors. It was hoped, of course, that, as their contribution to a quick end to the war, they would take the twenty to Second Lieutenant Fulmar and safety at Ksar es Souk. Which, of course, was treason.

More important, they would be compromised. Thereafter, the Americans would be able to demand other services—under threat of letting the SS know what they had done in Morocco.

When he had parachuted into the desert near Ksar es Souk three days before, Lieutenant Eric Fulmar would not have been surprised to find himself immediately surrounded by Waffen-SS troops. As it happened, German troops did not meet him; but this was no proof that Helmut von Heurten-Mitnitz and Müller were playing the game as they were expected to. They may well have been waiting until he had furnished the names of the French officers before arresting him.

As soon as the code word signaling that the invasion was about to begin came over the Zenith portable radio, he had called Rabat to order the delivery of the list of French officers to Müller. Then he had telephoned Müller and told him the list was in his mailbox. To Fulmar's surprise, Müller had told him the precise hour he expected to be at Ksar es Souk.

Müller was so clear and careful about the time of his arrival that Fulmar immediately suspected that when the truck appeared, it would be full of Waffen-SS troopers, not French officers. In view of that, he decided to change his plan to accompany the Berber force that would intercept the Müller convoy before it reached Ksar es Souk.

He decided he would watch the intercept from the palace tower.

Pawns are put in jeopardy, he thought. *That's part of the game. But nowhere is it written that they have to put* themselves *in jeopardy.*

When the announcer began to repeat the presidential proclamation, Fulmar searched through the broadcast band, hoping to pick up something else. There was nothing.

He turned off the radio and picked up the binoculars again. This time there was a cloud of dust rising from the desert floor. Right on schedule. Fulmar slid off the antique chair and knelt on the stone floor in a position that would allow him to rest his elbows on the parapet to steady the binoculars.

It was two minutes before the first of the vehicles came into sight. It was a small, open, slab-sided vehicle—a military version of the Volkswagen, Germany's answer to the jeep. Four soldiers in the black uniforms of the Waffen-SS rode in the Volkswagen. Behind it was a French Panhard armored car.

Fulmar frowned. The armored car was unexpected. It smelled like the trap he worried about. Behind the Panhard was a Citroën sedan, and behind that a civilian truck, obviously just pressed into service. The truck was large enough to conceal twenty French officers. Or that many Waffen-SS troops. Behind the truck were two other slab-sided Volkswagens holding more Waffen-SS soldiers.

About half a mile from Ksar es Souk, the convoy disappeared from sight in a dip in the terrain. And then it reappeared, rounded a turn, and skidded to a halt. The road had been blocked there by a four-foot-high pile of rocks.

From the tower, Fulmar could see the Berbers waiting for the convoy, but to the Germans the Berbers were invisible.

The Waffen-SS troops jumped from their Volkswagens and formed a defensive perimeter around the convoy.

The Panhard moved in front of the leading Volkswagen and then tried to climb the pile of rocks. Nobody left the truck. Which meant nothing; they might be trying to conceal the presence of more German troops as long as possible.

Fulmar saw the muzzle flashes of the Panhard's machine gun moments before he heard the sound. And then the Panhard burst into flame, and a huge plume of black gasoline smoke surged into the sky.

There were more muzzle flashes, followed moments later by the rattle of the weapons. Two of the Waffen-SS troopers rushed toward a Berber position before being cut down.

And then the others began to raise their hands in surrender.

One German and three French officers, plus a Waffen-SS driver, came out of the Citroën with their hands in the air. Then the truck disgorged a dozen more Frenchmen—officers, civilians, and, astonishingly, two women. The German officer almost certainly was Obersturmbannführer Müller.

A Berber on horseback appeared. He rode over to the Panhard armored car and took a long, meditative look at two of its crew who had escaped and were lying on the ground. He killed both of them with a burst from his Thompson machine-pistol. He then rode over to the place where the two Waffen-SS troopers had been cut down and fired short bursts into their bodies.

More horsemen appeared. The remaining Germans, including the officer who had been in the Citroën, had their hands tied behind them. A rope was looped around their necks, making a chain of them. And one of the Berbers on horseback started leading them toward Ksar es Souk.

The French officers and the women were left unbound, but they were still unceremoniously herded down the road toward the palace. The vehicles were left where they had stopped.

The operation hadn't gone exactly as planned, but it had worked, and the armored car hadn't been nearly as much of a problem as it could have been. And, obviously, Müller was doing what he had been told to do.

Fulmar put the binoculars case around his neck, picked up his Thompson machine-pistol, and wound his way carefully down the narrow stone stairs of the tower.

At the bottom, he emerged into the courtyard. Spotting a small boy, he ordered him in fluent Arabic to fetch the cognac, the coffee service, and the radio from the tower.

Then he started toward the gate from the inner to the outer courtyard. Just before he reached it, he covered his face below the eyes with part of the blue cloth of his headdress. The once-glistening parachutist's boots were now scarred and torn by the rocks and bushes of the desert; they looked like any old boots. He was quite indistinguishable from a bona fide Berber.

In the outer courtyard there were a hundred Berbers, a third of them women in black robes. The men had painted their faces blue, as was their custom, and most of them were armed as he was with a Thompson. Off at one side, handlers held about forty horses. Fulmar made his way among the men to a group of the leaders and told them what had happened.

And then one of the Berbers touched his shoulder and nodded toward the gate. The horseman with the string of prisoners was now in sight.

"As soon as he's inside, go get the trucks and cars," Fulmar ordered. "And see what you can do about hiding the armored car."

"Why?" the Berber asked.

"Just do it," Fulmar said.

The Berber made a mocking gesture of subservience.

"I hear and obey, O son of heaven," he said.

"May you catch the French disease and your member turn green and fall off," Fulmar said.

They laughed at each other, and the Berber walked to where the horses were being held. He swung easily into a tooled leather saddle, then called out the names of half a dozen men, who trotted to the horses and mounted. They rode out of the courtyard as the German prisoners were led inside.

The Germans appeared terrified.

What the hell, Fulmar thought, *I'd be terrified too if I was being led with a rope around my neck into a King Arthur and the Knights of the Round Table palace by a bunch of guys with blue faces and submachine guns.*

He turned to another Berber.

"The stocky one," he said. "The one without the leather equipment. Take him inside to the small room or the library. Leave someone with him and make sure that no one else goes into the room with him."

"And the others?"

"Take them into the main room and get them something to eat and drink. They are not to be bothered."

"Not even their boots?"

"Not even their boots," Fulmar said. "They fought well. They deserve honorable treatment."

When the French arrived and had been herded into the courtyard, Fulmar walked up to them.

"On behalf of His Excellency Sidi Hassan el Ferruch, Pasha of Ksar es Souk, I welcome you to his home. You will be fed and cared for, and when it is time, you will be taken behind American lines."

He spoke in French. They seemed to accept him as a French-speaking Berber. At least he got no surprised, wary looks.

He was a little puzzled at the lack of excitement. No joy. No cries of pleasure. Then he realized that these people had expected to be taken somewhere in the desert and shot to death by the SS. They were in shock. They hadn't quite understood yet that they would live.

One of them, a wiry, intense little man, pulled himself together enough to start questioning Fulmar.

But Fulmar turned and walked off without letting him finish. He went into the palace to the small room off the library.

There was a Berber outside the door, and another inside. The German officer was sitting awkwardly on a three-legged stool, his hands still tied behind him.

Fulmar walked over to him, took a curved blade knife from a jewel-encrusted scabbard on the gold cords around his waist, and cut him free.

"Have someone bring my cognac," Fulmar ordered. "And coffee and oranges and some meat."

"Sprechen Sie Deutsch?" the German officer asked as he rubbed his wrists.

"Absolutely," Fulmar said in flawless German. "I'm an Alt-Marburger, you know—an alumnus of Philips University, Marburg an der Lahn."

"You're Fulmar?" the German asked, genuinely surprised.

"At your service, Herr Obersturmbannführer," Fulmar said. "Where the hell did that armored car come from? That could have sent this whole operation down the toilet!"

"What was I supposed to say? 'Thank you, I don't need an armored car'?"

"It could have fucked things up," Fulmar repeated, repressing a smile. They looked at each other.

"This is a little strange, isn't it?" Fulmar asked.

There had been a brief moment's emotion. But as quickly as it had come up, both seemed anxious to restrain it.

"Are you going to live up to your end of the bargain?" the German asked.

"As soon as we get everybody safely out of sight, I'll take you back to your car," Fulmar said.

"And what happens between there and Ourzazate?"

"You're safe between here and there," Fulmar said. "If I were you, I'd be worried about getting from Ourzazate to Rabat."

The game was over, Fulmar thought. And the pawns had not been swept from the board.

He wondered why he had no feeling of exultation, and the answer came immediately: A new game had already begun.

[THREE]
The Franco-German Armistice Commission
Rabat, Morocco
10 November 1942

Helmut von Heurten-Mitnitz was not in his office when Obersturmbannführer SS-SD Johann Müller went there looking for him. But Müller found him calmly packing his luggage in his apartment, a high-ceilinged well-furnished suite overlooking a palm-lined boulevard in the center of town.

Von Heurten-Mitnitz was a tall, sharp-featured Pomeranian aristocrat, the younger brother of the Graf von Heurten-Mitnitz. He was the sixth generation of his family to serve his country as a diplomat.

"Good afternoon, Obersturmbannführer," von Heurten-Mitnitz said dryly as he placed a shirt in his suitcase. "You have doubtless come to tell me that our courageous French allies have driven the Americans into the sea?"

Obersturmbannführer Johann Müller snorted.

"In a pig's ass they have," he said.

"What is the situation?" von Heurten-Mitnitz asked.

Müller told him what had taken place just outside Ksar es Souk and of his meeting with Fulmar.

"Finally, face-to-face, eh?" Helmut von Heurten-Mitnitz said. "What's he like?"

"I thought he was an Arab at first," Müller said. Von Heurten-Mitnitz looked at him, waiting for him to go on. "And somehow I expected him to be older," Müller said. "Good-looking kid. Well set up. Smart. Sure of himself."

Von Heurten-Mitnitz nodded thoughtfully. The description was more or less what he had expected.

"And what of the other Americans?" von Heurten-Mitnitz asked dryly.

"I think the Americans will be here in Rabat in twenty-four hours," Müller said.

"Something is slowing them down?" von Heurten-Mitnitz asked.

"There's a reliable rumor going around that they had to waste two hours sinking the invincible French North African fleet," Müller replied.

"Well, it appears that you and I are to be preserved from the Americans in order to assist in the future victory of the Fatherland. Passage has been arranged for you and me, and not more than one hundred kilos of official papers, et cetera, aboard a Junkers at half past eight," von Heurten-Mitnitz said. "There is a fifty-kilo allowance for personal luggage."

"Why so late?" Müller asked.

"The Americans also wasted several hours sweeping the invincible French Service de l'aire from the skies," von Heurten-Mitnitz said. "It was a choice between a U-boat and the Junkers at night."

Müller walked to a table and picked up a bottle of Steinhager.

"May I?" he asked, already pouring some of the liquor into a glass.

"Of course," Helmut von Heurten-Mitnitz said. "And would you be good enough to pour one for me?"

When Müller handed von Heurten-Mitnitz the small, stemmed glass, he asked, "Did you know what the Americans had in mind?"

Helmut von Heurten-Mitnitz met his eyes.

"Not in the way I think you mean," he said. "I knew they were coming. It was the logical thing for them to do, and I knew they were capable of mounting a transatlantic invasion force. But they didn't tell me about it.

Murphy, in fact, went out of his way to lead me to believe the Americans intended to reinforce the British from Cairo."

"Then they didn't trust you," Müller said simply. "So why trust them?"

Helmut von Heurten-Mitnitz sipped at his Steinhager before replying.

"The simple answer to that, Johann," he said, "is that I have—*we* have—no choice but to trust them. Do you understand? I didn't expect them to tell me details of their invasion."

"We *could* arrange to be captured here," Müller went on doggedly. "Have you thought about that? We just don't show up at the airport."

"That would work for you," von Heurten-Mitnitz said. "If you want, you can do just that."

"It wouldn't work for you? Why not?"

"You would be considered a soldier and become a POW," von Heurten-Mitnitz said. "I have a diplomatic passport. I'm quite sure they would put me on a plane to Lisbon for return to Germany."

"Not if you said you didn't want to go," Müller said.

"But I have to go, Johnny," von Heurten-Mitnitz, said. "You understand that."

Müller snorted, drained his Steinhager, and poured another.

"You have to put things in perspective," von Heurten-Mitnitz said. "Although it just began, the invasion of North Africa is already history. What they want me for is the future."

Müller grunted again.

"What they want *us* for, you mean." He paused, frowning. "And aren't you afraid that you—and, for that matter, me—that we'll look bad in Berlin for not having done more than we did here?"

"Are we going to be blamed, you mean? Or regarded with suspicion?" von Heurten-Mitnitz asked and went on without waiting for a reply. "I don't think so. I think what happened here will be regarded as yet another manifestation of French perfidy and ineptitude in battle. And with the Americans in Morocco, I think the Führer and his entourage will want to put the unpleasant subject out of mind. Until, of course, the Führer in his good time decides to take Morocco back."

Müller snorted derisively.

"And have the Americans told you what they want from us in Germany?"

"To a degree," Helmut von Heurten-Mitnitz said. "But I think the less you know about that now, the better."

He closed his suitcase and buckled its leather straps.

"Are you packed?"

"I packed right after Fulmar telephoned me," Müller said.

"Well, then, let's collect your luggage and go out to the airfield," von Heurten-Mitnitz said. He looked at Müller. "Johnny, if you want to stay and be captured, I'll understand. I can also come up with a convincing story to explain it back home. You know, devotion to duty and all the rest of it."

"Jesus Christ, don't make it easy for me," Müller said. "I've almost talked myself into staying. Almost, shit! When I walked in here, I was going to tell you I *was* staying. And then I remember what those swine did in Russia. What they're doing in Germany, to Germans. . . ."

"Yes," von Heurten-Mitnitz said, understanding.

He looked around the room. "I rather hate to be leaving," he said. "There's much about Morocco I really like."

Müller looked at him.

"I wish we were going someplace besides Germany," he said.

[FOUR]
Washington, D.C.
12 November 1942

> OPERATIONAL IMMEDIATE
> SUPREME HEADQUARTERS ALLIED EXPEDITIONARY FORCE
> GIBRALTAR 1015 HOURS 12 NOV 42
> JOINT CHIEFS OF STAFF PENTAGON WASH DC
> FOR COL W J DONOVAN OLD FRIENDS SAFE STOP NEW
> FRIENDS GOING HOME STOP SIGNED MURPHY STOP END

The radio message was received and logged in at the Pentagon Message Center at 0515 hours, Washington time. Since it had been transmitted in the clear, no decryption was necessary. It was placed in Box G at 0517 hours.

Box G was emptied at 0528 hours, and its contents carried by armed messenger to the National Institutes of Health building, where it was logged in at 0605 hours. At 0615, the message was placed in a box marked DIREC-TOR, by which time it had a red tag stapled to it, identifying it as an "Opera-tional Immediate" message deserving the Director's immediate attention.

At 0619 hours, the messages in the Director's box were picked up by Chief Boatswain's Mate J. R. Ellis, USN, a ruddy-faced, heavyset man of thirty-eight whose unbuttoned uniform jacket revealed a Colt .45 semiautomatic pistol carried high on his hip in a "skeleton" holster.

Ellis read the sheaf of messages, then put them into a briefcase. He but-toned his uniform jacket and went to the parking lot, where a white hat sailor, a torpedoman second class, sat behind the wheel of a Buick Road-master sedan. Ellis got into the front seat beside him.

"How they hanging, Chief?" the torpedoman asked, and then, without waiting for a reply, asked, "Georgetown?"

"Georgetown," Ellis confirmed.

When Chief Ellis had joined the OSS—so early on that it was then the "Office of the Coordinator of Information"—he was a bosun's mate first class just back from the Yangtze River Patrol, and he had been the driver of the Director's Buick Roadmaster. His duties were different now, if some-what vaguely defined. Newcomers to the OSS, particularly senior military officers who might naturally tend to assume a chief petty officer was avail-able to do their bidding, were told two things about Chief Ellis: Only the Colonel and the Captain (which meant Colonel William J. Donovan, the Di-rector of the OSS, and Captain Peter Douglass, USN, his deputy) gave orders to Chief Ellis.

More important, if the Chief asked that something be done, it was wise to presume he was speaking with the authority of at least the Captain.

When the Buick pulled to the curb before a Georgetown town house, a burly man in civilian clothing suddenly appeared from an alley. It was clearly his intention to keep whoever got out of the Buick from reaching the door of the town house.

And then he recognized Ellis, and the hand that had been inside his jacket reaching for his pistol, came out and was raised in a wave.

"What do you say, Chief?" he asked as Ellis stepped out of the car and walked toward the red-painted door of the building.

"I thought you got off at six," Ellis said.

"So did I. Those sonsofbitches are late again," the burly man said.

Colonel William J. Donovan opened his own front door. He was stocky and silver-haired, and he was dressed in a sleeveless undershirt. Shaving cream was still on his face.

"The damned alarm didn't go off," he said. "How much time do we have?"

"Enough," Ellis said.

"You didn't have to come here, Chief," Donovan said. "I was going by the office anyway."

He turned and motioned for Ellis to follow him inside.

"Something important in there?" Donovan asked, indicating the brief-case.

Ellis opened it and handed Donovan the sheaf of red tagged messages. Donovan read them, carefully, and then handed them back.

"Douglass see these yet?" he asked.

"No, sir, I thought I would send them back with the driver," Ellis said. "You saw Murphy's radio?"

"Yes, sir."

"There never was any doubt in your mind about that, was there, Chief?"

"Not about Fulmar," Ellis said. "I wasn't too sure about the Krauts."

Donovan chuckled.

"Well, it worked," Donovan said. "And just between you and me, there was more to it than appears."

"I had sort of figured that out," Ellis said. "I haven't figured out *what* yet."

It was a subtle request to be told. Donovan, as subtly, turned him down. "Have you had breakfast?"

Ellis hesitated.

"There's a coffee shop at Anacostia," he said.

"Which means you haven't," Donovan said. "Which means that you've been up all night, too. Am I right?"

"I figured I'd better stick around."

"The cook's not up," Donovan said. "But I started the coffee. Do you think you could make us some ham and eggs without burning the kitchen down?"

"Yes, sir," Ellis said.

"I'll go put a shirt on," Donovan said, "and grab my bags. I won't be long."

He started up the stairs, then turned.

"Ellis, maybe you'd better check with Anacostia. I'd hate to go all the way out there only to find we can't fly out today."

"I checked just before I came over here," Ellis said.

"Yes, of course you would have," Donovan said. "What would I do without you, Ellis?"

"I don't know," Ellis said seriously. "Without one man who knows what he's doing, this outfit would be even more fucked up than it already is."

It took Donovan a moment to realize that Ellis, in his own way, was making a joke.

Then he laughed, a hearty, deep laugh in his belly.

"Sunny-side up, Ellis, please," he said. "And try not to burn the toast." And then he continued up the stairs.

Ellis turned to a telephone on a small table against the wall and dialed a number.

"Ellis," he said when the call was answered. "I'm at the Boss's. We should leave here in thirty minutes. If you don't hear from me again in two hours, tell the Captain that we're on our way."

Then he hung up, went into the kitchen, removed his uniform blouse, and, wearing an apron, he made breakfast for the two of them.

Ellis had learned to cook from a Chinese boy aboard the USS *Panay* of the Yangtze River Patrol. He often thought of that when he was pressed into cook service. That had been a long time ago. He'd seen a twenty-one-year-old seaman first striking for bosun third. Seventeen years ago.

But he'd only been back from China a short time. Just before the war started, they'd closed down the Yangtze Patrol and sailed what gunboats were left to the Philippines. They'd wanted to keep him in the Philippines, but his enlistment was up, and he didn't think he wanted to serve in the Philippines, so he told them he wanted out, and they'd sent him home.

They'd been pissed, of course. Everybody knew the war was coming, and they didn't want to let him out. But there was nothing they could do about it (enlistments had not yet been frozen). So they'd sent him back as unpleasantly as they could, making him work his way as supercargo on an old and tired coastal freighter headed for overhaul at San Diego. He'd thought then that since he would never see China again (he loved China), the best thing he could hope for was to keep his nose clean so he could get his twenty years in and retire with his rating.

That was not quite two years ago.

He had fallen into the shit and come up smelling like roses. The orders that were soon sending him back to China (and to Burma, and India, and

Egypt, and England) described him as "the administrative assistant to the Director of the Office of Strategic Services." Which meant that he was going to travel with the Colonel to all those places and take care of whatever he needed taken care of.

That sure beat what for most of his adult life had been his great ambition, to be the ranking chief on a Yangtze River gunboat.

Naturally, there had to be a price to pay for this beyond making life a little easier for the Colonel when he could arrange it—beyond even putting himself between the Colonel and whoever meant the Colonel harm—but he was prepared to pay that.

What exactly that price was going to be, Ellis didn't know. When he got the bill, he'd pay it. And in the meantime, if the Colonel wanted eggs sunny-side up before they got on the plane to go around the world, that's what the Colonel would get.

[ONE]
East Grinstead Air Corps Station
Sussex, England
3 December 1942

While he was in Cairo, Colonel William J. Donovan sent a courier ahead to London bearing material he did not wish to entrust to ordinary channels. Among this material was a personal message to David Bruce, Chief of the OSS London station, explaining that he would be leaving Cairo in the next few days. After that he planned to spend a day in Algiers and another day in Casablanca—"to see things for myself." From there he would fly on to London.

In addition to the Casablanca station chief, two familiar faces were waiting for Donovan and Ellis at the Casablanca airfield.

They were Richard Canidy and James M. B. Whittaker. Both men were in their mid-twenties and close to the same height—about six feet—and good-looking enough to turn most girls' heads in their direction. End of resemblance. Canidy was heavy of shoulder and large of bone, Irish dark-eyed and dark-haired, while Whittaker was pale blond and slender, with leopard-like moves.

Canidy and Whittaker had been close since they were schoolboys. Canidy was one of Donovan's more recent acquisitions, but Donovan had known Jimmy Whittaker since he had worn diapers. Whittaker's uncle, Chesley Haywood Whittaker, a Harvard- and MIT-trained engineer who had built railroads, dams, and power-generating systems around the world, had been a great friend of Donovan's all of his life. Before the war began, it had been Donovan's intention to make Chesty Whittaker his deputy. But on Pearl Harbor Day, while he was waiting at his Washington mansion for a summons to the White House, Chesty Whittaker had suffered a coronary embolism.

Canidy and Whittaker were readily recognizable as officer-pilots of the United States Army Air Corps. Both were wearing pilots' sunglasses and leather-brimmed caps whose crown stiffeners had been removed. That way, the caps and an aircraft headset could be worn simultaneously. Canidy wore a tropical worsted shirt, no tie, and olive-drab trousers. He had on as well a garment officially described as Jacket, Horsehide, Flying, A-2. The golden oak leaves of a major were pinned to his epaulets, and a leather patch embossed with his name and the wings of the Chinese Air Corps was sewn to the breast.

The entire back of the jacket had painted on it a representation of the flag of the Republic of China. Below that was written a lengthy message in Chinese informing the people of that country that the wearer was engaged in fighting the Japanese invaders and that a reward, payable in gold, would be given for his safe transfer into the hands of any Official of Generalissimo Chiang Kai-shek's Kuomintang government.

Before Pearl Harbor, Canidy had been a Flying Tiger, flying P-40s in Burma and China for the American Volunteer Group. He considered his jacket a lucky piece.

Whittaker was also wearing an A-2 jacket, but his was so new it still smelled of the tanning chemicals. On it were embossed leather representations of a captain's bars sewn to his epaulets, and to the breast was sewn a patch with a representation of Army Air Corps wings and his last name. He was wearing pink trousers and a pink shirt. And looked, Donovan thought, like a fighter pilot in a recruiting-service poster.

Canidy carried an issue .45 Colt automatic pistol in an issue holster on a web belt around his waist. Whittaker had a Model 1917 Colt .45-caliber ACP revolver jammed casually into his waistband under the A-2 jacket. The crude hilt of an odd-looking knife was visible at the top of Whittaker's Half Wellington boots. Donovan knew the knife. The blade, which was ten inches long and nearly black with oxidation, had a double edge cut in inch-long scallops. Jimmy Whittaker had brought the Colt and the Kris home with him from the Philippine Islands.

The two of them looked like pilots from a fighter squadron somewhere in North Africa who just happened to be at the Casablanca airport. They were in fact in the OSS, and they were supposed to be in England. Donovan wondered what the hell they were doing in Casablanca. He asked them.

Canidy gestured to a B-25 "Mitchell" twin-engined bomber parked on the grass not far from the terminal.

"Your personal chariot awaits your pleasure, Colonel," Canidy said. "We thought you and Chief Ellis might want to avoid the common herd on the commuter flight."

"That's not what I asked, Dick," Donovan said.

"Stevens sent us down here with three *very* heavy crates," Whittaker said. "And when we checked in, they told us you were coming."

Lieutenant Colonel Edmund T. Stevens was Deputy Chief of Station, London.

"It's also the plane we used to drop Fulmar down on the other side of Ourzazate," Canidy said. "Extra fuel tanks, even a couple of airline seats. The way we cleaned it up, it cruises right around 310 knots."

Donovan took a closer look at the airplane. The turret on top had been removed, and the opening faired over. The machine-gun positions in the sides of the fuselage were also gone, and faired over. It was no longer a bomber, but a high-speed, long-range transport. Canidy, Donovan reflected, sounded like he was trying to sell it to him. He wondered what that was about but didn't ask. Not only was he fond of both of them, but he trusted their unorthodox—sometimes even outrageous—style.

"I'll be here two days," Donovan said. "Won't they expect you back?"

"Absence," Jimmy Whittaker said solemnly, "makes the heart grow fonder."

Donovan grinned.

"Why not?" he said.

The B-25 arrived in England sixty hours later, having flown a circular route far enough out over the Atlantic to avoid interception by German Messerschmidt ME-109E fighter planes based in France.

Lieutenant Colonel Stevens, another old friend of Donovan's recruited for the OSS, was on hand to meet it. Stevens, forty-four, graying, erect, with intelligent hazel eyes, was a West Pointer who had resigned his commission and gone to work in his wife's wholesale food business. He had lived in England for several years before the war, and his ability to handle upper-crust Englishmen had proved even more valuable than his military expertise.

Stevens wasn't sure what he thought about their waiting around in Morocco so they could fly Donovan up on the B-25. Canidy, as usual, was treating orders and accepted procedures the way playboys treat women: Canidy knew damned well that he was expected to unload the crates, grab a few hours' sleep, and fly back to England. Both he and Whittaker had more important things to do than drive airplanes.

Canidy had been put in charge of the OSS base in Kent. Whitbey House, the requisitioned "stately home" of the Dukes of Stanfield, was both the "safe house" for the OSS and the training base for agents. And there Jimmy Whittaker ran what the OSS called "The Operational Techniques School," or what Canidy more accurately called the "Throat Cutting and Bomb Throwing Academy."

But separately and—more important—together the two were a *very* persuasive pair. When the problem of transporting the crates of radios and special explosives (earmarked for Casablanca but sent in error to England) came up at a staff meeting in London, Canidy and Whittaker had quickly made convincing arguments that the obvious solution was for them to fly the crates down to Casablanca in the B-25: There was no reason they couldn't be absent from Whitbey House for seventy-two hours; the crates would not be misdirected again; and there wouldn't be all the bureaucratic crap involved in arranging for the priority shipment through normal channels.

Stevens had let them go, though it was even money they wouldn't be back in seventy-two hours—Canidy and Whittaker being Canidy and Whittaker. But he had not expected they would return with Colonel Donovan aboard. Still, Canidy and Whittaker being Canidy and Whittaker . . .

And the truth was that what they'd done was a good thing. It had provided a more secret mode of travel than one of the courier flights from

Casablanca: There was no question in Colonel Stevens's mind that the Abwehr had a 90 percent accurate passenger manifest of VIP courier flights. And besides, Donovan was human, and there had to be some jolt of pleasure derived from traveling aboard "his own" aircraft, flown by two of "his own" pilots.

On receipt of the Air Corps message that "Colonel Williams" would be aboard a B-25 aircraft, Stevens had been so confident that "Williams" was Donovan that he had gone to East Grinstead with two cars. Donovan would be carried to Whitbey House in the long, black Austin Princess limousine assigned to the Chief of Station, while Canidy, Whittaker, and Ellis would go in a 1941 Ford staff car driven by Captain Stanley S. Fine.

Stevens had with him a thick sheaf of Top Secret messages that Donovan would want to deal with right away. Canidy and the others had no "need to know." Thus, separate cars.

When the B-25 landed, a checkerboard-painted "Follow Me" truck led it away from Base Operations to a remote corner of the field where the Princess and the Ford sedan were waiting.

Donovan was first off the airplane. He was wearing a simple olive-drab woolen uniform, with the silver eagles of a colonel and the crossed flintlocks of infantry. On his head was a soft "overseas" hat.

Technically, Donovan was assigned to the Joint Chiefs of Staff, and probably should be wearing the insignia of a General Staff Corps Officer and not the flintlocks. It was interesting to wonder why he wore infantryman's rifles: Perhaps he simply wanted to—and was confident no one would call him on improper insignia. In Europe, he was answerable only to Eisenhower, and Ike had much too much on his mind to notice the insignia Donovan wore.

But Stevens knew that as open-faced and disingenuous as Donovan appeared, there was more than a little subtlety in him: Donovan was a longtime mandarin in the political establishment and an old buddy of Franklin Roosevelt. Without these credentials he would never have been pegged by Roosevelt to create out of practically nothing America's first true spy network. But he was doing this in a country at war, and he was doing it officially as a soldier. Which meant working as much with the military establishment as the political one.

Which meant that all other things being equal, Donovan would have been treated like an amateur by the military establishment (an amateur being defined as anyone who had not been on active duty prior to 1938). Which meant that America's young spy organization would have had about as much chance of getting off the ground as a balloon in a needle factory. Thus the infantry rifles: Anyone who has commanded an infantry regiment in combat is, Q.E.D., not a military amateur. And Donovan had not only commanded a regiment (in War I with the "Fighting 69th" Infantry) but he'd won the Medal of Honor doing it.

The crossed flintlocks would subtly remind the senior officers with whom he dealt (including Eisenhower, who had spent War I at Camp Colt, New York) that he had seen more than his share of combat, which meant that he was not just a civilian politician in uniform who could be ignored because he "just doesn't understand what the Army is all about."

And the Army establishment was not half of the stone wall Donovan had had to break through before he could even begin to worry about the enemy. Long, long ago (that is to say, a few weeks earlier) during the hectic seventy-two hours between Colonel Stevens's orders to report to active duty and his departure by plane to London, Donovan half jokingly, half bitterly had looked at Stevens and sighed. "You know, Ed," he told Stevens, "I consider it a good day if I can devote fifty-one percent of my time to the armed enemy."

There was no doubt whom he meant by the "unarmed" enemy: a number of people, ranging downward from J. Edgar Hoover, who loathed William J. Donovan. The authority granted to Donovan by the President (which came with virtually unlimited access to nonaccountable funds) had turned him into a very real threat to long-established government fiefdoms. He was particularly a thorn in the side of the FBI, the ONI (the Office of Naval Intelligence), G2 (Military Intelligence), and the State Department Intelligence Division. These bodies had quickly proved to be a thorn in the side of William J. Donovan.

Lt. Colonel Stevens and Captain Fine saluted when Donovan walked over to them. Donovan returned the salute, smiled, and then shook their hands. Then he walked to the tail of the aircraft and met the call of nature. By that time, Canidy and Whittaker had climbed out of the aircraft and begun to unload the luggage. Fulmar, Stevens saw, was not with them.

As Canidy and Whittaker approached the Austin Princess, Donovan said, "Canidy would like to keep the airplane."

"I'll bet he would," Stevens said, smiling.

"He thinks he can get it in and out of the strip at Whitbey," Donovan said, seriously. "Would keeping it pose problems?"

"No, sir," Stevens said.

Donovan nodded. It was an order. Stevens would now have to somehow arrange for the transfer—or at least the indefinite "loan"—of the B-25 to the London Station. Another victory for the persuasive Canidy-Whittaker combination.

"I see you brought your lawyer with you, Colonel," Canidy said to Stevens as he offered his hand. "Been behaving yourself, Stanley?"

Prior to his entry into military service, Captain Stanley S. Fine, a tall, skinny, somewhat scholarly-looking man of thirty-three, had been Vice President, Legal, of Continental Studios, Inc. Before he had been recruited for the OSS, he had been a B-17 Squadron Commander.

"I see you brought this one back in one piece," Fine said, nodding at the B-25.

"We try to learn from our little mistakes," Whittaker said, wrapping an affectionate arm around Fine and then kissing him wetly on the forehead. Fine was torn between laughter and annoyance.

The trouble with Dick Canidy, Fine thought as Canidy hugged him, *is that I both like and admire the sonofabitch.*

If I didn't like him, both of them, the goddamned Bobbsey Twins, it would be very easy to stay pissed off, because they get to fly around in airplanes, while I sit on my ass and clean up the paperwork mess they leave behind them.

Fine was not just kidding when he needled Whittaker and Canidy about bringing the B-25 back in one piece. Not too long ago the pair had wrecked a Navy R-5D Curtiss Commando transport aircraft on takeoff from the airfield in Kolwezi in the Belgian Congo. And Fine had wound up dealing with the problem of how to explain the lost airplane.

Fine had flown one of the R-5Ds involved in the Kolwezi Operation. After that Operation was successfully (miraculously was a better word) completed, Fine had started to "make himself useful" in London, "until something else comes up." Before long he'd turned into something like Stevens's deputy. He wasn't sure how he felt about this: It was important work, but he was a pilot, and pilots should be flying.

Just before Canidy and Whittaker talked Stevens into letting them take the B-25 to North Africa, Captain Peter Douglass, Sr., USN, Donovan's deputy, made a two-day trip to London. Ten minutes after he arrived at Berkeley Square, he tossed a thick folder, red-stamped SECRET, on Fine's desk.

"Come up with how you think we should handle this, Stan," he said. Then, chuckling, he added, "It's right down your alley."

It was a thick file from the Navy's BUAIR (Naval Bureau of Aeronautics), with addenda and comments from the U.S. Army Air Corps and the War Production Board, expressing the Navy's bureaucratic outrage: An R-5D transport which they had loaned to the Army Air Corps had not only not been returned, but the Air Corps professed to have no knowledge of its whereabouts. Further, the Navy complained, in the absence of a Certificate of Loss Due to Enemy Action, the War Production Board refused to grant them anything higher than a "B" Priority for its replacement from the Curtiss Production Stream.

This wasn't as funny as it first appeared. Bureaucratically, it was necessary to find the Navy a replacement aircraft as soon as possible, which meant arranging an "AAA" priority for them. Otherwise, the next time the Navy was asked to loan the Air Corps an aircraft, it would find sufficient reason to delay indefinitely doing so, priority or no priority.

The "loan" process had to be kept moving smoothly not only for operational reasons but—at least as important—for security reasons. The OSS would in the end get what it wanted, but questions would be asked if it took a personal telephone call from the Joint Chiefs of Staff to the Director of BUAIR ordering him to immediately produce an airplane.

The mess was not helped by the fact that the R-5D Commando that Canidy and Whittaker had dumped in Kolwezi had been intended as a VIP transport and had been borrowed by the Air Corps for no longer than thirty days for use "in transporting senior U.S. and Allied military and civilian officials to, and within, the British Isles."

The Commando had been destroyed on a mission so secret that the full details were known to only the President, General Marshall, Brigadier General Leslie R. Groves, USA, Colonel Donovan, and Captain Peter Douglass, Sr., USN.

Fine still had no idea what the sacks he had transferred from Canidy's Commando to his had contained. And the operation was still classified Top Secret. Obviously, the Navy could not be told that the plane, accidentally overloaded, had crashed on takeoff in the Belgian Congo, and had then been burned to inhibit identification.

Meanwhile, the Navy wanted either the VIP airplane back, or one just like it. And they wanted it immediately.

Happily, a solution born of his experience in Hollywood came to Stanley Fine. For a moment, as a result of his training at Harvard Law, he had to reject the solution. But before long, expediency won out over ethics. At Harvard Law he had been taught that at the head of the list of Thou Shalt Nots for a member of the bar was "uttering, issuing, or causing to be uttered or issued a statement, written or oral, he knows to be false."

Fine's solution, anyhow, was a rewrite: If the Office of War Production and the Navy wanted a Certificate of Loss Due to Enemy Action, write them one.

He was a little uneasy when Captain Douglass—an Annapolis graduate and thus almost by definition a straight shooter—smiled, patted him approvingly on the shoulder, and told him to go to it.

As Fine typed out the revised scenario—the Navy's R-5D was missing and presumed lost following a takeoff from Great Britain bound for North Africa, with the presumption that it had been intercepted by German fighter aircraft based in France—Fine reflected upon the implied, if unintentional, slur behind Captain Douglass's joy at Fine's solution to the R-5D mess:

This was exactly the sort of thing a lawyer, for the obvious reasons, would immediately think up, while a professional officer, for the obvious reasons, would not. When Fine reached the signature block, he typed PETER DOUGLASS, SR., CAPTAIN, USN. If the Navy was to be lied to, let a sailor do it.

Donovan climbed into the back seat of the Princess. Stevens followed him, and the WRAC (Women's Royal Army Corps) sergeant driver closed the door after them and got behind the wheel.

As soon as they had left the airfield, Stevens laid his rigid briefcase in his lap, worked the combination lock, and opened it. It was full of yellow Teletype and cryptographic foolscap, all of it stamped either SECRET or TOP SECRET. There was also a .38 Special–caliber Colt "Banker's Special" revolver.

He handed the yellow messages to Donovan. Some were addressed to Donovan personally. Others were messages addressed to the chief of station that Stevens felt Donovan would wish to see.

Donovan read them carefully as the Princess limousine, trailed by the Ford, headed down narrow county blacktop roads toward Kent and Whitbey House. Stevens read over Donovan's shoulder, taking the messages back from him and often making notes of Donovan's reactions to them.

"Curiosity practically overwhelms me about that one," Stevens said when

Donovan came to one brief message. It was only classified "priority," which, because most of the other messages were "operational immediate" and "urgent," made it apparently of low import:

```
PRIORITY
SECRET


NAVAL COMMCENTER WASH DC 1800 HOURS 2 DEC 1942
STATION CHIEF LONDON FOR DONOVAN


REGRET TO INFORM YOU FOOTBALL STADIUM CHAINS CRACKING STOP
LT COMMANDER HUDSON USNR STOP


END
```

"Jesus!" Donovan said, and exhaled audibly.

"Bad news?" Stevens asked, surprised at the out-of-character blasphemy.

Donovan looked at him almost as if he didn't know who he was, and then shook his head. He folded the message carefully and put it in his breast pocket.

"You don't want to give that back to me?" Stevens said.

"I—uh—Ed, I'm keeping sort of a personal file of significant messages," Donovan said, then leaned forward to crank down the glass partition.

"Sergeant," he ordered, "the first chance you get, pull off the road and stop, would you, please?"

Then he pushed himself back against the seat. Lt. Colonel Stevens knew this was not the time to press him with questions.

A moment later, the Princess pulled onto the shoulder of the road and stopped. The WRAC sergeant twisted around to see what else was expected of her.

"Let's take a walk, Ed," Donovan said, and opened the curbside door.

As Stevens got out, he saw the Ford pull in behind them.

"Just stay where you are, please," Donovan called, as Canidy stepped out of the passenger seat in the front, followed a moment later by Fine. There was a "just do what you're told" tone in his voice.

He led Stevens fifty yards down the road, seemingly oblivious to the rain, which was now falling steadily. Then he stopped, looked around to make sure there was no chance of their being overheard.

"Lieutenant Commander Hudson is the President," Donovan began. "I guess he got the name from the Hudson River."

"And?" Stevens asked, confused.

"Ed," Donovan said. "The time has come for you to be brought in on this. It's—I don't know how else to put this—*the* big secret of this war. I am not bringing Dave Bruce in on this. I don't want to burden him with it. But one man here has to be told. And I've decided—actually President Roosevelt decided—that's you."

"Bill, knowing something that Dave Bruce doesn't puts me on a hell of a spot," Stevens protested. "He's the station chief."

"That can't be helped," Donovan said, so sharply that Stevens looked at him in surprise.

"I'll be as concise as I can," Donovan said. "In the summer of 1939, Albert Einstein sent a letter to Roosevelt through a man named Alexander Sachs. In the letter he said that he and others believed that if an atom of an element called uranium could be split under the right conditions, the splitting of this atom would send out particles which would knock into and then split other atoms. Those would split others, which in turn would split others. A chain reaction, in other words. Do you follow me?"

"I have absolutely no idea what you're talking about," Stevens said.

"Bear with me," Donovan said. "The thing about splitting atoms is that energy is released. If we can cause a chain reaction of atoms, a *tremendous* amount of energy would be released. The formula is 'energy equals the mass times the square of the speed of light,' which is one hell of a lot of energy. In other words, a bomb with a power that boggles the mind could be built. One bomb would have the explosive power of thousands of tons of explosives."

Stevens couldn't think of anything to say to that, so he said nothing.

"Roosevelt took a chance and authorized a program to see if the atom could indeed be split. A couple of thousand dollars at first, God alone knows how many millions so far. An Italian physicist named Enrico Fermi has been working on the project ever since. At the University of Chicago, in a laboratory under the stands of the football stadium. Taking an even greater chance, Roosevelt put Leslie Groves— You know him?"

"Only by reputation," Stevens said. "Army Engineer colonel?"

"Buck General," Donovan said, nodding. "Groves is now building a facility in the hills of Tennessee to refine enough uranium 235 to make such a bomb. Construction began before they knew for sure they could cause a chain reaction."

"And now they know?"

"That's what that message is all about," Donovan said.

"How does the OSS get involved?" Stevens asked, then paused. "I guess I'm wondering why you're telling me."

"The OSS has already been involved," Donovan said.

Stevens's eyebrows rose, but he said nothing.

"In the presumption that the people at the University of Chicago would succeed in making a chain reaction, we've started to build the bomb," Donovan said. "Let me make it clear: We're *years* away from having one. But now we know we can eventually make one. To make one, we need one hundred highly refined pounds of a uranium isotope called uranium 235. At the moment, the total supply of uranium 235 in the world, including that in the hands of the Germans—who are investigating 'nuclear energy' themselves—is one-millionth of a pound."

"I'm lost again, Bill," Stevens said. "I don't mean to sound so dense."

"Uranium 235 can be refined from uraninite," Donovan said. "There are two known sources of uraninite. One is in Pomerania, a state of Germany, and the other is in Kolwezi, in the Katanga Province of the Belgian Congo."

"Oh!" Stevens said, catching on.

Donovan nodded.

"It was not known for sure whether the uraninite in the Belgian Congo was (a) in fact uraninite or (b) if it was, whether it could be refined to produce uranium 235. But we had to try."

"That's what Canidy and Fine brought out," Stevens said. It was not a question.

"There was no way the ore could have been shipped out by sea, or by truck to South Africa. The only way to take it out was by air."

"I thought the Kolwezi Operation had something to do with the Norden bombsight," Stevens said.

"So does the Chief of Naval Operations," Donovan said. "He doesn't have the need to know. The President, alone, makes that decision."

"And the President wanted me brought in on this? Why?"

"Getting that bomb built before the Germans build one is the nation's highest priority," Donovan said. "Which can be looked at another way: Keeping the Germans from building one before Groves and his people can is OSS's highest priority."

"I'm confused again, Bill," Stevens said. "What's that got to do with my knowing about this?"

Donovan didn't seem at first to respond directly: "The OSS's second priority is to keep the Germans from even suspecting we're experimenting with an atomic bomb. God alone knows what they would do if they were to find out Fermi has actually caused a chain reaction."

"It is impossible to keep a secret," Stevens said, thinking out loud.

"This is going to have to be the exception to that rule," Donovan said.

"How many people know?"

"Maybe a dozen physicists under Groves. J. Edgar Hoover had to be told. A lot of his assets are to be diverted to keeping the secret. Marshall knows, of course. Pete Douglass knows. And now you do."

"That brings us back to 'Why me?'"

"You're privy to everything that will go on here," Donovan said. "It will explain to you certain things that I may do, or ask to be done," Donovan said. "And you will be able, now that you know the priorities, to stop anything that shouldn't be done."

"That authority belongs to the station chief," Stevens said.

"That's what I told the President," Donovan said. "He said Dave has enough on his mind as it is."

"What about the brass? What about Ike?" Stevens asked. "Certainly Ike must know."

"Three Army officers know. Groves, me, and you. And for the time being, that's it. I'll tell Dave Bruce that you are privy to a project of the highest priority, and that it has been decided in the interests of security that he not be made aware of the details."

"That puts me on a hell of a spot, Bill," Stevens said, again, without thinking.

"Your 'spot,' Ed, however uncomfortable you may feel," Donovan said coldly, "is not quite like mine. I'm charged with keeping the Germans from either finding out about our bomb, or building one of their own."

"Sorry," Stevens said. "I'm a little off balance."

Donovan laughed. Stevens looked at him in surprise.

"Your WRAC sergeant," Donovan said, "is studiously looking out the rear window. She obviously thinks we came out here to take a leak."

Stevens looked. As he did, the WRAC sergeant stole a quick look to see what they were up to, then quickly turned her head again.

"She must think we have the bladders of a whale," he said.

Donovan laughed heartily, then took Lt. Colonel Stevens's arm and prodded him back down the road toward the car.

[TWO]
Whitbey House, Kent
6 December 1942

Whitbey House, the ancestral seat of the Duchy of Stanfield, consisted of some 26,000 acres: Whitbey House itself—84 rooms and outbuildings; the village of Whitbey on Naer (pop. 607); the ruins of the Abbey of St. William the Martyr (Roman Catholic); St. Timothy's church (Anglican); a 4,600-foot gravel aircraft runway (built in 1931 by the father of the present Duke); an open aircraft hangar; as well as other real property that had come into the hands of the first Duke of Stanfield circa 1213.

As everyone expected, it was requisitioned for the duration of the war by His Majesty's Government. Few "stately homes" escaped requisitioning. His Majesty's Government's need for space was virtually insatiable. The situation became worse when the United States entered the war and began to ship air, ground, and naval forces (and their supply depots) to the British Isles. It was generally believed that the ducal airstrip would be expanded into an aerodrome for use by the United States Army Air Corps.

At every fifty feet around the perimeter of the lands of Whitbey House signs were mounted bearing the seal of the Crown and the legend "Government Establishment—Entry Prohibited."

Some of the signs were nailed to trees or affixed to stone fences, and some were mounted on stakes driven into the ground. The signs were cardboard. Already, after four months in place, they were growing ragged and illegible. A requisition for more-durable signs had been submitted, but it was a question of priority, and there was no telling when they would be made available.

Around the twelve-acre area that converged upon Whitbey House itself, out of sight of the roads outside the estate, was another barrier, coils of barbed wire called "concertina." Hanging from the concertina at fifty-foot intervals, more signs were painted on oblongs of twenty-four- by eighteen-inch plywood. On these signs was a representation of a skull and cross-bones with a simple legend beneath it: "Persons Trespassing Beyond This Line Will Be Shot on Sight."

Once requisitioned, Whitbey House had passed from the control of H.M. Office of Properties to the War Office, and from the War Office to the Special Operations Executive, and from SOE to a little-known American organization, the Office of Strategic Services, or OSS.

The mission of the OSS was known in full to no more than a handful of people. Even Lieutenant General Walter Bedell Smith, Chief of Staff to SHAEF Commander General Dwight D. Eisenhower, was not fully privy to the exact mission of the OSS, nor was Eisenhower's Intelligence Chief, although they both believed that they were.

What most senior brass did know was that Colonel William J. Donovan answered to the President by way of General George Catlett Marshall, Chief of Staff of the U.S. Army, though sometimes Colonel William J. Donovan answered to the President through no intermediary at all. That was enough to convince them that Donovan was the most powerful colonel the Army had ever known. But it did not endear Donovan to them.

The skull and crossbones and rolls of concertina were American. Just outside the barbed wire was a tent and hut encampment housing an American infantry battalion. On rotation, one of the four companies of the battalion provided a guard force between the concertina and a third barrier, enclosing just over three acres around Whitbey House itself.

The other three companies of the battalion carried on routine training but were of course available should there be a need.

The third barrier consisted of an eight-foot fence of barbed wire, with concertina laid on either side of the fence. There were in addition flood lamps, three to a pole, every hundred feet.

A constable of the Kent Constabulary was stationed in the gatehouse of Whitbey House. His function was to turn away casual visitors to the estate, but he was also equipped with a U.S. Army EE-8 field telephone. When the Princess and the Ford passed onto the estate, he cranked the telephone and told the sergeant of the U.S. Army Guard at the first barrier that he had just passed two authorized vehicles, one of them carrying an American colonel.

The limousine and the Ford rolled for almost a mile through a manicured forest on a road laid out centuries before. The road had been designed then to provide as level as possible a route for the heavy carriages of the aristocracy rather than the shortest distance between the gate and the house.

When they emerged from the forest, Whitbey House itself came into sight at the end of a wide, curving entrance drive. The House was a brick and sandstone structure three floors high. As they approached, it grew ever more impressive; and by the time they reached the final U.S. Army guard post, it was impossible to see all of it without moving the head.

The sergeant of the guard passed the two-car convoy inside his barrier, and the officer of the guard was waiting at the inner gate to check identification cards against a list of authorized personnel. Like the other officers of the infantry battalion, he had been told that Whitbey House housed a highly classified organization whose mission was to select bombardment targets for the Eighth Air Force. He had no reason to doubt what he was told, but he frequently questioned the necessity of guarding the establishment so closely.

When the two cars rolled up before the front door of Whitbey House, two officers were standing outside waiting for them. One was an American lieutenant, a pleasant, red-haired young man named Jamison. The other was a WRAC Captain named Elizabeth Alexandra Mary Stanfield.

Both saluted as Donovan got out of the car, and Lt. Colonel Stevens made the introductions.

Donovan found Captain Stanfield rather interesting. She was in her early middle thirties, a pale-skinned, lithe, sandy-haired woman whose tunic bore the insignia of the Imperial General Staff. Captain Stanfield had been assigned as liaison officer between the Imperial General Staff and OSS Whitbey House Station. Donovan knew that meant she had been sent to spy on the OSS—a job she was ideally suited for. For one thing, she knew Whitbey House intimately. Her identity card read "Captain the Duchess Stanfield."

Donovan was aware too that her husband, Wing Commander the Duke Stanfield, RAF, had been shot down and was carried as "missing in action" on RAF rolls. And he knew that Captain Elizabeth Alexandra Mary, the Duchess Stanfield, of the Imperial General Staff had crossed swords with Richard Canidy of the OSS almost immediately after she had reported to "liaise" with the new occupants of her ancestral home. Donovan wasn't privy to all the details of the encounter, except that it had ended with Canidy telling Her Grace that she acted as if she had a corncob up her ass.

However accurate Canidy's description might have been (and Donovan thought it was right on the mark, for the Duchess struck him as very aloof), voicing it was going a bit far, even for Canidy.

Interestingly, after Canidy had made his point, Her Grace blithely turned the other cheek rather than work herself into a ducal rage. If proof was needed, this served as confirmation that Her Grace's job was to report back to the Imperial General Staff and SOE anything they might find interesting. There was no other explanation for why the encounter had not resulted in a demand from His Majesty's government for a formal apology for the insult to an officer of the IGS who was not only a peer of the realm but whose godmother was the Queen Mother.

"I'm going to have a bath," Donovan said. "And then I'm going to write my wife a letter. Which Colonel Stevens will graciously carry back to London and place in tonight's pouch."

"Certainly, sir," Stevens said.

"In the morning, I would like the grand tour, but not tonight," Donovan said. "Could I have a sandwich sent to my room?"

"How about a New York Strip?" Canidy asked. "Lieutenant Jamison stole one especially for you."

"That would be fine," Donovan said, smiling at Jamison.

Jamison led Donovan up the wide main staircase to the second floor.

"I could use a drink," Canidy said after Donovan had disappeared. "By the authority vested in me as commander of this establishment, I declare the bar is now open."

Stevens chuckled.

"Your whisky or ours?" he asked. He correctly suspected that Canidy and Jamison had stolen four cases of whisky from the London Station.

"Now, Colonel," Canidy said. "I thought you'd given up on that."

"I'll have a drink, Dick," Stevens said. "Stolen or not."

"What about Your Gracefulness," Canidy said to the Duchess. "Will you have a wee nip with the peasants?"

She did not, Stevens saw, take umbrage.

"Thank you, no, Major," she said. "It's a bit early for me."

"And, inspired by the example of our leader, I'm for a hot bath myself," Whittaker announced.

"The next thing you know, he'll be changing his underwear more than once a week," Canidy said.

The Duchess shook her head and walked down the corridor toward the offices. Canidy led Stevens and Fine down the opposite corridor toward the Officers' Club, and Whittaker climbed the stairs to the second floor.

Whittaker walked down a wide parquet-floored corridor to a sturdy, paneled door, unlocked it, and went in. Before the OSS had taken possession of Whitbey House, this suite of three rooms had been the apartment of the Duchess. It was now his quarters. Canidy had assigned the Duchess to less impressive rooms.

He tossed his cap and jacket on the bed and walked into the bathroom. He turned on the tap, and water began to gurgle into a huge, black marble bathtub. When there was an inch or so of water on the bottom, a smile of pleasure crossed his face, a Eureka smile, as though a smashing insight had flashed into his brain. He walked out of the bathroom and returned naked several minutes later. His flesh was not as seamless as you might have expected from his flawlessly handsome face. He had been twice wounded in the Philippines, and there were more than a dozen scars where insect and leech bites had become infected.

In one hand Whittaker held a glass and the neck of a Scotch bottle and in the other a square tin of Pear's Finest Bubble Bath Crystals. He set the glass and the Scotch carefully on the tub rim, and then started shaking bubble-bath crystals into the now-about-half-full tub of water.

Some bubbles formed, but not enough to satisfy him. He added more salts, and finally shook the tin over the water to empty it. Then he somewhat delicately tested the water with his toe, withdrawing it quickly because it was hotter than he expected. He turned on the cold tap, and the combined hot and cold flow was sufficient to start bubbles forming. Once they had started, there seemed to be no end of them.

Whittaker's face took on a look of almost pure pleasure. He tested the water again and again until it was the right temperature, then climbed into the tub. The bubbles concealed all of him but his head. A hand appeared, grabbed the Scotch bottle, and poured whisky into the glass. He leaned back against the end of the tub, and his other hand appeared, this time to sweep bubbles away from his face.

Someone came into the bathroom.

"Odd, you don't look like the bubble-bath type."

"Nothing is too good for the well-born," Whittaker said.

"Someone like yourself?" his visitor asked, mocking.

"Kind, cheerful, obedient, reverent, et cetera," Whittaker said solemnly. "I have all the aristocratic virtues, I just can't remember them at the moment."

His visitor giggled and then thought of something.

"Where did you find the bubble bath?"

"Where do you think?" he replied.

"You bastard," Her Grace the Duchess Stanfield said, and then she walked to the tub and picked up the tin. "You triple bastard! That was my entire supply!"

"Well, I guess there's only one thing that can be done about that," Whittaker said.

"Don't tell me," she said, genuinely annoyed. "You'll have some airfreighted from the States."

"What I meant was that you should take advantage of it while there's still some left."

"You mean, climb in there with you? You're insane!"

"Don't knock it till you try it," Whittaker said. "Have you ever been diddled under the bubbles?"

"No!" she said.

He smiled wickedly at her.

"My God, what if somebody should come in!" she said softly.

"There's probably room for another couple," Whittaker said. "Whom did you have in mind?"

"That's not what I meant!" She stopped, knowing that he had tripped her again.

"Lock the door," he said.

She wet her lips, turned, and locked the door.

Then she turned and faced him, and met his eyes, and then very slowly and deliberately undressed. She knew that he liked to watch her remove her clothes, and letting him watch did something to her, too. She felt lightheaded and excited by the time she walked across the tiles to slip into the tub with him.

She tried to snuggle in next to him, but he forced his knee between hers and she found herself straddling him.

"I probably shouldn't tell you this," she said, "but I missed you."

And then she gave a little animal yelp as he entered her.

She moved on him, and then happened to glance beyond him. There was a mirror. She could see nothing of him but the back of his head. But she could see herself: wanton, she thought, jiggling up and down the way she was.

She looked down at him. His eyes were closed. *He is very young,* she thought. She felt incredible tenderness for him. He was young, twenty-four, twenty-five; and she was thirty-six and married and nothing could ever come of this affair.

But that doesn't change anything. The absurd truth is, I love him. Even though I'm just a convenient roll in the hay for him.

"I love you," she said.

He stopped moving under her and opened his eyes and looked at her.

For a moment she thought that he was going to reply, but he didn't. And then, very slowly and deliberately, he started moving into her again.

III

[ONE]
Whitbey House, Kent
6 December 1942

Canidy was sitting at an ancient desk he often thought should be in a museum, working his way through the ten-inch-high stack of paper that had accumulated while he'd flown to North Africa.

With the command of OSS Whitbey House station came a mind-boggling bureaucratic responsibility: The paperwork involved in simply housing and clothing and feeding the OSS personnel there would in more normal times have occupied the services of half a dozen secretaries.

As he signed his name for the fiftieth or sixtieth time over the signature block (RICHARD M. CANIDY, Major, USAAC Commanding), he thought again about how the responsibility for Whitbey House had dropped down upon him. The appointment had been as inevitable as it was surprising. And frustrating.

Canidy had been recruited as an agent for the OSS when it was still the Office of the Coordinator of Information. Not because he had any espionage skills or relevant experience—for he hadn't—but because he was an old friend of Eric Fulmar's and they wanted to recruit Fulmar. The way to do that had been to find an old pal who could sing "Auld Lang Syne" while waving the flag in Eric's face.

He had been so naive then that he had believed that his association with international espionage would end when that operation was over.

But then it had been made clear to him that since he was possessed of certain highly classified information—concerning not only the Fulmar operation but the workings of the COI itself—it would not be possible for him to just quit. So they had found something useful for him to do.

Despite the uniform he wore and the thousand times he had written his signature above the "Major, USAAC" signature block, he was not a major of the Army Air Corps. In June of 1941 he had been discharged from the Navy (as a Lieutenant, Junior Grade) and had gone off to Burma to fly P-40s for the American Volunteer Group. Which meant that he had been a civilian when he was hired on as a "Technical Consultant" for the COI.

Later it had been decided that military status was important for the Fulmar operation. So the Adjutant General's office had handed him an AGO card that made him a major. And "Major" he had remained. He was still paid as a "Technical Consultant," however, and had apparently been promoted, because the monthly checks were now over fifty dollars more than a major on flight pay with his length of service would be paid.

He didn't call attention to this peculiarity, because he suspected they would give him a bona-fide commission if he did. And he would continue what he was doing for several dollars less a month.

Whitbey House was not his first "command." "Major" Canidy had also commanded the COI "safe house" at Deal, New Jersey. Chesley Haywood Whittaker's oceanfront estate had been turned over to Donovan and the COI by Chesty's widow. And the COI had stashed there Vice Admiral de Escadre de Verbey of the French Navy until the time the admiral would be used against the Germans and/or General Charles de Gaulle, the difficult-to-deal-with head of the Free French.

Since it was felt the Admiral would be more comfortable with a military host than a civilian, it had been "Major" Canidy at Deal. And Major Canidy had recruited bona-fide Captain and B-17 Squadron Commander Stanley S. Fine for the Fulmar Operation.

Fine had fully expected to be returned to the Air Corps after the COI no longer needed his services. But the COI was just as reluctant to lose him as it was to lose Canidy. Since Canidy and Fine were already on the COI ros-ter—*and* pilots—they had been given the "fly the magic dirt for the Norden bombsight out of the Belgian Congo" mission.

When that operation was over, Fine had become for all intents and pur-poses Colonel Stevens's deputy. And Canidy was given command of Whit-bey House station. It was Canidy's opinion that—with the single, if very important, exception that they were "cleared" for OSS duty—his and Fine's current jobs had nothing to do with their qualifications but rather with their availability as more or less round pegs in the round holes of the OSS manning chart. There were dozens of empty holes; the OSS was growing al-most miraculously.

Canidy was amused and a little disconcerted to be regarded now by OSS recruits as a grizzled and legendary veteran.

There were perks, of course. He *was* commanding Whitbey House sta-tion, which meant—most important—that he didn't have to deal with a commanding officer. Stevens left him pretty much alone. And he had a car and a driver: If he wanted to go into London, he didn't have to ask permis-sion. And he was the Lord of the Manor and had established himself in the ducal apartment of Whitbey House: three large rooms, museum-quality fur-niture, an enormous bathroom, and even room service when he wanted it.

There was a loud knock at his door.

"Come!" Canidy called. It was more than likely Jamison come to lead him through the paperwork jungle. Jamison was the very bright lieutenant who did much of the administrative work for Canidy.

It was not Jamison.

"Am I interrupting anything, Dick?" Colonel Wild Bill Donovan asked as he walked into the room.

Canidy quickly stood up.

"Not a thing," Canidy said. "I was just sitting here letting this crap drive me out of my mind." He gestured at the paper-submerged desk.

Donovan chuckled sympathetically.

"You ought to see what Pete Douglass has waiting for me when I get back to the office," he said.

"Jamison is a lot of help," Canidy said. "Actually, he's perfectly capable of running this place all by himself."

"Jimmy about?" Donovan asked.

"Jimmy's spreading pollen," Canidy said. "Would you like me to find him?"

Donovan laughed.

"We'll send for him after a bit, and for Stevens and Fine," he said. "I want a private word with you first."

Canidy nodded.

"I'm tempted to ask about Ann Chambers," Donovan said. "Did I detect a little sour grapes about Jimmy's 'pollen spreading'?"

"Ann's in the North of England," Canidy said. "I finally got her on the phone about twenty minutes ago."

Ann Chambers was a war correspondent for the Chambers News Service. Her father was Chairman of the Board of the Chambers Publishing Corporation, of which the Chambers News Service was a wholly owned subsidiary. She was in England because Dick Canidy was in England, and she was in love with Dick Canidy. Between her bona-fide skills as a journalist and her father's influence, Ann got pretty much what she wanted.

"Give her my best regards when you see her," Donovan said.

Canidy chuckled.

Ann Chambers posed a continuing problem for Donovan and the OSS. Other curious journalists could be dealt with by suggesting quietly to their superiors that national security required their return to the States. More seriously curious journalists could be hospitalized for psychiatric evaluation. Brandon Chambers, however, would demand to know precisely how his daughter had endangered the national security and would then make his own judgment about that.

And if Brandon Chambers's daughter was put into a psychiatric hospital for evaluation—which had been the Attorney General's solution to the problem of habeas corpus—Brandon Chambers's eight newspapers, five radio stations, and the Chambers News Service could be counted on to put the admittedly constitutionally questionable practice before the American public until the Supreme Court dealt with its legality.

"Certainly," Canidy said, smiling. "I'll even tell her you want her for an exclusive, long, candlelit tête-à-tête maybe?"

Donovan had to laugh. "Okay," he said. "I confess I sometimes yearn for the days when the men went to war, and the women stayed home and knitted sweaters for them."

And then Donovan was suddenly all business.

"I'm curious about your reaction, your gut reaction, about putting Fulmar back into Morocco," he said.

"'Gut reaction'?" Canidy parroted. "Okay. When Fulmar jumped out of the B-25, I felt a little sick to my stomach."

"Fear or outrage?" Donovan asked conversationally.

"A little of both," Canidy said. "Was making him the bait really necessary?"

"Yes," Donovan said simply. "And it paid off. We are now reasonably sure von Heurten-Mitnitz is everything he claims to be."

"Well," Canidy said, "I suppose that's important."

"It's most important," Donovan said. And then when Canidy didn't reply, "You're not going to ask me why?"

"I think if you want to tell me, you will," Canidy said, smiling. "Otherwise . . ."

"You're learning, Dick," Donovan said, smiling back at him.

"*Are* you going to tell me?" Canidy asked.

"How much of a briefing about German jet aircraft did you and Ed Stevens get from the Air Corps? And how much specifically did they tell you about jet aircraft engines?"

"Not much," Canidy said. "Just that the Germans have, in the flight-test stage, aircraft powered by jet engines. The Air Corps feels that it's very unlikely that these will ever become operational."

"And what do you think?"

"I'm a fighter pilot," Canidy said. Then he paused. "An ex–fighter pilot? Anyway, from that position of ignorance, it seems to me that a fighter which can make five hundred knots and fire twenty-mm cannon well out of range of a B-17's or a B-24's .50-calibers is going to shoot down a lot of bombers."

"To the point," Donovan said, very seriously, "where the entire Air Corps strategy of bombardment of German industry may well have to be scrapped."

"The Air Corps brass didn't seem to be all that worried," Canidy said.

"If the Luftwaffe can come up with half a dozen squadrons of jet fighters," Donovan said, "our losses would be unacceptable. And it would be as much a public relations as a logistical disaster. In other words, if the Germans get those aircraft into production, the course of the war in Europe will be drastically changed. It may not mean we would lose the war, but it could bring on an unsatisfactory armistice."

"Jesus!" Canidy said.

"And there's something you haven't been told, Dick, because it's brand-new information. The Germans have begun testing—we still don't know where—at least one jet-propelled flying bomb. Or pilotless aircraft. You're an aeronautical engineer, think about that: Hundreds, perhaps thousands, of pilotless aircraft, faster than any fighter we have, each carrying five hundred pounds of high explosive, aimed at London or Manchester. Or, for that matter, launched from submarines and aimed at New York City."

Canidy thought aloud, "How would they be controlled?"

"I'm not an aeronautical engineer," Donovan said. "I thought maybe you could tell me."

"I have a degree as an AE," Canidy said. "That's all."

"Modesty becomes you, Richard," Donovan said, teasing him. "But I've heard you're pretty good. You really have no idea how they could be controlled?"

"Navigation wouldn't have to be that precise," Canidy said. "All you'd have to do would be to maintain a known heading. Over five hundred miles, you could put something like that within, say, ten miles of where you wanted it. London is a lot wider than ten miles. And if you knew the cruising speed, a simple timer could shut off the fuel when it was over the target."

He looked at Donovan, who nodded.

"That's just about the same answer I got from Professor Pritchard," Donovan said, "who sends his regards."

Matthew Pritchard had been one of Canidy's teachers at MIT. More than a teacher, almost a collaborator in Canidy's thesis.

"It's frightening," Canidy said. "The more you think about it, the more frightening it gets. And without having to worry about pilot safety, they could stamp them out like cookies. No landing gear, no communications equipment, a rudimentary stabilization system. . . . Just an engine and a load of explosive."

"Matt Pritchard told me that the engine is the only weak point he could think of," Donovan said. "As it is with the jet-powered fighters."

"I don't understand," Canidy said. "I agree, of course, that the engine is the most important component, but I don't see how that helps us."

"We keep them from building engines," Donovan said.

"How are we going to do that?" Canidy asked.

"I should have said, 'we delay, we interfere with,' the production of engines," Donovan said. "I think we can do that. How effectively remains to be seen."

"How delay? How interfere with?" Canidy asked.

"The priority is first delay the jet fighters and next the flying bombs. If we can delay the production of jet engines, we can delay the production of jet fighters, and then we pray the Eighth Air Force can use the time bought to destroy German industry before they can, as you put it, start stamping out flying bombs like cookies."

"And von Shitfitz can somehow help? How?"

"Specifically, by helping us bring out an expert who can tell us about the engines," Donovan said. "Not their design. But their metallurgy. According to Pritchard and others, this is a whole new technology. A whole new metallurgy. If we can find out what kind of alloys are needed and shut off the German supply of the raw material, then we can delay—or at least interfere with—engine production."

"Our own metallurgists can't tell us?"

"There're several ways to go, or so I'm told. We need to know which way the Germans are actually going before we can try to interfere with the raw-material-to-finished-engine process."

"And the guy you want to bring out can tell us?" Canidy asked.

Donovan nodded. He was a little uncomfortable. While everything he had said to Canidy was true, it was not the whole truth.

"Who is he?" Canidy asked.

"His name is Friedrich Dyer. Professor Doctor Friedrich Dyer, of the Department of Physics at Philips University in Marburg an der Lahn in Hesse."

"Which is where Eric went to school," Canidy said.

Donovan nodded again.

Canidy accepted what he was being told without question. There was no reason that he should be suspicious, but it was better that he not be.

If Friedrich Dyer could be successfully extracted from Germany he might well be useful. But that was not the reason a good deal of effort and a great deal of money was going to be expended to extract him. If he could be extracted, then others on a list in Donovan's safe could be extracted. The German chemists, physicists, and mathematicians on the list were those with expertise in the mathematics, physics, and chemistry of nuclear energy.

Getting them out *might* help Leslie Groves's Manhattan Project. It *certainly* would deny their knowledge to the Germans. But they had to be extracted in such a way as not to alert the Germans to the American interest in nuclear energy. They would, in other words, have to be mixed with people with no nuclear connection.

Since Canidy could not be told about the atom bomb, he could not be told any more than he had been about the Dyer operation. Donovan understood the necessity for this, but he disliked what in the final analysis was deception of his own people.

"The prototype production of engines has been assigned to a plant in Marburg," Donovan said. "The Fulmar Elektrisches Werk."

"Fulmar?" Canidy said. "Jesus!" And then: "*Electrical* plant?"

"Relatively small electric furnaces capable of great and precise heat are what's needed," Donovan said. "The critical parts are small."

Canidy grunted, as if ashamed he hadn't thought of that himself.

"If we can bring the first man out, we can get others out," Donovan said. "Dr. Conant of Harvard has made the point to the President that scientists are not a renewable resource."

"It would be easier to kill them," Canidy said. "Certainly cheaper."

Donovan looked at Canidy in surprise. Not that the thought had entered Canidy's mind—it was a thought that had of course passed many times through his own mind—but that he could talk about it so matter-of-factly, aloud.

And then Canidy met his eyes, and Donovan saw embarrassment in them, maybe even shame.

"Don't be embarrassed, Dick," Donovan said. "It may well be necessary to take some people out."

"Shit," Canidy said.

"The rationale, for what it's worth, is that any number of dead Germans are better than one dead American. A lot of innocent people are being killed in the bombing."

Canidy grunted again.

"Would it be all right if I had a drink, Colonel?" Canidy asked.

"I sort of hoped you'd offer me one," Donovan said.

That's another lie, Donovan thought. *I don't like to drink. But I will drink with you now, because I know it's important to you that I do that.*

Canidy walked across the room to a table on which sat half a dozen bottles of whisky and gin and bourbon.

"Scotch?" he asked.

"Please," Donovan said.

Canidy made two stiff drinks, walked back, and handed one to Donovan.

"Are we in touch with von Heurten-Mitnitz?" Canidy asked.

"*Von Heurten-Mitnitz,*" Donovan noticed, *not "von Shitfitz*"; Canidy was now thinking too hard to indulge his tendency to be clever.

"We have limited access to a British agent in Berlin who will make initial contact with him when the time comes. When that will be, I'll leave up to you."

"What exactly is my role in all this?"

"I thought you would have figured it out," Donovan said. "This operation is yours, Dick."

That wasn't the truth, the whole truth, and nothing but the truth, either. Donovan had planned to talk to Canidy, to feel him out. The decision as to who would run von Heurten-Mitnitz would be made later, after talking to Stevens and Bruce. Bruce wanted to give the assignment to Eldon Baker. Stevens thought Canidy should have it.

"Getting Professor Whatsisname out?" Canidy asked. "Or running von Heurten-Mitnitz?"

"Running von Heurten-Mitnitz," Donovan said, making the decision, and then immediately making another. "And running the entire pipeline, when we get that far. You have objections?"

Canidy didn't reply for a moment.

"I was talking to one of the SOE guys," he said finally. "He told me, with great pride, that the English spend their time between wars training their intelligence people. That way they have competent people available when they're needed. At the time, I just got mad. The sonofabitch was taking a shot at the OSS—they're good at that—but now I'm wondering why we don't do that. If we did, I wouldn't be sitting here now, unable to honestly come up with a name, except maybe Baker's, who could run von Shitfitz better than I can."

"I think you can do better than Eldon Baker," Donovan said. "That's why I gave the job to you."

"What happens next?"

"Plan to spend several hours with Ed Stevens after I leave. He'll give you all the details."

"I'll stay here?"

"Until it gets in the way," Donovan said. "You've done a good job here, Dick. I was nosing around before."

"Is that what they call 'throwing the dog a bone'?" Canidy asked.

Donovan laughed. "Actually it's called 'Putting the Other Side to Sleep, We Hope.' We know they're watching us pretty closely, so we're going to try to put them to sleep a little. Fine, for the time being, will continue as Stevens's administrator. And then we're going to send him to Switzerland, where we hope they will think he's going as an administrator."

"Switzerland? What for?"

"Do you know Allen Dulles?"

Canidy shook his head. "No."

"I thought maybe you'd met in Washington," Donovan said. "Dulles is station chief in Switzerland. Good man. We intend to use Stan Fine's contacts with the Zionists—as incredible as it seems, with what Hitler is doing with the Jews, they have a fine intelligence net inside Germany—to see what he can find out for us. And then, in time, we—which is to say you—will bring Fulmar up from Morocco, where he is working as a linguist, and work him here as a linguist for a while and then send him to Switzerland too."

"From where we can move him into Germany?" Canidy asked.

"You may conclude that it's necessary," Donovan said.

"That's already been decided, hasn't it?" Canidy asked, looking into Donovan's face.

"You may come to conclude that it's necessary," Donovan repeated.

"And Whittaker?"

"Whittaker will continue on running agent training," Donovan said.

"Oh," Canidy said with sarcastic innocence, "I thought maybe you'd come to conclude that it's necessary to send him back to the Philippines."

He was expecting a reaction from Donovan, but not the one he thought he saw in his eyes.

"Jesus Christ!" he said. "When? Why?"

"I think we've covered everything that has to be covered, Dick," Donovan said, very evenly. "Why don't we call it a night?"

[TWO]
Special Operations Executive Station X
7 December 1942

The meeting was held in a small, oak-paneled chamber on the second floor of a Georgian mansion that had been the country home of a ducal family. Before the home had been turned over to the Imperial General Staff of His Majesty's Forces, and then by the IGS to the SOE, the room was known as the "small bridge room."

Which was a euphemism. The truth was that His Grace, having been corrupted by the Americans, had turned the "small bridge room" into a salon for the play of much less reputable games. While visiting the 160,000-acre ranch his family had owned in Montana since 1884, His Grace had visited Las Vegas, Nevada, where he had been introduced to an American game of chance known as "poker." Though losing a bit ($18,000) before he got the hang of it, His Grace became enraptured with the game. And he soon came to understand the philosophy of play: He came to see that it was really a game that turned not so much on the luck of the draw as on the quick-wittedness of the players and upon their ability to judge the psychological makeup of their opponents.

His Grace found that far more interesting than waiting to see what card would fall next in Chemin de Fer or where the ball would come to rest after it bounced around a roulette wheel. Moreover, once he came to understand the game, His Grace was rather good at it. He left Las Vegas $22,000 richer than he had come.

It wasn't the money that pleased him—His Grace owned substantial tracts of land in Mayfair—but the sense of accomplishment. And he would be damned if he had to forgo that pleasure until his next visit to America, which might not be for another five years. He knew enough men who would not only be as fascinated with the game as he was (after he had overcome their initial resistance), but who also possessed both the intellectual bent and the financial resources (once *they* had the hang of it) to make formidable—and thus worthy—opponents.

His Grace had a word with the owner-manager of Harrod's Gambling Hall, a most obliging chap. When His Grace left Las Vegas, he took with him a heavy, oak, six-sided table with a green baize playing surface and rather clever little shelves around the edges in which one kept one's chips and one's glass; a light fixture designed to illuminate the playing surface and nothing else; six matching chairs with arms and cushions; a case of chips; two dozen green plastic eyeshades; and a case (20 gross) of plastic-coated cards. The latter two items were emblazoned with "Harrod's Gambling Hall, Las Vegas Nevada."

His Grace successfully taught the game to his friends, but he was not able to convince his butler—and thus, none of the other staff either—that poker was the sort of game His Grace should be playing. The butler, furthermore, felt that if it should become public knowledge that he was playing, His Grace might suffer the slings and arrows of outrageous rumors.

The room in which the poker table and the chairs and the special light fixture and the other accessories were installed was therefore referred to as "the small bridge room."

"C" (as he was then and now known), who had been at Oxford with His Grace, had later been one of those taught the game of poker by His Grace, and who was now head of MI-6 and de facto chief of all British Intelligence, told this story to Lieutenant Colonel Edmund T. Stevens and Major Richard Canidy when they first sat down at the six-sided baize-covered poker table.

"In the eyes of the staff," "C" concluded, "poker was rather like the young women the Duke brought here when he acceded to the title. We were still at Oxford then. He used to ship them over from Paris by the half dozen. The staff referred to them as his 'special weekend guests.' "

Canidy and Stevens both laughed out loud. "C" chuckled, pleased that he had amused them. And that he had put them at ease.

"C" was a gentleman and subtle. The story was intended not only to amuse Canidy and Stevens but to remind them of the differences between the British and American cultures. And to suggest that they were all playing poker: the British and the Americans versus the Germans, and the British versus the Americans. These points were not lost on either Major Canidy or Colonel Stevens.

In the First World War, the British and the French had agreed between themselves that since Americans knew nothing of war, the American entrance into the war would mean nothing more than an influx—albeit a massive one—of "colonial" troops and matériel to be used as the experts saw fit.

Things didn't go quite as the British and French experts had planned, the American Commanding General "Black Jack" Pershing being rather reluctant to follow their orders. He announced, and stuck by his decision, that when Americans went into combat, they would be led by American officers, and would not be fed piecemeal into either English or French formations.

The situation was changed in this war. An American general was in overall command, reflecting the reality that Americans would have otherwise sent their troops and matériel to the Far East. Japanese, not Germans, occupied American territory. Americans would go along with the notion that the war should be won first in Europe, but only if their man, Eisenhower, was in charge.

Since a large and powerful body of American opinion still held that the European war was none of America's business, it would have been politically impossible for Roosevelt to send a million American soldiers to Europe to be commanded by an Englishman.

The British understood this; but that did not change their devout belief that the Imperial General Staff, as well as MI-6 and the Special Operations Executive, were far better equipped to run military operations and intelligence than was Eisenhower and his American staff and the just-born, relatively speaking, Office of Strategic Services.

If the British had their way, all the assets—matériel, personnel, and financial—of the OSS would be directed by the various intelligence officers who, in one way or another, all reported to "C."

Colonel William J. Donovan was the World War II equivalent for espionage and sabotage—for "strategic services"—of General Black Jack Pershing and the AEF of World War I: Despite their inexperience and despite any other objection the Imperial General Staff—or Winston Churchill himself— might have, Americans, Donovan insisted—with the authority of President Roosevelt—would run their own covert operations.

And, to the surprise of some British, the Americans had done well, in an intelligence sense, in the invasion of North Africa. If they had failed, perhaps there would have been a chance to argue again for British control. But that hadn't happened. There was no way now to talk the Americans out of independent operation. There would be cooperation, nothing more.

And that, Stevens thought, was the real reason "C" was sitting across the poker table from him now. The ostensible purpose of this meeting had to do with certain operational details involving Helmut von Heurten-Mitnitz and Johann Müller. If the British had been running these agents, the personal attention of "C" would not be required. "C" was here now to ensure that his people understood that the decision had been made to cooperate with the independently operating Americans.

Photostatic copies of all the MI-6 files on Helmut von Heurten-Mitnitz and Johann Müller, on the von Heurten-Mitnitz family, on the Baron Fulmar, on the German rocket installation at Peenemünde, on German jet-engine experimentation, on everything the Americans had asked for, plus some things they hadn't asked for but which they would find of interest, had been brought to the meeting at Station X.

It took more than four hours before the Americans had examined the photostats and were out of questions; arranged the details of liaison with the British agents in Germany; and come to an understanding, an agreement, about where British support would end and the Americans would have to fend for themselves.

And then the Americans left.

The deputy chief of MI-6 sat alone with "C" at the poker table, a bemused look on his face.

"If you're about to say something witty, Charles, about our American friends," "C" said, "please spare me. Otherwise?"

"I had a rather profound thought, actually," the deputy chief of MI-6 said. "I confess to thinking about sending virgins off to do a woman's work. But then it occurred to me they all start off as virgins, don't they? All it takes is once."

"C" smiled.

"I knew I could count on you for something romantic, Charles." Then he added: "But I don't think you can fairly categorize either that Major Canidy or that half-German chap they're going to send in as virgins. They may not yet know how to run a professional like von Heurten-Mitnitz, but they're not virgins. They've both been operational."

"*Virgins,*" the deputy chief of MI-6 insisted. "*Deadly* virgins, perhaps. But *virgins.*"

[THREE]
The Hotel d'Anfa
Anfa, Casablanca, Morocco
8 December 1942

Though it was now functioning as officers' quarters for Western Task Force, the Hotel d'Anfa had lost none of its elegance or ambience. The pool and the tennis courts remained open, as did the only rooftop bar and night club in Casablanca.

Eldon C. Baker, a man of not quite thirty-two years with something of a moon face and thinning, sandy hair, sat in a corner of the bar. He wore an officer's uniform with the customary "U.S." lapel insignia but without insignia of branch of service or rank. On the shoulder of his green gabardine tunic was a square embroidered in blue. There was a triangle within the square and the letters "U.S." It was the insignia worn by civilian experts attached to the U.S. Army in the field.

Baker carried both orders and an AGO card in the name of James B. Westerman. The orders had been issued by the War Department and authorized priority military air travel from the United States to "Western Task Force in the Field" in connection with activities of the Office of the Comptroller of the Army. In the "RANK" block, the AGO card said, "ASS Lt/Col." This meant that Baker carried the assimilated rank of Lieutenant Colonel and was entitled to the privileges of that rank when it came to quarters, transportation, and so on. So far, no one else had thought "ASS Lt/Col" was at all amusing.

Baker also carried—in a safe place—a second identification card and a second set of orders. These had his correct name on them. The identification card, which came with a badge, identified him as a Special Agent of the U.S. Army Counterintelligence Corps, and the orders, issued in the name of the Assistant Chief of Staff, Intelligence, said that he was engaged in a confidential mission for the Assistant Chief of Staff, G-2, and any questions concerning him and his mission should be referred to that office.

While the second set of credentials was genuine—they had in fact been issued by G-2—Eldon C. Baker was not an agent of the CIC. He was in fact an employee of the State Department and was paid as an FSO-4. For more than a year, however, he had been on temporary duty with the OSS. He was listed on the OSS table of organization as "Chief, Recruitment and Training"; and it was in connection with this that he had come to Morocco. His primary mission was to recruit people, with emphasis on officers fluent in French, Italian, or German, for planned covert operations against Germany and Italy. He also intended to arrange for the parachute training of OSS agents by the U.S. Army. And he had a third mission, known only to Colonel Donovan and Captain Douglass: He was going to send a postcard.

The third mission had a higher priority than anything else that had brought Eldon C. Baker from Washington to the rooftop bar of the Hotel d'Anfa.

Baker saw Eric Fulmar before Fulmar saw him. As Baker expected, Fulmar came into the bar a little after five o'clock. The hint of a smile appeared on Baker's lips when he saw him. Eric Fulmar was rather obviously pleased with himself and his role in the scheme of things.

He was in olive-drab uniform: a shirt, trousers, and tie. His feet were in highly polished jump boots, which went with the silver parachutist's wings on his breast pocket just above his two ribbons. He was wearing the ETO (European Theater of Operations) ribbon with a battle star and the ribbon of the Silver Star medal. Hanging from his shoulder was a Thompson machine-pistol, a non-issue weapon.

As he sat down, he rather ostentatiously laid the weapon on the bar stool beside his and, in Arabic, ordered Scotch and water from the Moroccan barman.

He got strange looks from the other officers at the bar, who were young staff officers of one kind or another assigned to the various rear-area support services in Casablanca. Fulmar managed to remind them, Baker saw, that while they might be in uniform, they weren't *really* soldiers. Fulmar, with his Silver Star and parachutist's wings and Thompson machine-pistol, *was* a soldier.

Baker stood up from his table, walked to the bar, and slid onto the stool beside him.

"*Wie gehts,* Eric?" he asked in flawless German. "*Was ist los?*"

That got some attention from the other officers at the bar, too. It probably wasn't the smartest thing to do, Baker thought; but on the other hand, he felt sure that Fulmar would somehow already have let the others know that he spoke German.

Fulmar turned to look at him. His eyes were cold. Baker was made a little uncomfortable to be reminded that beneath the facade of self-impressed young parachutist hero, this was a very tough and self-reliant young man.

"What brings you here, Baker?" Fulmar asked. His eyes were contemptuous and wary.

"Westerman," Baker said.

Fulmar thought that over.

"Westerman, then," he said.

"Well, I had to come over here, and I thought I'd say hello," Baker said. He saw the chill deepen in Fulmar's eyes, and quickly added, "I heard about the promotion and the Silver Star. Congratulations."

"Bullshit," Fulmar said flatly.

"I need a word with you," Baker said, giving up. He wondered why he had bothered trying to be friendly. It had been necessary, twice, to cause unpleasant things to happen to Eric Fulmar. And Eric Fulmar was not the sort to let bygones be bygones.

Fulmar took a sip of his Scotch, then turned to look at Baker out of his cold blue eyes.

He would have made an SS officer to warm the cockles of Hitler's heart, Baker thought. Blond-haired, blue-eyed, muscular, erect, the perfect Aryan.

"Have your word," Fulmar said.

"Not here," Baker said. "Can we go to your room?"

Fulmar said something to the bartender, who picked up Fulmar's glass and pushed it into a bed of ice behind the bar. Then Fulmar picked up his machine-pistol and walked out of the bar. Baker followed him.

They rode wordlessly two floors down in an elevator and then walked down a corridor to Fulmar's suite, a small sitting room and a much larger bedroom with a balcony. The balcony overlooked the Atlantic Ocean and a rather stunning beach.

"I don't know if this place is secure or not," Fulmar said.

"It doesn't matter," Baker said. "This isn't going to take long."

He took from the breast pocket of his tunic two 3×8-inch sheets of corrugated paperboard, held together by rubber bands, and then a fountain pen, a large, somewhat ungainly instrument.

"Is that German?" Fulmar asked, his curiosity aroused. Baker nodded his head.

"I used to have one something like it," Fulmar said.

"Sit down, Eric," Baker said, nodding toward a small writing desk as he removed the rubber bands from the sheets of cardboard.

When Fulmar had seated himself, Baker handed him a postcard and two sheets of paper cut to the same size. Fulmar examined the postcard. It was a photograph of the Kurhotel in Bad Ems.

"What's all this?"

"I have only the one postcard," Baker said. "So we can't take the risk of fucking this up. What I want you to do is copy the message from the one sheet of paper onto the other sheet of paper. Copy what is written exactly."

Fulmar looked at the piece of paper. The postcard was to be addressed to Herr Joachim Freienstall, 74-76 Beerenstrasse, Berlin/Zehlendorf. The message (in German) was "Sorry I missed you. Please give my regards to my father and Prof. Dyer. Kindest regards, Willi von K."

"What the hell is this?" Fulmar asked. "Who's Freienstall? For that matter, who the hell is 'Willi von K'?"

"That has nothing to do with you," Baker said.

"Bullshit," Fulmar said. "Why do you need me to write it?"

"Let me put it this way," Baker said coldly. "You don't have the need to know, Eric."

"Then write your own fucking postcard," Fulmar said.

"Just do what I ask you, Eric," Baker ordered. "This is important."

They locked eyes for a moment.

"I'd like to know what scurvy trick this is," Fulmar said. "And on whom."

"At the moment, that's impossible," Baker said.

"Shit!" Fulmar said, but he took up the fountain pen and copied the message onto the blank sheet of paper.

When he had finished, Baker picked it up, examined it, nodded, and said, "Fine. Now do it exactly the same way on the postcard."

As Fulmar complied, Baker took a Zippo lighter from his pocket and burned the first copy. When he had examined the final version and found it satisfactory, he burned the original message.

"Get up," he ordered. After Fulmar complied, Baker sat down at the desk. He laid the cardboard sheets on the desk and then the postcard. Then he wet his index finger with his tongue and ran it over "Joachim Freienstall," rendering the name illegible.

Fulmar's eyebrows rose, but he didn't say anything.

Baker waited for the spit to dry, then very carefully wiped the postcard with his handkerchief, paying particular attention to the glossy side with the photograph of the Kurhotel. Next, holding it with his handkerchief, he extended the card to Fulmar, who made no move to take it.

"Now what?" Fulmar asked.

"Take the card and lay it on the cardboard," Baker said.

"Will my index and thumb prints be enough?" Fulmar asked sarcastically. "Or should I put the rest on it, too?"

"Pass it back and forth a couple of times between your hands," Baker said.

Fulmar did as he was told. Baker then laid the second sheet of cardboard on top of the postcard, replaced the rubber bands, and put the whole thing back in his pocket.

"You understand, of course," he said, "that you are to mention this to no one?"

"The thing about you, Baker," Fulmar said, "is that you're such a truly devious bastard that I really have no idea what you're up to."

"In our business, Eric," Baker said, "there are those who would take that as a first-rate compliment."

He put out his hand.

"That's it," he said, "unless there's something I could do for you in Washington?"

Fulmar pointedly ignored the hand.

"Not a thing you could do for me," Fulmar said. "You've already done enough for me. Or to me."

"I'm really sorry you feel that way, Eric," Baker said.

"Yeah, I'm sure you are," Fulmar said.

Baker shrugged and walked out of the room. Fulmar looked at the closed door for a full minute, his face lost in thought. And then a look of genuine concern crossed his face.

"Christ!" he said, and hurried out of the room.

He had remembered a Red Cross girl with absolutely marvelous eyes who had said she would meet him at quarter to six in the bar.

[FOUR]
The Wardman Park Hotel
Washington, D.C
16 December 1942

Major Peter "Doug" Douglass, Jr., who was short for a pilot and looked even younger than his twenty-five years, wanted to say good-bye to his father before he took off for Europe. The easiest way to do that would have been simply to land his P-38 in Washington. But Peter Douglass, Sr., was a captain in the United States Navy, and Doug Douglass did not want the "good-bye" to turn into a fatherly lecture on the hazards to an officer's career of flouting regulations forbidding "diversions en route to the aerial port of departure." The other easy alternative, declaring engine trouble over Washington, was just too much of a convenient coincidence.

Between Alabama and North Carolina, however, Doug Douglass found his answer. He had a good executive officer who could lead the rest of the group to Westover. And he really didn't think anyone would ask questions about carburetor trouble near Baltimore making a "precautionary" landing there necessary. So he used the in-flight communications system to relay a spurious message to his father: "Replacement package will arrive Baltimore 1330 hours." He was confident his father would know what it meant.

Charity Hoche was waiting for him with an OSS station wagon. He knew Charity fairly well. He had, in fact, rather casually made the beast with two backs with her on one of the few times he'd been able to make it to Washington. Charity worked for the OSS—that is to say, for his father—as sort of a housekeeper for the turn-of-the-century mansion the OSS operated on Q Street near Rock Creek Park.

She came out of the same very upper-echelon set as Donovan and Jimmy Whittaker and Cynthia Chenowith and Ed Bitter and his wife. A bright girl with a dim look, she had picked up from friends (most of them OSS types) and at parties more than she should have picked up about the OSS. So it was decided that the best way to keep an eye on her was to give her a job.

And she looked damn good, too, when he saw her. Marvelous breasts, long blond hair, and a pronounced nasal manner of speech he found enticingly erotic. But he had come to see his father, not for a casual roll in the hay.

"My dad's tied up?" he asked.

Charity told him that his father was indeed "tied up" but that he hoped Doug could wait until eight, at which time he might be free.

On the other hand, since my father is tied up, maybe a casual roll in the hay would steady my nerves for the arduous duty I am about to face.

So they went for a beer, except he didn't drink because he was going to have to fly, and Charity drank some concoction with fruit juice and a cherry and gin. It tended to make her emotional. By four o'clock, Doug had decided he would not fly on to Westover until tomorrow. Every hour on the hour, Charity called to see if his father had any word for them.

Then they had dinner someplace, but he didn't pay much attention to what they had to eat. They had started playing kneesy under the table pretty soon after their arrival, and that was more interesting than food. Around dessert or coffee or some damn thing, she leaned over to say something to him and rested her magnificent breast on his hand.

Finally, it was out in the open, although there was some imaginative use of euphemisms: They could not go to Charity's place for a "nap"—the euphemism here being that if he was going to fly to England the next morning, he would need his rest—because she lived at the house on Q Street, and people might get the wrong idea.

Anyplace but Washington, a hotel would have worked; but there were no hotel rooms to be had in Washington. (They spent a dollar and a half in nickels confirming that by telephone.)

And then Charity found a way: They would go to Ed and Sarah Bitter's suite in the Wardman Park Hotel. Not only could they call from there to see if there was word about his father, but Charity remembered hearing that Ed Bitter (who was a bit dense about such things) was out of town on duty.

Sarah was much more likely to understand how important it was for Doug to get that nap, and she would probably even displace her child Joe from his room so that Doug's nap would be both private and without interruption.

Sarah Child Bitter was indeed delighted to see Major Peter "Doug" Douglass, Jr., Army Air Corps. For Sarah's husband, Lieutenant Commander Bitter, was for a number of reasons particularly fond of Major Douglass.

In the days before the war, Ed Bitter and Doug Douglass had been "Flying Tigers" together. Right after the war started, Doug had saved Ed's life at considerable risk to his own neck. Wounded by ground fire while strafing a Japanese air base, Ed had managed to land his crippled plane in a dry riverbed. And then, defying the laws of aerodynamics, Doug had landed his P-40, loaded Ed into it, and taken off again with Ed on his lap. If Doug hadn't done that, Ed would have either died from loss of blood or fallen into the hands of the Japanese who regarded the "Flying Tigers" as bandits and be-headed the ones they caught.

Doug Douglass was welcome to Little Joe's room anytime he wanted it.

But not for the purpose Charity obviously had in mind. Sarah took her into the butler's pantry and told her so.

"I don't mean to be nasty about this, Charity," she said. "But if you insist on acting like a woman who goes to hotels with men, go to a hotel."

"If there were any vacant hotel rooms in Washington, and there are not, they would not rent one to an aviator and his blonde," Charity argued. "They demand marriage licenses."

"Then you are just going to have to restrain your impulses until you can arrange something," Sarah said. She giggled and added, "Either a marriage li-cense or your own apartment."

"Unfortunately, there's no time to do that," Charity said.

"Unless you get to roll around with him tonight, you'll go blind, right, or grow hair on your palms?"

"This time tomorrow night, he'll be in his little airplane somewhere over the Atlantic," Charity said.

"Did he tell you that?" Sarah asked.

"No, and I don't want him to know I know," Charity said.

"If it's a secret, why are you telling me?"

"What are you going to do, phone Hitler? The only reason I'm telling you is that I want you to know how important this is to me."

"Charity, I love you, but I know you. If I ever found out . . ."

"The reason I know is that Captain Douglass told me to get reports from the Navy on the progress of a flight of P-38s from Westover Field in Massa-chusetts tomorrow afternoon. They're flying via Newfoundland to Scotland. Doug told me he's going to Westover. I didn't have to be Sherlock Holmes to put two and two together."

"My God, if Ed found out, he'd kill me," Sarah said, weakening.

"He won't be home until Tuesday," Charity argued conclusively. "You told me that yourself. And if you don't tell him, I certainly won't."

"I'm going to take Joe for a walk," Sarah said finally, feeling very much the sophisticated woman of the world. "Do what you think is right."

And Sarah took Little Joe for a walk, although he didn't need one. What happened between Doug and Charity while she was gone was none of her business.

But she hadn't imagined they wouldn't be finished when she came back. Or that they would keep it up for hours.

She concluded that the best way to handle the situation was to just go to bed and say nothing until after Doug left in the morning. Then she would really give Charity a piece of her mind.

It was a lucky thing Ed wasn't home. Ed would have had a fit. But Ed had told her—with certainty—that his duty as aide-de-camp to Vice Admiral Enoch Hawley, USN, Chief Aviation Matériel Assignments Branch, BUAIR, would keep him out of town for at least the weekend and probably into Tuesday.

Lieutenant Commander Edwin Ward Bitter, USN, returned home three hours later, just before midnight.

When he found the baby's crib in their bedroom, his curiosity was aroused. "Who's here?" he asked when he crawled into bed beside Sarah.

Feigning a much deeper sleep than was the case, Sarah replied, "Douglass."

"Good," Ed said happily and went to sleep.

That bought her some time, Sarah thought, to consider how to handle the situation when it came up in the morning as it would as inevitably as the sun.

Being married to one herself, Sarah had come to understand that service academy graduates and career officers were just plain different from other officers. They saw things in another kind of light, they had more rigid codes of honor and standards of behavior than people like, say, Ed's (and Sarah's and Doug's) friend Dick Canidy.

Sometimes these differing perceptions were evident. For starters, both Doug, who was a West Pointer, and Ed, who had gone to Annapolis, were not amused—and let him know it—whenever Canidy characterized the Army-Navy Club as "The Old Farts Home." And both took offense whenever Dick or Jim Whittaker mocked the professional military establishment.

And now Doug Douglass had stepped over the professional line: It was another of those odd military customs that Sarah had so much trouble understanding. Ed certainly didn't expect Douglass, who was a healthy young bachelor, to play the celibate. But he fully expected him to obey the hoary adage that an officer must keep his indiscretions one hundred miles from the flagpole.

An officer did not take his loose women under the roof of a brother officer's house, much less sleep with them there. And by sleeping with Doug at all, Charity Hoche would lose her status in Ed's eyes. She could no longer be a "lady," even though she and his wife had gone to Bryn Mawr together.

In the morning when Ed got out of bed, Sarah pretended to be asleep. Fifteen minutes later, after changing Joe, he carried the baby into his and Sarah's bed, his wholly transparent purpose being to wake her up.

"When did Doug come in last night?"

"Very late."

"I'm getting hungry. Do you think I could wake him up?"

"I think you ought to let him sleep," Sarah said, hoping to delay the inevitable just a little longer.

"To hell with it," Ed said after a moment's thought. "He and Canidy have blasted me out of a sound sleep often enough. Now it's his turn."

"Go ahead, then," Sarah said. "I'll have room service send up a breakfast buffet." *And stretchers.*

She heard him go down the corridor to Joe's room and call Doug's name, happily, cheerfully.

She picked up the telephone and ordered a breakfast buffet for four.

When Ed Bitter called his name and banged on the door, Doug Douglass woke up snuggled against Charity Hoche, her back to his belly, his hand holding her breast.

He carefully withdrew his hand and rolled carefully onto his back.

Oh, my God, he's home! Good God, he's worse than my father. When he finds out we're both in here, he'll shit a brick!

He looked at his watch. Quarter past nine. He looked down at Charity Hoche.

A stiff prick, especially your stiff prick, you prick, he thought, *has no conscience.*

He walked quietly across the room, picked up his zipper bag, and took it into the bathroom, carefully and as quietly as possible closing the door after him. He took out a change of underwear and laid it on the sink. Then he adjusted the shower so that it was as cold as he could stand it, pulled the curtain in place, and climbed into the bathtub.

She's liable to hear the shower, he thought. *It sounds like the inside of a bass drum, and she's more than likely going to hear it and wake up.*

Charity Hoche had in fact been awake when he first stirred. She didn't want to stir then though; it was too nice the way she was. She'd experienced before a man's hand cradling her naked breast and a man's naked body warm against hers, and these had always been, she was willing to admit, rather pleasant. But this was somehow different. She didn't know how, but it was.

She remembered what she had said to Sarah the night before. Was it possible that she was telling the truth, *in vino veritas,* that this was something special to her? That Doug Douglass was not just one more terribly exciting young man?

She forced herself to breathe slowly, regularly, as if she were still asleep, and then she felt the bed rise as he left it. She waited until she heard the shower, then she rolled onto her back, twisted out of bed, and stumbled over to look at her face in the vanity mirror. Her eyes were puffed, and her hair was mussed, and she cupped her hand in front of her mouth in a futile effort to smell her own breath.

She combed her hair as well as she could with her hands and pushed her swollen eyes with the balls of her fingers. Then she returned to the bed, straightened the mussed sheets, puffed up the pillows, arranged them against the headboard, and stepped back in, propping herself against the pillows, wondering if she should modestly pull the blanket up under her chin.

She decided there was no point in trying to pretend that her body was still some sort of secret to him. This was not the first whack he'd had at it.

And he also knows, she thought bitterly, *that I pass it around like canapés.*

When he came out of the bathroom in his underwear, he did not look pleased to see her awake and half sitting up in bed. *He was going to sneak out of here,* she thought.

"Good morning," she said, and smiled at him.

"Good morning," he replied, smiling uncomfortably. Then: "Ed came home last night."

"I know," Charity said. "I've got lipstick. We can letter scarlet *A*'s on our foreheads."

"He is not going to think this is funny," Douglass said.

"I'm sorry if you are now overwhelmed with morning-after remorse," Charity said. "Should I jump out the window?"

"I was thinking of Sarah," he said.

He really is. He is, in addition to everything else, a nice guy.

"She told me he wasn't due until Tuesday," Charity said. Then a thought of genuine importance hit her. "Are you going to be all right to fly?"

He nodded, and then he thought of something. "My God, my father."

"I won't tell if you won't tell," Charity heard herself say. She was sorry, but the crack had popped out on its own.

"Jesus," he said impatiently.

"I spoke with him an hour ago," Charity said. "He will be tied up—he's at the base in Fairfax—until nine. He wanted to know if you could delay your departure until noon. I told him you could."

He looked at her in surprise.

"You're not taking off until about six," Charity said. "There's a front going through, and they will hold you until it does."

"You know, then?"

"Well, you know, what the hell, why be in the OSS if you don't get to know the secrets?"

"Is that why what happened last night happened?"

"What happened last night is standard V-Girl service," Charity said. "Just the standard patriotic contribution to the morale of the boys in uniform."

She wondered why she had said that, why she was acting as she was.

"I don't understand you at all," he said, almost sadly.

He turned and looked for his uniform. He found it where she had hung it in the closet and, with his back to her, started to put it on. He had, she saw, a very broad back.

After he pulled his trousers on, while still in the process of tucking his shirt in, he turned and faced her.

"I would be grateful when you come out, if you would control that clever mouth of yours. Don't make it worse for Sarah than it will be."

Then he finished zipping his fly and walked out of the bedroom.

Bitter, ever the gentleman, was sitting at the table drinking coffee. The table was covered with silver, china, and food; but he was waiting.

"Good morning," Douglass said, as jovially as he could manage.

Bitter stood up and they shook hands.

"Good to see you, buddy," he said.

"You too," Douglass said.

"What are you doing in Washington?" Bitter asked. "If you can tell me."

"Leaving," Douglass said. "I'm going from here to the airport."

"Sarah was so beside herself with pleasure, she ordered breakfast for four," Bitter said. "Dig in."

Sarah and Douglass looked at each other, and then away.

"As a matter of fact, Eddie," Douglass said as he helped himself to coffee, "I am about to test the premise that a lot of money and effort can be saved if we ferry P-38s to England."

"That's you?"

"You know? How did you hear about it?"

"The Navy is going to run Catalinas along your route," Bitter said. "I assigned the Catalinas."

"What are Catalinas?" Sarah asked.

"Long-range amphibious patrol planes," Doug furnished. "If we have to sit down, they'll pick us up."

"I wish I was going with you," Ed Bitter said.

"No, you don't," Douglass said.

"Am I allowed to ask questions about that?" Sarah asked.

"No," Ed Bitter said simply.

Charity walked into the room from the corridor.

Bitter looked at her, and then at his wife, and then back at Charity.

"Good morning, Edwin," Charity said matter-of-factly. "I didn't think you were due back until Tuesday."

"We came back early," Bitter said.

"Oh, good!" Charity said. "Sausage. I'm as hungry as a horse!"

She sat down and began to help herself.

Bitter looked at Douglass, who carefully avoided looking at him.

Charity ate a piece of sausage, made a pleased face, and then said, "Captain Douglass will meet Doug at the airport in Baltimore. I think Doug would prefer that you drove him. Can that be arranged?"

"Of course," Sarah said.

"I don't know what to do about gasoline," Ed said.

"Buy some on the black market," Douglass said.

"I don't deal in the black market," Bitter said.

"I thought everybody did," Douglass said.

"I don't think officers should," Bitter said.

"My, aren't we on our white horse this morning?" Douglass said.

"There are some things officers just don't do," Bitter said.

"Aside from black market gas, what did you have in mind?" Charity asked.

Bitter glowered, then got up.

"Will you please excuse me?" he said stiffly, and marched out of the room.

Charity looked at Douglass.

"I'm sorry," she said. "I promised to watch my clever mouth. I meant to. It just got away from me."

"Fuck him," Douglass said. "Self-righteous sonofabitch. Come on, let's get out of here."

"Please don't," Sarah said.

"I'm sorry I put you on the spot, Sarah," Douglass said. "You're a lovely woman. What I can't understand is why you married that self-righteous sonofabitch."

"I think maybe you'd better leave," Sarah said.

"Talk about uncontrollable mouths," Charity said to Douglass. Douglass walked around the table to her, grabbed her arm, and propelled her out of the apartment.

The door slammed and woke the baby. Sarah went to him and picked him up and carried him into their bedroom. Ed was standing at the window, looking down at the street.

"Have they gone?" he asked after a minute.

"I asked them to," Sarah said. "I told him that I would not tolerate his calling you a self-righteous sonofabitch in your home."

He looked at her and smiled uneasily.

"You self-righteous sonofabitch!" Sarah said. "How dare you behave that way? That man is your best friend, and he saved your life, and he's liable to be dead by this time tomorrow, and you dare to lecture him!"

It was the first time since he had met his wife that he had ever heard her use language stronger than a "damn."

When they got to the airfield in Baltimore, Douglass went into Base Operations and checked the weather and filed his flight plan. When he came out of the briefing room, his father was there with Chief Ellis.

"I'm sorry about last night," his father said. "I really would have liked to have dinner with you. Charity take care of you all right?"

"Just fine," Douglass said.

"And on that clever little line," Charity said, "Charity will fold her tent and steal away."

"You have to go?" Doug asked.

"It was nice to see you again, Major Douglass," she said, offering her hand like a man. "Take care of yourself."

"And it was nice to see you, too, Miss Hoche," Douglass said, and then laughed out loud. "Who do you think you're fooling?" he asked.

Lieutenant Commander Edwin W. Bitter, USN, came running down the marble corridor. He was out of uniform. He had no tie and no hat, and he was wearing a battered leather aviator's jacket with a Kuomintang flag painted on the back.

He saw Captain Douglass.

"I don't mean to intrude," he said.

"Rack his ass, Dad," Douglass said. "For the first time in his life he's out of uniform."

"I came to wish you Godspeed," Bitter said.

"Thank you," Douglass said, a little uncomfortably.

"And to remind you that I have been a self-righteous sonofabitch as long as you've known me, and therefore you should not have been surprised."

"You're an asshole," Douglass said, "but I love you."

"And I wish to apologize to you, too, Charity," Bitter said.

"That's all right, Edwin," Charity said. "I've known what a self-righteous asshole you are for a long time, too."

"I don't think I wish to know what this is all about," Captain Douglass said.

"No," Doug said, "you don't." And then he said, "I gotta go."

He put out his hand to his father, who shook it.

"Hug him, for God's sake!" Charity ordered.

They both looked at her, and then embraced.

Doug punched Bitter on the arm, then turned to Charity.

"Do I get a hug too?" she asked.

"A kiss, but only to shut your runaway mouth," Doug said.

"How dare you, sir?" Charity said, grabbing his ears and kissing him with mock passion on the lips.

It began as a joke, for the amusement of spectators, but it didn't end that way. When they finally stopped, Charity looked very much as if she was going to cry.

"It's cold," Douglass announced, "and two fans make a lot of wind. I think everybody ought to stay inside."

The ground crew was already at the glistening, somehow menacing twin-engine fighter airplane. There was a ladder against the nose of the fuselage, which sat between the twin-engine booms, and Doug Douglass quickly climbed up it. When he was in the cockpit, a ground crewman climbed the ladder and saw that he was strapped properly into the parachute. Then he climbed back down and removed the ladder.

There were ten meatballs, each representing the kill of a Japanese aircraft, painted on the fuselage nose above the legend "Major Doug Douglass." The first time Charity saw them, she had thought they were thrilling and very sexy. Now they made her cry, for they reminded her that he was a fighter pilot. What fighter pilots did, presuming they could indeed make it across the Atlantic Ocean, was fight. She wondered if she was seeing him for the last time.

"Clear!" Douglass called down from the cockpit. The starter ground, and the left engine started. The sudden loud noise startled Charity. Then the right propeller began to move, blowing away a cloud of light blue smoke. She saw Douglass pull a helmet over his head and then snap a face mask in place.

He raised his left hand in a very casual wave. One of the engines roared, and the P-38 moved off the parking stand.

He was almost immediately hidden from their sight by other parked aircraft, but they stood there against the glass of the terminal and waited. Two or three minutes later, they heard the sound of an airplane taking off. Douglass's P-38C, its wheels already up, flashed past them. The plane turned to the right and was out of sight in thirty seconds.

"He'll be all right, Charity," Ed Bitter said. "There are no better pilots than Doug."

Charity smiled at him. For him, that was a real apology.

IV

[ONE]
The Foreign Ministry
Berlin, Germany
20 December 1942

The return to Berlin of Helmut von Heurten-Mitnitz, recent German representative to the Franco-German Armistice Commission for Morocco, posed a problem at the highest levels of the Foreign Ministry: No one knew what to do with him.

In some circles, von Heurten-Mitnitz arrived under something of a cloud. There was a suggestion—ever so tactfully phrased; they were, after all, diplomats—that perhaps he had been just a bit too willing to accept the loss of Morocco to the Americans. He might after all have considered making his way to Tunisia. From there, when the Führer decided the time was propitious, the Wehrmacht would launch its counterattack for the recapture of Morocco.

His defenders, who included his brother, the Graf von Heurten-Mitnitz, who was not only a Party luminary but reputed to be one of the few aristocrats with whom the Führer was personally comfortable, pointed out, on the one hand, that transportation between Morocco and Tunisia was currently rather hazardous, and on the other, that Helmut had been *ordered* onto the Junkers transport which flew him to Italy.

He was defended as well by most of his peers in the Foreign Ministry. He was a career diplomat, as indeed members of his family had been for centuries. He had done his duty as he saw it, and his duty was to make himself available for further service to Germany rather than to enter American captivity. He certainly could not be held responsible for the Americans blatantly violating French neutrality, or for the French, true to form, flying the white flag the moment they had come under fire.

Some of the less politically savvy of these Foreign Ministry friends proposed that he go to the Reichschancellery to personally brief the Führer about what had happened in Morocco. His brother had gotten him out of that. The Graf von Heurten-Mitnitz knew that Adolf Hitler sometimes blamed the messenger for the bad news.

In the politically ill-conceived idea, however, was the seed of a good one: Since the Führer blamed the successful invasion on high-level French perfidy, there was obviously no one better qualified than Helmut von Heurten-Mitnitz to prepare for the Führer a detailed report. He would work closely, of course, with Obersturmbannführer Johann Müller, and between them they could come up with a detailed and balanced assessment that would lay the blame where it belonged. With Müller involved, the report could of course in no way be called a whitewash of Foreign Ministry failures or a condemnation of SS ineptitude.

Helmut von Heurten-Mitnitz was provided with an office overlooking the interior garden of the Foreign Ministry, a small staff, authorization for a personal automobile, and other perquisites befitting his rank as Minister. Talk of his too hasty departure from Morocco quickly dissipated. He was, after all, a member of the club, and gentlemen do not speak ill of their peers.

That left but one problem still to be resolved: his military status.

After graduation from the Gymnasium in Königsberg in East Prussia, Helmut von Heurten-Mitnitz served six months as an officer-cadet with the 127th Pomeranian Infantry Regiment. This was expected of him. The 127th Pomeranian Infantry traced its roots back to the Graf von Heurten's Regiment of Foot (1582). After his six months of cadet service, Helmut received a reserve commission as a lieutenant.

Two months later, he matriculated at Harvard, from which he graduated in 1927. From 1931 until 1933, he was attached to the German Embassy in Washington, first as a cultural attaché and later as a consular officer. From 1936 until 1938, he was the consul in New Orleans.

On his return from New Orleans to Berlin, by then already a medium-level diplomatic official destined for greater responsibilities in the Foreign Ministry, von Heurten-Mitnitz was courted by both Military Intelligence and the Sicherheitsdienst of the SS, each of which were as much interested in the internal operations of the Foreign Ministry as they were in any external threats to Germany.

Military Intelligence offered him a reserve commission as a major, with the subtle understanding that since he would be of more value to the Army where he was, there was little chance he would ever be called up. He politely declined the honor.

And the SS offered him a commission as Sturmbannführer (Major) in the Honorary SS. He declined this honor, too, mainly because he was well aware that the Honorary SS consisted of nothing more than those who did favors for or made substantial financial contributions to the SS. While the holders of honorary SS rank were entitled to wear the black uniform with the lightning-bolt runes and the death's-head, that really signified nothing.

His hope was to keep out of the military altogether and to continue serving his country in the diplomatic service. This required some fancy footwork, however, especially after his return from Morocco; for there were new regulations eliminating many military service exemptions, including those for members of the Foreign Service. It was finally resolved at the highest levels.

Still, it didn't hurt to be a member of the club: He was offered and accepted a reserve commission in the SS—*not* the honorary SS—as a Brigade-führer-SD, the secret service of the SS, with the understanding that he would not be called to active service and would remain with the Foreign Ministry.

Attired in a quickly tailored black SS uniform, he took the oath of personal allegiance to Adolf Hitler in a ceremony presided over by Reichsführer-SS Heinrich Himmler himself. Afterward, his brother was kind enough to hold a small reception for the new Brigadeführer at a home maintained by the family at 44-46 Beerenstrasse in Zehlendorf. Reichsführer-SS and Frau Himmler put in a brief appearance en route to the symphony, which the Graf von Heurten-Mitnitz told Helmut was an unusual honor.

Helmut von Heurten-Mitnitz considered asking Müller to be present at either the swearing in or the reception, but decided against it. If they appeared too chummy, that might provoke suspicion. After the reception, he took off the SS uniform and hoped that he would never have to wear it again.

After settling into his new work, he labored industriously on the report for the Führer without actually completing it. The point was to keep it on the burner until it was forgotten and they found something else for him to do.

His name almost immediately appeared on guest lists of allied and neutral embassies, and he dined out nearly every night. He was a bachelor and thereby in demand on that account: There were many widows in Germany. That satisfied what he thought of as bodily demands, but he took care not to form anything approaching an emotional relationship.

And then, on the nineteenth of December, the Americans sent him a message.

On the morning of the twentieth, when his secretary Fräulein Ingebord Schermann came into his office, his desk was piled high with dossiers "borrowed" from the French Deuxième Bureau (analogous to the FBI). These were to assist him in preparing his report to the Führer on French perfidy. What he was actually doing was reading a novel by the Viennese novelist Franz Schiller about a romance between an Austrian nobleman and a tubercular widow.

Helmut von Heurten-Mitnitz's secretary made him uncomfortable. She was intense. Worse, fanatical.

Ingebord Schermann's blond hair was parted in the middle, brushed tight against her skull, and then brought together in a tight bun at the base of her neck. What few words she uttered were delivered like orders, in a Hessian dialect even harsher than Obersturmbannführer SS-SD Johann Müller's.

Von Heurten-Mitnitz regarded Müller as the archetypal Hessian peasant: blunt, phlegmatic, practical, and dull. Like most Northern and Eastern Germans von Heurten-Mitnitz was convinced he spoke *German,* and that Middle—Hesse and the Ruhr—and Southern (Bavarian and Swabian) Germans spoke a vulgar patois only loosely based on that language.

Fräulein Schermann was a not unattractive woman of, he guessed, thirty or thirty-two. Her calves and ankles were a little thick—another Hessian peasant characteristic, von Heurten-Mitnitz thought—but she was not fat and really didn't need the "foundation garment" that encased her body from just above her knees to just below her neck.

It was difficult for von Heurten-Mitnitz to imagine Fräulein Schermann in the throes of carnal passion, although he had caught himself more than once thinking about her breasts. As a young man, he had once had a fling with a peasant girl, a Silesian, whose breasts had been nearly as firm as her tail.

He suspected that in the unlikely event some young man got his hands on Fräulein Schermann's breasts, he would find much the same thing.

Von Heurten-Mitnitz had not chosen Fräulein Schermann; she was thrust upon him.

"And I have just the girl for you, Helmut," the Chief of the Foreign Responsibilities Division had told him. "Very efficient. Very dedicated."

There were three reasons why Fräulein Schermann was assigned to von Heurten-Mitnitz. The first was innocent coincidence: She was available for assignment when his need came up. Second, Fräulein Schermann's dedication translated to mean she was an informer for the Gestapo or the SD. There was no reason he should be under suspicion, but that didn't mean he wasn't being watched on general principles. Third, Fräulein Schermann had made someone else in the Foreign Ministry as uncomfortable as she made him, and she had been gotten rid of as tactfully as possible.

Von Heurten-Mitnitz looked up from his carefully hidden behind paperwork novel while Fräulein Schermann delivered in the tones of a Feldwebel (Sergeant) with two long service medals the announcement that "Obersturmbannführer SS-SD Johann Müller wishes to see the Herr Minister."

"Would you ask the Obersturmbannführer to come in, please, Fräulein Schermann?"

Fräulein Schermann nodded her head, just once, an almost mechanical movement.

"Jawohl, Herr Minister," she said.

Müller marched into the office. He was wearing a black overcoat that reached almost to his ankles. There was a leather belt around the coat, from which hung a closed pistol holster.

"Heil Hitler!" Müller barked and gave the straight-armed salute.

"Heil Hitler!" von Heurten-Mitnitz said. "I'm pleased that you could fit me into your schedule, Obersturmbannführer."

"It is my honor, Herr Minister," Müller said.

"I have taken the liberty of reserving a table at the Adlon," von Heurten-Mitnitz said. "Is that all right with you?"

"The Herr Minister is most kind," Müller said.

"It was good of you to give me a ride," von Heurten-Mitnitz said. "Just let me get my coat and hat."

He had not quite reached the bentwood coat rack when Fräulein Schermann appeared, snatched the coat from the hook, and held it out for him. As he was shrugging into it, she handed him his hat.

"Obersturmbannführer Müller and I will be taking lunch at the Adlon, Fräulein Schermann," von Heurten-Mitnitz said. "If there are any important calls for the Obersturmbannführer or myself, please be good enough to transfer them."

"Jawohl, Herr Minister."

Müller's car, an unmarked Opel Kapitän, was parked in front of the Foreign Ministry. There were both uniformed Berlin municipal policemen and plainclothes SD men stationed there, walking slowly back and forth in front of the sandbags stacked against the building. None was willing to remind an Obersturmbannführer SS-SD that parking was prohibited in front of the Foreign Ministry.

Müller got behind the wheel, and they drove off.

"Drive by my house, will you, Müller?" von Heurten-Mitnitz said. "I have to go inside for a moment."

Müller nodded.

Going to Zehlendorf and then back downtown would give them a few minutes to talk in privacy. There was nothing suspicious in a man going home on his way to lunch to pick up something he had forgotten.

Müller drove past the Zoological Gardens and then down the Kurfürstendamm to Brandenburgischestrasse. Two blocks into it, the street was blocked by a mountain of rubble and two wholly unnecessary policemen waving directional signs to order them onto a detour. Von Heurten-Mitnitz saw the shell of a department store where he had once bought underwear.

A lane just a car wide had been cleared through the rubble on the side street, and Müller's Opel bounced over loose bricks and masonry. And then, as suddenly as it began, the destroyed area gave way to a neighborhood that, save for blacked-out windows and signs indicating air-raid shelters, seemed untouched by the war.

They'll be back, von Heurten-Mitnitz thought, *sooner or later, but inevitably. And this neighborhood, too, will be a mound of smoldering rubble.*

"The Russians have stopped von Manstein," von Heurten-Mitnitz said.

On 23 November, the German Sixth Army, which had reached the suburbs of Stalingrad, had been encircled by the Russian 1st Guards and 61st Armies. On Göring's assurance that the Sixth Army could be supplied by air, Hitler had forbidden any attempt to break out of the encirclement. When it became apparent that the Luftwaffe could not supply the Sixth Army, Hitler had ordered General Erich von Manstein to assume command of Army Group Don at Rostov, and to break through the Russian forces. Von Manstein had attacked with an armored corps from Kotelnikovo on 12 December. After suffering severe losses, the German attack had been stopped twenty miles short of Stalingrad on 19 December.

"Oh?" Müller responded, not very surprised. "Now what?"

"Now nothing," von Heurten-Mitnitz said. "Von Manstein has nothing more with which to attempt a relief. Von Paulus is doomed."

General Fredrich von Paulus was the Sixth Army's commander.

"So there goes another quarter of a million men," Müller said.

"Yes, that's true," von Heurten-Mitnitz said. It was almost a minute before he spoke again.

"There is some good news," he said. "You may now call me 'sir.' I have been appointed Brigadeführer (Brigadier General) in the SS reserve."

"I saw your picture in *Die Sturmer*," Müller said dryly. "How did you manage to pull that off?"

"Under the new compulsory service regulations, I was about to be ordered to join my regiment as Hauptmann von Heurten-Mitnitz."

"You may wish you were a captain in the Pomeranian Infantry," Müller said.

"I believe they are now part of Von Paulus's Sixth Army in Fortress Stalingrad," von Heurten-Mitnitz said, and then abruptly changed the subject: "We have heard, I think, from our friend Eric."

"What do you mean, 'think'?"

"I have received a postcard from Bad Ems," von Heurten-Mitnitz said. "I want you to have a look at it and let me know what you make of it."

Müller nodded his head and didn't say a word until, as he pulled to the curb before the small mansion in Zehlendorf, he said, "Bad Ems? What the hell is there in Bad Ems?"

"It is argued by some historians that a telegram sent from Bad Ems triggered the Franco-Prussian War," von Heurten-Mitnitz said. He handed Müller the postcard. "Here, you figure it out."

"Why is it in this?" Müller asked, indicating a glassine envelope.

"I thought perhaps there might be a fingerprint on it," von Heurten-Mitnitz said. "Or am I letting my imagination run away with me?"

Müller shrugged.

Helmut von Heurten-Mitnitz stepped out of the Opel Kapitän into the snow-covered street and walked up to the gate in the fence in front of his house. Inside, he told his housekeeper that he'd stepped into slush and soaked his feet. Then he changed his shoes and socks and went back to the car.

"'Willi von K'?" Müller said as they drove off. "And you don't even know this is for you! The name got wet; all you can read is the street number."

"Eric von Fulmar is the Baron Kolbe," von Heurten-Mitnitz said.

"That's reaching for it," Müller said.

"Not if you can find his fingerprint on it," von Heurten-Mitnitz said. "His father, obviously, could be his father. Professor Dyer? Is there a Professor Dyer at Philips University in Marburg? Did Fulmar know him?"

"I'm reasonably sure there's a set of Fulmar's prints in Berlin," Müller said. "I'm not sure I can get at them without raising questions."

"I think we have to take that risk," von Heurten-Mitnitz said.

"Okay. For the sake of argument, I dust this postcard, find a print, and match it with Fulmar. And it turns out there is a Professor Dyer at Marburg. Then what?"

"Then we do what it says," von Heurten-Mitnitz said. "We give his regards to his father and this Professor Dyer, presuming we can find him."

"Germans," Müller said, "people I know, are freezing to death right now in Russia. And we're . . ."

"We can't help the people in Russia," von Heurten-Mitnitz said. "The best we can hope for is to do what we can to end this insanity. I think of it as cutting off a gangrenous hand to save the arm."

"You have the advantage on me," Müller said. "You can think of this in philosophical terms. I'm just a simple policeman. I think of it in terms of being hung on piano wire to strangle in the basement of the Prinz Albrecht Strasse prison."

"I feel like saying I'm sorry," von Heurten-Mitnitz said.

There was the sound of a police siren behind them. They were by then back on the Avus, a perfectly straight, four-lane Autobahn. Müller looked down at his speedometer. He was well over the speed limit.

He slowed enough for the motorcycle policeman to draw abreast. The policeman looked just long enough to see the uniform cap with the death's-head insignia and the insignia of an Obersturmbannführer on Müller's overcoat. Then the whooping of his siren died suddenly, and he fell behind.

Their lunch at the Hotel Adlon was very nice. There was roast loin of boar as an off-the-ration bonus. Stapled to the menu was a card printed in gold saying the roast boar was provided through the courtesy of Master Hunter of the Reich Hermann Göring.

It wasn't free, of course, but Göring wanted the upper class of Berlin to know that he was sharing the bounty of his East Prussian hunting grounds, not keeping it all for himself.

[TWO]
Atcham U.S. Army Air Corps Base
Staffordshire, England
20 December 1942

It was Major Doug Douglass's prerogative as commanding officer to conduct the final briefing before his P-38s attacked the sub pens at Saint-Lazare, but he passed on that one. So the briefing was given by a light colonel from Eighth Air Force G-3 (Plans and Training), the sonofabitch who had thought up the operation. The idiot was so happy with it that he actually had the balls to tell Douglass he wished he was checked out in P-38s so he could make the mission.

The light bird was a pilot, but he was a bomber pilot. And now he had come up with an operation in which fighter planes were supposed to do what the bombers had been unable to do, take out the German submarine pens at Saint-Lazare.

There were a number of reasons the bombers had failed, including the Big One: Where the sub pens weren't under thirty feet of granite, they were under that much reinforced concrete. Conventional 500-pound aerial bombs chipped the granite and the concrete, but they didn't crack it, much less penetrate it.

During his initial briefing, Douglass was told that superbombs—weighing up to ten tons—were "in development," and that they would certainly take out the pens. But the pens had to be taken out now; the subs they protected while they were being fueled and supplied were sinking an "unacceptable" amount of shipping tonnage.

There were other reasons the B-17s and the B-24s had failed. The pens were ringed with 88mm *Flakkanonen* manned by the best gunners the Germans had available. These were effective at any altitude the B-17s could reach. And there were four fighter fields, capable of sending aloft as many squadrons of very capable pilots flying Messerschmidts.

All these factors had been weighed, and a new tactic devised:

No further attempt to destroy the pens through the roofs was going to be made. The bombs would be sent through the front door, so to speak. What that meant, Douglass quickly—if with a certain amount of incredulity—

came to understand, was that bombs would be *thrown* into the pen entrances from low-flying aircraft. And the low-flying aircraft picked for this task were the P-38Es of the 311th Fighter Group, USAAC, Major Peter Douglass, Jr., commanding.

Following the law of physics that a body in motion tends to remain in motion until acted upon by outside forces, a 500-pound bomb dropped from the wing of a P-38 would continue for a time to move through the air at the same speed as the aircraft. Wind resistance would slow it down, of course, and gravity would pull it toward the earth, but for a certain brief period of time, it would proceed parallel to the ground.

The idea was that it would be released at the precise moment when its trajectory would carry it into the mouths of the sub pens.

This new tactic, the bomber pilot turned strategy expert announced, would have several other desirable characteristics. The Germans, like the English, had a new radio device that bounced radio signals off objects in the sky. These signals returned to clever devices that could then determine the range of the object in the sky. The devices were not very effective, however, against objects that were just off the surface of the water.

So, as the P-38Es approached the sub pens a hundred feet off the water, the altitude necessary to "throw" their bombs into the pens, they would arrive undetected. German ack-ack and fighters would not be waiting for them. And as soon as the P-38s dropped their bombs, they would, aerodynamically speaking, be clean fighter aircraft again and could very likely start making strafing runs on the German fighter bases before the Germans could get airborne.

During the final briefing, Douglass could agree with only one thing that the light bird said: There was *truly* no need for extensive training for this operation. This was so because the fighter group had already trained in the States in low-level bombing attacks.

The training, in fact, had been for the support of ground troops, but Doug knew the result was almost the same: His men knew how bombs behaved when they were dropped at low altitude.

Further practice in England would almost certainly have alerted the Luftwaffe to what they were up to.

They would leave Atcham, the briefing officer concluded, one hour before sunset. That would permit them to land at Ibsley, the closest P38 base to Saint-Lazare, by nightfall. During the night the aircraft would be fueled and the bombs loaded onto the wing racks. At first light they would take off. They could expect to be back in England before nine in the morning.

Except for his professional officer's understanding that planners are not happy unless they can make the simple as complicated as possible, Douglass could see no reason for the overnight stop at Ibsley. But he also understood his was not to reason why. Into the valley of the sub pens would fly the 311th Fighter Group.

He took twenty-nine P-38Es to Ibsley on the evening of December 19 and lost the first of them the next morning ten minutes into the mission: The pilot lost control on his takeoff roll, went off the runway, tipped up on one wing, and rolled over and over. The bombs didn't go off, but the avgas did, and there was an explosion.

There were Messerschmidt ME-109s waiting for them twenty-five miles from Saint-Lazare. If the German Radar hadn't worked, then something else had tipped them off about what was coming off.

"This is Dropsy Leader," Douglass said to his microphone. "Firewall it and follow me."

The twenty-eight remaining P-38 pilots advanced their throttles to FULL EMERGENCY MILITARY POWER, which was both hell on the engines and caused fuel consumption to increase incredibly. But festooned with bombs the way they were, their only defense against the ME-109Es was to get to the target and dump the bombs as quickly as they could. At about six miles a minute, it would take them about four minutes to reach the drop point; the engines would probably not collapse before then.

Three of his P-38s, following orders he had given them out of hearing of the strategic genius, dropped their bombs that instant and turned to take on the Messerschmidts. The three were in the rear. In case it got as far as an official inquiry, all the others could truthfully swear they hadn't seen anybody drop bombs in contravention of specific orders not to do so.

That turned out to be a moot point anyway. There were forty-odd German fighters, and not one of the three P-38s who rose to meet them made it back to England.

The Germans had cleverly designed their 88mm aircraft cannon so the muzzle could be depressed for use against tanks and other ground forces. Thus, when the sub pens came into view, they were partially obscured by the bursts of ack-ack shells.

Six P-38s were shot down by antiaircraft fire. Three of them simply disappeared in a puff of smoke. These had obviously been hit by the 88s. There was no way to tell whether the other three were downed by 88s, 20mm Oerlikon automatic cannons, or machine-gun fire.

Twenty-two P-38s successfully completed the bomb run. Of the forty-four 500-pound bombs "thrown" toward the sub pen entrances, it was estimated that eighteen or twenty entered the sub pens. Aerial reconnaissance indicated that these had done little or no damage.

Two P-38s were lost on the return leg of the flight, one of them to a Messerschmidt ME-109E and the other to unknown causes. Possibly a wounded pilot lost consciousness. A final fatality occurred at Ibsley when a P-38 attempted a wheels-up landing and exploded on contact with the runway.

A story circulated through the officers' messes of the Eighth Air Force that the group commander of the 311th Fighter Group—"Those poor bastards who got the shit kicked out of them at Saint-Lazare sub pens"—committed a physical assault upon the Eighth Air Force Plans and Training Officer whose idea the mission had been.

According to the story, the assault had been hushed up. The Commander of the 311th was a West Pointer, for one thing, and he'd been a Flying Tiger with ten kills for another, and for a third, his own P-38 had been shot up so badly they didn't even consider repairing it. They just hauled it off to the boneyard.

[THREE]
Frankfurt am Main, Germany
24 December 1942

As the Berlin-Frankfurt train backed into Frankfurt's Hauptbahnhof, Obersturmbannführer Johann Müller stood in the aisle of the first-class coach looking out the window. The station platforms were covered by a glass-and-steel arch, as if an enormous tube had been slit in half lengthwise and placed over the tracks. The framework of the arch remained intact, but many, perhaps most, of the glass windows had been blown out by bombing. Snow had come through these openings, leaving a soot-colored slush over most of the platform.

Müller's policeman's eye saw, too, the security in place. At the far end of the station, in order to make sure that no one left the platform by way of the yards, there stood two gray-uniformed members of the Feldgendarmerie (Military Police) and a civilian wearing an ankle-length leather overcoat and a gray snap-brim felt hat.

In theory, the civilian was working in plainclothes to facilitate his efforts in defense of Reich security. In practice, since only persons with a special ration coupon had access to full-length leather coats, he might as well have worn a hatband with "Gestapo" printed on it.

As a general rule of thumb, Obersturmbannführer Müller did not have much respect for the Gestapo. There were some genuine detectives in its ranks, but the bulk of them were patrolman types promoted over their abilities. You didn't have to be much of a detective if you were armed with power to arrest without giving a reason, and could then conduct an "interrogation," which generally began with stripping the suspect naked and beating him senseless before any questions were put to him.

Near the station end of the platform were the checkpoints. One was manned by the Feldgendarmerie and the other by the Railway Police. The first checked the identity and travel documents of military personnel—Army, Navy, and Air Force—and the other checked everyone else. Two more men in leather overcoats and snap-brim caps stood where they could watch this procedure.

Müller was a little surprised to see two black-uniformed men as well, an SS-Hauptsturmführer (Captain) and an SS-Scharführer (Staff Sergeant) standing to one side behind the Railway Police checkpoint. The SS-SD rarely wasted its time standing around railway platforms.

When the train stopped, Müller took his leather suitcase from his compartment, stepped off the train, and walked the few steps to the checkpoints. Before he could take his credentials from his pocket, the Hauptsturmführer, smiling, walked up to him, gave the stiff-armed salute, and barked, "Herr Obersturmbannführer Müller?"

"I'm Müller."

"Heil Hitler!" the Hauptsturmführer said, and then barked again: "Take the Obersturmbannführer's luggage, Scharführer!"

The Scharführer took Müller's suitcase from his hand.

"Standartenführer Kramer sent us to meet you, Herr Obersturmbannführer," the Hauptsturmführer said. "He hopes that your schedule will per-

mit you to call upon him, but if you are pressed for time, we are at your service to take you where you wish to go."

"Very kind of the Standartenführer," Müller said. "I look forward to seeing him."

Müller knew Kramer slightly. He was the commanding officer of the
Hessian region of the SS-SD. He was a jovial man, fat, a politician, a man who
had become what he was because of who and not what he knew. Müller
wondered what the hell he wanted.

An Opel Admiral, obviously Kramer's own official car, was parked outside the Hauptbahnhof. With the cooperation of the policeman on duty,
it made an illegal U-turn and drove Müller to SS-SD headquarters for Hesse,
a turn-of-the century villa across a wide lawn from the curved corpo-
rate headquarters of the I.G. Farben Chemical Company. On the way, they
passed the Frankfurt office building of FEG, the Fulmar Elektrische Gesellschaft.

"My dear Johnny," Kramer said when he saw Müller in his office door,
and then he came from behind his desk, hand extended. "I'm glad they
found you."

He did not, Müller noticed, say "Heil Hitler!"

"Having me met was very kind of you, Herr Standartenführer," Müller
said.

"You don't know, do you?" Kramer asked happily. "I rather thought you
might not."

"Sir?"

"Geehr," Kramer said to the Hauptsturmführer, "will you give him his
Christmas present, please?"

Geehr clicked his heels and made a little bow as he handed Müller a
small, tissue-wrapped package.

As Müller unwrapped it, Kramer said, "I telephoned Berlin the moment
it came over the wire, Johnny, and they told me you were on leave. I took a
chance that you were coming home, and had Geehr meet the Berlin trains.
You were on the second one."

The box contained the shoulder boards and lapel insignia of an SS-
Standartenführer. When Müller looked at Kramer, Kramer beamed.

"May I presume, Herr Standartenführer," Kramer said, "that I have the
great privilege of being the first to congratulate you on your well-deserved
promotion?"

"I had no idea," Müller said, truthfully.

"With rank as of 1 December," Kramer said and snapped his fingers. Geehr handed him a sheet of Teletype paper, which Kramer then handed to Müller.

There was no question about it. He had his own paragraph:

SS-OBERGRUPPENFÜHRER REINHARD HEYDRICH ANNOUNCES WITH PLEASURE THE PROMOTION WITH DATE OF RANK 1 DECEMBER 1942 OF OBERSTURMBANNFÜHRER SS-SD JOHANN MÜLLER TO STANDARTEN-FÜHRER SS-SD.

"May I keep this?" Müller asked as Kramer first enthusiastically pumped his hand. Then, with a snap of his fingers, Kramer ordered Geehr to produce a tray with a bottle of cognac and glasses.

"Yes, of course," Kramer said, and then: "The timing is a little awkward."

"Sir?"

"If it weren't Christmas Eve, Johnny, I would insist on doing more than offering a glass of schnapps," Kramer said. "But I daresay you are anxious to get home."

"My train is at half past five," Müller said.

"Nonsense. We have a car for you, of course, Herr Standartenführer."

"That's very kind," Müller said.

"With a driver, of course," Kramer added.

"I don't want to be responsible for someone having the duty on Christmas," Müller said.

"That's very kind of you, then," Kramer said. "What have we the Standartenführer can drive?"

"We have that nice little Autounion roadster, Herr Standartenführer," Geehr said.

"Splendid!" Kramer said. "That all right with you, Johnny?"

"That would be fine," Müller said.

"And if you'll take off your tunic, Johnny, I'll have Frau Zern put the proper insignia on it."

As Müller handed his tunic to Kramer's secretary, Kramer said, "I realize this sounds odd, but I was about to say perhaps we can have a drink together at the funeral."

"I beg your pardon?"

"The remains of the Baron Steighofen have been returned from the Eastern Front," Kramer said. "They will be interred at the Schloss on December 28. They're making quite a do of it. The Prince of Hesse, in the name of the Führer, will make a posthumous award of the Knight's Cross of the Iron Cross. Steighofen's not far from Marburg. I'm sure the Baroness would be pleased if you could find the time to attend."

Translated, Müller thought, *that means he is telling me it would be politically smart for me to attend. Does that mean I have to?*

"The Steighofens are well connected, Johnny," Kramer went on, immediately confirming what Müller had guessed. "With Baron Fulmar of FEG, for one thing."

"The twenty-eighth, you said?"

"Yes."

"I'm sure I can make it," Müller said.

"Then I look forward to seeing you there," Kramer said. "And once again, my dear Johnny, my most warm congratulations on your promotion."

I am your "dear Johnny," Müller thought, *because it has occurred to you that the only way a Hessian peasant policeman like myself could get himself promoted is because I have powerful friends. I was not your "dear Johnny" before I went to Morocco.*

"I wonder if I might use your phone before I go," Müller said.

"Of course," Kramer said.

"Could you have me put through to Helmut von Heurten-Mitnitz in the Foreign Ministry?" Müller asked. "I think he might wish to attend the Baron's interment, and I'm sure he didn't know about it either."

Kramer nodded at Geehr, who picked up the telephone and placed the call.

Calling von Heurten-Mitnitz from Kramer's office, Müller decided, served to buttress Kramer's notion that he had highly placed friends. But perhaps more important, the funeral would permit von Heurten-Mitnitz to talk to Fulmar's father under unsuspicious circumstances. If Müller placed the call anywhere else, there might have been questions.

But there would be no questions if the call was made from the office of the commander of the Hessian Region of the SS-SD.

[FOUR]

The Autounion roadster turned out to be a sporty yellow convertible. Müller drove it up the Autobahn as far as Giessen, and then along the tranquil Lahn River to the ancient university town of Marburg.

Under other circumstances, he thought, it would have been a very pleasant way for him to go home, at the wheel of a fancy car, and with the corded silver epaulets of a Standartenführer on his shoulders.

He had been a lowly Wachtmann, an ordinary police patrolman, when he had left Kreis Marburg to go to Prussia. And he was thrilled then to be appointed a Kriminalinspektor, Grade Three. With a little luck and hard work, he'd thought at the time, he might make it to Kriminalinspektor, Grade One, or even Deputy Inspector.

It had never occurred to him then that he would go into the SS-SD, or that he would rise to Obersturmbannführer if he did. It was quite as difficult to believe that he was now a Standartenführer as it was to accept that he was engaged in treasonous activities against the German State.

Giessen had been bombed, probably as an alternate target when fog obscured Frankfurt am Main. But after he left Giessen, there was no sign of war damage, or, for that matter, of the war itself. Everything was in fact just about as he remembered it. There were fewer Christmas decorations than he expected, and there were *Winterhilfe* posters splattered all over, even on trees, appealing for warm clothing, both for bombed-out civilians and for the troops in Russia. But otherwise time seemed to have stopped.

As he turned off the main road onto Frankfurterstrasse, he allowed himself to dwell on the notion that there were men from Marburg at Stalingrad right now, doomed to surrender and probably death.

He drove past a barracks compound and pulled the yellow roadster onto the cobblestones before a three-story, turn-of-the-century building that housed both the headquarters of the Kreis Polizei for Marburg and the regional office of the SS-SD. He got out of the car and walked into the building. There was a small Christmas tree sitting on a table in the lobby.

The Scharführer on duty, visibly startled at the visit of so senior an officer on Christmas Eve, popped to attention. He didn't at first recognize Müller, but Müller knew who he was. His name was Otto Zeiman. When

Müller first joined the police as an Unterwachtmann, Zeiman had been his corporal. He, too, had joined the SS-SD and had risen to Scharführer.

"Heil Hitler!" Zeiman said. "How may I help the Standartenführer?"

"How are you, Otto?" Müller asked, offering the older man his hand. "It's nice to see you again."

"The Standartenführer is kind to remember me," Zeiman said, beaming happily at him.

"When no one's around, Otto, it's Johnny, like always."

The older man colored with pleasure. He would never, Müller knew, call him by anything but his rank, but the gesture had cost nothing, and it was always valuable for a man like Zeiman to think of himself as a special friend.

"Hauptsturmführer Peis is the officer on duty," Zeiman said. "Shall I tell him you're here?"

Peis, the SD officer-in-charge in Marburg and another face from a long time ago, was like Zeiman a professional, not a political, although Müller, who had checked his dossier in Berlin before leaving, had learned that Peis's devotion to the National Socialist cause had recently become almost fervent. That was something to keep in mind.

"The boss is working on Christmas Eve?" Müller asked, and then, before Zeiman could reply, added, "Please, Otto."

Wilhelm Peis, in what looked like a brand-new uniform, came into the foyer a moment later, gave the straight-armed salute, said "Heil Hitler!," and asked how he could be of service to the Herr Standartenführer.

He was surprised to see Müller, period, and even more surprised to see that he was now a Standartenführer. The approach he decided to take with him was, consequently, formal. As Standartenführer, Müller might resent any intimacy.

"Heil Hitler!" Müller said. "I had hoped, if it would not interfere with your duty, that we might have a drink for Christmas."

"I regret that I have nothing to offer the Standartenführer," Peis said.

"Then why don't we go to the Café Weitz?" Müller said.

"If the Standartenführer will be good enough to wait, I will get my coat," Peis said.

When he was in the car, Peis said, "This is very nice. Standartenführer Kramer has one very much like it."

"This is Kramer's," Müller said. "He was good enough to give me the use of it."

"May I ask if the Standartenführer is here officially?" Peis asked.

"Officially, Peis, I'm on leave," Müller said.

"I understand, Herr Standartenführer."

"It's Christmas Eve, Wilhelm," Müller said. "And we have known each other a long time. Don't you think you could call me 'Johann'?"

"Yes, of course," Peis said, pleased.

The proprietor of the Café Weitz, a pale-faced man in his sixties who wore a frayed-at-the-collar dinner jacket, greeted them enthusiastically, and Peis obviously relished being able to introduce Müller as his "friend."

The proprietor said he was honored and asked if Müller had ever been to Marburg before.

"I was born here," Müller said, and regretted it. The café owner looked as though he had committed a terrible faux pas by not recognizing Müller. "I've been away for years," Müller said. "But I came to see my mother at Christmas."

Two bottles, one of Steinhager and one of French cognac, were promptly delivered to their table.

"While I am here, as I say, unofficially," Müller began when the café owner finally left them, "there are a few things I would like to make discreet inquiry about."

"I am at your service, Herr Standartenführer," Peis said.

"Johann," Müller said with a smile.

"Johann," Peis parroted uncomfortably.

"Tell me about Professor Friedrich Dyer," Müller said.

Peis grunted, as if the inquiry did not surprise him.

"What do you want to know?" he asked. "We have a rather extensive file on him. If you had asked at the station, I could have shown it to you."

"Just tell me, Wilhelm," Müller said.

"Well, he knows Albert Speer pretty well," Peis said.

Müller was astonished to hear that, but he was a policeman, and his surprise showed neither on his face nor in his voice.

"I know that," he said impatiently. "What else is there?"

"He's a professor at the university, knows all about metal."

"Personally. What do you *know* about him?"

"Well, we caught him exporting money, for one thing," Peis said. "Is that what this is all about?"

Müller ignored the question. "Tell me about that. Why wasn't he prosecuted?"

Peis, Müller saw, was uncomfortable. He would have to find out why.

"You know how it is, Johann," Peis said nervously. "Some you keep on a string."

"What can he do for you?"

Peis was made even more uncomfortable by the question.

"Family?" Müller asked.

"One child," Peis said. "His wife is dead."

"And the one child is female, right? And you're fucking her?"

There was alarm in Peis's eyes, proving that was indeed the case.

"We're all human, Wilhelm," Müller said.

"I . . . uh . . . the way it happened, Johann, was before the war. We caught him shipping the money to Switzerland, and making anti-state remarks."

"She must be one hell of a woman," Müller said with a smile. "This is almost 1943."

"We had two students of official interest, two in particular, at the university," Peis said.

"Who?" Müller asked.

"There was an Arab, the son of some Arab big shot—"

"What was his name?" Müller interrupted. He had a very good idea, but he wanted to hear it from Peis.

"El Ferruch," Peis said triumphantly, after he had dredged the name from the recesses of his memory.

"Sidi Hassan el Ferruch," Müller said. "The son of the Pasha of Ksar es Souk. What about him?"

Peis was uncomfortable but did not seem especially surprised that Müller knew about el Ferruch.

"We had a request to build a dossier on him," Peis said.

"And did you?"

"He was living with—"

"Eric von Fulmar, Baron Kolbe," Müller interrupted. "I asked you if you managed to build a dossier on el Ferruch?"

"Yes, of course I did," Peis said. "I sent it to Frankfurt, and I suppose they sent it to Berlin after he left here."

"What does this have to do with Professor Friedrich Dyer?" Müller asked.

"His money business came up at the same time," Peis said. "I called his daughter in for a little talk, and used her to keep an eye on them."

"And then, when they left, you kept her around for 'possible use in the future,' right?" Müller asked. "Wilhelm, you're a rogue!"

"Well, you see how it is," Peis said, visibly relieved that Müller seemed to understand.

"Wilhelm," Müller said, "I'm going to be here for about a week. A week with my mother. Now, I love my mother, but a man sometimes gets a little bored. He needs a little excitement, if you take my meaning."

"You just say when and where, Johann," Peis said.

"I'll say when," Müller said. "And you say where."

[ONE]
Motor Pool, Naval Element, SHAEF
London, England
1600 Hours
24 December 1942

There were two white hats on duty in the small, corrugated-steel dispatcher's shack when the tall, dark-haired lieutenant (j.g.) pushed open the door and stepped inside. He was wearing an overcoat and a scarf. His brimmed cap was perched cockily toward the back of his head.

The white hats started to stand up.

"Keep your seats," the j.g. said quickly, and added, "Merry Christmas."

"Merry Christmas, sir," the white hats said, almost in unison.

"My name is Kennedy," the j.g. said. "They were supposed to call?"

"Yes, sir," the older—at maybe twenty-two—of the white hats said. "You need wheels?"

"That's right," Kennedy said.

"I hate to do this to you, especially on Christmas Eve," the white hat said. "But look around, there's nothing else."

There were three vehicles in the motor pool, a three-quarter-ton wrecker, a Buick sedan, and a jeep with a canvas roof but no side curtains. Kennedy understood the jeep was for him. Lieutenants junior grade are not given Buick staff cars, especially at the brass-hat-heavy Naval Element, SHAEF.

"Anytime you're ready, Lieutenant," the other white hat said. "Where we going?"

"Atcham Air Corps Base," Kennedy said. "In Staffordshire. You know where it is?"

"Only that it's a hell of a way from here," the white hat said.

Kennedy had a sudden thought, and acted on it.

"There's no reason that both of us have to freeze," he said. "I'll drive myself."

"Oh, I don't know, Lieutenant," the older white hat said. "You're supposed to have a driver."

"If anybody asks, tell them I gave you a hard time about it," Kennedy said. "It's gassed up, I suppose?"

"Yes, sir, and there's an authorization for gas with the trip ticket."

"Okay, then," Kennedy said. "That's it."

"Lieutenant, would you mind writing down that you wanted to drive yourself?"

"Got a piece of paper?"

It was half past four when he turned the jeep onto the Great North Road. He had lived in London for several years before the war and for the first couple of hours on the Great North Road, he knew where he was. But by half past seven—about the time it had grown dark and the rain blowing through the open sides had soaked through his woolen overcoat—he was in strange territory and had to admit (which angered him) that he was lost.

He had a map, one he had drawn himself with care, even carefully listed the distance between turns in miles and tenths of a mile, but it had proved useless. And there were no road signs. They had been taken down in anticipation of a German invasion in the summer of 1940, and only a few of them had been replaced.

At nine o'clock he reluctantly gave up, and spent the night on a tiny and uncomfortable bed in a small country inn. It was a hell of a way to spend Christmas Eve, he thought.

At first light he started out again, unshaven, in a damp uniform. There had been a stove in the room, and he had hung his overcoat, jacket, and trousers over two chairs and a bedside table close to it. It had done almost no good.

It took him two hours to reach Atcham. The MP at the gate was willing to accept his identity card and trip ticket as proof that he hadn't stolen the jeep, but warned him that Atcham Air Force Station was "closed in." Once he came inside, he would not be permitted to leave until 0600 hours 26 December.

That strongly suggested that an operation was in progress, that he had come all this way only to find that the man he wanted to see was somewhere over France or Germany. Then he found a faintly glowing coal of hope. It was raining again. Visibility was about half a mile. There was a thick cloud cover at 1,000 feet. It was likely that an operation would not be able to get off the ground because of the weather.

He decided that seeing Major Peter Douglass was worth a chance. He'd worry about getting off the base when it was time to leave.

As he drove the jeep through an endless line of rain-soaked P-38s in sandbag revetments, a B-25 flashed low over him, so low that he could see the fire at the engine exhausts. It touched down and immediately disappeared in a cloud of its own making as it rolled down the rain-soaked runway.

One of two things was true, Naval Aviator Kennedy thought professionally. Either his assessment of flying conditions was way off, or the pilot of the B-25 was a fucking fool flying in weather like this.

Headquarters, 311th Fighter Group, U.S. Army Air Corps was a Quonset hut surrounded by tar-paper shacks with a frame building used for a mess, theater, and briefing room.

There was no answer to his knock at the door, so he pushed it open. Inside, a baldheaded man was snoring under olive-drab blankets on a cot. The jacket with staff sergeant's chevrons draped over a chair identified him as the charge of quarters.

When he shook the sergeant's shoulder and woke him, Kennedy expected the man would be upset that an officer had caught him asleep. But the reaction was annoyance rather than humiliation.

"I would like to see Major Douglass," the lieutenant said.

"He's asleep," the sergeant said doubtfully as he reluctantly got off the cot and began pulling his trousers on. "He came in pretty late last night."

"It's important, Sergeant," the lieutenant said. "Would you please wake him?"

"He's in there," the sergeant said, pointing to a closed door and leaving unspoken what else he meant: *If you want to wake him, you wake him.*

Kennedy went to the door, knocked, got no response, and then pushed it open. Major Peter Douglass, Jr., Army Air Corps, was in a curtained alcove of the office. He lay on his back in a homemade wooden bed, his legs spread, his mouth open. A uniform was hung somewhat crookedly over a chair. The decorations on the tunic were a little unusual: A set of standard U.S. Army Air Corps pilot's wings was where it was supposed to be. But there was another set, which the young naval officer recognized after a moment as Chinese, over the other pocket. And under the Army Air Corps wings were the ribbons of two Distinguished Flying Crosses. One of them was the striped ribbon of the British DFC. The other was American.

Kennedy went to the cot and looked down at Douglass. He wondered how much truth there was to the story that Douglass had walked into the Plans and Training Division of Headquarters Eighth Air Force, politely asked the lieutenant colonel who had planned the disastrous P-38 raid on Saint-Lazare to stand up, and then coldcocked him.

Kennedy leaned down and shook Douglass's shoulder. Douglass angrily snorted and rolled onto his side.

"Major Douglass," Kennedy said.

There was no response.

Kennedy was about to shake him again when he heard voices in the outer office.

"Merry Christmas, Sergeant, we're the Eighth Air Force Clap Squad," a voice said. "Where do we find a character named Douglass? He's been infecting the sheep."

The charge of quarters laughed.

"He's right in there, sir," the sergeant said. "And Merry Christmas to you, too."

Two officers, a major and a captain, walked into the room. They looked at the sleeping Douglass, then at Kennedy, and then at each other. They smiled and went to the bed, picked up one side of it, and rolled Major Douglass out onto the floor.

Kennedy was suddenly sure that these guys were the ones who had just flown the B-25 through the soup.

Major Douglass, now wide awake on the floor, was piqued.

"You sonsofbitches!" he declaimed angrily.

"Hark," Captain James M. B. Whittaker said, "the herald angel sings!"

"You bastards," Major Douglass said, but he was now smiling.

"Get dressed," Canidy said. "We are going to spring you from durance vile."

"You know, I suppose," Douglass said, as he rose to his feet and quickly stripped to change his underwear, "that now that you're on the base, you're restricted to it until 0600 tomorrow?"

"Only the gate is closed," Canidy said.

"You've got an airplane? You're not flying in this shit?"

"Oh, ye of little faith!" Whittaker said.

"But get dressed, Doug, it's getting worse," Canidy said.

Douglass looked at Kennedy as he pulled on clean Jockey shorts.

"You realize, of course, Lieutenant," he said, "that running around with these two is going to ruin your naval career?"

"I don't know who these gentlemen are," Kennedy said somewhat stiffly, but smiling.

"We thought he was a pal of yours," Whittaker said.

"My name is Kennedy," the j.g. said. "I came here from London to talk to you, Major Douglass."

"Talk to me? About what?"

"Saint-Lazare," Kennedy said.

"You drove from London in the rain in that jeep?" Whittaker said incredulously.

"That's right," Kennedy said. "It's really important."

"I don't want to talk about Saint-Lazare," Douglass said coldly as he put his arms in the sleeves of a shirt.

"Your name is Joseph P. Kennedy, Jr.," Canidy said. "Right?"

"Yes, sir," Kennedy said, visibly surprised that the major knew his name.

"I thought you said you didn't know him?" Douglass asked.

"I know about him," Canidy said.

"May I ask how?" Kennedy asked.

"I'm not sure you have the need to know," Canidy said.

"I know him," Whittaker said. "You went to school in Cambridge, right?"

"If you mean Harvard, yes, I did."

"Jim Whittaker," Whittaker said, putting out his hand. "'Thirty-nine. I thought you looked familiar."

Kennedy shook the offered hand.

"I can't place you," he said. "Sorry."

"You more than once knocked me on my ass playing lacrosse," Whittaker said.

Kennedy still didn't make any connection. He shrugged and shook his head. "No."

"Well, I hate to cut off auld lang syne," Canidy said, "but we have to get off the ground in the next ten minutes, or we will be stuck here until to-morrow."

"With respect, sir, I drove all the way from London to see Major Douglass," Kennedy said. "I really have to talk to him."

"Sorry," Douglass said. "I am all talked out about Saint-Lazare."

"What it is, Joe Louis, is that Lieutenant Kennedy and some other free-thinkers in Navy Blue," Canidy said, "have the odd notion that the only way to take out Saint-Lazare is with a pilotless flying bomb."

"Major," Kennedy said sharply, angrily. "That's classified Top Secret."

"Yeah," Canidy said. "I know. Tell you what, Kennedy. Come along with us, and you can talk to Doug on the way."

"Dick, is that smart?" Whittaker asked.

"Lieutenant Kennedy's father used to be the ambassador here," Canidy said. "I think he can be trusted."

"Dick, I really can't leave here, for Christ's sake. I'm the group comman-der," Douglass said.

"The base commander devoutly believes you have been summoned to brief certain unspecified big shots on Saint-Lazare," Canidy said.

"Come along where?" Kennedy asked.

Canidy ignored the question.

"We'll get you back however we get Douglass back," Canidy said.

"I really would like no more than an hour of Major Douglass's time right here and now," Kennedy said.

"That's not one of your options," Canidy said. "Come or not, suit yourself."

"This is official business," Kennedy bluffed.

"No, it's not," Canidy said. "Doug is supposed to brief you people on Fri-day. You're jumping the gun, Kennedy."

Kennedy's face again registered surprise at Canidy's detailed knowledge of the project. Canidy saw it.

"Never lie to Canidy the Omniscient," he said. "You coming or not?"

"I'm coming," Kennedy said after a moment.

[TWO]
Whitbey House, Kent, England
1015 Hours
25 December 1942

As Lt. Colonel Edmund T. Stevens and Captain Stanley S. Fine stepped out of a 1942 Ford four-door staff car at the entrance to Whitbey House, they were somewhat disconcerted by the roar of aircraft engines. They looked around for the source of the noise and spotted a B-25 Mitchell twin-engine bomber emerging from the cloud cover at about 1,000 feet.

Lt. Colonel Stevens was not pleased: The B-25 was attempting to land on the dirt runway built before the war by His Grace the Duke of Stanfield for his personal aircraft, a four-passenger single-engine Cessna. Engineering officers of the Eighth United States Air Force had recently examined the field in some detail. Their judgment was that the single runway was too short and too close to Whitbey House itself to be used by anything larger than single-engine observation aircraft. Furthermore, the experts said, improvement of the field was not feasible, because of the topography of the land. The strip could not be lengthened at the north-northeast end because of Whitbey House, nor at the south-southwest end because of the River Naer, whose steep banks were 135 yards from the end of the runway.

The experts had concluded that the field did not meet minimum safety standards even for an emergency landing strip and that it should thus be marked at both ends with at least fifty-foot-high X's (whitewashed rocks were recommended) to warn aircraft commanders of the hazard.

There was no doubt in Lt. Colonel Stevens's mind that the B-25 attempting to sit down on the closed and hazardous runway was the one that (not without difficulty) Dick Canidy had recently procured on indefinite loan from the Eighth United States Air Force and that Dick Canidy was flying it.

Why? No flights of the B-25 had been scheduled or authorized. It was supposed to be sitting in a revetment on the U.S. Army Air Corps base at East Grinstead, some thirty miles away.

A look at Captain Fine told Colonel Stevens that Fine had been considering the same possibilities, and was worried.

Worried not only that Canidy was attempting a dangerous landing, but more important (should he survive it) that he was about to be caught with his pants down by the Deputy Chief of the London Station of the OSS.

Colonel Stevens chose not to play the outraged senior officer. He pretended he'd never heard the B-25, prayed for Canidy's safety, and walked inside the house and waited.

He was greeted at the door by Lieutenant Jamie Jamison and Captain the Duchess Stanfield, WRAC, who he suspected were considerably less than glad to see him, at this moment, than they attempted to be. Lt. Colonel Stevens did not ask about the present whereabouts of Major Canidy, nor did Lieutenant Jamison or Captain Stanfield volunteer any information.

Lt. Colonel Stevens and Captain Fine were led into the refectory of the mansion, where thirty officers and enlisted men who were undergoing training as OSS agents had gathered for a pre-Christmas-dinner drink. A huge silver punch bowl had been set up at a table, and everyone was holding a silver mug.

There was an Army tradition that the commanding officer of a unit and his staff took Christmas dinner with the troops. Whitbey House OSS station was not a line company, of course, and Stevens was not the battalion commander. But he was the senior commissioned officer of the OSS in England (Station Chief David Bruce was a civilian), and Stevens felt that his place was here.

When it was immediately evident that the trainees were pleased to see him, he knew that he had made the right choice.

Lt. Colonel Stevens and Captain Fine were offered, and took, a glass of punch. The taste was familiar to Lt. Colonel Stevens. It was Artillery Punch. One of the trainees had served in the prewar Artillery and come forth with the recipe. There were shortly going to be, Stevens knew, some very drunk people in this room, and tomorrow morning some monumental hangovers. Artillery Punch was judged by the smoothness with which it went down and by the jolt one got a few minutes later. This was, in his expert opinion, very good Artillery Punch.

He decided against warning Captain Fine of its potency. It might be good for Captain Fine to get a little drunk—both because it was Christmas and because it was good to know how people behaved when drunk. *In vino veritas* had a special meaning for those in the intelligence business.

Captain Fine was on his third glass—a little red in the face and silly of smile—and Lt. Colonel Stevens was still delicately sipping his first when

Major Canidy appeared in the refectory. He was accompanied by Captain James M. B. Whittaker, which was not surprising, and by Major Peter Douglass, Jr., which was. But this explained what Canidy had been doing with the B-25. He had used it to fetch Major Douglass.

But what was really surprising was the presence of Lieutenant Joseph P. Kennedy, Jr., USNR. Stevens wondered where the hell Canidy had found him, and why he had brought him to Whitbey House.

Two days before, Canidy had decided that it would be nice to have Major Douglass at the Christmas dinner at Whitbey House. Douglass was close to going over the edge (the "incident" at Eighth Air Force headquarters was all the proof needed of that). And, because of his father, Douglass was one of the two exceptions (Ann Chambers was the other) to the rule that visitors to Whitbey House were absolutely proscribed.

But when Canidy called young Douglass at Atcham to offer him a ride, Douglass told him the base commander had restricted everyone to the base over Christmas. The Eighth Air Force was determined to nip in the bud a recently surfaced British resentment toward their American cousins. As in: Americans are "overpaid, oversexed, and over here."

The base commander had decided it would not be in the best interests of Allied goodwill to turn loose his several thousand overpaid and oversexed officers and enlisted men to drown their homesickness on Christmas in English pubs. He had arranged activities for them on the base.

"If I wasn't the group commander," Douglass told him candidly, "I'd go over the fence. But I'm stuck, I'm afraid."

Canidy actually winced when he saw Lt. Colonel Stevens. Then Canidy shrugged, and walked over to face the music.

Completely out of character, Captain Fine threw an affectionate arm around Canidy's shoulders and asked, "How the hell are you, buddy?"

Canidy and Stevens smiled.

"Been at the punch, have you, Stanley?" Canidy asked.

"Noël, Noël," Fine said happily.

"I'm happy," Lt. Colonel Stevens said, "if a little surprised to see you, Major Douglass."

"There I was, snug in my own little bed, minding my own business," Douglass said. "When out of the blue—actually, it was out of the gray overcast—came Canidy in his airplane. He told the base commander I had been summoned to a briefing of VIPs. The base commander was very impressed."

"I believe you know Lieutenant Kennedy, Colonel?" Canidy said innocently.

"Hello, Joe," Stevens said. "It goes without saying that I'm more than a little surprised to see you here, too."

"Major Canidy gave me the option of talking to Major Douglass here, or not talking to him at all," Kennedy said.

"As you seem to have already learned," Stevens said, "Canidy often does annoying things." He turned his face to Canidy. "Was it smart to bring that airplane here, Dick?" he asked evenly.

"I didn't have any choice," Canidy said. "When I went to Wincanton, the MP at the gate told me that once I went on the base, I was restricted to it until December 26. Something to do with keeping the barbarians away from the natives at Christmas."

"I thought this field was unsafe," Stevens said.

"I wouldn't want to try to take off with a load of bombs," Canidy said, "but empty, it's all right."

Stevens reminded himself then that Canidy was not a fool. Not only that, he was an aeronautical engineer who fully understood the "flight envelope" of B-25 aircraft. Before he had decided to land the B-25 at Whitbey House, he had convinced himself that it could be done safely. Flight safety restrictions were based on the worst scenario, a fully loaded aircraft piloted by an aviator of no more than ordinary skill and experience.

According to the book, Canidy had made an unauthorized flight for personal reasons (which, making it worse, included aiding and abetting an officer to go AWOL), during which he had landed an aircraft on a field he knew had been officially declared unsafe. And he had brought with him an officer who was not (at least yet) cleared to visit Whitbey House.

According to the book, he should be tried by court-martial, if for no other reason than to set an example *pour les autres.*

There was another way to look at it: A highly skilled pilot had made a short hop to pick up a buddy, a buddy who had lost thirteen of the twenty-eight young pilots he had led on a suicidal assault on the German submarine pens at Saint-Lazare. Stevens decided, therefore, to forget the whole thing.

And so far as young Joe Kennedy was concerned, he was to have been told on Friday anyhow that overall responsibility for the flying bomb project had been assigned to the OSS.

"I'm dying to know what's going on in this place, Colonel," Kennedy said, "but I'm afraid to ask."

"We were going to bring you here on Friday anyway," Stevens said. "Candy just pushed up the schedule a little."

"Can I ask what's 'here'?"

"Whitbey House is under the Office of Strategic Services," Stevens said, "which is under your father's old pal Colonel Bill Donovan."

"And I was to be brought here, you said?"

"OSS has taken over the 'take out the Saint-Lazare sub pens' project," Stevens said, "to settle the squabble between the Air Corps and the Navy about who should do it and how. Candy's the action officer."

That was the official version, but it wasn't the entire truth. Candy had gone to Stevens and told him he had heard about the flying bomb project: There was no question in his mind that when the Germans started to produce jet aircraft engines, they would do so in plants as well-protected as the submarine pens. Which meant that he wanted to get in on the ground floor of the project.

Stevens had agreed with that and taken the proposal to David Bruce. Bruce had gone to Eisenhower that same afternoon; and Ike, over the objections of the Navy and the Air Corps, had turned the flying-bomb project over to the OSS.

"So that's how you knew so much about me," Kennedy said to Candy.

"I liked it better when you thought maybe I really was omniscient," Candy said. He looked at his watch. "We've got an hour or so before dinner. You want to talk now, or would you rather wait until we're a little drunk, and stuffed with the roast beef of Merrie Olde England?"

"Now," Kennedy said.

Douglass shrugged, accepting the inevitable.

One of the trainees had found the piano. Over the murmur of conversation, "O Little Town of Bethlehem" could be faintly heard.

"Kennedy," Candy said, "when Doug tells you what you're facing at Saint-Lazare, and when you tell Doug about your B-17s full of Torpex"—a new, very powerful British-developed explosive—"you both may wish you were soused."

"Christ!" Kennedy said softly.

"Something wrong, Joe?" Stevens asked.

"I guess I'm just surprised to hear discussed so openly what I thought was a secret," Kennedy said.

"I'm glad you brought that up," Stevens said.

"Sir?"

"Although he certainly has given you cause to think otherwise," Stevens said, "Canidy is not a complete fool, nor does he play footloose and fancy-free with security. Everyone within hearing is involved in this project, and cleared appropriately. But no one else here is. You understand?"

"Yes, sir," Kennedy said.

"And you understand, of course, Kennedy," Canidy said, "that that was a none-too-subtle reprimand?"

"Don't push your luck, Dick!" Stevens snapped. "Damn it, sometimes you go too far!"

Stevens held Canidy in an icy glance for a long moment, until Canidy said, "I'm sorry, Colonel. I guess I do."

"Guess?" Stevens snapped.

Here was another icy pause, then Stevens said, "I suppose the best place to talk is in your apartment, Dick. Shall we go there?"

"Yes, sir," Canidy said. He sounded genuinely contrite.

As they started out of the room, Stevens became aware that conversation in the hall had died down and that the trainees were now singing along with the piano. Eyes were on them, and he thought he saw disappointment—and perhaps displeasure—in them that the brass was walking out on the Christmas carols.

He put his hand on Canidy's arm.

"Don't say anything smart, Dick," he said softly. "Just turn around and sing."

Canidy met his eyes for a moment and nodded.

They sang "O Little Town of Bethlehem" and "Good King Wenceslaus," and as they were singing "Away in a Manger," Ann Chambers, in her war correspondent's uniform, came into the refectory, walked up to Canidy, kissed him on the mouth (which introduced applause into the caroling), and then stood with her arm around him.

They sang until it was time for dinner.

After dinner they went to Canidy's apartment and discussed killing the enemy.

[THREE]
Schloss Steighofen
Hesse, Germany
28 December 1942

Beatrice, Countess Batthyany and Baroness von Steighofen, woke shivering, her arms wrapped over her large, dark-nippled breasts for warmth. In her sleep, she had kicked the sheets and blankets off. She reached down for them, dragged them over her, and glanced at the other side of the bed. It was empty.

She had not, she concluded, taken the captain of the honor escort into her bed. She reconstructed the end of the evening: The captain had been the perfect German officer and gentleman. His training and standards had not permitted him to believe that sexual congress between himself and the widow of his late commanding officer, in the familial Schloss and on the eve of a memorial service to the late Oberstleutnant Baron Manfried von Steighofen, could possibly take place.

Beatrice was now pleased that sexual congress had not, in fact, taken place. It had seemed like a splendid idea around midnight, but in the cold light of morning, she was glad to avoid the consequent awkwardness.

She rolled on her side and looked at the clock on the bedside table.

It was not the cold light of morning. It was the cold light of almost two o'clock in the afternoon. With a sudden movement, she kicked the bedclothes down and swung her feet out of bed. She searched with her feet for her bedroom slippers for a moment. When she could not immediately find them, she stood up and walked to the window.

The apartment Manfried had built in the Schloss (with her money) looked down upon the snow-covered fields outside the Schloss wall. It was a beautiful day, clear and bright. She liked cold, crisp, clear days. What she would do was take a ride, perhaps even a fast ride, a gallop, if the paths were not icy. It would sweat the cognac out of her, and then she would return and take a long bath.

She walked to her chest of drawers and took out a rather unattractive pair of underpants. No one was going to see her in them anyway, she thought, so it wouldn't matter that the heavy cotton underpants concealed the curves of her belly and buttocks and hung down nearly to her knees. They would absorb the sweat of her ride. She put on riding breeches and sat on the floor to tug on English-made, knee-high riding boots.

She glanced at herself in a mirror as she walked to another chest of drawers for a blouse. In riding breeches and boots, and naked above the waist, she looked like a character in a blue movie she had been shown in Budapest. All she needed to complete the costume was a whip and a black mask over her eyes.

She put on a white cotton blouse and tucked it into her breeches. Her nipples pushed against the thin material, making them clearly visible. She was going to have to wear either a brassiere or a sweater, or face the disapproval of the servants and the captain (whose name, she realized, she could not remember) if she took off her tweed riding jacket.

She opted for the sweater, taking a tan woolen pullover from a closet and pulling it over her head.

Then she realized that she wasn't going to be able to make it to the stables, much less mount a horse, without help.

She went to the bedside table and poured two inches of Rémy Martin cognac (about the last cognac here; and she had not remembered to bring any from the house in Vienna) into a glass and drank it straight down. She held her breath as she felt the brandy burn her throat and stomach, and then exhaled as the warmth spread through her body.

After that she left the apartment, which was like stepping from the present into the past. A few years ago, she had hired a Berlin architect to do it over. The Bauhaus School was now frowned upon by the Bohemian corporal and his sycophants, but the architect had studied there, and that was obvious in what he'd done to this wing of the Schloss.

Outside the door she was back in the Dark Ages. The Cold Ages would have been a better term, she thought. The walls were stone, the floors wide oaken planks. There had been no way to install electricity except by bolting conduits to the walls. Crossed lances and crossed swords, ancient battle flags, and dark portraits of the Barons von Steighofen and their women hung on the walls above the conduits. A narrow carpet ran down the center of the corridor, but it did nothing to take the chill from the place, either physically or aesthetically.

There was no grand staircase, either. One moved from floor to floor in the Schloss via one of five semicircular sandstone staircases. A handrail fixed to the wall was a recent—say, around 1820—improvement.

She descended three floors to the level of the courtyard, entered it, and walked across the cobblestones to the stable door. The stables, too, were a recent improvement to the Schloss. Sometime in the early 1800s, these had been constructed outside the Schloss wall, and a hole forced through for access to them.

The smell of the horses was pleasant and reassuring. A groom was working on a saddle, which he had put onto a dummy. What he was doing, Beatrice realized, was working on Manfried's saddle. She remembered Captain Whatshisname telling her about that. Manfried's "caparisoned stallion" would be part of the memorial ceremony, standing there with Manfried's cavalryman's boots reversed in the stirrups, while they did whatever they were going to do to mark Manfried's passage into Valhalla.

The groom got to his feet and bobbed his head to her, obviously surprised to see her dressed as she was.

"Bring the Arabian for me, will you? What's his name, Voltan?"

"Voltan, Baroness?" the groom asked disapprovingly.

"I'll get him," she said. "You go find me a saddle and a blanket."

"Yes, of course, Baroness."

She decided not to correct him about her rank. So far as he was concerned, she was and would forever be the wife of the Baron, and thus the Baroness. It would be of little interest to him that, because she was his widow, she was no longer the wife of the Baron or that, in those circumstances, the title would pass to Manfried's nearest surviving male relative. Which meant that she was the "Baroness" only by courtesy. He would be even less interested to know that in the circumstances, she had reverted to being in her own right what she had been before she married Manfried, the Countess Batthyany.

She pulled open the heavy wooden door to Voltan's stall, pulled him out of it, and led him to the stable yard. The groom came out a moment later carrying a saddle and a blanket. She took the blanket from him and threw it on Voltan, and then, after the groom had put the saddle in place and tightened the girth, she mounted the horse and directed the adjustment of the stirrups.

Satisfied, she rode out of the stable yard, walking Voltan long enough to start his blood flowing. Then, touching her heels to his sides, she put him into a canter. He would like to have been given his head, put into a gallop, she sensed, but she didn't think that was wise. There might be ice under the layer of snow.

She allowed herself to think of nothing but the chill wind in her face, the drumbeat of hooves, and the animal beneath her until his heartbeat against her inner thighs told her that he had had enough. She turned his head then and started to walk him back toward the Schloss.

It was only then that she could begin to face the day ahead of her. She would much rather not have come to the Schloss at all. She had wept when they told her in Budapest that Manfried had been killed. Manny had been a good man, and he had died too young. He was—*had been*—thirty. She was twenty-nine. They had been married not quite seven years and she had come to like, even admire him. And he had loved her, which had been very sweet indeed. She mourned him in her own way, and that should have been enough.

But, of course, it was not. Manny had been Oberstleutnant Baron von Steighofen, and there would have to be a public memorial for the people on his lands, for the soldiers of his regiment, and for what Der Führer called "Das Volk" of the "Thousand-Year Reich."

And she was the Countess Batthyany and realized the obligations of her birth. In public, she would be the grieved aristocrat whose husband had made the supreme sacrifice for his country, his Führer, et cetera, et cetera.

An assortment of Manfried's relatives (none of hers; she had no living close relatives) headed by his cousin the Baron von Fulmar would be at the Schloss. Plus an assortment of dignitaries, local and from Berlin. They included Helmut von Heurten-Mitnitz, representing the Foreign Ministry, and two Standartenführers of the SS-SD. One of these, Kramer, was the SS-SD man for Hesse, and the other, representing the Reichsführer-SS, was a peasant named Müller.

Müller had arrived with von Heurten-Mitnitz, which the Countess had thought a little odd, until Kramer had announced at cocktails that the two of them had been together in Morocco and had barely managed to escape when the Americans had invaded North Africa.

War, like politics, makes strange bedfellows, the Countess thought wryly. She rather liked von Heurten-Mitnitz, the little she'd seen of him. There were two kinds of Pomeranians, the ugly kind and the other kind—lean, lithe, leopard-like. This one was the other kind. It was a shame that under current circumstances there would be no opportunity to get to know him better.

On the other hand, if he could procure an assignment in Budapest, as now seemed likely—

When there had been hints in Berlin that such an assignment might be available, he had made it as clear as he could that he was prepared to make whatever sacrifice asked of him.

"I was rather afraid, my dear Countess, that if I suggested in any way how pleased I would be to return to Budapest, they would send me to Helsinki. Or Tokyo."

She'd laughed, not because she was expected to, but because she liked his humor. She hoped he would be assigned to Budapest.

"If the Gods smile on me," von Heurten-Mitnitz said, "might I call?"

"I would be pleased to receive you," she said.

She had a strange feeling: Did his desire to call upon her have anything to do with her? Or was there something official in his interest?

When she returned to the Schloss—tired, sweaty, and in desperate need of a drink and a bath—she saw von Heurten-Mitnitz having a conversation in the formal drawing room with Baron von Fulmar. The Baron was visibly uncomfortable, which made the Countess wonder again if there was more to Herr von Heurten-Mitnitz's friendship with Standartenführer Müller than their escape from North Africa.

Two days before, Helmut von Heurten-Mitnitz had telephoned Baron Karl von Fulmar in his offices at Hoescht am Main, an industrial suburb of Frankfurt am Main.

Von Heurten-Mitnitz expressed his condolences then over the death of Oberstleutnant Baron von Steighofen and announced that the press of other duties made it impossible for the Foreign Minister to personally attend the Baron's memorial service. Thus he had been delegated as the Foreign Minister's personal representative.

"The family will be honored, Herr von Heurten-Mitnitz," Baron Fulmar had replied.

"I deeply regret intruding on your grief, Herr Baron," von Heurten-Mitnitz went on, "but do you think that while I am in Hesse, you might spare me, say, an hour of your time?"

The Baron von Fulmar hesitated.

"Either at your office, Herr Baron," von Heurten-Mitnitz went on, "or at the Schloss. Whichever would be most convenient."

"I gather this is of an official nature?" the Baron asked.

"Let us say I would like to discuss something with you personally," von Heurten-Mitnitz said. "Certainly not over the telephone."

"I'm sure that can be arranged, Herr von Heurten-Mitnitz," the Baron said. "And I think it would be most convenient to do so at Schloss Steighofen."

"Then I look forward to meeting you, Herr Baron, at the Schloss," von Heurten-Mitnitz said, "and once again, my most sincere condolences."

The Baron von Fulmar was apprehensive that a highly placed official of the Foreign Ministry wanted to talk to him privately. His concern took a quantum jump when von Heurten-Mitnitz arrived at Schloss Steighofen accompanied by a Standartenführer SS-SD.

And the next morning he actually broke into a sweat when a servant delivered von Heurten-Mitnitz's card:

HELMUT VON HEURTEN-MITNITZ
BRIGADEFÜHRER SS-SD

The Foreign Ministry
Berlin

On the back of the card was written: "May I suggest the drawing room at 9:30? von Heurten-Mitnitz."

The Baron, a large-boned, florid-faced man, whose thinning hair was cut so short that the veins in the skin over his skull were visible, was kept waiting until 9:40 before von Heurten-Mitnitz showed up.

The formal drawing room was not a pleasant place. The furniture was old (but not good), heavy, and comfortless. There was one well-worn and colorless Persian carpet. And dark portraits of barons past adorned the walls. The Baron elected to stand rather than torture himself on any of the chairs or couches.

"How good of you to find the time for me, Herr Baron," von Heurten-Mitnitz said, offering his hand.

"How may I be of service, Herr Brigadeführer?" the Baron asked, laying the card von Heurten-Mitnitz had sent him on a table. The act was meant to look casual.

"Oh, God, did I send you one of those?" von Heurten-Mitnitz said, chagrined. "I didn't mean to. I usually send them to people who are impressed with that sort of thing. I would much prefer, if you don't mind, that you forget that Brigadeführer title. My association with the SS-SD is hardly more than an official fiction."

"As you wish, of course," the Baron said. "What should I call you?"

"If it would not be presumptuous, my Christian name is Helmut. And let me emphasize this is by no means an official interview."

"What, may I ask, is on your mind, Herr von Heurten-Mitnitz?"

The moment he laid eyes on the Baron, von Heurten-Mitnitz decided that arrogance lay at the core of von Fulmar's personality (he was, in other words, a scarecrow in fine clothes). The only way to handle such arrogance was to "wear" greater arrogance. If he tried to fence delicately, von Fulmar would perceive it as weakness: He had to knock him off balance straight off. And there was one good way to do that: "I wondered if by chance you have been in touch with your son," von Heurten-Mitnitz asked.

The Baron's face tightened. "I have not," he said firmly.

"I was referring, Herr Baron, to your eldest son," von Heurten-Mitnitz said, as if he wanted to be absolutely sure they were talking about the same person.

"I presumed you were," the Baron said.

"He's been a bit of a problem for you, hasn't he?" von Heurten-Mitnitz said, making it more of a challenge than an expression of sympathy.

"Until just now, Herr von Heurten-Mitnitz," the Baron said, "I was under the impression that his case had been considered at the highest levels, and that it had been decided I could not fairly be held accountable for my son's actions."

Von Fulmar was challenging von Heurten-Mitnitz's right to ask questions. But the Baron's bluster was hollow. A well-connected Party member can get away with reminding a Foreign Ministry functionary that he has access to the "highest levels," but that is as far as he would dare challenge a Brigadeführer SS-SD.

"The subject, regrettably, has come up again," von Heurten-Mitnitz said coldly. He gave that a moment to sink in, then added, more kindly: "And I have been asked to look into it. Confidentially and unofficially, as I said."

"God, now what has he done?" the Baron asked. "I presume you know the basic facts?"

The bluster was more than a little diminished.

"I think it would be best if you repeated them to me in your own words," von Heurten-Mitnitz said. "If you wouldn't mind?"

"You didn't respond when I asked what he's done now," the Baron said.

"That's not really germane," von Heurten-Mitnitz said.

"My father sent me to America," he said, "to study electrical engineering at the University of Southern California, in Los Angeles."

"Why do you think he did that?" von Heurten-Mitnitz asked.

"In my day, a son went to school where his father sent him. I was first at Marburg for four years. And then my father sent me to Los Angeles. He felt that would be best for me, and I did not question it."

"I was sent to Harvard, actually," von Heurten-Mitnitz said with compassion in his voice. "I found it quite difficult to adjust to."

The Baron responded to that with a nod, then went on.

"And while I was there, I made a genuine ass of myself," the Baron said. "I became infatuated with a young woman."

"That would be 'Mary Elizabeth Chernick'?" von Heurten-Mitnitz asked.

"She had adopted the stage name 'Monica Sinclair,'" the Baron said. "She wished to become an actress."

"This is the same Monica Sinclair we used to see in American films? Forgive me, Baron, but wasn't she a bit young for you?"

"My former wife is six months younger than I am," the Baron said icily.

"I see. And may I ask why you married her?"

"I was a damned fool," the Baron said. "We had . . . been together . . . and she was in the family way."

"I see," von Heurten-Mitnitz said. "And you did the gentlemanly thing."

"I never had the intention of staying married to her," the Baron said. "Obviously, it would have been impossible to bring her to Germany."

"Obviously," von Heurten-Mitnitz agreed.

"Under American law, a child born to a woman within ten months of her divorce is presumed to be the legal offspring of her former husband. When my former wife was six months pregnant—You follow the arithmetic?"

Helmut von Heurten-Mitnitz nodded.

"—I obtained an initial decree of divorce. My father at the time advanced me a sum of money sufficient to satisfy her and to support the child until he was eighteen. I immediately returned to Germany, and was in Germany three months later when the divorce became final and the child was born. I never saw him in the United States, in other words, and for years—"

"When did you in fact see him?" von Heurten-Mitnitz interrupted.

"I saw him for the first time in 1934," the Baron said, "when he was sent to Switzerland."

"Tell me about that," von Heurten-Mitnitz said.

"My former wife's career, such as it is," the Baron said, "has been based on the same role, which she plays over and over. She projects an image of unsullied innocence, incredibly enough, and that image is inconsistent with either divorce or progeny. She sells virginity the way whores sell the opposite. It was proposed to *Miss* Sinclair by Max Liebermann of Continental Studios—and she did not object—that the boy be sent to Iowa and raised by her mother."

"She gave up her child that willingly?" von Heurten-Mitnitz asked.

"I daresay the grandmother could not have been a worse mother than my former wife," the Baron said. "The reports from our legal counsel in America said she was a simple, decent woman."

"I see," von Heurten-Mitnitz said.

"And then she died, and other arrangements were necessary," the Baron said.

"Other arrangements?"

"I was approached, not directly, you understand, but through our lawyers in America, by a representative of Continental Studios, who led me to believe that now that her mother was no longer around, my former wife was willing to give me uncontested custody of the child. I am more than a little ashamed to admit that I turned down the offer. I had recently remarried, my son Fritz had just been born. I did not want the intrusion in my home. . . ."

"I understand," von Heurten-Mitnitz said, his tone suggesting that he both understood and disapproved.

"Our legal counsel reported to me that it was my wife's intention to place the boy in a private school, St. Paul's, run by the Episcopal Church, in Cedar Rapids, Iowa. They paid the school high compliments, and I was able to convince myself that he would be better off there than he would have been either with his mother—which in any case was out of the question— or with me here."

"I'm sure you were right, Herr Baron," von Heurten-Mitnitz said.

Von Heurten-Mitnitz was more than a little bored with this recitation of von Fulmar's. But the Bad Ems postcard had mentioned the Baron, and there was certainly a reason for that. He could only hope he'd be able to pull that from what von Fulmar was telling him.

"I was wrong, Herr von Heurten-Mitnitz," the Baron said. "Quite wrong. I should have brought the boy to Germany, no matter the difficulty, and raised him and seen to his education. If I had done that, we would not be standing here having this embarrassing conversation."

"I regret that you find it embarrassing, Herr Baron," von Heurten-Mitnitz said. "That is not my intention."

"Obviously, he has been up to something shameful, or you would not be here," the Baron said.

"You were explaining to me how he came to Switzerland," von Heurten-Mitnitz said.

"The school in Iowa was only a primary school," the Baron said. "But my son became friendly with a classmate, the son of the headmaster, in fact. When it was learned that this classmate was to attend a school for gymnasium-aged boys in Massachusetts, we decided my son should go with him."

"Do you happen to recall the headmaster's name?" von Heurten-Mitnitz asked, fishing.

"As a matter of fact, I do. He took it upon himself to send copies of the boy's grades to me. And an invitation to his graduation. His name was Canidy. The Reverend Dr. Canidy."

"I see," von Heurten-Mitnitz said.

It wasn't much, and he had no idea what it meant, but the OSS agent who had dealt with Fulmar in Morocco was named Canidy.

"Is that important?" the Baron asked, sensing that the name had somehow clicked in von Heurten-Mitnitz's mind.

"No. But odd details sometimes take on importance."

"As I was saying, my son was next sent to a school, St. Mark's, in Massachusetts. He was there two years. I was again approached by a representative of Continental Studios, this time directly. A very young and very brash young Jew. He had gone to Harvard, I must tell you."

"Then he must have been a very bright, as well as a very brash, young Jew, Herr Baron," von Heurten-Mitnitz said.

"He explained to me that in order to preserve my ex-wife's public reputation, it had been decided to send the boy out of the United States."

"To you?"

"No. What he said was that Max Liebermann, who owned Continental Studios, wanted the best possible education for the boy. It turned out, by the way, that the young Jew lawyer was Liebermann's nephew."

"Was his name Liebermann?"

"No, Fine," the Baron said. "Stanley S. Fine."

"Go on," von Heurten-Mitnitz said.

"It was put to me that Die Schule am Rosenberg, in Switzerland . . ."

He looked at von Heurten-Mitnitz, who nodded to show he knew about "Rosey."

". . . was the sort of place where Eric belonged," Fulmar went on. "Fine solicited my influence in getting him admitted."

"And did you use your influence to do so, Herr Baron?"

"Yes, I did. After consulting with some friends of mine in the Party, and with, of course, the Baroness."

"Officially or unofficially?"

"At first unofficially, and then officially. It was necessary to settle the question of whether or not the boy was Aryan."

"And?"

"My former wife is descended on both sides from good, solid, Silesian peasant stock. My son is unquestionably Aryan."

"And how does that affect his standing in the Almanac de Gotha?"

The Almanac was a quasi-official publication listing royal and noble bloodlines.

The Baron gave him an icy look.

"It has not yet come up," he said. "If it does, and if he were a German, he would be in his own right Baron von Kolbe. And, of course, as my eldest male child, he is heir to my title."

"Under German law, he is German," von Heurten-Mitnitz said.

"As I said, Herr von Heurten-Mitnitz, so far as I know the matter has not come up."

"Yes," von Heurten-Mitnitz said. "So you got him into Rosey?"

"Not only that, but I paid for it. I couldn't have it said that a Jew was paying for my son's education, could I? I paid for it, and I was happy to do so."

"Did you intend to finally bring the boy to Germany?" von Heurten-Mitnitz asked.

"That's precisely what I had in mind," the Baron said. Von Heurten-Mitnitz looked at him, waiting for amplification.

"On his graduation from Rosey," the Baron went on, "I arranged for him to matriculate at Philips University in Marburg an der Lahn. As I had, and my father had. At some time during his college years, when it appeared to me that he was sufficiently mature to understand the circumstances, I planned to discuss his future with him. I had come to believe the best thing for him would be to enter military service, either with my regiment or perhaps even the Waffen-SS."

"And your plans for him," von Heurten-Mitnitz said dryly, "somehow went awry?"

"Since I was naturally unable to meet him when he came to the university," the Baron said, "I asked the manager of our plant in Marburg—we make 'special' aircraft engines there—to ease his path. The manager is also an alter Marburger. He went to the president of our Brüderschaft (fraternity) and explained the situation. Accommodation was arranged for him in the dormitory, that sort of thing, and he agreed to look out for him."

"I see," von Heurten-Mitnitz said.

"My son wanted nothing whatever to do with my Brüderschaft," the Baron said.

"Excuse me?"

"My son appeared in Marburg in the company of a young Moroccan named Sidi el Ferruch, who was the son of the Pasha of Marrakech. They had been roommates at 'Rosey.' They arrived in a Delahaye touring car bearing diplomatic license plates. The car was driven by el Ferruch's personal bodyguard. The bodyguard and el Ferruch's manservant, as well as el Ferruch himself, were traveling on diplomatic passports. They were also armed."

"Astonishing," von Heurten-Mitnitz said.

"They established themselves in three connecting suites in the Kurhotel," the Baron said. "And when my man finally found them there and explained to my son the arrangements we had made for him, my son announced that he was perfectly comfortable where he was. He had no intention of moving into a student dormitory or, for that matter, joining a Brüderschaft."

"He was not quite what your man expected, eh?" von Heurten-Mitnitz chuckled.

"When I heard what had happened," the Baron went on, ignoring the remark, "I simply made time to go to Marburg to talk to my son. I tried to explain that, while someone like el Ferruch might exempt himself from normal undergraduate customs and regulations, it behooved him to remember that he was my son, a von Fulmar, and was expected to behave as such."

"I gather that he was not receptive?" von Heurten-Mitnitz said.

"He told me bluntly that he was an American and didn't much care how Germans were expected to behave. As for behaving like a dutiful son, he told me it was ludicrous of me to suddenly appear out of nowhere and start acting like a father to him."

Helmut von Heurten-Mitnitz shook his head sympathetically.

"I then told him I had no intention of maintaining him in a resort hotel and that he could either move into the student dormitory and do what he was told or leave the university. He actually laughed. It was all I could do not to slap his face."

"He laughed at you?"

The Baron nodded.

"On his eighteenth birthday he had entered into a contractual arrangement with Continental Studios. So long as he remained outside of the United States and maintained an absolute silence regarding his relationship with Monica Sinclair, there would be deposited monthly to his account with Thos. Cook & Sons the sum of five hundred dollars, which would be more than enough for his personal expenses."

"How difficult for you," von Heurten-Mitnitz said.

"He went on to refuse any help from me in any way. He wanted no part of me, or of his German heritage. At that point, Herr von Heurten-Mitnitz, I am ashamed to tell you, I lost my temper."

"You struck him?"

"No. But I called him 'an arrogant, ungrateful bastard' and told him that I washed my hands of him, once and for all."

"And his response?"

"He told me to go fuck myself, is what he said."

"I'm surprised you didn't strike him," von Heurten-Mitnitz said.

"During the entire conversation, el Ferruch's bodyguard stood behind my son's chair. He was an enormous Negro with a pistol in his belt. Frankly, I was afraid. Not so much physically, you understand, Herr von Heurten-Mitnitz, but because of the political and diplomatic ramifications of a confrontation with him. Because of his diplomatic status."

Helmut von Heurten-Mitnitz managed to restrain a smile. His mind's eye saw the Baron nervously eyeing N'Jibba, el Ferruch's enormous, shining black Senegalese bodyguard. What had kept the Baron from doing something foolish was not his awareness of political and diplomatic ramifications, but a menacing robed character two meters tall and weighing 150 kilos.

"I gather the discussion concluded soon?" von Heurten-Mitnitz asked. "And that was the end of it?"

"It wasn't the end of it, but yes, I left," the Baron said. "As soon as I could, I discussed the situation with my legal counsel. He confirmed my belief that

I had the legal right under German law to bring my son to heel. But he also pointed out that the matter wasn't quite that simple. He therefore made a few discreet inquiries of highly placed persons within the Foreign Ministry and the Party."

"And?"

"The matter came to the attention of the Foreign Minister himself, who thought it would be 'ill-advised at the present time' to either exercise my parental rights or to seek to have my son declared a German. Under American law, since he was born there, he is an American. The Americans were liable to become highly indignant if a German court were to declare otherwise."

"And I would think," von Heurten-Mitnitz added, "that others had in mind the possible usefulness of el Ferruch should war come and we find ourselves in possession of French Morocco."

"I thought it might be something like that," the Baron said.

"I was the German representative to the Franco-German Armistice Commission for Morocco," von Heurten-Mitnitz said. "In that capacity, I came to know your son, Herr Baron."

"Did you?" the Baron asked, surprised.

"Before we get into that, let me ask, how often did you see your son after your first encounter? Or should I say 'confrontation'?"

"I never saw him again," the Baron said firmly.

"And you had no idea that the last time he left Germany, he had no intention of returning? There was no telephone, not even a postcard?"

"I never had any contact with him after that meeting."

"But you did pay his tuition at Marburg?"

"It was suggested to me that I do so," the Baron said.

"And gave him an allowance of— How much was it?"

"Five thousand Reichsmarks monthly," the Baron said. "But that, too, Herr von Heurten-Mitnitz, was at the recommendation of highly placed persons."

"So I understand," von Heurten-Mitnitz said.

He fixed the Baron with a stern look.

"Herr Baron, it goes without saying that what I will now tell you is a state secret. You are to tell no one."

"I understand," the Baron said.

"There is reason to believe that your son is now connected with American military intelligence."

The Baron's face went white. "I can't tell you how ashamed that makes me."

Helmut von Heurten-Mitnitz let him sweat a moment.

"The information we have is considered highly reliable," he said.

"Certainly, no one thinks—" the Baron began, and stopped.

"Certainty not," von Heurten-Mitnitz said. "There is no suspicion that in any way reflects on your own loyalty."

"Then . . . what?"

"It is considered possible that he will attempt to contact you, most probably through third parties, but perhaps in person," von Heurten-Mitnitz said. "FEG is involved with much that is of interest to the Americans."

"I must strenuously protest even the suggestion—"

"Herr Baron, there is no question whatever in my mind of your loyalty. But he is your flesh and blood!"

"If he is connected with American military intelligence," the Baron said, "he is an enemy of the German state. That transcends anything else."

"I am going to give you my private telephone number," von Heurten-Mitnitz said. "And the private telephone number of Standartenführer Müller, who is handling this matter for the Sicherheitsdienst. If there is any attempt by your son to contact you, or if anything comes up that arouses your suspicions in any way, I want you to contact either of us immediately."

"Yes, of course," the Baron said.

Helmut von Heurten-Mitnitz wrote the numbers on the back of another of the calling cards identifying him as Brigadeführer SS-SD, and handed it to the Baron.

"Thank you for giving me your time at this period of grief," he said.

"I thank you for your understanding, Herr Brigadeführer," the Baron said.

The Baron, von Heurten-Mitnitz thought, *is fully prepared to denounce his son to the authorities if given the chance. And Eric von Fulmar and Colonel William J. Donovan of the OSS certainly had known he would. What, then, is the meaning of the postcard from Eric von Fulmar asking that his father be given his regards?*

"One final question, Herr Baron," von Heurten-Mitnitz said. "Are you acquainted with Professor Doktor Friedrich Dyer?"

He saw on von Fulmar's face that the question struck home.

"I am not personally acquainted with him," the Baron said. "But he is, at the request of Reichsminister Speer, serving as a consultant to our Marburg Werke."

"So I understand," von Heurten-Mitnitz said smoothly. "But you're not personally acquainted with him?"

"No," the Baron said.

Von Heurten-Mitnitz now understood that the answers to the questions posed by the Bad Ems postcard had to lie with Professor Dyer of the University of Marburg, his relationship with the Fulmar Werke there, and most important of all, his relationship with Albert Speer. Müller was going to have to go to Marburg, while he himself tried to find out why Reichsminister Speer was interested in an obscure professor there.

VI

[ONE]
The U.S. Navy Bureau of Aeronautics
Washington, D.C.
31 December 1942

The second-ranking officer in the United States Navy was formally known as the Deputy Chief of Naval Operations (DCNO). The DCNO was a busy man.

When he had business, for example, with the Director, U.S. Navy Bureau of Aeronautics, the DCNO's aide-de-camp would call the Director BUAIR's aide-de-camp and tell him the DCNO wished to see the Director, BUAIR, and that if it was convenient, he would like to do so from, say, 1420 hours to 1445 hours on that day, or maybe the next. The DCNO's aide-de-camp was very rarely told that the "suggested" time and date would be inconvenient.

The chain of command was considered very important to the smooth administration of the Navy Department in Washington. If the DCNO had business with a subordinate of the Director, BUAIR (which rarely happened), the word would be passed through the Officer of the Director to the subordinate in question.

Lieutenant Commander Edwin Ward Bitter, USN, was aide-de-camp to Vice Admiral Enoch Hawley, USN, who was Chief, Aviation Assets Allocation Division, of the Bureau of Aeronautics. He was very surprised that the aide-de-camp of the DCNO would telephone his office at all, and even more surprised at the conversation that followed:

The DCNO wished to see the Chief AAAD as soon as it would be convenient. When would that be?

"I'm sure the admiral can be in your office in thirty minutes, Commander," Lt. Commander Bitter said. "Can you tell me anything that will help the admiral prepare?"

In other words, what does the DCNO want to know?

"The admiral will come to *your* office, Commander," the aide-de-camp to the DCNO said. He then apparently consulted his watch. "It is 1455. The admiral will expect to be received by Admiral Hawley at 1525. Thank you very much, Commander."

The phone went dead.

Bitter cocked his head in curiosity, then stood up from his desk and walked to Admiral Hawley's open office door. The office was neither large nor elegantly furnished. The desk was wood, but it was scarred, and utilitarian rather than ornamental. An American flag and a blue flag with the three silver stars of a Vice Admiral hung limply from poles against the wall. On the desk were In and Out boxes and three telephones, and an old Underwood typewriter was on a fold-out shelf. Bitter knocked at the door.

Admiral Hawley, a silver-haired man in his late forties, glanced up and made a "come in" gesture with his hand. Then, as Bitter walked into the room, he returned his attention to the stack of papers on his desk, reaching several times from them to punch buttons on his Monroe Comptometer, then waiting with impatience as the automatic calculator clicked and spun through its computation process.

Finally, he looked up at Lt. Commander Bitter.

"Admiral, DCNO will be here at 1525. His aide just telephoned."

"Here?" Admiral Hawley asked, demanding confirmation.

"Yes, sir," Bitter said. "I told him that I was sure you could be in his office in thirty minutes, and he said DCNO would come here."

Admiral Hawley made a strange noise, half grunt, half snort.

"Is the Chief still here?" he asked.

"No, sir. I gave him liberty," Bitter said.

"Then I suppose you had better make a fresh pot of coffee," the admiral said.

"Yes, sir."

"Is there anything stronger around?"

"There is the emergency supply, Admiral," Bitter said.

"This may qualify—I am presuming, Ed, if you knew what he wants, you would have told me—as an emergency."

"I asked," Bitter said. "He avoided the question."

Admiral Hawley nodded.

"Make sure it's available, and ice and glasses and soda, but don't bring it out until I tell you to. The only reason I can imagine why he's coming here is that he's so ticked off at me that he doesn't want to wait until I could get over there."

"I'm sure it's nothing like that, Admiral," Bitter said.

"Then you enlighten me, Ed," Admiral Hawley said.

Bitter thought about it and finally shrugged. He then went to prepare the coffee and to make sure the Chief had not made a midnight requisition upon the bottle of Scotch and the bottle of bourbon, the emergency rations, in the filing cabinet behind his desk.

Admiral Hawley stood up, pulled a thick woolen V-necked sweater off over his head, stuffed it in a cabinet drawer, and then put on his uniform blouse. After that, he made an attempt to make his desk look more ship-shape than it did.

And then he stopped.

To hell with it. If I've done something wrong, it was an honest mistake, and I'll take the rap for it. I am no longer a bushy-tailed ensign. For that matter, no longer a bushy-tailed captain. If the DCNO didn't understand that my desk is crowded with stacks of paper and a clerk's comptometer because I'm working, fuck him.

The door from the corridor was opened at 1523 hours by the DCNO's aide-de-camp. The DCNO marched in.

"Good afternoon, Commander," he said, and quite unnecessarily identified himself. He was a large man, tanned, who looked like—and indeed was—an ex-football player.

"Good afternoon, Admiral," Bitter said. "Admiral Hawley expects you, sir, and has asked me to show you right in."

The DCNO's aide-de-camp, a full commander who looked like a younger version of his boss, nodded at Bitter, and Bitter nodded back.

Bitter walked quickly, ahead of the DCNO, to Admiral Hawley's door and pushed it open.

"The Deputy Chief of Naval Operations, sir!" he announced.

"Good afternoon, sir," Admiral Hawley said as he rose to his feet behind his desk.

"Hello, Enoch," the DCNO said as he walked, with hand extended, across the room. "How the hell are you?"

"I'm very well, sir. Yourself?"

"Overworked and underpaid and wishing I was anywhere else but here," the DCNO said. He sounded sincere, if resigned.

"May I offer you some coffee, Admiral?"

"Only if you have something to put in it besides milk and sugar," the DCNO said.

"I'm sure we can take care of that, Ed, can't we?" Admiral Hawley said.

"Aye, aye, sir," Bitter said.

When he was out of the room, the DCNO said, "He's limping."

It was a question.

"He took a Japanese .50-caliber, or parts of one, in his knee," Admiral Hawley said.

"And what does he have pinned to his chest?"

"They're AVG wings, Admiral. Commander Bitter was a Flying Tiger."

"I find that absolutely fascinating," the DCNO said.

Admiral Hawley had no idea what the DCNO meant.

"Bitter is a very good man," Hawley said loyally. "Class of '38, and he was nearly a double ace—he had nine kills—when he was hit. By ground fire, I think I should add."

"Hummmpph," the DCNO said.

Bitter came back into the room carrying a napkin-covered Coca-Cola tray and two cups of coffee. When he extended the tray, the DCNO said, "The name 'Canidy' mean anything to you, Commander?"

"Yes, sir," Bitter said, surprised at the question.

"You were in the Flying Tigers with him?"

"Yes, sir."

"That all?"

"We were stationed together at Pensacola, sir, as IPs, before we went to China."

"That all?"

"I don't know what the admiral is asking, sir," Bitter said.

"Is he a good man?"

"Yes, sir."

"Friend of yours, you would say, Commander?"

"Yes, sir."

The DCNO looked at his aide.

"Charley, I think we have just been given a late Christmas present," he said. "Would you agree with that?"

"Yes, sir, Admiral, it certainly looks that way."

"Commander, get some of that coffee for Charley and yourself, and then sit down."

Bitter left the room, quickly returned with two mugs of coffee, and sat down, somewhat stiffly, beside the DCNO's aide-de-camp.

"We came here, Enoch," the DCNO said, "more or less directly, from a meeting of the Joint Chiefs of Staff. The CNO was tied up, and so was Colonel William J. Donovan. A Navy captain named Douglass was sitting in for Donovan."

The DCNO took a swallow of his coffee and then looked at Bitter.

"Are you familiar with either of the gentlemen I just mentioned, Commander?"

"Yes, sir."

"How?"

"Captain Douglass's son was in the AVG, sir," Bitter said. "I had occasion to meet the captain here in Washington. I met Colonel Donovan before I went to China."

"You know what they do now?" the DCNO asked.

"Yes, sir."

"Charley," the DCNO said, "I think we just climbed out of you-know-where smelling like a goddamned rose."

"It's really beginning to look that way, sir," the DCNO's aide said.

"One of the items, actually several of the items, on the agenda, Enoch," the DCNO said, "was the German submarine pens at Saint-Lazare. First, there was a rather disturbing report about what hell those subs are raising with shipping, both in terms of shipping per se—they're sinking ships almost as fast as we can build them—and in terms of matériel that is not reaching England.

"Then the subject turned to what's being done to take the submarines out. That was not a bit more encouraging. At that point, I got egg on my face."

"Sir?" Admiral Hawley asked.

"Another proof, if I needed one, that, unless you know what you're talking about, you keep your mouth shut," the DCNO said. "I opened my mouth and announced before God and the JCS that the last information I had on the Navy project to take out the pens with torpedo bombers based in England looked very promising, and that I would fire off cables exhorting them to even greater effort."

The DCNO looked around the room, then shrugged.

"At that point, rather tactfully I must admit, Captain Douglass told me that the torpedo-bombing idea hadn't worked out—you can't get enough explosive into a torpedo to take on that much concrete—and then he let me know that the OSS had been given the responsibility for taking the pens out. I had the definite feeling that there were senior officers at that table who felt that the DCNO should know something like that. And, of course, I should have."

"Sir," Hawley said, "there was a message on that. . . ."

"I'm sure there was, and I'm sure that I should have seen it, but I didn't, so there I was with my ass hanging out. But I learned a long time ago that once part of your ass is hanging out, no further harm can be done, so you might as well let it all hang out. So I asked how come the job had been taken away from the Navy and why it was thought the OSS could do something the Navy and the Air Corps couldn't."

"Admiral," Admiral Hawley said, "it was my decision to recall the torpedo planes. We needed them in the Pacific. They were in Europe only because of the high priority of the submarine pens project. . . ."

The DCNO interrupted him by holding up his hand.

"No criticism was intended about that. What bothered me was that we were just as much as hanging up a banner saying, 'The Navy Can't Handle Its Own Problems.' "

"Sir," said Admiral Hawley, "if I may say so, it wasn't considered a Navy problem. It was considered a Theater problem. And I have been led to believe that it was given to the OSS to make that point."

"Don't hand me that crap, Enoch," the DCNO said. "Protecting the sea-lanes is the Navy's business. Submarines, friendly or hostile, are Navy vessels. Enemy submarine pens are the Navy's business. Bombardment of enemy shore bases, either by naval gunfire or aircraft, is the Navy's business."

"Yes, sir," Hawley said.

"The Air Corps wants to be its own branch of service, Enoch," the DCNO said. "And sooner or later, it will be. When that happens, I don't want the Air Corps saying, 'You might as well give us naval bombardment aviation, too. They have proved that they can't handle it. Remember when we had to come in and take out the German submarine pens for them?'"

"I take your point, sir," Hawley said.

"You can't blame a man for honestly speaking his mind, but I was pretty uncomfortable sitting there and hearing a man in the uniform of a Navy captain assuring me that now that the OSS had the responsibility, a handful of civilians in uniform was going to do something the Navy couldn't."

He paused and shook his head, as if the memory was painful.

"I said something else I shouldn't have said," he went on. "I made a smart-ass remark. An unfair and smart-ass remark. I said that I just had a hard time believing that Donovan's Dilettantes were going to be able to do something the Navy couldn't. Whereupon the Commandant of the Marines, that disloyal sonofabitch, joined the opposition."

"Sir?"

"He said, 'What the hell, Jake, they stole a battleship. If all else fails, they can steal the Kraut submarines.' Which of course got a big laugh. And then the Chairman asked if we could move on to something else. And then I got control of my runaway mouth and said that all I was trying to do was offer the Navy's cooperation to the OSS in any way possible to solve the problem. Then the Chairman indulged me. He said that he certainly appreciated the offer of cooperation and suggested that I get together with Captain Douglass after the meeting adjourned.

"Douglass told me, of course, that he would welcome any help the Navy could give the project. And he went on to say that there's still one Navy officer on the project, a lieutenant named Kennedy. His 'action officer,' this man Canidy, is also a former naval officer. He's no dummy—Douglass, I mean—and I think he understands my concern. He said he would have a word with Canidy and that there would be no objection if we beefed up our liaison staff with the project."

"I see," Admiral Hawley said.

"So I came to see you with two questions in my mind, Enoch," the DCNO said. "First, I wanted the name of an officer of suitable rank and experience we can send over there to represent the Navy's interests, and second, in the profound hope that you could disabuse me of the notion that there is no aircraft in the Navy inventory that can do what has to be done."

"The bad news first, Admiral," Admiral Hawley said. "The problem is the weight of explosive throw. The submarine pens have been carved out of rock and then reinforced with concrete. It's going to take tons of explosive, very precisely placed, to cause any real damage. Skip bombing has been tried, and it failed. Torpedoes you know about. If the pens could be taken out with bombs, it would have to be a bigger bomb than anything now available. A bomb far too large to be carried in any Navy aircraft. I think this flying bomb concept, turning a B-17 into an explosive-filled drone, is going to be the only answer."

"Someone has to pilot the drone from the control aircraft," the DCNO said thoughtfully. "There's no reason he cannot be a naval officer." He looked at Bitter: "Are you on flying status, Commander?"

"No, sir," Bitter said.

"Medically grounded? Because of your knee?" the DCNO asked.

"Yes, sir."

"There are such things as medical waivers," the DCNO said. "Is there any reason you can see, Commander, why you could not control a drone from an aircraft piloted by this Lieutenant Kennedy?"

"No, sir," Ed Bitter said.

"Did I detect a moment's hesitation, Commander?" the DCNO asked.

"Sir," Bitter said. "The question would be whether I would be permitted to do so."

"Captain Douglass has said he will have a word with your friend Canidy," the DCNO said.

"Major Canidy is sometimes difficult, sir," Bitter said.

"Christ, Commander, he's a major. Majors, even Army Air Corps majors, do what they're told."

"Sir," Bitter said. "The thing is, he's not really a major. He's really OSS and wears a major's uniform because it permits him a certain freedom of movement. I doubt if Captain Douglass would order him to let me fly the drone. Or if he did, that Canidy would accept the order if he didn't think it was the thing to do."

"Hmmph," the DCNO snorted. "Well, let me put it this way, Commander. When those submarine pens are taken out, I want them taken out by naval officers. Preferably by Navy officers in Navy aircraft. But in any event by Navy officers. How you arrange that, I leave up to you. If necessary, start singing 'Auld Lang Syne' and 'Anchors Aweigh.' Do I make my point?"

"Yes, sir," Bitter said. "I'll do my best, sir. I'm grateful for the chance."

"How soon can you leave for England?" the DCNO asked.

"Immediately, sir," Bitter said.

The DCNO sat for a moment tapping the balls of his fingers together.

"I think the way to handle this, Enoch," he said, "is to put the Commander on temporary duty. That way, if it becomes necessary, he can hoist your flag. And you can approve his application for waiver of physical condition and get him back on flight status."

"Aye, aye, sir," Admiral Hawley said.

"Take a couple of days at home, Commander," the DCNO said. "And then get yourself to England. You know what's expected of you."

"Aye, aye, sir," Bitter said.

[TWO]
Marburg an der Lahn, Germany
31 December 1942

Hauptsturmführer Wilhelm Peis had had to consider the possibility that once he actually met Fräulein Gisella Dyer, Standartenführer Johann Müller might not like her. Or that he would be put off by her negative attitude: More than once Fräulein Dyer had forgotten her situation. She did not in these moments become openly defiant. But with some alcohol in her she tended to lose her sweetness and innocence and turn into a flippant and sarcastic bitch.

Obviously, Standartenführer Müller had to be entirely pleased with the evening: Peis hoped there would be an opportunity afterward to discuss his future with the Standartenführer. Peis had nothing specific that he wanted from the Standartenführer; he simply wanted the Standartenführer to look upon him favorably. There was no overestimating the influence of a Standartenführer SS-SD on the staff of the Reichsführer-SS in Berlin. A favorable—or unfavorable—word from a man like that in the right ears would have a pronounced influence on his career. A few little words could mean the difference between staying here with maybe a nice promotion or being assigned to the Eastern Front.

Peis had to keep reminding himself that underneath, Müller was probably a man much like himself, that Müller had in fact once been a lowly Wachtmann on the Kreis Marburg police. A man didn't change his spots, even if he came to wear the corded silver epaulets of a Standartenführer.

Since he was a man, he wanted to spend a couple of pleasant hours on New Year's Eve over drinks and dinner with an attractive young woman. And afterward he wanted to snuggle up with her in bed. It was little enough for him to expect of Peis, and he would likely be annoyed if things didn't go well.

Because of the very real possibility that Fräulein Dyer might show up in one of her difficult moods, Peis considered that it might be best for her not to show up at all and to solicit the help of Frau Gumbach.

Frau Gumbach operated a whorehouse near the Bahnhof, a regular whorehouse with resident whores. She also had available a dozen women who operated outside the law—that is, who didn't have the prostitute's yellow identity card. These girls were available by appointment to men who could not afford being seen in the whorehouse, or picking up whores in bars or along the street.

The problem was that Standartenführer Müller had expressed a specific interest in Fräulein Dyer. If Fräulein Dyer did not appear at supper at the Kurhotel, Standartenführer Müller might conclude that Peis was saving her for himself. It would not be desirable for Müller to harbor any such suspicions.

When he telephoned Frau Gumbach, she assured him that she understood his dilemma perfectly and that it would be her pleasure to help. She knew just the girl: She had been bombed out of her home and employment in Kassel and the Hessian Labor Officer had sent her to work in the aircraft engine plant in Marburg. Not only would she be pleased to make a little extra money, but she would like the opportunity to associate with important people.

"You're not suggesting that I pay her?" Peis asked incredulously.

"Of course not, Herr Hauptsturmführer," Frau Gumbach said. She was fully aware that Peis's friendship kept her house open and her girls free not to "volunteer" to become manual laborers for the Todt Organization. "I will, of course, give her a little something, but you should consider this to be a simple gesture between friends."

"I'll be in the parking lot behind the Café Weitz at quarter to seven," Peis said.

Frau Gumbach was usually reliable, but he wanted to see the girl from Kassel before he took her to the Kurhotel to meet Standartenführer Müller.

He then called Fräulein Dyer and invited her to spend New Year's Eve with himself and Standartenführer Müller. Müller, he pointedly told her, was a very important officer from Berlin. He asked her to be at the Kurhotel at seven. If he was not yet there, she was to wait for him at the bar.

He did not offer to pick her up. Riding the streetcar and then walking almost a kilometer up the hill to the Kurhotel through the snow would give her time to reflect on her situation.

[THREE]

Gisella Dyer was twenty-nine years old. She was tall and rather large-boned, the kind of woman described as "statuesque" by those whose perceptions of statues are based on the baroque school. That is to say, she had broad shoulders and sturdy thighs, large, firm breasts and buttocks, but little fat.

Gisella Dyer and her widowed father lived in a large and comfortable house close to the ancient fortress and later abbey that had been seized from the Papists and turned into Philips University by Philip, Landgrave of Hesse-Kassel, after his conversion to Protestantism by Martin Luther.

The house had been her grandfather's, and he had left it to Gisella's father and mother; but it was no longer entirely theirs. She and her father (her mother had died when she was fourteen) lived in four large rooms, with private bath, on the second floor, twenty-five percent of the house. The rest of the space had been requisitioned (temporarily, until victory) by the Housing Office and was now occupied by three families and a bachelor, an engineer at the Fulmar Werke.

Her grandfather had been Professor of Mathematics at Marburg. Her father was an instructor in metallurgy in the College of Physics. If it had not been for the War/National Socialism (which were in Gisella's mind interchangeable), her father would have been Professor of Metallurgy. And three years ago, Gisella would have become Gisella Dyer, D.Med.

But with National Socialism, there had come "Party considerations." In addition to one's academic credentials, one needed the blessing of the Party in order to be promoted to a distinguished position. Prof. Dr. Friedrich Dyer's academic credentials were impeccable, but he was not in good standing with the National Socialists of Stadt und Kreis Marburg. Quite the reverse.

Professor Dyer had been opposed to the Nazi Party from the days when it had been just one more lunatic, amusing fringe party. He had thought then—and worse, said—that it was more dangerous than other batty groups primarily because of its intellectual dishonesty. The National Socialist belief in "Aryanism" and "Aryan Purity" especially aroused his contempt.

In the fall of 1938, he had made unflattering remarks about Professor Julius Streicher, the Party's virulent anti-Semite intellectual, in the presence of some people he innocently thought of as friends. They had promptly reported him to the Sicherheitsdienst. In the course of the investigation that followed, it was discovered that he had illegally transferred funds to Switzerland and was planning not to return to Germany after a seminar to be held in Budapest.

The Sicherheitsdienst officer who conducted the investigation was SS-Obersturmführer Wilhelm Peis, a former Kreis Marburg policeman whose Party affiliations had led to his duties as deputy commander of the SS-SD office for Stadt und Kreis Marburg.

Peis summoned Gisella to his office, offered her a glass of Steinhager, and then outlined to her the severe penalties she could expect her father to suffer. The least of these was punishment under the criminal statutes. But it was more likely that he would be tried under the "enemy of the state" laws before a "People's Court." If that happened, he certainly—and she herself more than likely—would be sent off to a concentration camp. On his release he would be permitted to make his contribution to the New Germany with a forester's ax or a laborer's shovel.

Peis then matter-of-factly let Gisella know there was a way out of the predicament: She would undertake to keep her father on the true National Socialist path; she would report regularly to Peis treasonous or defeatist statements made by their friends and associates; and she would come, when he wished, into his bed.

Gisella gave only passing thought to refusing him.

If Peis wanted her, he could have taken her right there and then, ripped her clothes off, slapped her into submission, and done it on his office couch. To whom could she have complained? The SS-SD was the ultimate law in Stadt und Kreis Marburg an der Lahn, and Peis was the number-two man in the SS-SD there. The question she faced was not whether Peis would have her body, but how to make the circumstances most advantageous to her and her father.

She went that afternoon to Peis's apartment, allowed him to get her drunk, and fell into his bed.

An honorable man after his fashion, Obersturmführer Peis lived up to his end of the bargain. The charges against her father remained "unconfirmed, under investigation." As long as she behaved, her father's well-being was assured.

After the initial novelty passed, Peis required her to perform only infrequently. He had other young women similarly indebted, plus a small harem of others who considered it an honor to share the bed of an SS-Obersturmführer. Whenever he did send for her, it was less a hunger for her body than a desire to humiliate her. He made sure she was aware of this.

Gisella now realized that if she had been clever enough to pretend that she welcomed his attentions, he would more than likely have grown bored with her. But she hadn't been able to do that, and Peis sensed her contempt. This he repaid with humiliation.

Six months after he originally called her into his office, she became a kind of occasional gift from Peis to his friends or else to someone he wanted to watch. By then, he had been given command of the Marburg SS-SD.

One evening he "invited" her to take dinner with him at the Kurhotel on the mountainside south of Marburg.

The Kurhotel, a small, recently built, Bauhaus-style building, was the nicest place around and Peis liked to be seen there in the company of "respectable" young women. He had "invited" her there before; after supper there would be a session in a room set aside by the management for Peis's use.

He was not there when she arrived, so she took a seat alone at one of the tables in the barroom to wait for him. When the waiter appeared, she ordered a glass of white wine. When the waiter returned, he had a bottle of Gumpoldskirchner '32 wrapped in a towel in a basket.

"Compliments of His Excellency, Fräulein Dyer," the headwaiter smirked.

"I beg your pardon?"

He nodded toward a table across the room. Three men sat there, an Arab, a Nordic blond, and a huge Negro. She had seen them before both here and at the university, where they were known, somewhat derisively, as "the Arab Prince and his boyfriend." The boyfriend, a rather good-looking young man—a *very* young man—caught her eye and raised his glass. She quickly looked away.

"Thank you, no," she said to the waiter in a rage. "Take it away!"

She might be forced to prostitute herself to Peis, she thought bitterly, but she was not available to be picked up in a hotel barroom.

"His Excellency may take offense, Fräulein," the waiter said.

"Not nearly as much as Hauptsturmführer Peis will," she snapped.

She was still humiliated and angry when Peis came in. When he sat down, she told him what had happened. But he was not, as she expected, furious that someone was making advances to one of his ladies.

"Which one has the yen for you?" he asked. "The Arab or the Baron?"

"The Baron?"

"The young one is the Baron von Kolbe," Peis said.

"I thought he was the Arab's 'little friend,'" she replied.

"That's what I thought at first," Peis said. "But they are apparently not homosexual."

"You seem quite sure," she said, now annoyed with him too.

"My dear Gisella," Peis said, "of course I'm sure. It is my business to be sure."

"I don't think I understand you," she said.

"Among my duties is the surveillance of people of interest to the Berlin headquarters of the SS-SD," Peis said, obviously pleased with the opportunity to reveal his importance. "One of these is the Arab, actually a Moroccan. His name is Sidi Hassan el Ferruch. The other is Eric von Fulmar, the son of the Baron von Fulmar, as in Fulmar Elektrische Gesellschaft."

"And they are being watched? Why?"

"Reasons of state, of course," he said. "I can't get into that, of course."

"Naturally not," she said, hoping he thought she sounded very impressed with him.

"But I can tell you something rather interesting about them," he said.

Whatever that was would have some sexual connotation, she knew. He liked to embarrass her.

"Really?"

"They like their women shaved," Peis whispered.

"What?" Gisella asked, but then she understood. "Wilhelm," she said, somewhat surprised to realize she was really quite curious, "how could you possibly know that?"

"Frau Gumbach told me," he said, "that when His Excellency sends his bodyguard for girls once or twice a week, payment is generous and in advance, but before the girls can leave, they have to show N'Jibba, the body-guard, that they have shaved their most intimate places."

"I don't believe that," Gisella said. "Why?"

"I haven't the faintest idea," he said. "But I'm going to find out."

"How? Are you going to walk over there and ask him?"

"No," he said. "I'm leaving. You're going to find out for me."

"I don't think this is funny, Wilhelm," Gisella said.

"I'm not teasing you, if that was your question," he said. "I've been trying to think of a way to meet both the Arab and the Baron. Socially, I mean. And I just worked out how to do it. I'm going to go over there with your apologies for refusing their wine. I'm going to tell them you are a respectable girl who didn't know who they were. And then I'm going to leave."

"I told you, I don't think this is funny," she said.

"I told you I wasn't teasing you," Peis said. "Let me phrase that another way. I want you to get to know one or both of them intimately. Preferably the Moroccan. And I hope you can do that with discretion. Because if you can't, Gisella, the next time N'Jibba fetches whores from Frau Gumbach, one of them is going to be you."

She fought back tears. He was obviously serious, and besides, her tears only pleased him.

"Will you tell me why you want me to do this?"

"I will expect a full report from you," he said.

"About what?"

"About anything interesting they do," he said.

She watched in her compact mirror as Peis bowed and clicked his heels at their table. When she saw them glance in her direction, she quickly snapped the compact closed and studiously looked away. Peis then walked across the room, but stopped just outside the door and nodded his head to signal that he had arranged things.

Three minutes later, with a triumphant smirk, the waiter brought the bottle of Gumpoldskirchner '32 back to the table.

"Compliments of the Baron, Fräulein Dyer," he said.

"Thank you," she said.

Then von Fulmar was standing beside her.

"I thought perhaps, since you are alone, I might ask to sit with you," he said. There was sarcasm in his voice.

He was quite self-confident, which was strange and even a little funny.

He was not a day over twenty, if that, despite the well-tailored English suit. She was twenty-five. Quite a gap as far as she was concerned, but he seemed oblivious to it.

"Please do," she said, and gestured to a chair.

The waiter immediately produced a glass. Fulmar waved it away.

"I'm drinking the cognac," he said. "Would you fetch my glass, please?"

"Jawohl, Herr Baron," the waiter said.

An odd combination of sophistication and boyishness.

"Where're your friends?" Gisella asked.

"They were already engaged," Fulmar said. Gisella was sure this boy and the Arab had decided between them who was coming to her table. Perhaps they had even flipped a coin over her. And this boy had won.

"And Hauptsturmführer Peis was called to duty," Gisella said.

"What's going on, Fräulein?" Fulmar asked.

"I'm not sure I know what you mean, Herr Baron," she said.

"Why do you call me that?" he asked, turning unfriendly. But after a moment, she also realized he was not acting like a young boy making a play for an older woman.

"I was told your father is the Baron von Fulmar."

"Well, true. But I'm an American, and Americans can't be barons."

"Your German is perfect," she said. "You could easily pass for a German."

The compliment rolled off him quickly. "Languages come easily to me," he said matter-of-factly. "I even speak pretty good Arabic. But what I asked is 'what's going on, Fräulein?' "

The waiter returned with the brandy glass. Von Fulmar sniffed at it, sipped at it, and set it down. Then he looked at her for her reply.

"I really don't know what you mean," she said uncomfortably.

"I know who Peis is," he said, almost impatiently, and with obvious contempt, "and I know who you are. Why is the local Sicherheitsdienst thug offering me his girlfriend?"

Gisella felt her face flush.

She blurted what came into her mind. "You can get in trouble calling him a thug," she said.

Fulmar dismissed that with a wave of his hand.

"Do you work for him?" Fulmar asked.

She met his eyes but didn't say anything.

He shook his head. "What does he want to know?" he asked.

She was frightened now. This was not going at all the way she had expected it to.

"Just fishing, huh?" Fulmar said.

Gisella blurted, "I'm not his girlfriend."

"I thought you were," he said matter-of-factly, and she believed him. And that meant that he really was unafraid of Peis. He had sent the wine to her without caring whether Obersturmführer Wilhelm Peis would like it or not.

"I think I understand," Fulmar said. "He's got something on you, right?"

She nervously, softly, licked her lips before she spoke.

"I think he wants to be friends with you and your friend."

Fulmar laughed unpleasantly.

"I'll bet he would," he said. "That sonofabitch!" Then he looked at her curiously. "What's he got on you?"

When she didn't reply, he shrugged. "Sorry, none of my business. I shouldn't have asked."

"Please," she said softly, "don't make trouble for me."

He looked at her again, and she realized she liked his eyes.

"No," he said. "Of course I won't. We'll sit here and have a couple of drinks and dance. If he has somebody watching us—the goddamned waiter seems very curious—he will report that we seemed to be getting on famously."

She smiled.

"You have a very nice smile," he said.

"Thank you," she said, and realized that her face was warm, that she was blushing.

"How do you know who I am?" she asked, a moment later.

"You were pointed out to me at the university," he said. "I've had a couple of lectures about tungsten from your father. I'm studying electrical engineering."

Then he stood up.

"May I have the pleasure of this dance, Fräulein Dyer?" he asked with exaggerated courtesy.

While they were dancing, he seemed determined to keep distance between them, and after a moment she understood why: He had an erection. Uncharacteristically—but on purpose—she moved her midsection close to his for confirmation.

When they were back at the table, his knee brushed hers and then quickly withdrew. A moment later, her knee found his. This time his did not withdraw.

"Is that on orders, or not?" he asked, looking into her eyes.

Shamed, she withdrew her knee.

"I didn't mean I don't like it," Fulmar said.

She averted her eyes from his, but moved her knee against him again.

"Would you care to see my etchings, Fräulein Dyer?" Fulmar asked. She smiled. "It would give the waiter something interesting to report."

"Where are your etchings?" she asked.

"Here. Upstairs. I live here."

She picked up her wineglass and drained it, and then stood up.

"Shall we go, Herr Baron?" she asked.

As they waited for the elevator, the waiter came to the dining room entrance to see where they were off to.

She took more pleasure than she expected to from coupling with Eric von Fulmar. That was probably because he was kind and straightforward, and enthusiastic. Peis made a point of looking bored as he pumped away at her.

When Peis phoned the next day to ask how things had gone, she replied: "It made me feel like one of Frau Gumbach's whores."

"I asked you," he said, obviously taking pleasure from that, "how things went, not whether or not you liked it. For instance, did you have to shave?" He let that sink in for a moment, and then added: "You went to Fulmar's room at seven-thirty. You came back down at quarter to nine and had dinner. You went back to his room at half past ten and stayed there until three in the morning. He drove you home then in the Arab's Delahaye."

She was stunned.

"I'm happy for you, Gisella," Peis went on, "that you have formed this new relationship. And I would be very unhappy if it were broken off."

"Wilhelm, he's twenty years old!"

"I don't care if he's fourteen," Peis said.

"Damn you!"

He laughed and hung up. But what was really funny was that she had outwitted him. As long as von Fulmar stayed at the university, she more than likely would be able to exchange sleeping with Peis, and whoever else it amused him to offer her to, for a really decent kid, with nice eyes, who didn't treat her like a whore.

The only thing that finally went wrong with Gisella Dyer's relationship with Eric Fulmar was that it had to end.

And after it ended, of course, she went back to her role as whore-on-call.

[FOUR]

Gisella Dyer was distressed.

It was bad enough that on the Eve of the New Year she had to charm and then sleep with a complete stranger, who, since he was a Standartenführer, would almost certainly be in his fifties. But what made it really bad was that she'd just about allowed herself to believe she no longer had to be one of Peis's whores-on-call.

She had not jumped at this hope without reason: Because of her father's knowledge of titanium and other exotic alloys, the Reichsminister Albert Speer had sought him out—*personally* sought him out—when he had come to the Fulmar Werke in his private train a month before and had installed him, at a flattering honorarium, as "consultant" to the Fulmar Werke.

Her father was obviously now rehabilitated in the eyes of the government. And that should have been clear to Peis.

Despite the virtually limitless power Peis had as the local SS-SD officer, he was a peasant, very much aware of who his betters were. And very much the servant in their presence. After the Reichsminister's departure, her father told Gisella that Peis looked like he was wetting his pants every time Speer spoke to him.

It just seemed logical that Peis would leave her alone, would probably go out of his way to avoid her in the fear that her father would get him in trouble with Speer.

It had been nice to think about. And then as the days and weeks passed and Peis didn't call her, it began to seem possible that she was free of Peis for good. She had not been "invited" to any of the pre-Christmas parties he staged for his close friends. Or, until just now, to a New Year's Eve gathering.

But it was starting all over again. Nothing had changed. And she felt foolish for having hoped.

She did what she could with her hair and dressed carefully (as a whore should, she thought bitterly), even to underwear that was no protection against the cold but would be pleasing to a man.

When the time came, she left the apartment and stood on the snow-covered street wondering which would be the better route to catch the Strassenbahn, which would take her to the Südbahnhof.

The Strassenbahn ride would be shorter if she turned left and went down the hill—the Marburg—that way. But the walk was almost twice as far as it would be if she went off the Marburg in the other direction and caught the Strassenbahn on the other side of the Marburg, by the City Baths.

She decided that since it was snowing, the shorter walk made more sense even if the ride was longer, and she started down the street toward the City Baths, her hands jammed in the pockets of her coat.

After the Strassenbahn put her off into the snow in front of the Südbahnhof and she started walking up the ice-slippery cobblestone road to the Kurhotel, Gisella thought of Eric Fulmar. Probably because she was going to the Kurhotel; she had spent a good deal of time with him in the Kurhotel.

She wondered if he ever thought of her, wherever he was. Probably on the Eastern Front, but possibly, because he was able to walk through raindrops, in Berlin. Or, for that matter, in Paris or Budapest, safe, warm, and in bed with some woman. Right now she would have been pleased to have been that woman.

She then wondered about the Standartenführer she would be entertaining tonight. Would she be just a little bit lucky, and would he be reasonably young and pleasant? Probably not. Christmas was over.

As she walked into the foyer of the Kurhotel, already crowded with drunk and exuberant New Year's Eve revelers, she remembered how furious Peis had been—and what Peis had done to her—when one day in the early spring of 1940, after returning for his fourth year at the university, Eric von Fulmar had simply vanished.

Peis had been unable to accept that Fulmar had said nothing to her about that. She still remembered Peis's words, between brain-jarring slaps:

"You sucked his cock for two years, and he just took off without a whisper? You don't really expect me to believe that, you stupid cunt!"

Gisella Dyer gave her coat to the attendant and entered the dining room. The room was full, and extra tables had been crowded into it to accept the New Year's Eve crowd.

She wondered, *What does anyone have to celebrate?*

She saw Peis at a table across the room. There was a thin, long-haired blonde with him, doubtless some whore of Frau Grumbach's. And a stocky man in the black uniform of the SS.

She fixed a smile on her face and made her way through the crowded room.

"Heil Hitler!" she said, making the gesture. "Good evening. Happy New Year!"

"My dear Gisella," Hauptsturmführer Wilhelm Peis said, rising and kissing her hand. "You look very lovely tonight."

"Thank you," she said.

"Herr Standartenführer Müller, may I present Fräulein Gisella Dyer?"

Müller shook her hand, then held her chair out for her.

He was neither as old as she had feared, nor as unattractive. And he had intelligent eyes, with neither sexual interest in them nor contempt for a rounded-heels female. The blonde from Frau Gumbach's smiled at Gisella warmly, as if they were old friends.

Shortly after one in the morning, Gisella found herself in the suite the Kurhotel had made available to Standartenführer Müller. She had known this was going to happen, but the way it was happening was making no sense. During the evening he had been formal and correct, which she suspected was because he did not want to act incorrectly in public with a woman whose morals might be questioned.

But once he had locked his bedroom door, the correctness did not end.

She had steeled herself to be pawed, but he made no move to touch her. He was in fact acting as if she were not in the room.

He took off his tunic and hung it up, then sat on the bed and pulled off his boots. Next he arranged his breeches on the couch so as to preserve their crease.

"How much have you had to drink?" he asked suddenly. "Are you sober?"

"I'm a little happy," she said.

"Are you drunk is what I'm asking," he said, looking at her.

"No, I don't think I am."

"I have a message I want you to deliver," he said.

She looked at him with the unspoken question in her eyes.

"From Eric von Fulmar. He wishes to express his best wishes to your father."

She felt a chill.

"I don't quite understand," she said, her voice faint.

"But you heard what I said?" Müller asked, somewhat impatiently.

"Yes, but I don't understand the message," she said.

"It is a very simple message. When you go home in the morning—I think it will be best if you stay the night—you will give that message to your father, and then at two o'clock tomorrow afternoon you will go to the Café Weitz. I will meet you there and you will relay his answer to me."

She felt the tears start, and she couldn't stop them.

"Herr Standartenführer," she said, "I swear on my mother's grave that my father doesn't know who Eric von Fulmar is!"

"But you know him?"

"Yes, I knew him."

"That's all?"

"He was my lover when he was at the university," she said.

"You were in love with him?"

"I . . . I was performing a service to the state at the request of Hauptsturmführer Peis," she said.

Müller went to her and grabbed her shoulders and put his face close to hers.

"It would be very dangerous for you, my girl, to lie about von Fulmar's relationship to your father," he said.

Gisella was now shaking.

"I swear before Christ he never met him," she said.

"He was your lover and he never even met your father? Why not?"

"Because I didn't want him involved," she said.

"When was the last time you heard from Fulmar?"

"I've been over this again and again and again. I don't know where he went, and he never told me he was going."

"And you have not had any contact with him since May of 1940?"

"No. I swear, I don't know anything about him. My God, why won't you believe me?"

Müller let her go, walked to his tunic, and took out a package of cigarettes. He handed her one and lit it, then lit another for himself.

"Gisella," he said, almost in a fatherly tone, "I want you to consider your answer very carefully before you give it. If you should be contacted in any way by Eric von Fulmar, in any way at all, would you promptly notify Hauptsturmführer Peis?"

She took a deep breath.

"Yes, of course I would," she said, "if that is what is desired of me."

"I don't believe you," Müller said matter-of-factly.

She looked at him in horror.

"Peis would. I don't. Which is a good thing for you."

"I don't know what you mean," she said helplessly.

"Eric von Fulmar is now an officer in the United States Army," Müller said. "He sent a postcard, postmarked Bad Ems, to a mutual friend, asking that his regards be given to your father—"

"I tell you," she said desperately, interrupting him, "he doesn't know my father!"

And then the implications of what he had said sank in. He didn't sound as if he were a security officer looking for a spy or a spy's accomplices. Gisella stared at Müller in utter confusion.

"—and I want to know what he meant by that," Müller finished.

"He didn't know my father," she wailed. "He doesn't know my father."

"Fulmar sent his regards," Müller said flatly. "We have to find out what the hell he meant by it. My life, and now yours, Gisella, may damned well hang on that."

"I don't understand—" she began, and he shut her off.

"Yes, you do." he said. "You're a very intelligent young woman."

"Has this anything to do with Reichsminister Speer?" Gisella asked. She saw immediately in his eyes that the question confused him. "I don't know," he said. "If you're asking if I am making inquiries on behalf of Speer, no. Quite the opposite, Gisella."

She looked at him curiously, and he nodded his head to confirm her suspicions.

"I want you to ask your father, right out, if he can think of any reason why Fulmar would send him his regards," Müller said. "Do you understand? If he can't think of anything, have him guess. Whatever he tells you, you tell me. I'll decide whether it's important or not."

He kept looking at her until finally she nodded her head, and said, very softly, "All right. All right."

He nodded, then turned from her and stripped down to his underwear and got in the bed.

Baffled, she crawled in bed beside him, careful not to touch him.

Was Müller up to something with Peis? Or was he up to something deeper than Peis was ever capable of?

She had a nightmare. Peis was slapping her face, and this time Müller was watching. When Peis ripped her blouse and brassiere off and applied the tip of his cigarette to her nipple, she woke up, breathing heavily, soaked in sweat.

"What's the matter?" Müller asked.

"I had a nightmare," she said.

He sort of chortled. But it was not unkind.

"I was in it?"

"You and Peis," she said. "He was burning my breast with a cigarette."

"He did that to you?"

"Yes, when Eric disappeared and I had no idea where he was, or even that he was going."

"That may happen again," Müller said, "I am sorry to say."

She started to shiver.

He rolled over and put his arm around her.

He held her until she stopped shivering, then started to turn away from her.

"Don't let go of me," Gisella said.

"I'm not a fucking saint," Müller said.

"Neither am I, Herr Standartenführer," she heard herself say faintly, but very clearly.

VII

[ONE]
Washington, D.C
5 January 1943

Although Ed Bitter was about to leave his wife and child and—*at last*—approach, at least, the field of battle, he, and they, were in much better shape than other families whose head had been ordered overseas.

For one thing, he didn't have to worry about where Sarah and Joe would live. Just after Ed announced he was going overseas, his parents and Sarah's father began a very polite but quite serious competition for the privilege of housing Sarah and Joe until Ed came home.

Thus, Ed's mother argued that there was more than enough room in the Lake Shore Drive apartment. And besides, she'd love the chance to get to know her grandson better.

Joseph Child, on the other hand, argued that while it was of course up to Sarah, he thought she would be more comfortable in New York, as she had so few friends in Chicago. And besides, happily, a very nice apartment had just become vacant in a building "the bank owned" not far from his own apartment.

Sarah, Solomon-like, announced that if there was no objection, she would like to go to Palm Beach. Her father's house there was, of course, closed. But there was the guest house, right on the beach, which could be easily opened. Six rooms were more than enough room for the two of them. And even for her father or the Bitters, if they decided to drop in for a week or ten days. Besides, she said, Florida would be good for Joe.

With exquisite courtesy, the grandparents split the problem of transporting Sarah and Joe to Palm Beach. Joseph Child would come to Washington and provide Sarah company until the guest house in Palm Beach could be made ready. Pat Grogarty, who had been the Childs' chauffeur more years than Sarah was old, would then drive Sarah and Joe to Florida, where Ed's mother (who now liked to be referred to as "Mother Bitter") would be waiting, "to help Sarah get settled."

Meanwhile, Ed had managed to convince both Sarah and the grandparents that he was simply moving from one desk assignment to another. Not, in other words, to sea, much less to war. Though their anxieties about his safety annoyed him, he was nevertheless a little touched as well. He was, after all, a professional naval officer, and the nation was at war. He had obligations on that account.

But on the other hand, there was no point correcting their belief that because of his wound, he would no longer be required to go in harm's way. So he had not let Sarah know that he was now back on flight status, despite the still-stiff knee.

The funny thing was that leaving Sarah and Joe turned out to be difficult, more difficult than Ed had imagined.

While he wasn't madly, passionately in love with Sarah, he respected and admired her more than any other woman he had ever known. She had character. She'd handled the shock of her pregnancy, for instance, in a really decent way. She'd accepted her share of responsibility, and told him straight off—and he was sure she had meant it—that he had no obligation or duty to marry her.

He had accepted, of course, his duty to legitimize his child, and would adhere to his wedding vow to "keep only to her, forsaking all others." For her part, Sarah had agreed not only to an Episcopal wedding ceremony but also to raise Joe in the Christian faith. She was a splendid woman and a splendid mother, and she loved him.

On balance, their marriage was a good thing for both of them, even without considering Joe.

Ed had come, and this was rather unexpected, to really love his son.

That experience, in fact, was one of the reasons he was sure he didn't love Sarah. He had never felt for her anything like the emotion he felt when his son smiled at him or gave him a wet kiss. Such things really made Ed melt. With Sarah, he never melted. Yet marriage seemed a very cheap price indeed for having a son like Joe.

Ed's new assignment was incredible good luck: He was getting back in harm's way, and this previously had seemed out of the question. Up to now his only reasonable expectation was to spend the war as a staff officer, a shoreside staff officer, far from action. He was a crippled aviator, who stood virtually no chance of passing a flight physical again. And alas, he was a very good staff officer. Very good staff officers are usually much too important to send to sea. A very good crippled staff officer was a double kiss of death.

As the work he was doing for Admiral Hawley had become less and less important, his feeling of frustration had grown. When he first went to work for the admiral, the disaster at Pearl Harbor had still been a bleeding wound, and the assignment of Naval Aviation assets had been critical. There had been neither many planes nor the spare parts and support equipment for them. Thus the appointment of these throughout the world had been very much like an intensive, indeed, deadly, game of chess.

As aircraft and equipment had trickled from assembly lines, daily decisions—based on losses—and educated guesses—based upon less than complete understanding of war plans—of requirements had to be made. A wrong guess—or estimate, as it was called in the trade—was at the time a genuine threat to the conduct of the war. Sending more aircraft, or fewer, than the tactical situation required could have lost more than a battle.

But that situation had changed. Everybody was still screaming for more aircraft; but in point of fact, the major problem for the last several months had been scrounging shipping space rather than equipment to ship. The trickle had become a flood. Aircraft manufacturers who had been delivering four aircraft a day were now delivering twenty. Or forty. The Naval Flight

Training Program, vastly expanded, was delivering a steady, and steadily growing, stream of pilots.

Bitter knew that his job could just as easily have been accomplished—perhaps been better accomplished—by one of the directly commissioned civilians who had entered the Navy in large numbers, men from automobile and furniture factories, grocery distribution, railroads, even five-and-ten-cent-store executives. These people were skilled and practiced in moving "supply line items" from Point A to Point B in the most efficient manner.

The need for someone qualified to base the supply decisions on tactical considerations had ceased as soon as the American industrial complex began to stamp out airplanes with the same efficiency that it spit out automobiles and refrigerators.

As often as he dared, he had asked Admiral Hawley to have him returned to aviation duty or to a ship. He was a naval officer first and an aviator second, and he could hold his own on a ship, as executive officer or even as captain, with luck.

Admiral Hawley had always courteously but firmly refused. The Navy needed him most where the Navy had put him, the admiral kept telling him.

And, as things had turned out, the admiral had been proved right. He was going overseas, going in harm's way, back on flight status, because that was what the Navy needed.

Four days after the DCNO marched into Admiral Hawley's office, Sarah drove Ed to Anacostia Naval Air Station in the Cadillac, as she had fifty times before. The only difference was that this time he wouldn't be back in a couple of days. Otherwise, it was the same routine. He traveled in a blue uniform, carrying two suitcases (his priority orders waived weight restrictions) and a stuffed leather briefcase.

Sarah clung to him when the public address system announced the boarding of the Air Force C-54, and the pressure of her breasts against his abdomen reminded him that he was going to miss that part of their marriage. Joe cried, and there were tears in Ed Bitter's eyes when he kissed his son.

The plane refueled at Gander, Newfoundland, and again at Prestwick, Scotland, after fighting a headwind across much of the Atlantic, and then took off again for Croydon Field outside London, where it was scheduled to land at half past ten in the morning London time.

[TWO]
U.S. Army Air Corps Station
Horsham St. Faith
0185 Hours
6 January 1943

Major William H. Emmons, who was the commanding officer of the 474th Photo Reconnaissance Squadron of the Eighth United States Air Force, was more than a little curious about Major Richard Canidy.

Canidy was preceded at Horsham St. Faith by a telephone call from Brigadier General Kenneth Lorimer of Eighth Air Force Headquarters.

Mission 43–Special-124 was a photographic reconnaissance of the German submarine pens at Saint-Lazare, General Lorimer said. And it was being flown at Major Canidy's request. Special-124 was a high-priority mission, he emphasized. Which meant that there was to be no delaying it or canceling it or getting around it except maybe for some overwhelming catastrophe (such as, say, the end of the world). Which meant that if Major Emmons had problems mounting it, equipment problems, say, it would be necessary to take an aircraft from another scheduled mission so that Special-124 could go.

Major Canidy himself would come to Horsham St. Faith to personally brief the flight crew (Major Emmons was always pissed when some chair warmer showed up to tell his people how to do what they were ordered to do) and would remain at Horsham St. Faith while the mission was flown. After the mission the film magazines would be turned over to Major Canidy, who would arrange for the necessary processing.

"Under no circumstances, Bill, is Major Canidy to be permitted to go along on the mission," General Lorimer said finally. "You understand me?"

"Yes, sir."

Later Major Emmons as much as said it straight out to his friend Captain Ross that Canidy was one more of the glory-hunting headquarters sonsofbitches who liked to pick up missions (twenty-five missions and you got an Air Medal and went home) by inviting themselves along as "observers." They got in the way, and they added two hundred pounds to the gross weight, and they picked and chose the missions to observe, generally short, safe ones.

Emmons was a little sorry that General Lorimer had this Canidy's number. Special-124 was going to be short, but it wasn't going to be safe. A P-38 group attempting to skip-bomb the Saint-Lazare pens had lost sixteen of twenty-nine attacking aircraft. Major Emmons would be happy to send some chair-warming sonofabitch trying to pick up a mission out on one like this.

Major Canidy arrived at Horsham St. Faith at three o'clock in the morning, sleeping in the back seat of a Packard driven by an English woman sergeant. Major Emmons was surprised to see that the sonofabitch did have wings pinned to his tunic. But that was all. Just wings. No ribbons. The sonofabitch apparently hadn't even been here thirty days. If he had been, he would have had the ETO (European Theater of Operations) ribbon.

First Canidy asked for coffee and then something to eat, then promptly began to tell the crew how to fly this mission. And right in front of the WRAC sergeant, too. *That* pushed Emmons over the edge.

"Excuse me, Major," he said. "This mission is classified."

"I know," Canidy said. "I classified it." And then he understood. "Does Agnes look like a German spy to you, Major?"

"How much B-26 time do you have Major?" Emmons flared. "If you don't mind my asking? To tell my men how to fly this mission?"

"Actually no B-26 time," Canidy said.

"But he does have several thousand hours of pilot time," the WRAC sergeant said sweetly. "And both the American and the English DFC."

"Shut up, Agnes," Canidy said.

"And before we came here, we were with Major Douglass, who led the P-38 strike on the pens. He and Major Canidy were Flying Tigers in China."

"I told you to shut up," Canidy repeated.

"Richard," the WRAC sergeant said, undaunted, "the major obviously believes—and, worse, is communicating his belief to these gentlemen—that you're a . . . How does Jimmy put it? A candy ass."

"Cahn-dy Ah-ss" in the WRAC sergeant's dignified, precise English was comical. That broke the ice a little, and both Emmons and Canidy chuckled. The B-26 pilot, a lieutenant who looked as if he belonged in high school, laughed out loud, like a boy.

"I guess I owe you an apology, Major Canidy—" Emmons began.

"Don't be silly," Canidy interrupted.

"—but when General Lorimer said that you were not under any circumstances to go on this mission, I got the idea you were one of those guys who like to collect missions by going on the easy ones."

"Lorimer said what?" Canidy asked.

"That you are not under any circumstances to go along on this mission," Emmons said.

"Oh, that sonofabitch!" Canidy said.

"He meant it, too," Emmons said. "I'm sorry."

"He outfoxed you, Richard," the WRAC sergeant said, obviously pleased to learn that. "He knew very well all along that you planned to go."

Canidy looked at the boyish B-26 pilot and shrugged his shoulders.

"You just tell us what you want, Major," the young pilot said. "And how you think is the best way to get it. We'll give it the old school try."

Saint-Lazare was on the English side of the Brest Peninsula, 375 air miles from Horsham St. Faith. The B-26 stripped for aerial photography cruised at 325 knots. It would take a little over two hours in all for the trip. The boyish B-26 pilot broke ground at 0538, and the B-26 reappeared at Horsham St. Faith a few minutes after eight. The return trip had taken longer than the way out. The port engine had been ripped off by flak.

A "wounded aboard" flare went up from the B-26 as it lined itself up with the runway.

When the wheels came down, even from where they stood watching, it was clear to both Emmons and Canidy that the starboard gear had been damaged and was not going to lock in place.

An attempt to radio the pilot to go around, pull up his gear, and belly it in failed. And in any event, there wasn't time. It came in, in a crawl, and touched down, skidded off the runway, toward the bad gear, and spun around and around and around across the grass.

When Canidy and Emmons, in a jeep, reached the aircraft sixty seconds ahead of the crash truck and ambulances, the air was heavy with the smell of avgas. Thirty seconds after they pulled the limp body of the boy pilot through the canopy, the gas ignited.

But the photographers had tossed the film canisters out of the gun-and-camera ports in the fuselage the moment the plane had stopped moving, and thus MA (for Mission Accomplished) could be written in the records after Mission 43–Special-124.

[THREE]
Croydon Air Field
London, England
1035 Hours
6 January 1943

As the C-54 taxied to Base Operations, Ed saw two U.S. Army buses and a limousine waiting. There were three or four full colonels aboard the C-54, and one of them was apparently important enough to be met by a limousine. Not without a little thrill, Ed saw in the limousine a couple of symbols that he was now in the war zone. Except for a narrow slit, its headlamps were painted black, and its fenders were outlined in white so the car would have more visibility in a blacked-out-against-the-enemy city.

He waited impatiently until there was room enough in the aisle for him to stand and put on his uniform cap and overcoat and collect his luggage. Then he walked down the stairs, following the line of people toward the buses.

Then his name was called.

"Commander Edwin Bitter!"

He looked around.

There were five people in uniform (no two uniforms alike) standing in a line by the limousine. Four of them were standing at attention, and the fifth was saluting. Three of them, including the one saluting, were female. It took him a moment to place her. He had never before seen his cousin Ann Chambers in her war correspondent's uniform.

But he had immediately recognized the two broadly smiling American officers with her. The one in a green blouse and trousers was Dick Canidy. The one in a rather startling all-pink (trousers, shirt, and cut-down blouse) and totally illegal variation of an Air Corps captain's "pinks and greens" was Captain James M. B. Whittaker. He had no idea who the two Englishwomen, a captain and a sergeant, were.

The other debarking passengers were fascinated with the odd little greeting party. Most were amused, but two of the full colonels failed to see anything entertaining.

Bitter was more than a little embarrassed as he left the line headed for the buses and walked to them.

"The King was tied up," Canidy said, "so he sent the Duchess to welcome you."

"Damn you, Dick," the British female captain said.

"Commander Bitter," Canidy said, "may I present Her Gracefulness, the Duchess of Stanfield? And Sergeant Agnes Draper? I believe you know everyone else."

"The commander seems a bit underwhelmed to see you, Dick," the British captain said, as if this pleased her.

She's a good-looking woman, Bitter thought. *Somehow aristocratic. I wonder—it wouldn't surprise me—if she might indeed be a duchess.*

"That's because he hasn't been kissed, Your Gracefulness," Canidy said.

"Will you stop calling me that?" She laughed.

Canidy moved quickly to Bitter, grabbed his arms at the moment Bitter grasped what he was up to, and kissed him wetly on the forehead.

"Welcome to England, Edwin," Canidy said loudly. "We who have preceded you, plus, of course, those who have been here all along, will be able to sleep soundly now that the Pride of the U.S. Navy has arrived."

"What are you doing here?" Bitter asked.

"We came to fetch you, obviously," Jimmy Whittaker said. "To spare you the two hours of 'How to Behave Now That You're in England' lectures you'll be given if you get on one of those buses."

"How's Joe, Eddie?" Ann Chambers asked.

"They're going to Palm Beach," Ed Bitter said.

"War is hell, isn't it?" Canidy said dryly.

"You seem to be having a good time," Bitter said. "How did you know when I was coming?"

"I'm omniscient," Canidy said.

"You're what?"

"I'm omniscient," Canidy repeated. "Tell him, Your Gracefulness, that I'm omniscient."

The captain put out her hand to Bitter.

"How do you do, Commander?" she said. "My name is Stanfield."

"How do you do?" Bitter said.

"On your knees, you uncouth swabbie," Canidy said. "That's a duchess you're talking to."

Bitter looked in confusion at the captain and saw in her face, and then in a nod of her head, that she was indeed a duchess. He looked at the sergeant and was convinced he saw in her eyes sympathy for his discomfort.

It was just like Canidy to embarrass him in front of an enlisted man. Woman.

He looked away from the sergeant, but not before he had noticed that despite the ill-fitting uniform, she was as good-looking as the captain, toward the buses. An Army officer with a clipboard was looking at him impatiently.

"I'd better get on my bus," Bitter said.

"You weren't listening to Captain Whittaker, Commander," Canidy said. "If you do that, they will carry you into hours of durance vile, or some damned thing like that: Following the short-arm inspection, there will be bullshit lectures on how you're supposed to treat the natives. Tell him you're going with us."

"Natives, indeed!" Captain the Duchess Stanfield said.

"What's a short-arm inspection?" Ann Chambers asked.

"I'll show you later," Canidy said, grinning at Whittaker.

"I'd better follow the SOP," Bitter said. "Where are you going to be later?"

"You don't have to go, Eddie," Canidy said.

"I can't just go AWOL," Bitter protested.

"What are they going to do, send you overseas?" Canidy replied.

"Where are you going to be later?"

"God, you are a stuffed shirt," Ann Chambers said.

"We're going to drink our lunch at the Savoy Grill," Jimmy Whittaker said. "Then we'll be in the bar at the Dorchester from about five. Can you remember that, or should I write it down for you?"

"I'll do what I can to be there," Bitter said. He turned to Captain Stanfield: "I'm happy to have met you, Your Grace."

"Thank you," she said.

"Dick!" Ann Chambers protested as Bitter picked up his bags and started to walk to the buses. "Don't let him go!"

"I told him he didn't have to go," Canidy said. "But he's in one of his Commander Don Winslow of the Navy moods. You can't argue with him when he gets that way."

As he hurried toward the buses, Ed heard Whittaker laugh. Then the duchess asked, "Commander Winslow?"

Canidy told her of Commander Don Winslow, the dauntless, perfect, true-blue hero of a daily radio program for children. Just before he boarded the bus, Ed heard the duchess laugh.

The bus carried the C-54 passengers to a hotel requisitioned as a billet for newly arrived officers. He was given a small room that was furnished with a cot and a chair. Before long a bored major delivered an hourlong lecture extolling the ancient virtues of the British people and their culture. He made it quite clear that being assigned to England, where one would have the opportunity to actually mingle with these people, was a great privilege. The major was followed by a bored medical captain who delivered another hourlong lecture, enlivened with color slides, of typical genital lesions one could expect if one became too friendly with English ladies.

When the lectures were over, a sergeant found him and sent him off to Naval Element, SHAEF. A bus ran on a thirty-minute schedule between the transient hotel and Supreme Headquarters, Allied Expeditionary Force. The sergeant told him he'd better take his luggage with him, since the Navy had their own officers' quarters.

Repacking and claiming his luggage made Ed miss the first bus to Grosvenor Square. And it was ten past two—and he hadn't had any lunch—when he finally found Naval Element-SHAEF. A captain there told him that he had been placed on further TDY with the Office of Strategic Services, which was a supersecret outfit located on Berkeley Square. He could wait for a car if he wished, but it was only a couple of blocks away.

A London bus splashed gritty slush over his overcoat as he walked to Berkeley Square, and he had to stand for several minutes outside a firmly closed door before he was finally permitted inside.

But the things turned immediately and vastly better.

A Lieutenant Colonel Stevens greeted him. A good-looking, older officer. He was wearing a West Point ring. Ed was among his own.

"We've been expecting you, Commander Bitter," Stevens said. "Let me welcome you."

"Thank you, sir."

"I wonder what happened to Canidy," Lt. Colonel Stevens said.

"Sir?"

"He borrowed our limousine to meet you at Croydon and spare you the 'Be Kind to Our British Cousins' lectures," Colonel Stevens said. And then before Bitter could frame a reply, he raised his voice and asked, "Has Major Canidy checked in?"

"Sir," a man's voice, somehow familiar, called back, "he said when you're through with Commander Bitter to send him over to the Dorchester."

"He must have gotten tied up at SHAEF," Colonel Stevens explained. And then he added, "Eighth Air Force did a photo recon of the Saint-Lazare sub pens yesterday. Canidy wanted to see what, if anything, they got."

"Yes, sir," Bitter said.

"Commander, I believe I'm supposed to brief you, but I would imagine that you're pretty well briefed on the problem itself already. As well as its ramifications. I think I should tell you this, however: Despite what the DCNO thinks—he had a talk with Colonel Donovan—OSS was given this mission because Ike thought it was the sensible thing to do. It is not a conspiracy to make the Navy look foolish."

"Yes, sir."

"Dick said he proposes to send you to see your friend Douglass, who has unfortunately become the expert on the target and its defenses. And then you'll go see how the Aphrodite project is coming along at Fersfield. How does that sound?"

"'Aphrodite project'?" Bitter asked.

Stevens chuckled. "The drone aircraft," he explained. "Dick Canidy is apparently well read in mythology. Aphrodite, he informed us, is not only the goddess of love, she is the protectress of sailors. He further suggested that when they heard that name, as they certainly will, the Germans would be prone to associate Aphrodite with the WAC, who use her as their lapel insignia. We were all so dazzled that no one could think of an objection. The Aphrodite Project it is."

"Canidy is full of surprises," Bitter said.

"Dick speaks very highly of you, Commander," Lt. Colonel Stevens said. "Despite the motive behind your assignment to us, he thinks you'll be very useful."

Stevens watched Bitter's face for a reaction. When he could detect none, he went on, as if he was doing something reluctantly that had to be done, "Commander, I think I should tell you that Canidy has been ordered to keep a close eye on you. The first time he suspects your primary loyalty is not to the Aphrodite Project—bluntly, that you consider yourself under a greater obligation to the Navy—he is to send you back to the United States on the next available aircraft. Do you understand?"

"Yes, sir," Bitter said.

"Captain Fine has an identity card for you, Commander, and a set of orders that will permit you to move freely around without many questions being asked. Once you have those, there's nothing else for you to do here. You'll work out of Whitbey House."

"Yes, sir," Bitter said.

"Can you come in, Stan?" Stevens called. A moment later, Captain Stanley S. Fine came into his office.

"You know Commander Bitter, Stan?" Stevens asked.

"Yes, sir," Fine said. "Good to see you, Commander. Welcome to the lunatic asylum."

"Take care of the paperwork, will you, Stan? And then take the Commander over to the Dorchester."

"Yes, sir."

"And, Stan, I want the Princess back."

"I understand, sir."

On the way to the Dorchester, Bitter was given the answer to the question he dared not ask. The Princess was the Austin Princess limousine Canidy had had at the airport.

The entrance to the Dorchester Hotel was protected by sandbags stacked high around the revolving door, and the plate-glass windows that looked out onto Park Lane and Hyde Park were painted black and crisscrossed with tape to keep glass shards from flying if a bomb struck nearby.

But inside, the hotel was much as Bitter remembered it. The only difference seemed to be that most of the men and many of the women in the lobby and bar were in uniform.

Bitter was surprised that the British lady sergeant was at the table against the wall with the others. Another manifestation of Canidy's contempt for military customs. Enlisted people were not supposed to socialize with officers.

And officers were not supposed to demonstrate affection in public, either, he thought, when he saw that Ann Chambers was cuddled affectionately against Dick Canidy.

"Commander Don Winslow of the Navy," Canidy said, "and his ambulance chaser."

"The ambulance chaser," Fine said, "has been sent to reclaim the Princess."

"Oh, damn," the British enlisted woman said. "And it's such fun to drive!"

"Besides," Whittaker said, "the steering wheel is where it's supposed to be, right?"

Whittaker, Bitter saw, was holding the duchess's left hand, on which she wore a wedding ring.

"Now that you've had your lectures, Edwin," Canidy said, "show us how you can charm the natives."

"Richard," the British woman sergeant said, "for Christ's sake, leave him alone."

That was astonishing behavior for an enlisted woman, Bitter thought, precisely the reason the customs of the service kept enlisted people separated socially from officers.

"Commander," the duchess said, "it seems only fair to tell you that for the last four days, we have heard nothing from Richard but glowing reports about you. I can't imagine why he's being such a shit to you now that you're actually here."

A waiter appeared with one chair.

"I'm terribly sorry, Your Grace," he said. "But this is the only chair."

Bitter saw that she quickly pulled free the hand Whittaker had been holding.

"We'll manage," the duchess said. "Thank you very much."

Bitter found himself sitting beside the English female sergeant. That made him uncomfortable, but there seemed to be nothing he could do about it.

Whittaker reached under the table and came up with two gray paper sacks.

"Scotch and applejack," Eddie," he said. "We're out of bourbon and rye."

"I hate to admit this," Fine said, "but I'm growing to like the applejack."

Under the circumstances, Bitter decided that he could not refuse a drink, even though he really didn't want one.

"Scotch, please," he said.

The English sergeant shifted on the banquette seat so she could reach the ice bucket. With long delicate fingers she dropped ice in a glass, then extended it to Whittaker for the Scotch.

Bitter remembered her name: Agnes Draper.

When she handed him the glass, their fingers touched, and he wondered if Canidy was actually capable of trying to fix him up with a female sergeant.

He decided that he was.

Fifteen minutes later, Lt. Colonel Stevens came into the bar.

"I hate to break in on this happy little gathering," Stevens said. "But I need a word with you, Dick. And you too, Stan."

Fine and Canidy immediately got to their feet. Ann slid over on the banquette, and then Agnes Draper followed her, which meant that her hip was no longer pressing against Ed's.

Bitter watched Canidy, Stevens, and Fine elbow their way through the crowded bar to the lobby.

"They do that all the time, Eddie," Whittaker said. "Have their private little chats. I'm not sure if they really have anything secret to talk about or whether they do it for the effect."

"Oh, come on, Jimmy," the duchess said. "That's unfair!"

"Hey," Whittaker said. "You're supposed to be my girl. You keep taking his side, Ann'll come after you with an ax."

"No, I won't," Ann said. "Anybody on Dick's side is on my side."

"Will you watch your mouth!" the duchess said to Whittaker. But she reached her hand out and rubbed the balls of her fingers over the back of his hand.

There was no question about it. Whittaker was emotionally involved with the duchess, and the duchess was a married woman. And she didn't really care much who knew about it. He told himself that it was none of his business, yet he wondered what Colonel Stevens, who must know, thought of it. And then he wondered what Colonel Stevens wanted to tell Canidy and Fine.

Stevens, Canidy, and Fine went by elevator to the fifth floor of the hotel, then into a suite guarded by an American wearing a uniform with civilian technician insignia. Inside the suite, Stevens led them into a small study.

He took a manila envelope from his briefcase, and a page of a newspaper from the envelope. He laid it on a table.

"That came in an hour or so ago from Sweden," he said.

"You're not going to ask how things went at Horsham St. Faith?" Canidy asked.

"Eighth Air Force called and said the mission was accomplished," Stevens said. "Is there something I don't know?"

"I was at Horsham St. Faith when the photorecon plane returned," Canidy said icily.

"I didn't know that," Stevens said, evenly.

"It was pretty badly shot up. The copilot brought it back, but he dumped it on landing. The pilot died in the ambulance. Probably that was best. He had a large chunk of steel in his head. He would have been a vegetable anyway."

"Jesus, Dick!" Fine said.

"Dick, you can't think that you're in any way responsible," Stevens said.

"No, of course not. The Good Fairy ordered that recon mission. Not me."

"It was necessary," Stevens said.

"I should have flown it," Canidy said. "Not some kid who graduated from high school last year. Some kid with maybe a hundred fifty hours total time."

"You know why that's out of the question," Stevens said.

"Tell that to the kid's mother," Canidy said. "I say 'mother' because he didn't look old enough to have a wife."

"Like you, Dick," Stevens said, "he was a volunteer. And we could afford to send him."

Canidy looked at him for a long minute.

"Was it Lorimer's idea that I couldn't go, Colonel," he asked, "or yours?"

"Mine," Stevens said. "If that angers you, I'm sorry."

Canidy nodded. Visibly changing the subject, he went to the newspaper Stevens had taken from the envelope and looked at it. Then he pointed his index finger.

"Well, I'll be damned," he said. "Our old pal Helmut Shitfitz."

Stevens chuckled. He was relieved that Canidy was going to let his un-happiness about the B-26 pilot drop.

"What's it say, Stan?" Canidy asked, handing the clipping to Fine.

"It's the *Frankfurter Rundschau*," Fine translated. "Of December 30. The caption says 'Dignitaries gathered at the memorial service for Oberstleut-nant Baron von Steighofen.' It lists them. One of them is von Heurten-Mitnitz. And Eric's father. And our friend Müller, who is now a Standartenführer, it would seem."

"What's a Standartenführer?" Canidy asked.

"Colonel," Fine said. "The SS organization comparable to a regiment is a 'standart.' Standartenführer, regiment leader."

"You think that they went to see Eric's father?" Canidy said. "That they got the postcard, in other words, and are still with us?"

"Müller spent New Year's Eve," Stevens said, "—spent all night in the Kurhotel on New Year's Eve—with Gisella Dyer."

"The professor's wife?" Canidy asked incredulously.

"The professor's daughter," Stevens corrected him.

"How do you know that?"

"The British have an agent in Marburg. There's a fighter base outside.

We asked him to keep an eye on the professor. He thought this was interesting, and sent it along."

"They're watching Dyer for us?" Canidy asked, surprised.

"No. Not the way you suggest. If they fall into something, they pass it along if they can. He must have been at the hotel and thought Dyer's daughter's association with a Sicherheitsdienst colonel might interest us. But our English brothers have made it clear that what we've gotten is all we're going to get. No more help from them from their guy in Marburg, in other words."

Canidy took that in and gave it a moment's thought. "Okay," he said, "so what do we do now?"

"The first thing is to get Fulmar back here from Morocco," Stevens said. "I hope Gisella remembers his handwriting."

"And we can't get the Limeys to help? Is that what you just said? Beneath their dignity, or what?"

"There are other priorities, Dick," Stevens said.

"Did the new aerial photos show you anything, Dick?" Fine asked.

"Yeah," Canidy said. "That Douglass's mission was a waste of effort. It's true that Doug's guys managed to put a few five-hundred-pounders where they were supposed to be. But the Air Corps' position that these did some damage is wishful thinking. I think they'll be willing to admit that before long, although they've got their 'experts' still looking for something."

"You sound pretty sure," Stevens challenged.

"I'm a former naval person myself, Colonel," Canidy said dryly. "When I see a photograph of a sub being fueled while a crane loads torpedoes, I am expert enough to deduce the maintenance facility is functional."

He waited until Stevens nodded, then went on. "It's going to take several of those flying bombs to take out those pens, and the small problem there is that I don't think Aphrodite's going to work."

"Why not?" Fine asked.

"Controlling those airplanes by radio is a lot easier said than done," Canidy said. "Particularly when they're old and shot up and worn out."

"Is there a reason for that?" Stevens asked.

"Yeah, if you mean an aeronautical, or aerodynamic reason," Canidy said. "Control surfaces are activated by cables. Even in a brand-new airplane, you may have to apply more pressure to get, say, the desired amount of left rudder or up-aileron than you do to get that much right rudder or down-aileron. The B-17s Kennedy's working with are old airplanes that should be in the boneyard. In many cases, they're made up of parts cannibalized from three, four, five airplanes. They're harder than hell for a pilot to fly. Trying to fly them with radio-actuated servomechanisms is damned near impossible. Power enough to put one into a dive, power enough for that much cable movement in other words, often won't raise the nose perceptibly when it's applied the other way. But servomotors give you the same pull in both directions. You follow?"

Stevens nodded.

"And that's empty," Canidy said. "We haven't even tried flying them with a load."

"Would it be easier—more possible—if Kennedy had new airplanes?" Stevens asked.

"Some, not much, but some," Canidy said.

"I'll check on that," Stevens said. "And Dick, you just said 'we' haven't tried flying. You are not to fly Aphrodite aircraft. If that sounds like an order, it is."

"I know," Canidy said, dryly sarcastic. "Like a vestal virgin, I'm being saved for something important, right?"

"Yes," Stevens said, "as a matter of fact, you are."

Stevens took the front page of the *Frankfurter Rundschau* from the table and put it back in its envelope.

"That's it," he said. "You can go back to your party."

[FOUR]
Broadcast House
London, England
1015 Hours
8 January 1943

The producer in the booth pointed his index finger at the left of two men sitting in the studio. The man he pointed at leaned barely forward.

"This is the overseas service of the British Broadcasting Corporation," the man said.

The producer pointed his index finger at the engineer in the booth beside him. The engineer lifted the balls of his fingers from the edge of the phonograph record he had cued.

The chimes of Big Ben went out over the air.

The producer pointed his finger at the man sitting at the right of the table in the studio.

"And now some messages for our friends in Germany," the man said to his microphone. He read down a neatly typed list of brief, cryptic messages until he came to number eight.

"The Kurfürstendamm is slippery with ice," he read, then read it again, slowly, with precision: "The Kurfürstendamm is slippery with ice."

The message sounded meaningless. But it would be carefully recorded in Berlin by radio operators of the several German intelligence agencies, including the SS-SD, and by the Ministry of Information, who would study it in an attempt to take some meaning from it. It would be compared with all other messages mentioning the Kurfürstendamm, or Berlin, or slippery, or ice. All possible meanings would be noted, however far-fetched, and copies would be made and distributed, so *that* information would be available for reference when the next "message for our friends in Germany" using any of those words came over the air. All the effort would be futile, for that message was in fact meaningless.

The BBC announcer did not read message number 9. For there was an insert mark between number 8 and number 9. The message he read next had been given to him less than thirty minutes before. And a notation at the bottom of the sheet of paper instructed him to read the message each night for ten nights.

"Gisella thanks Eric for the radio," he read very carefully, and then again, "Gisella thanks Eric for the radio."

Then he returned to his original sheet:

"Bruno sends greetings to Uncle Hans. Bruno sends greetings to Uncle Hans."

[FIVE]
Whitbey House
Kent, England
8 January 1943

Somewhat chagrined to be wakened by a sergeant with the message that if he wanted breakfast, he'd better shag ass, Lt. Commander Edwin W. Bitter dressed quickly and went looking for the mess. When they arrived the night before, he had been led to a room by another sergeant, and he had been sleepy and a little drunk. So when he went into the corridor now, he didn't remember which way to go to return to the main hall.

Whitbey House reminded him of a museum. He would not have been astonished to see uniformed guards standing around, or a group of schoolchildren being given a tour down the wide corridors.

He turned the wrong way and had to retrace his steps after finding himself at a dead end. When he finally found the main hall, he felt like a fool. It was equipped with a direction sign. Lettered arrows had been nailed to the pole. Two of them pointed to "Washington" and "Berlin." And near the bottom was one with "Mess" lettered on it.

As he got close, he heard the murmur of voices and could smell coffee and bacon. At the entrance to a long, high-ceilinged room a PFC sat at a table and collected thirty-five cents for the meal.

He saw that the mess at Whitbey House served both enlisted and commissioned personnel, and there were far more people than Bitter had expected. He made a quick guess of one hundred fifty, including twenty-five or thirty uniformed women. He wondered at first if this was yet another manifestation of Canidy's disdain for those customs of the service that decreed separation by rank.

But then he saw subtle differences: Although there were officers and men (of both sexes) sitting together at the eight-chair tables, the enlisted personnel were going through a serving line, while the officers were served by waiters. And there were separate tables for both enlisted and commissioned instructors. And one table at the far end of the room was separate from all the others. This one was reserved for the commanding officer and his staff, which was to say Canidy, Whittaker, Jamison, and Captain the Duchess Stanfield, WRAC.

Canidy saw Bitter standing in the door and motioned him to the head table. As he started across the room, someone greeted him.

"Good morning, Commander," Sergeant Agnes Draper said.

She was at a table with several other enlisted women, American WACs and British.

"Good morning, Sergeant," Bitter said.

Sergeant Draper, Bitter noticed, was not wearing a tunic, just a khaki uniform shirt and knit khaki necktie. Her breasts stretched the khaki noticeably.

"I have known Commander Don Winslow," Canidy greeted him, "since

Christ was an apprentice seaman, and this is the first time I've ever seen him needing a shave."

"Sit down, Commander," the duchess said. "Ignore him. He's in one of his rotten moods."

"Overslept, did you?" Canidy pursued.

"I guess I did," Bitter said as a GI waiter handed him a mimeographed menu. He was impressed with the array of food offered. "Very impressive menu," he said.

"A well-fed sailor is a happy sailor," Canidy said piously. "Thank Jamison for the food. He is a first-class scrounger."

"So I see," Bitter said. He ordered poached eggs and roast beef hash, then poured himself a cup of coffee from a silver pitcher.

"We have a reputation to maintain here, Commander," Canidy said. "Your commanding officer expects you to be shaved and shined and in every way to measure up to our well-known spiffy sartorial standards."

Bitter looked at him. Canidy was wearing an open-collared khaki shirt with no insignia of rank, and over that an olive-drab sleeveless sweater with the neck and arm holes bound in leather. It was, Bitter decided, British rather than American issue.

"Yes, sir," Bitter said. "I will try not to disappoint you, sir."

"That's the spirit!" Canidy said. "When you go to see the admiral, I want him to look at your freshly shaven chin and sharply creased trousers and say to himself, 'Now, *this* young officer is clearly one of our own.'"

"What admiral?" he asked.

"On our part, we are so concerned about what the admiral thinks of you that we are going to let you use the Packard," Canidy said.

"What admiral?" Bitter repeated.

"The Deputy Commander for Air, Naval Element, SHAEF," Canidy said, "called Colonel Stevens first thing this morning. He told the colonel he deeply regretted not having been on hand to properly welcome you to the European Theater of Operations. Translated, that means he wants to remind you of your naval heritage, and why you have been sent here."

"If I have to say this, Dick," Bitter said, "I consider that I work for you. Period."

Canidy nodded.

"He asked Colonel Stevens if there was any way you could possibly find time in your busy schedule to give him a few minutes of your time. When

Stevens told him he thought that might be difficult, the admiral sweetened his offer. He announced that he is an old friend of General Lorimer and would be happy to introduce the two of you."

"You're losing me, Dick," Bitter said.

"Bear with me, Commander," Canidy said. "Now, as a trade-school graduate himself, Colonel Stevens is well aware of the hoary military adage: 'Beware of admirals bearing gifts.' So he did not tell the admiral that we had already discussed you with General Lorimer and had in fact planned to send you over there this morning for a little chat. He decided that it might well be in our interest to see what the admiral has in mind. So he thanked the admiral profusely for his interest and suggested that you meet him there at noon."

"Where's 'there'? and for the third time, who is General Lorimer?"

"'There' is London. Brigadier General Kenneth Lorimer, of the Eighth Air Force Headquarters at High Wycombe, is what the Eighth Air Force chooses to call the 'cognizant officer' for the Project Aphrodite," Canidy said.

"Okay," Bitter said.

"The admiral's concern for your welfare apparently goes beyond introducing you to the old boy network," Canidy said. "He volunteered to provide you with a car and driver. Now, that really made Colonel Stevens suspicious, as cars and drivers are about as scarce as fifteen-year-old English virgins."

"Thank you very much, Dick," the Duchess Stanfield said.

"No offense, Your Gracefulness," Canidy said, "but please don't interrupt your commanding officer when he is speaking."

"I don't understand," Bitter said.

"Dick suspects, Commander," the duchess said, "that the car will come with a driver."

"And we don't need a sailor spy around here," Jimmy Whittaker said. "We have our hands full as it is with French and German spies. And English ones."

"The pair of you can go to hell!" the duchess said.

"Present company excepted, of course," Whittaker said.

"I have the feeling, I can't imagine how, that my leg is being pulled," Bitter said.

"No, it's not," Canidy said. "We spend so much time spying on each other that it's a bloody miracle we have any time left to spy on the Germans."

"It's unfortunately true, Commander," the duchess said.

"In order to forestall you finding yourself in debt to the admiral, or the Navy generally, Her Gracefulness suggested, and I agreed, that the thing to do is send you to London, and then High Wycombe and Fersfield, in my personal Packard. With the faithful Agnes at the wheel, of course, to lend a final touch of class."

"Your 'personal Packard'?"

"You don't want to hear about that," the duchess said.

"Yes, I do."

"It is a matter of some delicacy," Canidy said. "But what the hell, Your Gracefulness, we either trust him or we don't."

The duchess shrugged.

"Lieutenant Jamison was prowling the premises, Commander, and came across a door in the stables, hidden behind hay bales. Curious chap that he is, he moved the hay bales and opened the door, and lo and behold, there was a Packard automobile up on blocks and otherwise preserved for the duration and six months. Somehow, Her Gracefulness had simply forgotten about it when His Majesty's Government came around requisitioning motorcars."

The duchess, Bitter saw, was embarrassed.

"Once the car surfaced, however," Canidy said, "she was of course anxious to put it to work in the war effort. And who was the most deserving person we could think of?"

Bitter chuckled.

"So we painted 'U.S. Army' on the doors, and Whittaker's serial number on the hood."

"Whittaker's serial number?"

"We haven't figured out how to get the proper papers for it yet," Whittaker said. "We are trusting in the hunch that very few MPs are going to demand the trip ticket of a U.S. Army Packard driven by an English lady sergeant."

"Stevens has chosen to look the other way," Canidy said. "But I suppose there are those who would consider my personal Packard violates some petty regulation or other."

"So be careful, Ed," Whittaker said.

"There's a moral in this tale, Edwin," Canidy said.

"I'd love to know what it is."

"If you hadn't been nosy and asked questions, you would not now possess potentially damaging information. If you should now encounter an overzealous policeman, you can no longer honestly proclaim innocence."

"What am I supposed to say if I get stopped?" Bitter asked.

"Don't get stopped," Canidy said. "That would be easier."

"Jesus!" Bitter said.

"When Jamison and I stole the Ford," Whittaker said, "and Colonel Stevens caught us, Dick told him it was part of the agent training program. I don't think we could get away with that one again."

"Normally, I would deliver a lecture reminding you to tell the admiral nothing you don't absolutely have to," Canidy said. "The only reason you're not getting it is that you haven't been here long enough to learn anything."

Bitter looked at Whittaker.

"Welcome to the other side of the looking glass, Ed," Whittaker said.

"I'll be damned," Bitter said.

"Are you going to tell him about our agent-in-place at Fersfield?" Whittaker asked.

Canidy smiled.

"I don't think so," Canidy said. "Let's see if he can guess."

Shaved and in a freshly pressed uniform, Bitter stood an hour later in the entrance foyer of Whitbey House. He had still not quite made up his mind whether his leg was being pulled, either about illegal Packards or stolen Fords, or whether or not Canidy—and by contagion the others—was a little paranoid about being spied upon by the French and the English as well as the Germans.

But there was undoubtedly a Packard, a custom-bodied, right-hand-drive, 1939 Packard. The driver's compartment was canvas-roofed, and the front fenders held spare tires. It was the kind of car that belonged at a mansion like Whitbey House, and it now seemed credible that the duchess had hidden it, that Jamison had found it, and that Canidy had appropriated it for his own use.

U.S.ARMY was lettered on the passenger compartment door, and numbers that probably were indeed Whittaker's serial number were neatly lettered on the hood. A strip of white paint edged the lower fenders, and the headlights were blacked out except for a one-inch strip. People grudgingly conceded Whittaker's contention that neither a British policeman nor an American MP was likely to stop this car and demand its papers.

Sergeant Agnes Draper stepped out from behind the wheel and walked up the shallow stairs to the door.

"Good morning, Commander," she said. "Let me have your bag, sir."

"I can handle the bag, thank you," Bitter said.

She walked ahead of him to the car and opened the door for him. He wondered if she knew that the car was illegal. He put his small bag on the thickly carpeted floor and stepped in. She closed the door, then got behind the wheel.

On the way to London, Sergeant Draper told him that High Wycombe had been a girls' school before requisitioning. Then she delivered sort of a travelogue on the villages they passed through.

Bitter was having trouble dealing with Sergeant Draper. He had always had trouble dealing with enlisted men on a personal basis, and it was worse when the enlisted man was a woman. He remembered the soft warmth of her hip against his in the Dorchester bar. And, he thought a little bitterly, Canidy's refusal to treat her as an officer is supposed to treat an enlisted man/woman made things even more difficult.

To put her at ease, he asked the ritual questions: Where was she from? And did she like the service?

She told him that she was from the country—"actually not far from Whitbey House"—and that she "rather liked the service now" but that "before Elizabeth arranged to have me transferred, it was bloody rotten."

After a moment, Bitter realized that Sergeant Draper was referring to Captain the Duchess Stanfield by her first name.

"You customarily refer to the captain by her first name, do you?" he blurted without thinking.

She turned and smiled at him.

"Only among friends, of course," she said.

She had a very nice smile. And really nice boobs.

Goddamn it, he thought, *I wish she was an enlisted man. I could damned well tell an enlisted man that enlisted men don't call officers by their first names, and that friendship—of the kind she meant—between officers and enlisted men is against the customs of the service.*

VIII

[ONE]
Supreme Headquarters
Allied Expeditionary Force
Grosvenor Square, London
1115 Hours
9 January 1943

The Packard rolled grandly up Grosvenor Square, and Sergeant Agnes Draper signaled her intention to turn into the curb before the main entrance to the redbrick building. An English policeman, his gas mask slung over his shoulder, took a quick look and decided that a Packard with a WRAC sergeant at the wheel was entitled to use the front entrance. He signaled for her to turn.

There was not much room in front of the building. People had to be gotten out of and into their staff cars quickly or there would be a traffic jam. Only Eisenhower's Packard Clipper was given a parking space (on the sidewalk) in front of the place. Everybody else's car had to be parked either across the street or in a basement parking lot.

An American MP, tall and natty, wearing white gloves and leggings and a white crown on his brimmed cap, walked quickly and militarily across the sidewalk to open the door. When he had it open, he saluted crisply as Bitter got out.

Bitter returned the salute and walked toward the door. His second visit to SHAEF in less than twenty-four hours was more than a little different from his first. The first time he had arrived by bus at the back door, staggering under the weight of his luggage.

Inside the building, a WAC receptionist called Admiral Foster's office and then reported that the admiral's aide would come to get him.

The aide, a lieutenant, startled him by calling him by his first name. It took a moment to recall his face from Annapolis.

"I don't know what went wrong," the aide said as he led him down long corridors to Admiral Foster's office. "I'd planned to pick you up at Croydon and get you through initial processing without the standard lectures. But we never got confirmation of your ETA."

"No problem," Bitter said. He thought: *Canidy knew what plane I would be on.*

Admiral Foster, who had an office overlooking the snow-covered park, greeted him warmly, and a sailor quickly produced coffee.

"So far the schedule's fine," the admiral said. "Ken Lorimer can't see us until half past three or four, so we'll have time for a quick tour of this place, a little lunch, and for the trip to High Wycombe."

"Yes, sir," Bitter said. "Admiral, I'm brand-new. I'm concerned about my driver getting her lunch."

"*Her* lunch?"

"Yes, sir. She's a British Army sergeant."

"You and Eisenhower," Admiral Foster said.

"Sir?"

"General Eisenhower also has an English female sergeant for a driver," Foster said. "Damned good-looking woman."

"So is this one," Bitter said.

Foster told his aide to "make sure Commander Bitter's driver gets her lunch," and then he gave Bitter a tour of the Naval Element, SHAEF, introducing him to senior officers as "the man DCNO has sent off to represent the Navy in that 'delicate project.'"

It was clear that in his eyes Bitter was the round peg in the round hole, someone who not only had a "distinguished combat record" but was also a career naval officer who "understood the situation" better than someone else might. Bitter was no fool: He realized he was being given the treatment.

After lunch, when Sergeant Agnes Draper brought the Packard to the door, Admiral Foster suggested they take it to High Wycombe. His aide followed them in his car.

As soon as they were out of London, Foster asked if the divider could be raised, then got down to business.

"Damned good luck that you and this Canidy fellow are old friends, Bitter," the admiral said.

"Admiral," Bitter said, "when I reported into Berkeley Square, Colonel Stevens made a point of telling me that Canidy is under orders to send me home the minute he suspects I'm reporting to the Navy."

"You don't think your friend Canidy'd really do that to you, do you?"

"Yes, sir, I think—I know—he would."

"What the Navy expects you to do, Commander, is to do what you can to make sure the Navy comes out of this—by this I mean all operations in the European Theater, not just the submarine pen project—looking neither foolish nor like poor relations. And what you can do is let me know what the Army is up to that they've chosen not to tell the Navy about. From everything I've heard, the OSS has its nose in everybody's tent."

I'll be damned, Bitter thought. *Canidy was right.*

"Admiral," Bitter said, "do you know what the OSS does to people they suspect can't be trusted to keep what classified information they have been made privy to?"

"No, I don't," the admiral said. "And for God's sake, Commander, we're talking about the United States Navy."

"In the States, they send them to St. Elizabeth's Hospital for psychiatric evaluation."

"Excuse me?"

"And over here, they have a similar facility in Richodan, Scotland."

Admiral Foster looked at him incredulously.

"Apparently, sir, the principle of habeas corpus does not apply to persons undergoing psychiatric examination," Bitter said.

"Commander, I don't know where you heard that, but I wouldn't pay much attention to it. For one thing, it's illegal. Let me put it another way: If you should wind up in a psychiatric hospital, in possession of your faculties, the Navy will get you out. Do I make my point?"

"Yes, sir," Bitter said. "That's encouraging to hear, sir."

It was Canidy who had told Bitter about St. Elizabeth's hospital and the Richodan, Scotland, facility. And Bitter knew that Canidy had not been pulling his leg about either place.

All his good feeling about his assignment now vanished. For political reasons having nothing to do with the prosecution of the war, he had been asked by a two-star admiral to spy on the OSS. He knew that he could not do that, even though his failure to do so would be regarded by the Navy as disloyalty.

He suddenly understood that the OSS could have been given its extraordinary authority only by someone of extraordinary authority within the government. And that would not have happened if there was not some extraordinary reason for it. A reason that transcended matters as unimportant as the Navy looking foolish or like poor relations.

When Stanley Fine gave him OSS identification, he had thought it a bit amusing, a touch of schoolboy melodrama. It no longer seemed that way. The truth was that without realizing it, he had just left the Navy again, just as he had left it when he went off to the Flying Tigers.

Well, not quite. I volunteered for the Flying Tigers, and I damned sure didn't volunteer for this.

[TWO]

At Headquarters, Eighth Air Force, at High Wycombe, they paid the ritual courtesy call on the senior officer present. The lieutenant general was formally correct, managing to convey the impression—without, of course, ever openly stating it—that giving the sub-pen-busting mission to the OSS was a lousy idea, but that, as a dutiful soldier, he would comply with his orders to cooperate fully.

Then they went to meet Admiral Foster's friend, the Eighth Air Force officer charged specifically with supporting the project. Kenneth Lorimer turned out to be a very youthful brigadier general, who was wearing the same spectacular all-pink uniform Whittaker had been wearing at Croydon.

Foster introduced Bitter as the Navy man who would be dealing with Project Aphrodite on a day-to-day basis. He did not fail to mention that Bitter was Annapolis, '38.

It was pretty clear that Foster was suggesting to Lorimer that the ring knockers, the graduates of the service academies, join ranks to repel the temporary warriors who were intruding in the real business of warfare.

General Lorimer looked a little uncomfortable.

"G.G.," he said, "I'm sort of on a spot with you."

"I don't understand," Admiral Foster said.

"I hate to say I'm pressed for time, but I am," Lorimer said. "And, as embarrassing as it is for me to say this to you, G.G., you don't have the need-to-know what Commander Bitter and I are going to talk about."

"For Christ's sake, Ken, I'm the Chief, Naval Aviation Element, SHAEF."

"But you're not on Canidy's list, I'm sorry to say."

"What the hell is that?"

"It's the list of those people authorized access to Project Aphrodite operational information," General Lorimer said. "'Candy's List,' because Canidy drew it up."

"We're in a pretty fucked-up condition when a rear admiral is told to butt out," the admiral flared, "by a major."

General Lorimer shrugged his shoulders helplessly.

Admiral Foster checked his temper.

"Anything the Navy can do to help, Ken," he said. "And you remember that, too, Commander. Anything at all. Keep in touch."

"I'll walk you to your car, G.G.," General Lorimer said.

"I'll find it, thank you," Admiral Foster said, and shook their hands and left.

When the door had closed after him, Lorimer turned to Bitter and waved him into a chair.

"So what can I do for the OSS, Commander?"

"General," Bitter said. "I am somewhat embarrassed to confess that I think I have just been made a pawn in a game of some sort between Major Canidy and the Navy. I just got here. It was Admiral Foster's idea to bring me, to introduce me to you. I have no idea what I am supposed to do here."

Lorimer looked at him for a moment and then smiled.

"Let me clear the air between us, Commander," General Lorimer said. "I don't really give a damn one way or the other who runs this sub-pen-busting operation. I want to see it done right for selfish reasons. Eighth Air Force has lost a lot of airplanes and men with no apparent results. We're already starting to feel the pinch of short supplies because of the shipping those subs are sending to the bottom. I want the submarines gone, and if helping the OSS get them gone is what it takes, you just tell me what the OSS wants."

He paused, then went on: "And with Canidy running this, I am at least satisfied he's acting as I think an officer should."

"Sir?"

"I was taught as a second lieutenant that an officer should not ask anyone to do anything he is not willing to do himself. Canidy showed up at Horsham St. Faith yesterday, before daylight, all ready to fly a photo recon mission of the sub pens. We were ready for him. Colonel Stevens had called me and told him he was likely to try something like that, so, at my orders, he wasn't allowed on the plane."

"I wasn't informed—" Bitter said.

General Lorimer shut him off by raising his hand.

"Canidy called me this morning and told me I owed him one, and I could pay it back if I got the admiral off your back and sent you on to Fersfield. That's where the drones are. I did what I could."

"May I ask why Canidy believed you 'owed him one'?"

"Because when Colonel Stevens said he thought Canidy was planning to go on the mission and that was not a very good idea, I made sure that he didn't go," General Lorimer said. "But what *I* had in mind, Commander, was that when the B-26 that made it back crashed and burned on landing at Horsham St. Faith, Canidy damned near got himself blown up pulling the crew out of it."

"He didn't say anything about that to me, sir," Bitter said.

"Nor to me," Lorimer said. "He painted a pretty glowing picture of you, however. He said you're quite a fighter pilot. And he said he thinks you just might be able to carry off the sub pen project."

"I don't know what to say, sir," Bitter said.

"Well, I took him at his word, Commander. I don't know Canidy well, but well enough to know that he approves of few people. And I think we both know that he's in a business where he can't use 'Auld Lang Syne' as a personnel selection criterion."

Bitter looked into Lorimer's face but didn't reply.

"They've had you flying a desk, I understand?" Lorimer said.

"I came here from BUAIR, General."

"You want to get back to flying?"

"Yes, sir."

"Well, a worn-out seventeen isn't a P-38, of course," General Lorimer said. "But it's better than flying a desk. Have you got any multi-engine time?"

"A few hours in a twin-Beechcraft," Bitter replied. He realized that General Lorimer had, perhaps naturally, concluded that he was to fly in this operation. He really hadn't considered that before, but now that it had come up, he was excited.

"I was thinking, this morning as a matter of fact," General Lorimer said, "that the most dangerous part of the whole thing will be bailing out of the aircraft. You ever use a parachute?"

"No, sir," Bitter said.

"You were in the lucky half, huh?"

"Sir?"

"I was talking to one of my fighter group commanders, you probably know him, come to think of it, Doug Douglass; and he told me that one of two AVG pilots was at least once either shot down or had to make a forced landing."

"I flew with Douglass, sir," Bitter said, then blurted: "When I was hit and had to make a forced landing, Doug set down beside me, loaded me into his plane, and took off. If it wasn't for him, I wouldn't have made it."

Lorimer looked at him thoughtfully.

"So that was Douglass, was it?" he said. "I heard that story, but until just now, I thought it was so much public relations bullshit. How the hell did you both get into the cockpit of a P-40?"

"He put me in first and then sat on my lap. I don't know how he managed to work the rudder pedals."

"I'll be goddamned," General Lorimer said thoughtfully, and then, after a moment, returned to the present:

"Did Canidy tell you Douglass's group took heavy losses trying to skip-bomb these goddamned sub pens?"

"I heard about it," Bitter said, "but not from Canidy."

"Which brings us back to the drones," Lorimer said. "I had the chance to drop in at Fersfield, and had a couple of minutes to talk with two officers—Navy officers, by the way—a Commander Dolan and a Lieutenant Kennedy."

He paused, looked at Bitter to see if there was a response to the names, and when Bitter shook his head "no," went on:

"Basically, they have two problems. One of them is control of the drone itself, which they're working on. They have already decided that it will be impossible to get them off the ground without a pilot. There's no way they can install radio-controlled mechanisms that will permit really flying the aircraft. So a human pilot will take it off the ground, bring it to altitude, trim it up, synchronize the engines, set it on course, and then turn it over to the drone pilot in the control aircraft. That's when they start the radio controls working."

"The pilot would then parachute from the drone?" Bitter asked.

"That's the second problem," General Lorimer said, "getting the pilot out. How familiar are you with the seventeen?"

"I've never been in one," Bitter said.

"Well, that can be easily fixed," General Lorimer said. "I can arrange for you to participate in a crew training exercise. For that matter, I can send you as an observer on a mission."

"I would appreciate that, sir," Bitter said.

"Well, you'll understand this better after you've ridden in a B-17. But the exit problem, in brief, is that when they pack the fuselage with as much explosive as they need to crack the sub pens—and they can put a lot in there: without the bomb casings, Torpex doesn't weigh very much—it blocks the hatches normally used to bail out. You're going to have to solve that problem, too."

Bitter realized suddenly that General Lorimer had stopped speaking and was looking at him either curiously or impatiently. He had been lost in thought, not of solutions to the problems General Lorimer had outlined, but of his own inadequacy to solve them. He knew nothing about explosives, or parachutes, and he had never been in a B-17.

"I won't take any more of your time, General," Bitter said. "I think the thing for me to do is to get over to Fersfield and see for myself."

Lorimer nodded, then stood up and offered Bitter his hand.

"Let me know what I can do for you," he said.

When Ed walked out of the building, Sergeant Agnes Draper was across the street leaning against the fender of the Packard. When she saw him, she started to get in. But he signaled for her to wait for him there and walked over to her.

When he reached her, she was holding the door to the tonneau open for him.

"Fersfield, Commander?" she asked.

"Yes," he said, then added, "I think I'll drive, if you don't mind."

"I don't think you're supposed to do that," Sergeant Draper said.

"Nevertheless," he said, "I will drive."

"Yes, sir," she said.

He got behind the wheel and started the engine.

"If I may be so bold, Commander," Sergeant Draper said. Bitter looked at her.

"Yes?"

"Might I remind the Commander that we are in England? Where, as Major Canidy puts it, 'the natives drive on the wrong side of the road'?"

"Thank you, Sergeant," he said. "I'll try to keep that in mind."

It occurred to him a few minutes later that there was probably a European Theater driver's license, and he didn't have one.

What's the difference? If we are caught with this illegal automobile, the fact that I don't have a license to drive it won't matter.

He wondered why he had suddenly had the urge to drive, and, as important, why he had given in to it. Probably because he always seemed to be able to think clearly while he was driving, he concluded after a moment, and he certainly had a lot to think about.

And then he knew that wasn't true. The reason he was driving was that he had wanted to ride up front. With Sergeant Draper. And driving was the only way he could think of to do that.

"Would you like a cigarette, Commander?" Sergeant Draper asked. "I have both Players and Camels."

"A Camel, please," Bitter said.

When she seemed to be taking an inordinate amount of time to find the cigarettes, he turned his head to look at her.

She had two cigarettes in her mouth, and was lighting both of them at once.

She handed him one. He nodded his thanks and puffed on it.

A moment later, he glanced at his hand on the wheel. On the cigarette he was holding in it was a faint but unmistakable ring of lipstick.

When he puffed on the cigarette again, it seemed to him that he could just faintly feel the lipstick against his lips.

[THREE]
Fersfield Army Air Corps Station
Bedfordshire, England
9 January 1943

A blackened hulk of a B-17 lay in a farmer's field just outside the Fersfield airfield. It had apparently crashed while trying to land, and it more than likely had not been pilot error: The fuselage was torn in several places, and stitched with bullet holes in others.

The MP at the gate was impressed with both the Packard and its naval officer driver, but even more impressed with the passenger; he took a long time examining her identity documents.

Bitter was annoyed. Compared with the crisp and disciplined Marines to be found at Navy bases, Army guards were slovenly and insolent. Marine guards would never act as if they were trying to pick up a female sergeant right under the nose of an officer.

The salute the MP rendered after he had made absolutely sure Sergeant Draper was not a German spy—and after telling her she would be very welcome indeed at the base NCO Club if she had a little time—was more on the order of a casual wave than a proper salute.

There were a great many B-17s on the base, some shiny and new, others battle worn. And some skeletons were shoved together in a corner of the field, with mechanics here and there cannibalizing them for usable parts.

At the far end of the field, Bitter stopped the Packard before a four-by-eight-foot sign identifying six frame huts and a hangar at the 503rd Composite Squadron.

"This must be it," he said.

"Unless we have been misled," she said.

He looked at her in surprise. She was smiling at him.

"Sergeant," he said. "I'll find out what I can about billeting arrangements for you."

"Thank you," she said.

"You have been told that we may be here for a day or two?"

"Yes, sir," she said.

"You are prepared? I mean in terms of . . . uh . . . clothing? That sort of thing?"

"Captain Stanfield told me to be prepared for anything, Commander," she said.

Bitter decided there was no double entendre intended. And besides, she had this time referred to Captain the Duchess Stanfield as "Captain Stanfield," not "Elizabeth."

"Good," Bitter said, then left the car and marched up to the hut closest to the sign.

While there was a place for women in uniform, he thought on the way—Sergeant Draper was obviously releasing an able-bodied man for more active service—there were nevertheless problems because of their sex. Overnight accommodations for a male driver, for instance, would be much less difficult to arrange.

When he pushed open the door of the hut, a seaman spotting the gold braid of a senior officer on Bitter's cap brim called "Attention!"

"As you were," Bitter said, a reflect action. He had just located an interior door with a sign reading LT CMDR J. B. DOLAN nailed to it when Lieutenant Commander Dolan himself appeared to see who had come into the office.

"I'll be goddamned," Lt. Commander Dolan said. "Look what the tide washed up!"

He walked quickly across the room, his hand extended. He was a heavy-set, balding man in his middle forties, and a broad smile was on his face. The last time Bitter had seen Dolan was in China: John Dolan had been on one end of the stretcher that carried Bitter aboard the transport plane that flew him to the Army General Hospital in India. Dolan had been one of the leg-endary enlisted Navy pilots, a gold-stripe chief aviation pilot. In China he was the maintenance officer of the First Pursuit Squadron of the American Volunteer Group.

Canidy's cryptic remark about the "agent-in-place" at Fersfield now made sense.

"Chief, I'm glad to see you," Bitter said warmly.

"Chief, my ass, it's commander, Commander," Dolan said, grinning broadly and pointing to the gold oak leaf he had pinned to his collar. "How the hell are you, Mr. Bitter?"

Old habits die hard, Bitter thought. Dolan could not break the habit of referring to junior naval officers as "Mister." And then he admitted: *And I could not instantly or easily accept seeing him as a commissioned officer whose rank equals my own.*

"I'm doing pretty good, John," he said. "I'm back on flight status."

"I saw you limping when you came up the walk," Dolan said, making it an accusation.

"That's the damp weather," Bitter said.

"That sonofabitch," Dolan said, laughing. "He told me the new skipper was a candy-ass from the Pentagon."

"Well, the Pentagon part is right," Bitter said.

"Goddamn," Dolan said, "I am glad to see you. This operation is strange enough without some paper-pusher coming to run it."

"I'm glad to see you, too, Dolan," Bitter said.

"And maybe just a little surprised to see me in uniform?"

"Yes," Bitter confessed. When he'd last seen him, Dolan had been wag-ing a futile battle to get back on flight status. He had a bad heart.

"I tried to get recalled from retirement when I came home from China. BuPers says 'No way.' So I went to work for Boeing; I knew some guys there from the old F-4B. Then this candy-ass commissioned civilian from BuPers shows up and tells me that the Navy has changed its mind. I told him to go fuck himself. Two days later, he's back. If I will come back with the under-standing that I will go overseas immediately, the Navy will make me a lieu-tenant. So I figure what the hell, if they want me that bad, they want me bad enough to make me a lieutenant commander. I know the regulation, and the regulation is that you retire in the highest grade you held for thirty days in wartime. So I figure that I can put in thirty days before my medical records surface and they retire me again. But this time it'll be as a lieutenant com-mander, which pays a hell of a lot better than what I was getting as a retired chief. So I tell him, 'Lieutenant commander, and you got a deal.'

"Two days later, he's back with the commission and swears me in. And he's got my orders. I'm to report to Norfolk for further shipment. Apart-ments are hard to come by in Seattle, so I don't even give mine up. I buy two sets of blues and a couple of shirts, leave my car in the gas station, and get on a plane to Norfolk. I figured my medical records will catch up with me right away, but that I can stall them for thirty days. So I'd be back in Seat-tle in five, nor more than six weeks.

"When I get off the plane in Norfolk, I am met by a good-looking blonde with hair down to her ass who talks like Katharine Hepburn. She drives me to Andrews Air Corps Base outside D.C., and thirty minutes later, I'm on my way here. Canidy was waiting for me at Croydon with a shit-eating grin from ear to ear."

"And you came here?"

"Right."

"How are things going?"

"Not too hot," Dolan said. "You wouldn't believe the assholes that were here when I got here. I think we may be getting things shipshape, though, now that we shipped the experts out."

"And what about your medical records?" Bitter asked.

"As I'm sure you've learned yourself, Commander," Dolan said, "the re-sults of a flight physical depend on who gives the exam."

"Flight physical? You're flying?"

"Who would have ever thought," Dolan asked, innocently, "that you and me would wind up flying B-17s?"

It was a question and a challenge, and Bitter recognized it.

"Nothing you do would surprise me, Commander Dolan," he said.

"Good," Dolan said. "You used to be sort of a starchy sonofabitch, if you don't mind my saying so."

Bitter told himself that he would deal with the problem of Dolan's physical condition later. And then he realized he was lying to himself about that.

I'm going to need Dolan, and the only way I can have Dolan is on Dolan's terms. If Dolan can't fly, he'll simply retire again. Or ask Canidy to find something else for him to do.

"I have grown older and wiser, Dolan," Bitter said.

"Tell me about the Limey broad with the marvelous breasts," Dolan said. "She going to stay? How'd you talk Canidy out of his Packard?"

"Canidy wanted to impress a SHAEF admiral with the car," Bitter said.

"G. G. Foster," Dolan said. "He was a prick when he was a j.g. Watch out for that sonofabitch."

"You've seen him?"

"He was nosing around," Dolan said. "Treated me like a long-lost buddy. He thinks this war is between the Army and the Navy. He wanted me to be a spy for the good guys. I told him if I ever saw his ass around here again, I'd turn his ass in."

"I had lunch with him today," Bitter said.

"Did Canidy say anything to you about a place called Richodan?"

"He mentioned it in passing," Bitter said.

"Pay attention, Commander Bitter," Dolan said. "Very careful attention."

"I read you loud and clear, Commander Dolan," Bitter said.

Dolan punched him affectionately on the arm.

"You were telling me about the Limey sergeant with nice breasts," he said.

"Canidy sent her to drive the car," Bitter said. "And probably to report on what I said to Admiral Foster and vice versa. Is there some place we could put her up tonight, maybe for two nights?"

"You'll be crowded, two to a GI cot," Dolan said. "But sure."

"Dolan," Bitter snapped, "I'm not sleeping with her."

"I thought you got shot in the knee," Dolan said. "What the hell is the matter with you? That's the best-looking Limey I've seen since I've been here."

"For one thing, Dolan," Bitter said. "I'm a married man. And for another, she's a sergeant."

"Oh, I see," Dolan said, and smiled, and Bitter knew that Dolan thought he was a fool.

You can put an enlisted man in an officer's uniform, Bitter thought self-righteously, *but that doesn't make him an officer.*

"Come on in your office," he said. "I've got some good bourbon."

"I don't think that's my office, Dolan," Bitter said. "I'm just here to look around."

"Canidy said you would be around for a while," Dolan said. "And you're senior."

It didn't seem worth arguing about, and he didn't think he should refuse the drink Dolan offered when he had ushered him into the small office. Dolan poured an inch of bourbon into two water glasses and handed one to Bitter.

"Welcome aboard, sir," he said. He drank it down neat, then raised his voice and called out, "Go find Mr. Kennedy. Ask him to come meet the new skipper."

"Who's Kennedy?" Bitter asked.

"He's the only original asshole I kept," Dolan said, then corrected himself. "He was the only one of the originals who was not an asshole, I mean. That's why I kept him. He's a reservist, and he doesn't have much time, but he's a good man. And, considering the few hours he's got, he's a pretty good pilot."

A few minutes later, Commander Bitter, watching Lieutenant Joseph P. Kennedy, Jr., USNR, through the hut window, saw that he was first and foremost a gentleman. Kennedy stopped by Sergeant Draper and asked at some length if he could be of some assistance to her. But finally he came into the hut.

"Joe," Dolan said, "this is the Pentagon candy-ass Canidy sent us. He flew with Canidy and Douglass in the AVG. He got nine kills before he caught a slug."

"I think maybe I better go out and come in again and report properly," Kennedy said. "I thought I was being summoned to meet yet another of Dolan's old salts for yet another tale of the Old Navy."

"So far as you're concerned, Lieutenant Kennedy, Commander Bitter is an old salt," Dolan said.

Kennedy was unrepentant.

"In that case, I suggest we go splice the main brace before we chow down," he said. "How's that for old salt talk?"

"Remind you of anybody we know, Commander?" Dolan asked.

There was obvious affection between the two, Bitter saw. That spoke well for Kennedy. Dolan, like Canidy, liked few people.

"MIT, Mr. Kennedy?" Bitter asked. Kennedy had, like Canidy, a slight Massachusetts accent.

"Across the street," Kennedy said. "Harvard."

"Commander Dolan and I will try not to hold it against you," Bitter said, offering his hand.

"I like your driver, Commander," Kennedy said.

"So do I," Bitter said, then realized he was sounding proprietary. Quickly he backed away from that. "Why don't we go get a drink?"

[FOUR]

The 503rd Composite Squadron, the name assigned for bureaucratic purposes to the Aphrodite Project, had too few officers and men to justify its own mess hall. Thus the officers and men were fed in the messes that served the B-17 Heavy Bombardment Group based at Fersfield.

Dolan's rank entitled him to a place at the senior officers' table in the mess. But because of Kennedy, who would not be welcome at the senior officers' table when they went to dinner, Dolan led them to a table in a corner.

Almost immediately, a very young-looking major and an even younger-looking lieutenant colonel, both wearing high-altitude sheepskins, joined them without invitation. The colonel turned his chair around and rested his arms on the back.

"Dolan," the colonel said, "I've told you and told you that when you don't eat with me, everybody thinks you're mad at me."

Dolan stood up.

"Colonel D'Angelo, this is Commander Bitter," Dolan said. "Colonel D'Angelo is the Group Commander."

"And the base commander, Dolan," D'Angelo said. "Don't forget that."

"How do you do, sir?" Bitter said. "It was my intention to call on you in the morning."

That isn't exactly true, Bitter admitted, but he rationalized that by telling himself he probably would have thought of a courtesy call tomorrow.

"Danny Ester," the major said, offering his hand. "I'm the exec."

"Actually, Commander, we knew you were coming," D'Angelo said. "General Lorimer called a while ago. He said three fascinating things about you: That you are riding in a Packard. That the Packard is driven by a gorgeous sergeant. And that you were a Flying Tiger."

Bitter was uncomfortable.

"Guilty on all counts, sir," he said.

"He also said I was to cooperate with you," D'Angelo said. "Do you suppose he just said that? Or have you been carrying tales, Dolan?"

"No, sir," Dolan said.

"Danny," D'Angelo said, "I think it would be easier all around if you went and brought over the 'Field Grade Officers' sign than for us to change tables."

"Yes, sir," the major said. He walked across the room, picked up the sign, and walked back with it. When the other officers saw what he was doing, there was laughter and applause. Major Ester turned and bowed deeply from the waist.

"'Every cooperation,'" Colonel D'Angelo said, "and for that matter, the drinks I would love to have with you. But that's out of the question for tonight. We're scheduled for tomorrow. Unless there's anything really important?"

"That's very kind of you, Colonel," Bitter said, "but there's nothing I can think of now. Tomorrow, Commander Dolan and Lieutenant Kennedy are going to show me around. When you get back, however, I would like to ask a favor."

"Name it," D'Angelo said.

"I'd like to go along on a training mission," Bitter said. "I've got almost no experience with bombers. I've never even been inside a B-17."

"You know how to fire a .50-caliber Browning, Commander?" Major Ester asked.

"Sure," Bitter said.

"Unless you've got your heart set on a training mission, Commander," Ester said, "there's one way to get a hell of a lot of experience in a hurry. Come along with us in the morning."

"Wouldn't I be in the way?"

"You'd replace one of the waist gunners," Ester said.

Bitter was aware that everybody at the table was waiting for his response.

"I'd like that very much," he said.

Actually, he didn't want to go on a B-17 mission in the morning. And this bothered him a lot. He could already feel his stomach tighten with the fear.

"I'll get you a copy of the Dash-One," Colonel D'Angelo said. "You might want to glance through it later tonight."

"Thank you," Bitter said again and smiled at him, wondering if D'Angelo could see how frightened he was.

The manual, *TM-B-17F-1 Operating Manual B-17F Aircraft,* was produced before he left the officers' mess.

On the way back to their area, Dolan said, "That was a shitty thing for that little shit to do to you. If I were you, I'd tell him to go fuck himself."

"Meaning what?"

"You've paid your dues," Dolan said. "You already know what it's like to get shot at. You don't have to get shot at while you're taking a familiarization hop."

"If I didn't go, Dolan, you know what that little shit would start saying."

"Fuck him! What do you care what he thinks?"

"I'll go," Bitter said. "Leave it at that."

"Aye, aye, sir," Dolan said.

There was something in Dolan's tone that annoyed Bitter. And then he remembered what General Lorimer had told him about Colonel Stevens ordering Canidy grounded when he wanted to fly the photorecon mission.

"Dolan, you stay off the phone tonight," Bitter said.

"What?"

"You know what I mean," Bitter said.

"Shit," Dolan said.

" 'Shit, sir,' Commander."

"Canidy'll have my ass if you get yourself blown away," Dolan said.

"And I'll have your ass if I don't make that flight tomorrow," Bitter said.

When he got to the hut, he could see Sergeant Agnes Draper through a window. Inside, he found her room and knocked on the door. She answered it with her hair down, wearing a heavy, old, and unattractive bathrobe, obviously chosen for warmth, not style.

"You'll have to amuse yourself tomorrow," he said. "I'll be spending the day with the base commander. You fixed all right for everything? Money, in particular?"

"Yes, thank you, I am."

"Good night, then, Sergeant."

"Good night, Commander," she said.

He went to his room, arranged the light as best he could over the bunk, and started to read the manual. Compared to what he had been used to in the Navy and the AVG, it was astonishingly simple, like a children's book. The manuals Bitter had used presumed that the reader was a qualified pilot with a fairly advanced knowledge of aerodynamics, physics, meteorology, and mathematics. The Dash-One for the B-17 presumed the opposite.

This one was closer to the owner's manuals in glove compartments of new cars than anything else. He quickly grew bored with it and turned the light off. But he couldn't sleep. And he decided he couldn't just lie in the dark and worry. That made things worse. So he turned the light on again and read the Dash-One until his eyes teared.

At three o'clock in the morning, he was awakened by a sergeant who told him he was Colonel D'Angelo's driver and that he had been sent to take him to the briefing. The sergeant was carrying an armful of high-altitude clothing, bulky, crudely made sheepskin trousers, jacket, boots, and helmet.

As he walked down the narrow aisle of the hut, somewhat awkwardly because of the boots, Sergeant Draper's door opened and she looked out. Her heavy bathrobe was unfastened, and he could see her nipples standing up under her cotton nightgown.

"I don't think going on a mission was quite what Dick had in mind for you, Commander," Sergeant Draper said.

"Is that your concern, Sergeant?" Bitter snapped.

"I suppose not," she said, taking his words as a question and not a reprimand.

He nodded curtly to her and went out to the jeep.

The briefing was well under way by the time D'Angelo's sergeant led him to the briefing room. He immediately understood that he could not catch up by listening to the officer delivering the lecture, so he began to study the map covering the wall. He couldn't read the name of either the target or the alternate from the map, but they were well inside Germany. The bomber path was jagged rather than in a straight line. He guessed this was in order to fly around known heavy antiaircraft installations.

And then the lieutenant colonel on the little stage was holding his pointer in both hands in front of him—like a cavalry officer's riding crop, Bitter thought—and said: "That's it, gentlemen. Good luck."

D'Angelo came to him.

"Good morning, Commander," he said.

"Good morning, sir," he said.

"You're going with Danny Ester," D'Angelo said. "Come on, I'll give you a ride out to the line."

D'Angelo dropped him without a word under the nose of a B-17F sitting just outside its sandbag revetment. Bitter saw that it had been christened "Danny's Darling."

The enlisted members of the crew were already there beside a pile of parachutes. They were wearing unfastened sheepskin high-altitude gear.

"Good morning," Bitter said.

The only response was a nod from one of them.

He took a closer look at "Danny's Darling" itself. It was almost new, but there were seven bombs (each signifying a mission) and four swastikas (each signifying a confirmed downed German aircraft) painted on the fuselage just below and forward of the cockpit windshield. Just below these was a painting of a raven-haired, long-legged, hugely bosomed female. There were three large patches on the fuselage. The ship had been hit, and by something larger than machine-gun fire.

For the first time he remembered that he had not, as he had promised, written Sarah the moment he arrived in England. And he also realized that he was right now torn between two obligations: There would have been no question of flying a mission he had been ordered to fly. He was an officer. But he hadn't been ordered aboard this B-17. As Sergeant Draper had pointed out, it "wasn't what Canidy had in mind for him." And if he got killed, that would deprive Joe of his father, as well as Sarah of her husband. Did he have any right to endanger his life when it affected the lives of other people? Did he really have to make this mission so as to better discharge his duty with the flying bombs, or was he simply being a romantic fool?

It was very easy for Ed Bitter to conclude that he was a professional warrior, and what professional warriors did was go to war. He put Joe and Sarah from his mind. Major Danny Ester and the officer crew arrived on a weapons carrier a few minutes later. Ester introduced him, then went through a perfunctory examination of the crew's gear, and then ordered everybody aboard.

IX

One of the crewmen helped Bitter put the Browning .50-caliber machine gun in its mount, then asked him if he had ever fired one before.

"Yes," Bitter said.

That was not the truth, the whole truth, and nothing but the truth. But at Annapolis he had fired an air-cooled .30-caliber Browning machine gun. Functionally they were the same. And he'd fired enough rounds from the two fixed .50-caliber Brownings mounted in the nose of his Curtiss P-40 Warhawk in Burma and China to acquire some expertise with the trajectory and velocity of the bullet. The only difference was that if he had to fire this weapon, he would aim the weapon itself rather than the whole airplane. That would probably be a good deal easier.

The crewman took him at his word.

"Major Ester said when you were squared away, you could go up front," the crewman said.

Bitter nodded and smiled. Then he heard the roar of a B-17 taking off. He looked out the oblong window and saw a wildly painted B-17 just breaking ground. The fuselage and wings were painted bright yellow, and on the yellow background was painted a series of black triangles. The paint job obviously had been designed to make the aircraft extraordinarily visible, but aside from concluding that it was used in some sort of training, Bitter had no idea what it could be, or why a training aircraft should be permitted to be taking off at the same time as a bomber group.

He made his way forward and stood just behind the pilot's and copilot's seats, then looked at the controls and instrument panel. There was an awesome array of instruments and levers, but that was because there were four engines, each requiring its own gauges and controls. The panel really wasn't all that complicated. When the time came, he imagined he'd be able to make the transition into B-17s without much difficulty. An airplane was an airplane. Five or six hours in the air with a competent instructor, and he could be taught to fly a B-17.

He watched Major Danny Ester go through the checklist and get the engines started. When he decided he could do it without getting in the way, he asked him about the yellow B-17.

"Some people call it the Judas Sheep," Ester said. "Because it leads the lambs to slaughter."

"I don't understand," Bitter confessed.

"We use it to form up," Ester told him, and then explained. Most B-17 pilots were pretty inexperienced. Only a very few of them had 300 hours in the air. Many of them had become aircraft commanders with no more than 150 hours total time, including their primary flight training. And there were very few really skilled navigators. So the wildly painted aircraft were used to form the squadrons once they were airborne. The Judas Sheep took off first and then flew in shallow climbing wide circles around the airbase. One by one, as the bombers of the mission rose, they formed up behind it. When all the aircraft were in the formation and at altitude, the Judas sheep took up the course the bombers were to take to France, or Germany, or wherever, and then dropped out of the formation. The system, Major Ester told Bitter, had greatly reduced in-flight collisions, which had caused nearly as many casualties as enemy fighters and antiaircraft.

Ester shut down all but one engine—to conserve fuel, Bitter reasoned—and there was then a five-minute wait until a flare rose into the early morning from the control tower. Then Ester started a second engine and began to taxi. By the time he reached the end of the line of aircraft waiting to take off, all four engines were turning.

He stopped behind another B-17 and checked the engine magnetos. When it was finally their turn to move onto the runway, Ester didn't even slow at the threshold, but turned onto the runway as he pushed the throttles to TAKEOFF power. The plane immediately began to accelerate. There was not the feeling of being pushed hard against the seat that came in a fighter plane, but the available power was still impressive.

Bitter remembered from his study of the Dash-One that at TAKEOFF power the B-17's four Wright Cyclone engines each produced 1,200 horsepower, 150 horses more than the 1040 Allison in a P-40.

On the ground, the B-17 seemed lumbering and ungainly, but once Ester lifted it into the air, it immediately became surprisingly graceful. Ester climbed steeply to the right, and Bitter could see the triangle-marked yellow B-17 above them. Ester took up a position just behind it, then spent some time working with the flight engineer. They were synchronizing the engines and setting the fuel–air mixture at the leanest workable mixture.

They circled the field as they climbed to mission altitude, passed through the cloud cover at about 9,000 feet, and emerged into the light of early morning. When Bitter looked out the window and saw the aluminum armada that filled the sky, he was far less impressed than he had thought he would be. There was none of the elation he'd felt in Burma and China when he'd climbed out of the cloud cover and scanned the sky for the Japanese. He felt, in fact, very uneasy.

Uneasy, because he was helpless. This was more like being carted off to an operating room than flying a plane.

Just before they reached the Thames Estuary, their fighter escort appeared. Shining little dots that climbed out of the cloud cover became identifiable P-38s and P-51s as they climbed past the bomber formation, and then became little dots again as they took up protective positions above the formation, some to the front of the bombers and some to the rear.

"Maybe you better go back and get on oxygen, Commander," Ester said. "We just passed through 11,000."

Bitter returned to his gun position and put on an oxygen mask, and then a set of headphones.

A five-plane V of P-51s appeared on their left, apparently throttled back to keep pace with the much slower B-17s. The flight leader of the P-51s raised his hand and waved.

That's where I belong, in the cockpit of a fighter plane, not as super-cargo on a B-17.

There was nothing to be seen below them but clouds. He wondered where they were. From what he understood of the briefing, and from the quick glance he'd had at the map before D'Angelo took him out to the flight line, they were to fly a northeast course that crossed the Thames Estuary twenty miles southeast of Southend-on-Sea, then took them seventy-five miles on a more easterly course to a point in the North Sea where a Royal Navy destroyer was stationed. From there the route turned right, nearly due east, to Dortmund.

They were likely to be attacked by German fighters from two bases in Holland (Zwijndrecht and Hertogenbosch) and three in Germany (Duisburg, Essen, and Recklinghausen). The big map had shown known and suspected antiaircraft emplacements and German fighter bases; and it was marked with arrows indicating where Intelligence believed they would be first attacked, where they would be attacked later when the Germans computed their target, and later still en route home.

After dropping their bombs on Dortmund, they were to turn right and fly a straight course back to England, a course south of the attack course that passed nearly over Eindhoven and north of Antwerp and left the European coast at Knokke on the Dutch-Belgian border.

Ester's voice came over the earphones, answering his question: "We're approaching the coast, test your guns."

Bitter worked the action of the Browning, chambering a cartridge, then put his hands on the handles, aimed above the B-17 to their left, and pressed the trigger. The noise and recoil were startling.

Ester and his crew seemed to be taking the whole thing very calmly. Bitter wondered if this was a reflection of their courage, or whether they had grown used to what he was doing. Or whether it was a carefully nurtured facade.

Five minutes later, holes appeared in the cloud cover. He was trying to peer through one of these when he became aware of puffs of black smoke in the sky. That was antiaircraft. As he looked around the sky to see how much of it there was, an antiaircraft shell struck the port wing of a B-17 flying behind and below "Danny's Darling."

It exploded between the engine nacelles, taking off the outer portion of wing and the outboard engine and detonating the fuel tanks. The B-17, in flames, fell off to the right, went into a spin, and then disappeared from sight.

Bitter felt sick to his stomach.

Five minutes later, German fighters appeared; long before Air Corps Intelligence thought they would. There was a running air battle, first between the P-51s and the Messerschmidts, and then between the B-17s and the Messerschmidts that, inevitably, made it through the P-51s.

Bitter began to fire at a German fighter as it approached, and then he watched a double line of tracers from an aircraft behind him trace the path of the P-51 chasing the Messerschmidt through the bomber formation.

The P-51 seemed to stagger, and then blew up.

Bitter turned his attention to another Messerschmidt making a diving pass from the rear. He saw his tracers going where he wanted them to, but the enemy plane was out of sight before he could see any signs of having hit it.

And then, as quickly as it had begun, the skirmish was over. "Danny's Darling" droned on and on in straight and level flight, waiting for something else—antiaircraft or fighter—to try to knock it from the sky. The feeling of helpless terror returned. And despite the cold of their altitude, he was sweating.

As they approached the outskirts of Dortmund, where their target was the Krupp steel mills, the antiaircraft fire resumed. It seemed to be much heavier than it had been the first time. There were far too many black bursts to count.

The three-minute bombing run was the longest period in Ed Bitter's life. He was desperately afraid that he was going to lose control of his stomach, if not his bowels. He had been afraid, and often, flying against the Japanese, but nothing like this. Here, it was like being tied to a stake before a bull's-eye target on a rifle range. You could neither dodge nor fight back.

His sense of relief was enormous when he felt the B-17 shudder as it was freed of the weight of the bomb load, a moment before the bombardier's voice came over the earphones: "Bombs away!"

"Close bomb-bay doors," Ester ordered as he moved the B-17 into a climbing turn to the right.

In the middle of the turn, Bitter looked back at the still-oncoming bomber stream. They seemed to be suspended on the black puffs of smoke the exploding antiaircraft shells made. As he watched, two planes fell out of formation: One exploded violently a second after he noticed it. The second fell into a shallow spin.

Five minutes later, Ester's composure left him. There was not just excitement but unmistakable fear in his voice as he cried on the intercom, "Bandits, dead ahead. Christ, there's four of them."

Bitter watched in terror as one after another, four Messerschmidt fighters flashed past the B-17, their unbelievable closing speed moving them much too fast for him to get a shot at them.

He could hear the belly gunner's and the tail gunner's twin fifties firing as they went away, but somehow he knew that was futile.

Then there was a strange whistling noise, a wave of icy air, and the B-17 made a steep diving turn to the right. Bitter thought it was high time Ester made an evasive maneuver, then he remembered that bombers were trained not to make evasive maneuvers but to hold their formation, to preserve their "box of fire" at whatever cost.

And then the flight engineer, his voice hollow with horror, came on the intercom:

"Navy guy," he said, "can you come to the cockpit?"

Supporting himself against the centrifugal force of the steep turn, Bitter made his way forward.

Ester was leaning forward, against the wheel. The top of his head was gone, but his earphones, incredibly, remained pinned to what was left of his head. Bitter could see the gray soupy mash of his brain.

The copilot, blood streaming down his face, was taut against his shoulder harness as he tried to pull the wheel back against the weight of Ester's body and the aerodynamic forces of the dive itself.

Bitter pulled Ester's body back in the seat and started to unfasten the blood-slippery harness latches. When he turned to the flight engineer to get him to help move Ester's body out of the seat, he saw that the copilot, who had just barely managed to force the airplane into a nearly level attitude, was looking at him with glazed, terrified eyes. His yellow rubber "Mae West" inflatable life jacket was streaming blood.

The flight engineer was looking at Ester's open skull, then he threw up.

"Help me get him out of there!" Bitter ordered.

When there was no response, Bitter decided to move the body himself. Ester was a lot heavier than he looked. And once his head tilted backward, a thick, glutinous mess spilled out of it onto Bitter.

But he dragged him into the aisle between the seats and slipped into the pilot's seat. The copilot was now slumped unconscious.

And the B-17 was entering a spin.

If he couldn't bring it out of that, they would all die. Centrifugal force would pin them where they were; they couldn't even bail out.

[TWO]

Lieutenant Commander John B. Dolan, USNR, wearing a fur-collared horsehide naval aviator's jacket, stood on the observation platform of the control tower of Fersfield Army Air Base. He was holding a china mug of Old Over-holt rye whisky–sweetened coffee in one hand and a pair of binoculars in the other. From time to time, he would put the binoculars to his eyes with the practiced skill of an old sailor and examine the cloudy sky to the east.

Both the aviator's jacket and the binoculars were prewar. The leather patch sewn to the breast of the jacket was stamped with a representation of naval aviator's wings and the legend CAP DOLAN J.B. "Cap" stood for chief aviation pilot. Dolan had decided that it would fuck up the patch if he corrected the rank to reflect his current status, and besides, he suspected there were few people around who had any idea what "Cap" stood for. He had guessed correctly. Many of the Air Corps guys mistakenly interpreted it as the abbreviation for "captain," and so addressed him.

The binoculars bore two identification labels. One read "Carl Zeiss GmbH Jena" and the other "Property Aviation Section USS Arizona." Chief Aviation Pilot John B. Dolan had once flown Vought OS-2U "Kingfishers" off the catapults on the battleship Arizona.

The planes of the two squadrons based at Fersfield were thirty minutes late, but Dolan was not yet worried. His opinion of the skill of the Army Air Corps pilots was not high. It was not a chauvinist opinion, Navy vs. Army, but a professional judgment. Dolan was not surprised that they flew so badly, but that with so little training and experience they flew as well as they did.

It was a magnificent accomplishment on their part that they could fly seven hundred–odd miles into Europe, find and bomb a target, and then find their way home again. Without considering any trouble they ran into en route, he expected them to be an hour or so off their estimated time of arrival.

Forty minutes after they were expected, a sloppy formation of B-17s appeared to the southeast. When Dolan saw through the binoculars that the lead plane had begun a course correction toward Fersfield, he felt sure it was their squadron. He stepped to the window, tapped on it with his mug to get the Aerodrome Officer's attention, and raised the mug in the direction of the formation.

Three of the twenty-odd aircraft detached themselves from the formation and began to drop toward the base. Flares erupted from the first and last planes of the trio, the signal for wounded aboard.

Dolan heard the peculiar sound of the English-built fire and crash trucks starting, and then the more familiar sound of Dodge ambulances.

The planes with wounded aboard turned on final and came in for a landing. Dolan studied their numbers through his binoculars. Commander Bitter was in K5, "Danny's Darling." "Danny's Darling" was not among the three planes with wounded aboard.

The first two ships made it in all right, but the right landing gear of the third ship collapsed on touchdown. The B-17 skidded sideward but did not leave the runway as it screeched to a stop. It blocked the runway, however, and there was a ten-minute delay—during which the remaining B-17s circled slowly and noisily above—until a tractor could push the crash-landed B-17 off the runway.

Then the landings resumed, at roughly one-minute intervals. Dolan was not impressed with the pilots' skill in bringing their ships in. In what he judged to be a fifteen-mile crosswind, several of them had to make frantic last-minute maneuvers to line the planes up with the runway.

He looked for "Danny's Darling" among the circling and landing B-17s but could not find it. In the belief that the squadron commander was likely to stay up until the last of his chickens had gone to roost, Dolan was not particularly concerned about it. So he didn't expect it when he felt a tug at his sleeve and turned to find Major Dumbrowski, the junior of the two squadron commanders, standing there with pain in his eyes.

"'Danny's Darling,'" Major Dumbrowski said, "didn't make it. I'm sorry, Commander."

Dolan nodded his head. "What happened?" he asked. Neither his face nor his voice showed any emotion.

"Four Messerschmidts got through the fighters and hit us head-on. 'Danny's Darling' was flying lead. I guess it was cannon fire. One moment they were straight and level, and the next they were in a spin."

"You see any parachutes?" Dolan asked.

"No," Dumbrowski said. He held up his left hand and demonstrated the attitude of the stricken plane. "When it gets in a spin like that, you almost never see anybody get out."

"Yeah," Dolan said. "No chance he could have recovered?"

"One of two things happened, maybe both," Dumbrowski said. "A cannon round took out the controls, otherwise it wouldn't have gone into that spin. Or it took out the pilots. That's what they've learned to do, make a frontal assault and take out the pilots or the controls. Both, if they can."

"How far could you follow them down?" Dolan asked.

"There were scattered clouds at three thousand feet," Major Dumbrow-ski said. "My belly and tail gunners reported they lost them when they went into a cloud bank."

Dolan nodded, but said nothing. That was it. If they had dropped to 3,000 feet in a spin, they were through. It was surprising the wings hadn't come off long before they went into the clouds. And taking a plane as big as a B-17 out of a spin was beyond the capability of Ed Bitter, even if he had made it to the cockpit, and even if the controls hadn't been shot away. He was a goddamned good pilot, but he was not a bomber driver. And he had never flown a B-17.

"Commander," Major Dumbrowski said. "I'm not sure what I'm sup-posed to do. About notifying the right people, I mean. I mean about Com-mander Bitter being aboard."

"I'll handle it," Dolan said evenly.

Major Dumbrowski patted Dolan's arm in a gesture of sympathy.

When Dolan came down from the tower, Ed Bitter's Limey woman sergeant driver pushed herself off the fender of Canidy's Packard.

"Is there word?" she asked.

"Sergeant," Dolan said, "you might as well put your gear together, and Commander Bitter's. He's not coming back."

Her face went white.

"What happened?" she asked faintly.

"They was hit, is what happened," Dolan said, angrily. "The last time they was seen, they was in a spin."

"Oh, God!" she said.

"He never should have let that little shit talk him into going," Dolan said, still angry.

"No parachutes?" Sergeant Draper asked.

"What happens is that when a plane like that goes into a spin," Dolan ex-plained gently, "is that it pins you inside, like water in a bucket when you swing it around your head. You can't get out."

"Oh, my God," she said. "Did it explode when it hit?"

"Probably," Dolan said, and then, when he saw the question in her eyes, added, "Nobody actually saw it hit."

She considered that for a moment.

"Then we don't know, do we, that it *did* crash?"

"That's what happens," he said.

"How much fuel did they have? I mean to ask, when is the latest they could possibly return?"

He looked at his watch and made the computation.

"Another two hours and thirty minutes," he said. "Maybe two forty-five."

"Then I will wait, if you don't mind, Commander," Sergeant Draper said, "for another two hours and forty-five minutes. I seem to have more faith in Commander Bitter's ability than you do. And if I were gone when he returns, he would be furious."

Hard-headed Limey is the first thing he thought. But then, *Jesus Christ, she's in love with him.*

What the hell, I'm the senior officer. It's up to me to decide when I start making casualty reports.

[THREE]

Ed Bitter knew the technique for getting a fighter plane out of a spin, but he doubted that a bomber was stressed for the forces it required. You put the nose down and give it all the power available in the hope that velocity will overcome the aerodynamic forces of the spin.

But there was nothing to do but try. After what seemed like a very long time with the needle well past the NEVER EXCEED red line on the airspeed indicator, he felt a lessening of the centrifugal force pressing him into his seat, and then saw that the world had stopped spinning. They were in a steep dive.

And there was a frightening pain in his knee and lower leg. The pain was intense, but what frightened him was the possibility that his shot-up, still-stiff knee was about to collapse on him.

He didn't remember pain as he had applied pressure to the rudder pedals. But there was a reason for that: The adrenaline fed into his system by fear had overcome the pain.

Now that he was no longer quite so terrified, the pain had registered. It was a strange pain, dull, like a toothache, and with it came an uncomfortable sensation he couldn't quite describe. It was as if the bones of his leg and knee were collapsing. When he pushed on the rudder pedal, the upper leg seemed to fold downward into the knee and lower leg.

It was perhaps only a sensation. There had been extensive nerve damage when he had taken the Jap slug in his knee, and the doctors had told him that he could expect to experience "ghost" sensations while nerves that were not wholly destroyed regenerated. So maybe faulty nerves were sending the brain erroneous signals.

He hoped that was the case. If his knee collapsed, they were in deep trouble. It would be impossible to fly this airplane with only one functioning leg.

He reached up and pulled back on the throttles, then forced himself to very slowly bring the bucking, screaming aircraft from its near-vertical dive to lesser angles, and finally to something approaching horizontal.

But the airspeed indicator showed he was near stall speed. And when he looked out the window, he was horrifyingly close to the ground. He pushed the throttles forward and felt almost instantly the surge of power, then a pull to the right. His eyes flew up to the instrument panel and out the window. The outboard engine on the port side had stopped, and the inboard engine was smoking.

Desperately, he searched the overhead control panel for the ENGINE FIRE switches, and threw the ones for the portside engines. Then he cut the smoking engine and feathered its prop.

He was 500 feet off the ground on two engines, but he was in straight and level flight. His hands were shaking on the wheel, and he felt a strange coolness in his lap. He had pissed his pants.

He checked the instrument panel. The master artificial horizon was at a crazy angle. He looked over to the horizon on the copilot's panel and saw that the burst of machine-gun fire—or was it a cannon shell?—that had killed Ester had taken out the copilot's panel as well.

He glanced around for the flight engineer: *I need some help to fly this sonofabitch!*

The flight engineer was nowhere in sight. But Ester was: As Bitter watched, a fist-size lump of his brain tissue slipped out of his shattered head and then hung there, suspended by a vein or something.

Bitter threw up before he felt nauseated, the vomitus landing in his lap.

He grabbed the intercom mike.

"Somebody come up here!" he ordered.

He looked at the magnetic compass mounted on the top of the windshield. The Plexiglas window had been shattered within an inch of the compass, but the compass seemed to be working. He checked by steering right and then left.

The compass responded by swinging. That meant, since it was working, that he was headed northeast—in other words, into Germany, in the direction of Berlin.

The flight engineer appeared, looking dazed.

"Navigator and bombardier are dead, sir," he said.

"Get the copilot out of his seat," Bitter ordered. "And then get Major Ester out of the way."

Bitter started the B-17 on a slow and level 180-degree turn. It took all of his concentration. His inexperience with B-17s was made incredibly worse by having all his power on one wing. And when he applied much rudder pedal pressure, a burning pain shot up and down his leg from his ankle to his crotch.

When he next had time to look up, he saw that the flight engineer had pulled Ester along the narrow aisle and covered his head and torso with his sheepskin jacket. A moment later, another of the crewmen appeared, and between them they manhandled the copilot from his seat.

The odds, Bitter thought, strangely calm, *against getting this airplane back on two engines are staggering. And even if I can get it to a decent cruising altitude, there will be swarms of fighters waiting to take us out. The only chance we have is to keep doing exactly what I'm doing now: flying it 500 feet off the ground, headed in the general direction of England.*

The flight engineer leaned over him.

"Everybody in the back is okay," he said.

"What about the copilot?" Bitter asked.

"He's bleeding bad," the engineer said, and then asked what was on his mind: "Are you going to crash-land it, sir?"

"If we lose one of the two engines we still have, we'll crash, period," Bitter said without thinking.

He looked at the inboard port engine. The propeller was turning slightly in its feathered condition. The switch was still on, but there was no smoke.

He thought it over a moment, and decided there was nothing to do but try. If it caught on fire again, there was no more CO_2 to put it out. But maybe it wouldn't catch on fire; maybe it would even run.

He took it out of feather, and the propeller started to turn. He found the gauge and saw there was some indication of oil pressure. He moved the throttle half open, then threw the feathering switch again. The blades began to turn, and then began to rotate, forced by the wind.

He looked at the ENGINE RPM indicator, aware that he had no idea at all whether it was operating.

And then, before he heard the burst of noise, the indicator needle leapt. Now he had three engines. That might be enough.

He looked at the airspeed indicator. He was making 230 miles per hour. The fuel gauges, if they were working, showed just over half full. There was no reason he shouldn't try to make it back to England, even if he didn't know where England was, except in the most general terms: *somewhere west of where he was.*

He saw a fighter plane above him and ahead of him. Without thinking about what he was doing, he pushed the nose forward. It was a fighter pilot's response, a dazed fighter pilot's response: If you don't have a chance to get above your enemy, go down on the deck and pray he doesn't see you.

He was now 200 feet off the ground, close enough so there was the sensation of speed.

God takes care of fools and drunks, he thought. *If I set this thing down anywhere here, I'm liable to kill myself trying. If I don't kill myself and everybody on here, we'll all wind up as prisoners. What I'm going to do is try to take this sonofabitch home on the deck. When I get to England, we can all bail out.*

An hour later, he passed a coastline; and an hour after that, with his fuel gauge indicators approaching zero, he saw another coastline ahead. By then he had calmed down. If he had managed to take the airplane three or four hundred miles 200 feet off the deck—sometimes actually flying between hills and around church steeples—there was no real reason he couldn't get it on the deck at the first airfield.

He pulled gently on the wheel. What he needed now was some altitude so that he could see an airfield. He picked up the microphone and summoned one of the crewmen to the cockpit.

"I've never landed one of these things before," he said. "And there is a good chance that the landing gear is damaged. When I find a field, what I suggest you do is bail out. Tell the others."

The crewman came back in five minutes, just before he spotted a group of B-17s circling an airfield, obviously landing.

"We'll ride it down, sir," he said.

"Then you sit over there and read me the landing checklist," Bitter ordered. The crewman looked in revulsion at the ghastly, bloody flesh-and-brain-matter-splattered copilot's seat, but he finally sat gingerly down and started looking for the checklist.

Bitter tried the radio but got no response. The only thing to do was simply break into the circle of landing aircraft and chance that he wouldn't get into a collision. Then he realized there was no greater danger breaking in among the aircraft about to land than waiting around at the end of the line.

"Skipper," a voice came over the earphones, startling him. "That's Horham. If you think you can make it, Fersfield is about twenty miles. Steer 270."

Bitter decided that trying to make another twenty miles was less risk than breaking into the traffic here, and turned so the vertical marker on the compass covered the 7 in 270.

There were no airplanes in the air over Fersfield, which was a relief. Which was immediately replaced by terror when there was a sharp blast right beside him in the cabin. He looked and saw that the flight engineer had fired a flare out the copilot's side window.

"What was that for?"

The flight engineer gave him a strange look.

"Wounded aboard," he said. "We fire a flare when we have wounded aboard."

Ignoring the pain that shot through his knee and leg when he worked he rudder pedals, Bitter turned the B-17 onto its final approach path, retarded the throttles, and had several hasty, terrifying thoughts:

Flaps! What the hell kind of flaps do I use? Are they working?

The gear! How is this big sonofabitch going to handle when I put the gear into the slipstream?

The flaps and the gear.

Am I now going to dump it, after having brought it this far?

How am I going to steer this sonofabitch on the ground if my knee goes out?

Or I faint?

Should I go around and pick up altitude and let the others bail out?

One of the questions was immediately answered: "Gear going down," the flight engineer's voice said, then: "Gear down and locked."

"Twenty degrees flaps," Bitter ordered.

The airspeed immediately began to drop, and control went mushy. He pushed the throttles forward.

"Twenty degrees flaps," the flight engineer reported.

He was now lined up with the runway, approaching the threshold.

He was afraid to cut power. He suspected the seventeen might sink like a stone without it. He would fly it onto the ground, as a fighter is landed on the deck of an aircraft carrier, and pray that he would be able to stop it once he was there.

But almost instantly he recognized that had been the wrong decision. The B-17 was high above the runway. He reached out for the throttle quadrant and pulled the levers toward him. And still it wanted to fly. He pushed the wheel forward and the wheels touched and chirped, and then it bounced into the air again. His hands on the wheel were shaking.

He touched down again and raised the nose, and it bounced again into the air, then touched down a third time and stayed down. He tapped the brakes, tapped them again, and again, and was aware that every time he pushed hard he was making an animal-like noise—a cross between a moan and a shriek—when the knee flamed with pain.

But finally, with five hundred yards of runway left, the B-17 shuddered to a stop.

He gunned the port inboard engine enough to get him off the runway, then he chopped the throttle again and flipped the MASTER switch to off.

He exhaled. When he inhaled, he smelled the vomitus in his lap, and something else foul. And there was a stabbing pain in his knee and leg. And he felt a clammy sweat soak his face and back and was sure he was going to pass out.

But instead, without warning he threw up again. He was dimly aware that crash trucks, and ambulances, and a parade of other vehicles were heading toward the airplane. He looked at his wristwatch. His whole arm was trembling so severely that he could not see where the hands were on the face of his watch.

[FOUR]

When Lt. Commander Edwin H. Bitter, USN, exited the aircraft, Lt. Commander John B. Dolan, USNR, was there to greet him. But his welcome was not exactly what Bitter expected.

When Bitter put his arm around Dolan's shoulders to take the weight off his knee, Dolan's strong arm went around Bitter, and he looked at him with concern and compassion. But what he said was:

"Goddamn you! I told you, you should have told that little shit to fuck himself!"

"The little shit's dead, Dolan," Bitter said, and made a vague gesture toward the airplane.

"We thought you were all dead," Dolan said furiously. "The last time anybody seen you, you had two engines on fire and you was in a spin. The Air Corps's not too smart with spins. I was just getting up my courage to call Canidy."

"Did you?" Bitter asked. Over Dolan's shoulder he saw Sergeant Agnes Draper, standing beside the Packard.

"I was about to, goddamn it," Dolan said.

Bitter saw medics carrying a blanket-covered body to an ambulance.

He looked at Sergeant Draper. She was chewing her lips. And then she started to walk toward him.

And then Lt. Colonel D'Angelo was there.

"Are you all right, Commander?" he asked. "Something wrong with your leg?"

"I hurt it in the Orient," Bitter said. "I must have strained it again. I wasn't hit. I'm all right. I was lucky."

D'Angelo went into the aircraft, then returned as Sergeant Draper walked up and said, "I'm very glad to see you, Commander. Are you all right?"

"Sergeant Haskell just told me you brought it home," D'Angelo said.

"I didn't have much of a choice, did I?" Bitter said.

D'Angelo handed him a miniature bottle of Jack Daniel's bourbon. Bitter unscrewed the cap and drank it down. He felt the warmth in his stomach. D'Angelo handed him another and he drank that down, and that was a bad idea, for he threw up again without warning.

The humiliation was bad enough, but he saw pity in Sergeant Draper's eyes and that made it worse.

"Get a jeep, Dolan," Bitter ordered.

"A jeep?"

"Look at me, for God's sake!" Bitter said, gesturing at his blood-covered flight gear. "I don't want to mess up Canidy's goddamned Packard!"

"We'll just get that high-altitude gear off you, Commander," Dolan said, and very gently started to undress him.

"When he's through with the crew," D'Angelo said, "I'll send the debriefing officer over."

"I don't know what the hell I can tell him," Bitter said.

"I'll tell him to make it brief," D'Angelo said. "What I want to know is how you got it out of the spin."

Bitter looked at him.

"The last sighting had you in a spin," D'Angelo said.

Bitter was genuinely astonished at his response, which came without thinking.

"I'm a naval aviator, Colonel," he said. "They teach us how to get out of spins."

D'Angelo's face flashed surprise and even annoyance. Dolan chuckled heartily, and D'Angelo glowered at him, but then smiled.

"Dumb question," he said, "dumb answer."

"I'm sorry, sir," Bitter said. "I don't know why I said that."

"Raise your leg, Commander, please," Sergeant Draper said, and Bitter felt a tug at his leg. Sergeant Draper was on her knees in the muddy grass. His sheepskin trousers were down around his ankles.

Colonel D'Angelo put his arm around Bitter's shoulders to steady him.

"Right now, Commander," D'Angelo said, "I think you have the right to say any goddamn thing you want to."

Sergeant Draper pulled the sheepskin trousers off his feet, and then stood up and smiled at him.

"You're in pain, aren't you?" Agnes Draper asked—challenged—softly.

"If Dolan can come up with some ice and a rubber sheet, it will be all right," Bitter said.

"Well, let's get you home, Commander," Dolan said, and wrapped his arm around him. Agnes took Bitter's other arm and put it around her shoulder. And between them, Bitter hobbled to Canidy's Packard.

[FIVE]

When they got to the BOQ, Dolan sent a white hat after ice: "I don't want any excuses, just come back with ice."

Then they set Bitter down gently on his bed.

Dolan gave him three ounces of rye, straight, with an almost motherly admonition: "Drink it all; it'll be good for you."

The ice arrived in a garbage can carried by one of the white hats and Lieutenant Kennedy. A moment later, the other white hat came in with an oilskin tablecloth.

"I didn't know where to get a rubber sheet," he said.

Bitter raised the lower part of his body so the tablecloth could be put under it, while Dolan made an ice pack with a torn sheet. Then, very matter-of-factly, Sergeant Draper ordered Commander Bitter to loosen his belt and undo his fly.

She took off his shoes, then pulled his trousers off.

There was only a moment before a major arrived for postflight debriefing. He handed Bitter a miniature 1.5-ounce bottle of medical bourbon. Surprising himself, Bitter twisted the cap off and drank it down.

Agnes Draper took the ice pack from Dolan and gently patted it in place on Bitter's leg.

The debriefing officer was good at his work. He skillfully drew from Bitter the story of what had happened on "Danny's Darling." Twice, Agnes Draper took Bitter's glass from him and added rye.

And both times he found himself looking into her eyes.

And then he caught himself staring at her as she stood leaning against the wall, her breasts straining the buttons of her blouse, her stomach pressing the front of her skirt. And he sensed that she knew what he was looking at and didn't care.

But she left with the others when the debriefing officer was finished.

"If the leg is still giving you trouble in the morning," she said on the way out, "you'd better send for the flight surgeon. Right now, what you need is another belt of rye, and some sleep."

Bitter fell asleep wondering what Sergeant Agnes Draper's belly looked like when she wasn't wearing a uniform skirt.

When he woke up, Sergeant Agnes Draper was sitting on his bed, pinning his shoulders down.

"You were having a nightmare," she said.

"Yes," he said.

"It will pass quickly, I think," she said.

He pushed himself up in the bed, so that his back was resting against the wall of his room.

"It wasn't about today," he said.

"Oh?"

"Years ago, flying with Dick as a matter of fact, I rolled a trainer close to the ground. When I was upside down, the engine quit. That's what I was dreaming about."

"I see."

"I'm sorry I woke you, Sergeant," he said. "I'll be all right now."

"Actually," she said levelly, "you didn't wake me. It was only that when I came in here I found you thrashing about."

"I appreciate your concern, Sergeant," he said.

"Do you think you could bring yourself to call me by my Christian name? Or would you rather I left?"

"I don't quite understand," Bitter said.

"Yes, you do," she said.

He met her eyes but found himself unable to speak. After a long moment she nodded, then stood up and walked to the door.

"Agnes!" Bitter called.

She stopped and was motionless for a moment, and then turned around and ran quickly to the bed.

[SIX]

At 2115 hours Lieutenant Commander Edwin H. Bitter, USN, came to the attention of the Public Affairs Office of the Naval Element, SHAEF.

Commander Richard C. Korman had the duty. Six months before he had been Vice President, Public Relations, of the Public Service Company of New Jersey. Korman was writing a letter to his wife on his typewriter when he received a telephone call from a public information officer of Headquarters, Eighth United States Air Force.

"Commander," his caller announced, "this is Colonel Jerry Whitney. I'm in the PIO shop at Eighth Air Force."

"What can the Navy do for the Eighth Air Force?"

"We're about to decorate one of your officers, and the Chief of Staff said it would be a good idea to touch base with you."

"Tell me about it."

"Are you familiar with our Impact Award program?"

"I can't say that I am," Korman said.

"Very briefly, when one of our people does something that clearly de-serves recognition—when there's no question about what he's done and there are witnesses who can be trusted—we make the award just as soon as we can: the same day or the next day, and let the paperwork catch up later."

"And you say one of our people is involved? What did he do?"

"He was riding as an observer in a B-17 on a raid we made on Dortmund today. Kraut fighters blew the nose off his airplane, killing the pilots, the bombardier, and the navigator. The plane was last seen in a spin with two engines on fire. We put it down as a confirmed loss. But then, at five o'clock this afternoon, it came in at Fersfield with your man at the controls. All by his lonesome he'd flown it and navigated it all the way from Germany with one engine out and the fuselage shot full of holes."

"I'm surprised Kraut fighters didn't pick him off as a straggler," Com-mander Korman said.

"He avoided the fighters by flying it two hundred feet off the ground."

"Fucking incredible!"

"It gets better," Colonel Jerry Whitney said. "He's a pilot, of course, but not a B-17 pilot. The Group Commander, who put him in for the DFC, said it was the first time the guy had even been inside a B-17; and that's what he was doing on the mission, getting familiarized. Talk about on-the-job train-ing!

"So when I heard about it, I immediately saw the public relations poten-tial. So I called the Group Commander and told him not to give him the medal, we'd take care of the presentation ceremony."

"How do you plan to handle that?" Commander Korman asked.

"As soon as I touch base with you, I'm going to call over to Fersfield and tell this guy to move his tail to London. And first thing in the morning, I'll be at SHAEF, trying to find somebody senior to make the award. Maybe set up a special press briefing. Get the Signal Corps newsreel cameramen in. Using GI cameramen, we'll have prints to give Pathé, the March of Time, all the newsreel outlets."

"Sounds fine," Commander Korman said.

"I'll get the Navy a print, too, of course—interservice cooperation, right?—and I thought maybe the Navy would like to have a senior officer there, representing the Navy."

"I'm sure we would," Commander Korman said. "Who did you say is actually going to make the presentation?"

"That's not firm yet," Colonel Whitney said. "But I should know first thing in the morning. I'll touch base with you again then."

"I really appreciate your thoughtfulness," Commander Korman said. "By the time you call me, I'll have Navy representation firmed up. What's this guy's name?"

"Bitter, spelled the way it sounds. Edwin H. Lieutenant Commander."

"Where's he assigned?"

"Naval Aviation Element, SHAEF."

"Got it," Commander Korman said, "I'll tell you what I'll do, Colonel. I'll pull his records here, and by the time you get him here in the morning, I'll have a biography mimeographed, next of kin, hometown, what he did as a civilian, and maybe with a little bit of luck, there'll be a negative of him in the file. There's supposed to be, but sometimes there isn't. If there is, I'll have our photo section run off a couple of dozen eight-by-tens."

"We'd sort of like to keep control of this, Commander," Colonel Jerry Whitney said firmly.

"Don't misunderstand me, Colonel," Lt. Commander Korman said. "All I want to do is cooperate. This is obviously your show. I understand that we're getting a free ride."

"Just as long as we understand each other," Colonel Whitney said, not mollified.

"Absolutely," Commander Korman said. "I'll have whatever I can come up with by 0800 tomorrow. You just come in and I'll turn it all over to you. I'm really grateful for your cooperation."

"Well, what the hell, we're all in the same war, right, Commander?"

When Colonel Whitney was off the line, Commander Korman pulled his letter to his wife from the typewriter, crumpled it up, and tossed it into a wastebasket. It would just have to wait.

Next Commander Korman called the duty officer at Naval Aviation Element, SHAEF, identified himself, and said he was coming right over and would be grateful if the file of Lieutenant Commander Bitter, Edwin H., had been pulled by the time he got there.

When he arrived, he was informed that the only thing they had on Lieutenant Commander Bitter, Edwin H., was that he had only a few days before he arrived in Europe; that his service records were not to be found; that the only thing they knew about him was that he was involved in some Top Secret project; and that the only person who knew anything about that was Rear Admiral G. G. Foster.

Thirty minutes later, Commander Korman found himself standing at attention in the Connaught Hotel suite of Admiral Foster. Upon hearing Korman's recitation of the facts, Foster turned white. A moment later he informed him that while he admitted he knew nothing about public relations, he could see at least a half dozen ways that Commander Korman had fucked this up.

"Goddamn it, Korman, Bitter is a *naval* officer! His exploits should reflect on the *Navy,* not the goddamed Army Air Corps! That Air Corps public relations officer played you like a goddamned violin!"

"Sir," Commander Korman began.

"You just stand there, Commander," the vice admiral said, shutting him off, "and keep your ears open while I try to salvage what I can from the mess you've created."

The admiral made several telephone calls, including one to General Walter Bedell Smith, whom he addressed as "Beetle," and finally turned to Commander Korman.

"Now, here's what you're going to do, Commander," he said. "And listen carefully, because I don't want to repeat myself. You're going to get in a car, and you're going to drive to Fersfield, and you are quietly going to locate Commander Bitter. You are going to tell him that I personally sent you for him. And *nothing* else. Do you understand?"

"Yes, sir," Korman said.

"In the Navy, Korman, when a subordinate wishes to signify that he understands an order and is prepared to carry it out, he says 'Aye, aye, sir.'"

"Yes, sir. Aye, aye, sir."

"You will bring Commander Bitter to London. You will see that he is in a blue uniform and wearing all of his decorations, including in particular his Flying Tiger wings . . ."

"Sir?"

"What?"

"What kind of wings, sir?"

"Flying Tiger," Admiral Foster said impatiently. "You did know, Commander, did you not, that Commander Bitter was a Flying Tiger?"

"No, sir, I did not," Commander Korman confessed.

"Well, I can't say that surprises me," the admiral said, coldly sarcastic. "But from a layman's point of view, Commander, correct me if I'm wrong, it would seem to me that would be just the sort of thing they call 'human interest.' Something that would suggest that a naval aviator is really something special. That a naval aviator who has nine Japanese kills as a Flying Tiger can easily shift gears and take over the controls of a badly damaged Army Air Corps B-17."

"I take the admiral's point, sir," Commander Korman replied. He wondered how the admiral knew that Commander Bitter had nine kills. The Air Corps PIO guy hadn't mentioned that. Had he known? Had he planned somehow to use that fascinating piece of information to sandbag the Navy?

"General Smith is going to try to see if he can fit Commander Bitter's award of the DFC into General Eisenhower's schedule tomorrow. If he can't, he'll arrange for Bitter to get it from General Eaker, or give it to him himself. I will be there, of course. Now, can you handle this, Commander, or would you like me to send one of my aides with you?"

"I'll check in with you just as soon as I have Commander Bitter in London, Admiral."

[SEVEN]
London Station
Office of Strategic Services
0800 Hours
11 January 1943

"I'm almost afraid to ask why you're dressed like that, Dick," Chief of Station David Bruce said to Richard Canidy.

Bruce was a tall and handsome man, silver-haired, expensively tailored. Whittaker had told Canidy of a remark Chesley Haywood Whittaker had once made about Bruce: "I always feel like backing out of his presence." The remark had stuck in Canidy's mind because Bruce was indeed more than a little regal.

Lt. Colonel Edmund T. Stevens chuckled.

Canidy looked like a page from the Army Regulations dealing with prescribed attire for commissioned officers. He wore a green blouse and pink trousers. The shoes were regulation brown oxfords, suitably polished. The cap he had placed on the conference table in the chief of station's office was a regulation overseas cap. And the proper insignia of rank and qualification were affixed to the blouse in the proper places.

At the last division chiefs' conference he had shown up wearing a khaki shirt, a sheepskin flight jacket, olive-drab pants, sheepskin flight boots, and a leather-brimmed felt cap that, according to Colonel Stevens, looked to have just been rescued from five hours of being run over by traffic in Picadilly Circus.

"I have been shamed by Captain Fine," Canidy said, "who is psychologically unable to deviate by so much as an unshined button from 'What the Properly Dressed Officer Should Look Like.'" He paused, then went on:

"Actually, we have a little publicity problem, and I thought I should try to blend into the woodwork at SHAEF when I go over there."

"Since we don't go seeking publicity," David Bruce asked dryly in his soft and cultured voice, "quite the opposite, how can we have a problem?"

"This one came looking for us," Canidy said. "At 1115, some big shot, as yet unspecified, is going to pin the DFC on Ed Bitter. And from what I have been able to find out so far, it will be done before newsreel cameras and fifty or sixty reporters."

"What the *hell* are you talking about?" Colonel Stevens asked, a little impatiently.

"Bitter went to Dortmund yesterday," Canidy said. "As a waist gunner on a B-17."

"He did what?" Bruce demanded.

"He was sort of suckered into it, according to Dolan, which is where I am getting my information. Anyway, he went. They were hit. The pilot was killed, and the bombardier and the navigator, and the copilot wounded. Bitter, who had never been in a B-17 before, took it over—it was by then in a spin—and brought it home. The bomber group commander, a light bird name D'Angelo, decided to hang a DFC on him. Deserved, by the way, for it was really some distinguished flying. Then it got out of hand."

"How out of hand, Dick?" Bruce asked softly. Canidy could sense that Bruce was angry.

"D'Angelo," Canidy explained. "I talked to him about four this morning. He sent a routine TWX to High Wycombe asking routine permission to give him the medal. Some hotshot PIO guy—and I talked to him, too—got his hands on it. And he had some kind of notion that a Navy pilot flying an Air Corps bomber was more newsworthy than most DFCs, and decided to make a big deal of it. He talked to the Navy PIO and the Navy PIO talked to Colonel Stevens's good pal, Admiral G. G. Foster, and Foster sent a full commander to Fersfield in the wee hours of the morning. He stood Bitter and Dolan tall, and carried Bitter here to London."

"Where's he now?" Stevens asked.

"I don't know," Canidy said dryly. "Admiral Foster is in conference, and has been since 0800. Between 0345, when I first called him, and 0800, he was 'unavailable.' If I were a cynical man, I would begin to suspect that the admiral has no intention of letting us keep the heroic saga of Commander Bitter under wraps."

"I'll fix his ass," the chief of station said. Canidy raised his eyebrows. He was not used to either visible anger or any vulgarity from Bruce. "Have you called the Chief Censor?"

"That was my first thought," Canidy said, "fixing the admiral's ass, I mean. But sometime in the wee hours, it occurred to me that it's lovely disinformation. All Bitter has to say to the press is that he has been sent here to— what the hell, 'coordinate Navy bombing with the Air Corps.' That's credible, and it would take attention away from Fersfield."

The chief of station looked at him for a long moment without speaking, and then made a come-on movement with both his hands.

"The reason for all the secrecy with the sub pen project has nothing to do with the sub pens," Canidy went on. "It has to do with using the drones to take out, probably, the German rocket-launching sites, and possibly the heavy-water facilities in Norway and the jet-engine factories in Germany," Canidy said. "That's the secret we want to keep."

"I don't follow you, Dick," Bruce said impatiently.

"So we give them a secret we don't care they have: We can presume the Germans will get very nosy about what Bitter's doing at Fersfield and will send at least one Friendly Son of Saint Patrick down there to find out what he can."

Bruce shook his head and smiled at the description of the IRA agents.

"I'm going to throw a little security around Fersfield," Canidy said. "Not too much, but enough to make the IRA work a little to find out we plan to blow up the sub pens with drones. They're liable to feel clever as hell when they find that out, and stop there."

The chief of station thought that over for an even longer moment, then turned to Colonel Stevens.

"Ed?"

"We've got a turned agent in that area," Stevens said. "A fellow who used to live on Prospect Park in Brooklyn, incidentally. We could feed that to the Abwehr through him. Rumors of an all-out, very secret operation to take out the sub pens."

"I don't think we can stop the public relations business," Fine offered. "Once something like that starts—"

"I was about to say the same thing, Captain Fine, thank you," the chief of station said, a little stiffly. "And what do we do about Admiral G. G. Foster?"

"Leave him there," Canidy said. "He thinks he's won, and Dolan tells me Bitter has decided where his loyalty belongs."

"You willing to trust Dolan about that?" Bruce asked.

"Absolutely," Canidy said.

"Okay, we'll do it your way," the chief of station said. "What's next?"

"We have four teams for Greece sitting at Whitbey House about to go crazy," Canidy said. "What the hell are we waiting for?"

"We're waiting to make sure we don't parachute them into the arms of the Germans," Bruce said impatiently. "The same answer applies to the Yugoslav teams, to forestall your next question."

"Actually, I was going to ask about Fulmar," Canidy said innocently.

"He arrives from Casablanca early this afternoon," the chief of station said. "Fine wants to keep him in London until we get the messages ready, and then I think he should be sent to Richodan. Do you agree, Canidy?"

"No," Canidy said flatly.

"Eldon Baker feels there is too much of an emotional relationship between you and Fulmar, and Fulmar and Jim Whittaker. And Fulmar and Stanley."

"Eldon Baker is an asshole," Canidy said.

"Jesus Christ, Dick!" Stanley Fine protested.

Colonel Stevens decided that Canidy knew full well that "asshole" was the sort of word certain to offend the chief of station. He wondered if Canidy had used it on purpose, decided he had, and then wondered why.

"Presumably," Bruce said icily, "there is a professional, as opposed to personal, reason behind that little outburst?"

"If you send Fulmar to Richodan," Canidy said, "you get Eldon Baker to talk him into what I think you have in mind. I won't. I will not run von Shit-fitz if Baker keeps putting his two cents in."

"Sometimes, Canidy," the chief of station flared, "the thought runs through my head that maybe you should be at Richodan."

"Sometimes I wish I was there," Canidy said, matter-of-factly. "I didn't ask for the jobs you've given me, and the more I do them the less I like them. I'll do them, but not if I'm to be second-guessed by Baker."

"Both of you stop it," Stevens said firmly.

They both looked at him in surprise.

"Or we don't get any cookies and milk, right?" Canidy asked after a moment.

The chief of station looked between them, and then he laughed.

But David Bruce did not seem truly amused.

"Well, let's get on to other things," Bruce said, as if the exchange simply had not taken place, "if Dick has to be at Grosvenor Square by eleven-fifteen."

Stevens wondered why the chief of station had backed away from the confrontation. And then he understood: A sequence of events would follow if the chief of station relieved Canidy, which would automatically mean sending him to Richodan:

Donovan would demand an explanation. He would get the chief of station's version, and then Canidy's, and then he would ask for Stevens's.

Stevens would back Canidy, and the chief of station knew it. It would not be disloyalty on his part to do so, but rather loyalty to the OSS mission, which transcended the traditional loyalty to one's immediate superior.

The truth was that Canidy had become what no one was supposed to be, damned near irreplaceable.

There would be resentment bordering on mutiny on the part of Whittaker and Dolan if Canidy were relieved and sent to Richodan.

There was no telling what damage to the morale of the agents-in-training there would be if Canidy was relieved. They had faith in the OSS and what they were being asked to do largely because of Canidy. He had been "operational," and they believed he asked them to do nothing he didn't think was necessary and nothing he wouldn't do himself. And they believed he was their advocate.

That was true, of course. And the other truth was that Canidy had just played his hole card, and it was an ace.

There was no question in Stevens's mind or, apparently, in the chief of station's, that it was going to be necessary to send Eric Fulmar into Germany. If Canidy was relieved, it was entirely possible that Fulmar's reaction would be to refuse to go to Germany. They couldn't order him in; he really had to be a volunteer. And he could not be replaced with another German-speaking agent.

Stevens wondered if Canidy had thought this all through. It was certainly entirely possible that he had. Or whether the outburst had been as spontaneous as it had appeared.

Whichever it was, Canidy had offered David Bruce just two options: The chief of station could laugh at the whole thing. Or else he could pay the price of demanding polite, unquestioning obedience to his authority. He had elected to laugh, and in doing so, earned himself Stevens's respect.

[ONE]
44-46 Beerenstrasse
Berlin-Zehlendorf
0915 Hours
12 January 1943

The three-story stucco villa the von Heurten-Mitnitz family had built in the upper-class suburb of Zehlendorf in 1938 was never intended to be home. It was a pied-à-terre for those times when Graf and his wife—or the brothers and their wives—happened to be in Berlin. Otherwise, they preferred their Pomeranian estates and traveled to Berlin only rarely.

The downstairs, including the kitchen, had been designed to entertain large numbers of people in a way that would reflect the stature of the family. Anyone could rent a ballroom at the Adlon or the Hotel am Zoo for a dinner dance. Only a few could feed fifty at a sit-down dinner in their private residence.

The entrance foyer, designed to hold one hundred people for cocktails, was just inside the front door. It was illuminated by an Austrian crystal chandelier hanging from a roof beam. On either side of the far wall, over the double doors that led to the dining room, were curving stairs leading to the apartments upstairs. The host and his wife could make an impressive entrance down the stairs.

Helmut von Heurten-Mitnitz didn't like the house. The apartment he lived in there reminded him of a lesser suite in a second-rate hotel. But there were few decent apartments to lease in Berlin; and besides, living in the house would give him greater freedom of movement than an apartment or a suite in a hotel would.

He checked his appearance in the mirror in his bathroom: He was wearing a well-fitting gray suit, one of the last three he'd gotten from London before the war started. Next he patted his pockets to make sure he had his cigarette case and wallet, then started down the curving stairs to the foyer.

Halfway down, he called out:

"How good of you, Herr Standartenführer!"

Johann Müller was standing in his overcoat beside von Heurten-Mitnitz's housekeeper just inside the foyer. Melting snow from his boots formed small puddles on the tile floor.

"My pleasure, Herr Minister," Müller replied.

"Nevertheless, I am grateful to you," von Heurten-Mitnitz said. "I really don't know how I would get to the office before noon otherwise."

"My pleasure," Müller repeated.

The housekeeper went to the foyer closet and took a fur-collared overcoat and a homburg from it. She handed von Heurten-Mitnitz the homburg first, and he put it on before a mirror over a radiator, then held his arms behind him so she could help him with the coat.

"Thank you, Frau Carr," he said.

He made a courteous gesture, waving Müller through the foyer ahead of him. An Opel Admiral sat at the curb.

"New car, Johnny?" he asked as he got in.

"New to me," Müller said. "It's got ninety thousand kilometers on the meter. And I don't know how practical it is," he added as he climbed behind the wheel and started the engine. "It's conspicuous. Someone in my line of work should not be too conspicuous."

"You look well in it," von Heurten-Mitnitz said, then: "Why don't we take the Avus?"

Müller nodded and headed for the superhighway.

"Frau Carr, you know," Müller said, "has reported you for listening to the BBC. I saw the Zehlendorf SS report for the week."

"I rather thought she would," von Heurten-Mitnitz said dryly. "Her vigilance and devotion to the state are commendable. What do they tell her, by the way, when she does make such reports?"

"In this case, she was asked if anyone was with you," Müller said, "and told that since you have a Propaganda Ministry permit, further reports would not be necessary unless someone was with you when you listened."

"I wonder if she was relieved or disappointed?" von Heurten-Mitnitz mused. "I gather you're leading up to the 'Gisella Thanks Eric' message?"

"You're sure it's our Gisella and our Eric?"

"Oh, I'm sure it is," von Heurten-Mitnitz said.

"What the hell does it mean?" Müller said. "That we're to get her a radio so that she can listen to the BBC?"

"How could that be done?" von Heurten-Mitnitz asked.

"I thought you were going to tell me," Müller said.

"I have an idea," Helmut von Heurten-Mitnitz said. "I'm not sure how you will react."

"Let's hear it."

"Fräulein Dyer has attracted the eye of a senior SS-SD officer," von Heurten-Mitnitz said. "They met while he was home on Christmas leave. They were introduced by an SS-SD officer. A bachelor, somewhat older than the lady, he is rather badly smitten with her. He wants to give her a little present."

Müller laughed, then was silent for a moment before he replied:

"I was in Peis's apartment," he said. "Peis had a very nice, very ornate Siemens radio. I rather doubt he went to a store and bought it. It was probably 'taken into protective storage.' There are probably others."

"Perhaps you could steal a few hours from your busy schedule to pursue a little May and December romance," von Heurten-Mitnitz said.

"Goddamn it, Helmut," Müller said. "There's not that much of an age difference between us."

"And you know, of course, what Oscar Wilde said," von Heurten-Mitnitz said.

"I don't even know who he is, much less what he said."

"He was an Englishman," von Heurten-Mitnitz said. "A writer who said some interesting things, one of which was that 'celibacy is the most unusual of all perversions.'"

Müller snorted appreciatively.

"Now I know," he said. "He went to prison for being a fag, right?"

"Yes, he did."

"A man could get in trouble, Herr Minister, quoting the philosophy of an English pansy to a Standartenführer SS-SD," Müller said.

"Yes, I daresay he could," von Heurten-Mitnitz agreed.

"What the hell do they want, Helmut?"

"I've given that a lot of thought," von Heurten-Mitnitz said.

"And?"

"It may have something to do with the professor," von Heurten-Mitnitz said. "Or with the Fulmar Werke in Marburg. I can't imagine what else it would be."

"And by getting her a radio, we let them know we're ready to put our necks on the block? Is that how you figure it?"

"Yes," von Heurten-Mitnitz said. "They must have someone in Marburg. Or the Dyers are already in touch with an agent—"

"She's not," Müller interrupted. "And I don't think her father is, either."

"Then there is an agent in Marburg watching them," von Heurten-Mitnitz repeated, "who will report we're doing what we've been asked to do."

"It makes me sick," Müller said. "That may be just fear. But it may be that I don't like treason."

It was a moment before von Heurten-Mitnitz replied.

"While I was waiting for you, Johnny," he said, "I was listening to the radio. The Americans bombed Dortmund last night. According to the Propaganda Ministry, damage was light—"

Müller snorted.

"—and," von Heurten-Mitnitz went on, "if we are to believe Reichsmarschall Göring, as of course we all do, the Luftwaffe downed twenty-nine of the attacking force of two hundred bombers."

"Call me 'Meyer,'" Müller said.

In the early days of the war, Göring had assured the German people that if Allied aircraft ever bombed German soil, they were free to call him "Meyer," a Jewish name and thus a pejorative.

"I was asked to comment," von Heurten-Mitnitz went on, "on an Abwehr report from an agent in New Jersey, which estimated the Americans were flying upward of fifty aircraft to England every day."

"New Jersey?" Müller asked.

"A state. Right next to New York City," von Heurten-Mitnitz said. "In other words, roughly speaking, the Americans are sending to England approximately twice as many aircraft as the Luftwaffe can shoot down."

"What did you say about the Abwehr report?" Müller asked.

"It's rather delicate," von Heurten-Mitnitz said. "If I tell the truth, that makes me sound very wise in some quarters. And like a defeatist in others."

"I asked what you said," Müller said.

"I said that I would tend to believe the aircraft figures," von Heurten-Mitnitz said. "But I added that the Americans could be expected to make a desperate effort to replace the terrific losses inflicted upon them by the Luftwaffe, and that clearly such effort would be at the expense of other war production."

Müller grunted and shook his head.

"I think the next time the Americans bomb Dortmund," von Heurten-Mitnitz said, "there will be five hundred B-17s. And I think the next time we hear from our agent in New Jersey, he will estimate that a hundred B-17s are leaving every day for England."

"Shit," Müller said.

"What we are doing, Johann," von Heurten-Mitnitz said, "is trying to end this unwinnable war before the Americans run out of cities to bomb into rubble."

"They still call it treason," Müller said.

"Can you get a radio that will receive the BBC to Fräulein Dyer?" von Heurten-Mitnitz asked.

"You said, or at least suggested, that you think it would be a good idea if it appeared that I was somehow involved with the Dyer woman," Müller said.

"Yes, I did," von Heurten-Mitnitz said.

"I just might go see my family again this weekend," Müller said.

"It should be a pleasant drive, in your new car," von Heurten-Mitnitz said.

[TWO]
Supreme Headquarters
Allied Expeditionary Force
Grosvenor Square, London
1145 Hours
12 January 1943

"That went well I think, Korman," Rear Admiral G. G. Foster said to Commander Korman after the award ceremony. "Even Meachum Hope of Carlson Broadcasting."

"Thank you, sir," Korman said. He did not think it necessary to inform the admiral that he had learned that Bitter was the nephew of the man who owned Carlson Broadcasting. He rather doubted that Meachum Hope would have otherwise come to SHAEF to watch one more officer get one more medal. But that had mushroomed. When Carlson News Service had been ordered to the presentation by the London bureau chief, and word got around that Meachum Hope was making a recording for his nightly broadcast to the States, the other news services and radio broadcasters decided they might be missing something and showed up themselves.

And they were happy, for Eisenhower himself made the award, gave a little speech, and, with his arm around Lieutenant Commander Edwin H. Bitter, USN, smiled his famous smile. Ike was always good copy.

The admiral stepped away from Commander Korman and had a brief private word with General Eisenhower, then he came back to Korman.

"Arrange for Commander Bitter to be at my quarters around 1730," he ordered. "General Eisenhower said he might be able to drop by for a minute. Ask Mr. Meachum Hope and that woman reporter— What's her name?"

"Chambers, Admiral."

"Ask Mr. Hope and Miss Chambers if they would like to take a cocktail with me. And see if you can get Lieutenant Kennedy to be there."

"Who, sir?"

"Lieutenant Joseph P. Kennedy, Jr.," the admiral snapped. "Tell Commander Bitter I would be pleased if he could arrange it."

"Aye, aye, sir," Korman said. That was a mixed bag. It would certainly be good public relations for Meachum Hope and the Chambers girl to take a drink on the admiral. If he hadn't been so leery of the admiral, he would have made precisely that suggestion himself. He wondered who the hell this Lieutenant Kennedy was.

But there was nothing to do but find out who he was, and get him to the Connaught Hotel at 1730. It hadn't been a suggestion from Admiral Foster; it had been an order.

[THREE]
London Station, Office of Strategic Services
Berkeley Square

"Colonel Stevens would like to see you right away, Major," the sergeant major said when Canidy walked in.

"He say why?" Canidy asked. When the sergeant major shook his head, he asked: "Fulmar get in all right?"

"He's with Captain Fine," the sergeant major said.

Canidy went up the stairs two at a time, then raced down the corridor of the house to Colonel Stevens's office. The stairs creaked, and the carpet was threadbare. London Station, compared to Whitbey House, was crowded, dirty, and run-down. Stevens's private office was dark and small.

"You wanted to see me, sir?"

"How did things go at SHAEF?" Stevens asked.

"Very nicely," Canidy said. "I managed to get a word in with Bitter—I was right, he was being stashed by the Navy PIO—and he gave a nice little speech about interservice cooperation. He is taking cocktails with Eisenhower. Or at least with Admiral Foster, and Ike has promised to drop by. The admiral also wanted Kennedy there, so I called him and told him to go."

"I'm beginning to think like you," Stevens said, "that is to say, scatologically. When I saw this, I thought, 'My God, publicity is like the clap. It comes as an epidemic.'"

He handed Canidy a copy of the tabloid-size *Stars & Stripes*.

There were two photographs on the front page. One was of the President of the United States, smiling broadly, his cigarette holder sticking up jauntily. The second showed a good-looking female standing on the lower step of an aircraft loading ladder. She was wearing a USO uniform, and she was waving. There was a caption beneath the two-column photo:

AMERICA'S SWEETHEART IN UK—Monica Sinclair waves as she debarks a MATS transport at London's Croydon Airfield to begin a fourweek tour of American military bases in the UK.

She was greeted by Col. R. J. Tourtillott [left] of
SHAEF Special Services.

"Couldn't this have been stopped?" Canidy asked, shaking his head. "I
don't like it. For reasons that may seem a little far-fetched—a connection being made with her and Eric, for example. But I have a gut feeling that this is
bad news, and I'd rather go on the gut feeling."

"I have the same gut feeling," Stevens said, and then went on: "If we had
known about it, we could have stopped it. But until just now, it never entered my mind to have a liaison officer at Special Services. What do you
think we should do about her, if anything?"

"How do you feel about assassination?" Canidy replied.

Stevens chuckled. "I don't think we could keep that out of *Stars &
Stripes,*" he said. "How do we handle her short of assassination?"

"I thought you'd tell me," Canidy said. "Fulmar know?"

"Not yet," Stevens said. When Canidy looked at him quizzically, he
added: "In the words of our sergeant major, he has never seen 'such a
fucked-up service record.' He and Fine are wading through all the paper
now. Among other things, Fulmar's never been paid, and he doesn't have his
National Service Life Insurance—that sort of thing."

"Well, now he can put his mommy down as his beneficiary," Canidy said.

"What do we do, Dick?" Stevens asked.

"I don't know," Canidy confessed.

"Do you know her?"

"No," Canidy said. "But I think Eric met her once."

"Maybe he won't even want to see her," Stevens said. "Or vice versa."

"Well—before he sees *Stars & Stripes* himself—he'll have to be told that
she's here. In the meantime, you and me will pray that he doesn't want to
see her."

Stevens nodded.

"Anything else?" Canidy asked.

Stevens shook his head. "Good luck, Dick," he said.

Canidy picked up *Stars & Stripes,* folded it so that the front page was
not visible, and left Stevens's office.

He found Fulmar in Fine's office. He was sitting at a table with Fine and
Master Sergeant Ed Davis, the sergeant major.

"Ali Baba, I presume," Canidy said, "and the two thieves."

Master Sergeant Davis, a stocky, jowly man in his late thirties, was Regular Army. He had once been in a battery of Coast Artillery commanded by then Lieutenant Edmund T. Stevens. Stevens had bumped into him in the PX. Two days later, Davis had reported for duty at Berkeley Square.

Eric Fulmar, his jacket unbuttoned and his tie pulled down, stood up, smiled warmly at Canidy, then walked to him with his hand extended. But the intended handshake turned into an embrace.

"Has he been checked for clap and other social diseases, Davis?" Canidy asked.

"They wouldn't let him out of Morocco before they checked on that, Major," Davis said. Davis was privy to the fact—he was, among other things, the London station finance officer—that Canidy was not a major, but was in the employ of the United States government as a "Technical Consultant, Grade 14."

Even so, he treated Canidy with the regard of a longtime professional noncom for an officer he respects.

"Then it's okay to kiss him?" Canidy asked innocently.

"I wouldn't go quite that far, Major," Davis said.

"How's the paperwork coming?" Canidy asked.

"Give me another ten minutes, and we'll be finished," Davis said.

Canidy nodded, sat down at the table.

He went through the stack of forms that seemed to be completed and picked up the Application for National Service Life Insurance. As the beneficiary of the $10,000 the government would pay on his death, Fulmar had put down "Rev. George Carter Canidy, D.D., St. Paul's School, Cedar Rapids, Iowa." In the relationship block he had entered "Friend."

The Rev. Dr. Canidy was Canidy's father. Canidy thought of Eldon Baker's conviction that he and Eric were too close emotionally.

What was too close?

Finally, Davis was through.

"He's got a bunch of dough coming, Major," Davis said. "Both Army pay and OSS pay. Colonel Stevens said to pay him as a Technical Consultant, Grade 10, from the time of the first contact."

That was, Canidy thought, *a nice gesture on Stevens's part.*

"And you didn't even know you'd enlisted, did you?" Canidy said.

"More than I've got in the safe," Davis said. "I'll have to go over to SHAEF finance and get the money."

"Well, Captain Fine is rich," Canidy said. "We'll just sponge on him until you get it."

"I've got money," Fulmar said.

"Then I'll sponge on you," Canidy said. "Has this room been swept lately, Davis? We have deep secrets to discuss with the Sheikh of Araby."

"Yes, sir," Davis said. "The Signal Corps was here yesterday."

"What kind of secrets?" Fulmar asked as Davis cleared the table of the forms and other papers.

"We thought we'd start with your sex life," Canidy said, "and then go on to other, more interesting things."

"What the hell is that supposed to mean?" Fulmar asked, exasperated.

Canidy shrugged, a signal that he would not go on until Davis, who did not have the need-to-know, had left them alone.

When he had gathered up all the papers, Davis said, "Any time after lunch tomorrow, Lieutenant, come by and I'll have your money."

"Thank you," Fulmar said. He waited until Davis had left, then turned to Canidy. "On the subject of money, is my bank account still blocked?"

"I don't know," Canidy said. "But I'll find out."

He walked to Fine's desk, picked up the telephone, and called Colonel Stevens.

"Eric wants to know if his New York bank account is still frozen," he said, "and if so, why. Could you send a cable and find out?"

"Thank you," Fulmar said.

"What's all that about?" Fine asked. "Or can't I ask?"

"Not that Eric wasn't willing to risk his all for Mom's Apple Pie, et cetera, and the American Way of Life," Canidy said, "but Donovan promised him that if he joined up and did good, he would get both the IRS and the Alien Property people to take their hands off the money Eric has in the National City Bank."

"What money?" Fine asked.

"I made a few bucks in the 'export-import' business, Stan," Fulmar said, just a little smugly.

"Right, at a hundred and twenty grand," Canidy said. "It is one of the reasons he's not too popular in Germany. The export business he's talking about is smuggling cash and jewels out of Occupied France under the noses of the Germans. For a percentage."

"I didn't know about that," Fine said. "That you made so much money, I mean."

"And you are now going to learn some astonishing things about his sex life, Stan," Canidy said.

"You keep saying that," Fulmar said. "What the hell are you talking about?"

"Gisella Dyer," Canidy said.

Fulmar looked at him out of eyes that suddenly turned cold.

"That fucking postcard!" he said. "I wondered what the hell that was all about. Are you doing Baker's dirty work again, Dick?"

"What I'm doing is my job," Canidy said. "At the moment, I'm keeping Eldon Baker out of it. How long I'll be able to do that depends on you."

"Stop beating around the bush," Fulmar said. "Let's have it."

"We are, through your friends Shitfitz and Müller, establishing contact with Gisella Dyer."

Fulmar thought that over a moment before replying.

"You mean with her father," he said. "That was on Baker's postcard."

Canidy nodded.

"You sonofabitch!" Fulmar said. "Dick, if I'd known you were going to involve her in this OSS shit, I never would have told you about her."

"OK, let me handle that first," Canidy said. "The first thing is that all's fair in love and war."

"Fuck you," Fulmar said. "I told you about her as a friend."

"And the second thing is that it would have come out anyway."

"How?" Fulmar snorted derisively.

"There is interest in Professor Dyer," Canidy said.

"What kind of interest?"

"I don't know," Canidy said. "We have a file on him, and so do the English. They—'they' being the powers that be that don't confide in me—want to get him, and his daughter, out of Germany."

Fulmar looked at him suspiciously.

Canidy raised his right hand to the level of his shoulder, three fingers extended—the Boy Scout's salute.

"Boy Scout's Honor," Canidy said. "Cross my heart and hope to die. Okay?"

Fulmar chuckled.

"Okay," he said.

"They would have made the connection," Canidy went on. "He's at the University of Marburg. You went to Marburg. That connection would have come out on the punch cards."

"On the what?"

"The IBM cards," Fine explained. "Little oblong pieces of cardboard. They punch holes in them, and then stab them with what looks like an ice pick. They can sort them that way. Understand?"

"I'll take your word for it, Stan," Fulmar said.

"It would have come out. You would have been asked if you knew Professor Dyer."

"And I would have said 'No,'" Fulmar said.

"Oh, goddammit, no, you wouldn't have," Canidy said.

"Yeah, I would have, Dick," Fulmar said.

"Okay," Canidy said. "So I would have been asked if I had ever heard you mention the Dyers, and I would have said: 'Yes, Fulmar told me he was screwing his daughter.'"

"That's what I meant when I said, 'Fuck you, buddy,'" Fulmar said.

"We're kicking a dead horse," Canidy said. "We know about you and the Dyer girl. It has been decided to use that connection."

"Shit!" Fulmar said.

"I know what you're thinking," Canidy said.

"Do you? When was the last time you were in Germany?"

Canidy happened to be glancing at Fine when Fulmar said that. Their eyes locked for a moment.

"I don't want to come across all sweetness and light," Canidy said. "But since the intention is to get the professor and his daughter out of Germany, I suggest that we're the good guys."

"What makes you think you can get them out?"

"There are ways."

"What I see is Gisella waving bye-bye to the airplane, or the boat, or whatever. The way you and I waved bye-bye to the submarine off Safi," Fulmar said.

"So long as I'm running this," Canidy said, "that won't happen."

"But you can't, or won't, tell me why they want him out?" Fulmar asked.

"Can't," Canidy said. "And if I have to say this, Eric, you and I both got out of Morocco eventually."

"What do you think would happen to her if her father suddenly disappeared?" Fulmar asked. "And what makes you think she'll go along with this, anyway? What's in it for her? And don't wave the flag. That won't wash."

"Getting out is what's in it for them," Canidy said. "He's still considered dangerous, I'm sure. Sooner or later, they'll arrest him. The both of them. They know that."

"So long as she's 'being nice' to Peis," Fulmar said, "or his successor, they're probably reasonably safe."

"Peis?" Fine asked.

"The local cop," Canidy said. "Gestapo."

"No," Fulmar said, "SS-SD. There's a difference."

"What about Peis?" Fine pursued.

"What I thought was my irresistible charm in wooing the fair Gisella," Fulmar said, "turned out to be this Peis character telling her to be nice to me."

"I don't suppose he's still there, but it should be checked out," Fine said. "Have you got a first name, Eric?"

"Herr Hauptsturmführer," Fulmar said. "He's not too bright, but he's a real prick. Think of a stupid Eldon Baker in a black uniform."

Canidy laughed.

"You haven't told me what you want me to do," Fulmar said. "That would be nice to know before I tell you to go fuck yourself."

"What we want to do right now is prove to Gisella (a) that you're in England, and (b) in a position to send messages over the BBC."

"'Pigeons are pissing in the Seine,' that kind of message?"

Canidy nodded.

"And something only I could know, right?" Fulmar asked, and when Canidy nodded again, asked, as if he had just thought of this, "And what makes you think she'll be listening to the BBC? That's a sure way to get sent to a *Konzentrationslager.*"

"We're taking care of that," Fine said.

Fulmar looked at him curiously.

"Müller's going to get her a radio," Canidy said.

Fulmar's look turned incredulous. Then Canidy nodded.

"Jesus," Fulmar said, impressed.

"Think of something, Eric," Canidy said gently. "Something intimate, something she would remember, something they would not, of course, connect with her."

"In other words, something happened in bed, right?" Fulmar snapped.

"Anything that will do the job," Canidy said. "Sex is intimate and private. That's why I got into that. And for obvious reasons, we're going to need more than one message. But we need one now."

Fulmar shrugged.

"I don't really know why I'm going along with this shit at all," he said.

He had thought of something. Just before he'd left Marburg, they'd had a picnic on the Lahn. They'd rented a canoe, floated downriver with the current, and stopped and picnicked on the riverbank. He had been debating that day whether to tell her he was going. In the end, he decided it would be better if she didn't know.

He closed his eyes and exhaled.

"Eric wants to paddle Gisella's canoe again," he said.

"What?"

"'Eric wants to paddle Gisella's canoe again,'" Fulmar said. "With your filthy imagination, you figure out what it means. She'll know."

"Don't be too clever. You're sure she'll know?"

"I said, she'll know it's me."

"What's it mean?" Canidy asked.

"None of your fucking business, Richard," Fulmar said.

"What about a pet name?" Fine asked. "Something that would at once further identify you, and not use your real name. Or hers."

Fulmar gave him a withering look.

"Bübchen," he said finally.

"'Boobchin'?" Canidy quoted. "What the hell is that?"

"Little boy," Fine made the translation. "With overtones of affection that don't come across in English."

"And what did you call her?"

"Fuck you, Dick!" Fulmar said. And then, a moment later: "'Bübchen would like to paddle Gisella's canoe again.' And that's it, Dick. If that doesn't satisfy you, stick the whole thing up your ass."

Canidy stood up.

"Let's get the hell out of here," he said. "Let's go get something to drink."

"Are you sure that's all, Dick?" Fine asked.

His eyes moved, just perceptibly, to the *Stars & Stripes*.

"Christ, I forgot about that," Canidy said.

Fulmar misunderstood him.

"Whatever it is, it's going to have to wait," he said. "I need a bath and a drink. I have had enough of this shit for one day."

Canidy unfolded the newspaper and handed it to Fulmar.

Fulmar read the story about America's Sweetheart's arrival in England.

"What do you want to do about it, Eric?" Canidy asked gently.

"You weren't listening, Major," Fulmar said.

"Huh?"

"I just said, 'I need a bath and a drink. I have had enough shit for one day.'"

"Captain Fine," Canidy said. "If anyone should inquire, Lieutenant Fulmar and I will be in the bar at the Dorchester. When the press of your duties permits, feel free to join us."

"Give me three minutes," Fine said, "and I'll go with you."

[FOUR]

As Canidy, Fulmar, and Fine walked up from the direction of Tilney Street and crossed Deanery Street, there were half a dozen official limousines and staff cars parked in the small lot between Park Lane and the door to the Dorchester. Their drivers stood, smoking, in a knot by the front fender of a Rolls Royce.

"Excuse me," Canidy said, and walked toward them.

They all came to attention, and one of them stamped her foot, saluted, and barked, "Sir!"

"Would you come with me, please, Sergeant?" Canidy said as he crisply returned the salute.

"Sir!" Sergeant Agnes Draper barked and stamped her foot again. When Canidy marched in a military manner toward the sandbags around the door, she marched in a military manner after him.

Making him more than a little uncomfortable, Sergeant Draper relieved Lieutenant Fulmar of his luggage. Staggering a little under the weight, she followed the three officers across the lobby into the elevator.

They rode to the fourth floor. At the entrance to one of the corridors there, a man wearing an American uniform with civilian technician insignia dropped his *Stars & Stripes* to the carpet beside his upholstered chair and rose at their approach.

"This is Lieutenant Fulmar," Fine said. "He'll be staying here on and off."

"Yes, sir," the man said as he pulled his olive-drab jacket over the snub-nosed Colt Detective Special on his belt.

"And you know Major Canidy and the sergeant?" Fine said.

"Oh, yes, sir," the American said.

"They also serve who sit in hotel corridors reading the *Stripes*," Canidy said.

"Better this, Major," the CIC agent said, smiling, "than standing around in the snow guarding the castle."

"Virtue, doubtless," Canidy said, "is its own reward."

Fine unlocked a door. As he pushed it open, the CIC agent called, "The Signal Corps swept it this morning, Captain."

"Thank you," Fine said, and motioned the others into the suite ahead of them.

"I wondered where the hell you were," Canidy said to Agnes.

"Commander Whathisname dismissed me," Agnes said. "I think he suspected I was going to carry Commander Bitter off before he got to cocktails with Ike. And you told me not to take the Packard to Berkeley Square. I knew you would show up here eventually, so I came here."

"Good thinking, Sergeant," Canidy said, "you are a credit to the noncommissioned officer corps."

"Oh, I'm so pleased you think so," Agnes said. "Do you think I've earned a drink of your whisky?"

"Fix us all one while the Sheikh of Araby has his bath," Canidy said.

"No one," Fulmar said, beaming at Agnes, "has seen fit to introduce us, Sergeant. My name is Fulmar."

"Rein it in, Lone Ranger," Canidy said. "The lady is spoken for."

Agnes Draper blushed. Both Fine and Fulmar looked at Canidy in surprise.

"I thought Ann was here," Fulmar blurted.

"Indeed she is," Canidy said. "She'll be here, with Eddie Bitter, about five-thirty or six. That's one of the reasons I am being so . . . indelicate."

"Dolan told you?" Agnes said. Canidy nodded. "Damn him!"

"I'm sure you're a big girl, Agnes," Canidy said. "I'm not so sure about Bitter."

"You make me sound . . . predatory, Dick," Agnes said.

"I didn't mean to, honey," Canidy said gently. "I don't think that. I just wanted to be sure you understand what you're into. Eddie is liable to erupt in paroxysms of regret. He's an Annapolis man, you know. And officers and gentlemen—"

"Particularly married officers and gentlemen," Agnes interrupted. "Are you being oblique, Dick? Is this in the nature of a reprimand?"

"Ann is Eddie's cousin," Canidy went on. "She went to college with Mrs. Bitter."

"I didn't know that," Agnes said.

"Forewarned, to coin a phrase, is forearmed," Canidy said. "Having done my paternal duty as your commanding officer, my dear child, I consider the matter closed."

"Now that you have managed to let Captain Fine know? And Lieutenant Fulmar?"

"Don't be a bitch, Agnes," Canidy flared. "Fine has the need-to-know, and I didn't want Eric and Eddie getting into anything over the prize of your charms." He glared at her, then warmed to his subject: "I have enough on my mind without worrying about the impact of your getting the hots for one of my officers."

She glared at him, tight-lipped.

"Now that I think of it, Agnes," Canidy said, "and now that we've exhausted the subject, Lawrence of Arabia can wash behind his ears without supervision. Put a couple of bottles in bags, and we'll go downstairs to the bar."

There was a moment's hesitation before she smiled.

The bar off the Dorchester lobby was full, already on the edge of being crowded. As they stood just inside the doorway looking for a place to sit, there was the snap of fingers and a man's voice calling, "Over here!"

Canidy saw two Englishmen at one of the few six-seat tables. One was a private in a mussed and ill-fitting uniform, and the other a very natty, mustachioed, vaguely familiar, major. British majors, especially ones like this one, who looked as if he had just marched in from Sandhurst, simply did not drink with private soldiers.

Except, of course, he thought, *if they were in SOE, where service customs were ignored whenever they got in the way. Clearly, these two were SOE, and he'd probably met the major while he was "liaising" with SOE at "Station X."*

Well, they have a table. Getting a table was worth whatever liquor they would drink. And I'm already on shaky ground for not being as friendly as expected to my British counterparts.

Canidy put a smile on, took Agnes's arm, and propelled her across the room.

"Good to see you again," he said. "Have you room for us?"

"By all means," the major said.

"Do you remember Sergeant Draper?" Canidy asked.

"No, I'm afraid I don't," the major said. He offered his hand to Agnes. "My name is Niven," he said. "And this is Private Ustinov."

Fine caught up with them.

"Stan, I'd like you to meet Major Niven," Canidy said.

Fine was smiling strangely.

"I have the privilege of the major's acquaintance," he said. "But where the hell did you meet each other?"

"At . . . that place in the country," Canidy said.

"What place in the country would that be?" Major Niven said.

"*That* place in the country, of course," Private Ustinov said.

"Oh, of course," the major said. He smiled benignly at Canidy. "*That* place in the country."

"Why do I feel I'm making an ass of myself?" Canidy asked.

"David and I are friends from Los Angeles," Fine said. "Peter, too."

"By Los Angeles, you mean 'Hollywood'?" Canidy asked. He turned to the major. "You're in the movie business?"

"Not anymore," the major said. "But yes, I was."

"He was an elocution coach," Private Ustinov said. "I was a ballet instructor."

"Oh," Canidy said.

"I taught them, you see, to walk, and then David took over and taught them how to talk," Private Ustinov said.

"Well, I've obviously made a mistake," Canidy said. "You looked like a British officer I met. Sandhurst type."

"Well, I'm guilty of that," the major said. "I went to Sandhurst."

"Oh," Canidy said, "no offense intended, of course."

"And certainly none taken," the major said.

"You have seen Major Niven before, Dick," Fine said.

"I knew I had," Canidy said.

"On the great silver screen," Fine said. "This is the actor."

"Actors, if you please," Private Ustinov said. "Currently not on the boards, of course, but actors, plural, nonetheless."

Only at that moment did Canidy recognize David Niven.

"I know what I'm going to do," he said. "I'm going to go back to the lobby, and then come in again, and walk over and ask for an autograph."

"I would much prefer a taste, if you don't mind," Niven said, "of what I suspect Lady Agnes has in the bags."

"There is no booze," Private Ustinov said. "David and I came here in the hope that Stanley, who has some mysterious but steady source of intoxicants, would show up sooner rather than later."

"Booze, Sergeant!" Canidy said.

"Sir!" she said, and produced a bottle of Scotch.

"Have we met, Major?" Agnes asked when she had poured everyone a drink.

"Your father is the Earl of Hayme, isn't he?" Niven asked. Agnes nodded. "I thought so. I've been privileged to shoot over your estate in Scotland several times. The last time I saw you, you were a little girl. A spectacular little girl, obviously; you stuck in my mind."

"I didn't know you were a blue blood, Agnes," Canidy said.

Agnes flashed him a brilliant smile.

"Begging the major's pardon, sir, there is a good deal about me the major doesn't know," she said sweetly.

[FIVE]

It was nearer to seven than six when Commander Edwin W. Bitter and Miss Ann Chambers reached the bar at the Dorchester. Once they had left Admiral Foster's Connaught Hotel suite, they sent Mr. Meachum Hope, Lt. Commander Dolan, and Lieutenant Kennedy on ahead of them to the Dorchester. Then they went to the London bureau of Chambers News Service.

There Bitter wrote a short, awkward letter to his wife. The gist of the letter was that Sarah, despite what she was going to read in the newspapers tomorrow, or what she was liable to hear on Meachum Hope's "Report from London" broadcast, was not to worry. What he had done was neither as heroic nor as difficult as they were making it sound.

She should, he wrote, think of it as an automobile accident. He had been a passenger in a wrecked car, so to speak, and when the driver couldn't drive it himself, he simply took the wheel and drove it to the garage for him. He was not making regular bombing missions. He had thought, however, that he should make one mission as a passenger, so that he would understand what was involved. As far as he knew, he would never make another.

He gave it to Ann, who sat down at a teletype machine and retyped it, sending it to the SHAEF press center for censorship, then transmitting it by radio to Brandon Chambers, editor-in-chief of Chambers News Service, as a service message. He would see that it got to Sarah in Palm Beach.

"I don't think she'll believe you, Eddie," Ann said. "But I will write her and tell her that Canidy told me he's grounded you."

"Where did you hear that?" he asked.

"I didn't," Ann said. "I just made it up. But now that I think about it, it seems like a good idea."

"Just mind your own business, please, Ann."

"Just how long do you think you can— What is it you say? 'Harm's way'? Just how long do you think you can go in harm's way without getting harmed?"

"Isn't that a moot point? We're in a war, and I'm a naval officer."

"You're a horse's ass," Ann said. "Worse, you're a horse's ass with courage. That can get you killed. It *will* get you killed."

They locked eyes for a moment, and then Ann broke the silence: "Come on, let's get to the Dorchester before someone starts making eyes at Dick."

"Does that happen often?" he asked. "How is the great romance?"

"I don't know if you'll believe this or not," Ann said. "But if I can ever get him out of this war and up in front of an altar, I really believe he will be the perfect husband. His eye doesn't wander when I'm around."

"Why don't you marry him now?" Bitter asked.

"The way that works is that the boy asks the girl, Eddie," Ann said, "and Dick hates having to tell me that over and over."

"Aren't you worried about . . ."

"About what?"

"Getting in the family way."

"Eddie, that's in the category of none of your goddamned business!" Ann snapped. "God, I can't believe *you* asked me that!"

She gestured impatiently toward the door.

When he saw Canidy's Packard in front of the Dorchester, he knew he would have to face Agnes. And do so in front of the others. He hadn't had a chance to speak to her at all after Dolan came to his room at Fersfield and told him that Commander Korman had arrived from London.

Dolan, of course, knew that Agnes had been in his bed. He wondered if Dolan had decided that Canidy would be interested in that little bit of interesting information. And he wondered what Canidy's reaction would be if he knew. Canidy might tell Ann, certainly would tell Ann, unless he went to him and expressly asked him not to.

He decided he would have to do that. If Ann knew, it would get back to Sarah.

The way to handle the situation was to tell Canidy and Agnes the truth. He would tell Agnes that he was deeply ashamed, that he had been, as she knew, under terrible strain. He would tell her there was no excuse for what he had done, but that it would not happen again.

And he would tell Canidy much the same thing. That he was deeply ashamed, not of getting laid especially, but of taking advantage of an enlisted person. It was a violation of the officer's code that he had not thought himself capable of.

The bar was now jammed with shoulder-to-shoulder drinkers, and it took them several minutes to find Canidy and the others.

Canidy was half in the bag, with one arm around Agnes's shoulders and the other around a rotund English private whom he introduced to Ed Bitter as a Hollywood ballet master with a Russian name.

There was an English major at the table who wasn't feeling any pain either. And Fulmar, resplendent in pinks and greens and glossy parachute boots and wearing the Silver Star. And Fine, also a little tight, which surprised Bitter.

"Agnes," Ann said, "that man with his arm around your shoulders belongs to me."

"I have more than enough to go around," Canidy said grandly.

"That was before me," Ann purred. "Out of there, Agnes. You can sit with my cousin the hero."

Agnes didn't look at him as she came around the table and a chair was found for her.

"Excuse me, Major," Bitter said, "haven't we met?"

"Possibly," Major Niven said. "Congratulations on your DFC. Dick's been telling us about it."

"You ever go to a bar in New York called the '21' Club, Eddie?" Canidy asked. "Dave was just telling us he used to work there."

"Yes," Bitter said. "As a matter of fact, I have. My father goes there all the time. The place that used to be a speakeasy?"

"Right," Major Niven said. "On West Fifty-second Street."

"Then that must be it," Bitter said.

"Ed," Ann said, "you can be such an ass. This is David Niven, the actor."

He felt his face flush as he saw in Canidy's delighted grin that he had been had.

"Dick's no better," Agnes said loyally. "He thought he was from SOE and walked over and greeted him like a long-lost brother."

"I'll get you for that, Lady Agnes," Canidy said.

Bitter found himself looking into Agnes's face.

"What's that about? What's he up to now?"

She shrugged but said nothing. And then their knees brushed. And then a moment later their hands found each other under the table. As her fingers curled with his, he felt his heart jump.

"And what brings you to London, Major Niven?" Bitter asked.

Canidy laughed out loud and hard.

"Lend-lease elocution lessons," the English private said.

At about eight they all crowded into the Packard, and Agnes drove them across town to a black-market restaurant she had heard about from the other limousine drivers. Canidy and Niven talked their way in.

The food was neither good nor plentiful, but it was expensive. Meanwhile, under the table, Agnes slipped her foot out of her shoe and ran her toes over Bitter's ankle.

As they were having a fourth bottle of wine to go with the Stilton cheese, a microphone was turned on in Broadcast House. At the third of thirty messages, an announcer with impeccable diction solemnly proclaimed:

"Bübchen would like to paddle Gisella's canoe again. Bübchen would like to paddle Gisella's canoe again."

XI

[ONE]
Marburg an der Lahn, Germany
15 January 1943

Hauptsturmführer Wilhelm Peis stood at rigid attention and extended his right arm from the shoulder at a forty-five-degree angle.

"Heil Hitler!" he barked.

Standartenführer SS-SD Johann Müller casually raised his right arm from the elbow and let it drop.

"*Wie geht's,* Wilhelm?" he asked.

Müller's manner of returning the now-required straight-armed Nazi salute—or, more accurately, of *not* returning it—was intentional, an affectation that he had learned from Helmut von Heurten-Mitnitz.

They had been having lunch, as they did at least twice a week, in the Adlon Hotel; and they had to wait for a table because of an official luncheon. A steady procession of military, security service, and party dignitaries came into the lobby and exchanged greetings.

Helmut von Heurten-Mitnitz leaned forward and spoke softly.

"You will notice, Johnny," he said dryly, "that, with a few exceptions, the crispness of the salute is in inverse proportion to the importance of the saluter."

Müller laughed. Von Heurten-Mitnitz had put into words what he had himself noticed, especially that the whole salute and "Heil" business had become mandatory. Young officers—and especially young SS officers—and zealous Party officials came to attention and saluted so crisply they almost quivered.

Senior officers, both military and Party, were almost to a man far more sloppy. As often as not they "forgot" the "Heil, Hitler," or said it in a mumble.

It was as if they were saying, "That little dance is of course necessary for you underlings, but certainly not for someone like myself, of unquestioned loyalty and importance."

Müller then rose to his feet. "I am going to piss," he said, giving a very sloppy Nazi greeting to von Heurten-Mitnitz. "Heil Hitler, Herr Minister."

"Heil Hitler, Herr Standartenführer," von Heurten-Mitnitz replied, returning an even more casual salute.

And as he walked across the marble-floored lobby of the Adlon to the men's room, two Gestapo agents and an SS-SD Sturmbannführer, standing in conversation by one of the tall marble columns, recognized him and gave the Nazi salute in a manner that would have pleased Adolf Hitler himself.

And they smiled with pleasure when he returned it with a casual movement of his lower arm and said, *"Was ist los?"* instead of "Heil Hitler."

Now Müller thought of that incident in the Adlon. And thought again that he had learned a good deal from the Pomeranian aristocrat since he had come to know him. Helmut von Heurten-Mitnitz was a very smart fellow.

He hoped von Heurten-Mitnitz was smart enough to keep them from being caught, doing what they were now doing.

"I'm doing fine, Herr Standartenführer," Peis said. "And may I say that it is a pleasure to see you so soon again?"

"I had a very good time on New Year's Eve, Wilhelm," Müller said. "A very good time."

"I'm glad," Peis said, then added: "I thought you might like her."

"And they've given me a new car, and I thought I should take it for a run and see how it handles, and here I am, Wilhelm."

"A new car, Herr Standartenführer?"

Müller motioned him to the window and pointed out the Opel Admiral.

"Very nice," Peis said. "You must have a friend in the transport office, Herr Standartenführer. A good friend."

"You know how it goes, Wilhelm," Müller said, "one hand washes the other."

Peis nodded understanding.

"First things first," Müller said. "I forgot to apply for gasoline coupons. You know how it is."

"No problem whatsoever, Herr Standartenführer," Peis said. "We'll fill it up here, and then I'll give you whatever ration coupons you require."

"Very good of you, Peis," Müller said. "I will be in your debt."

"Not at all, Herr Standartenführer. My pleasure."

"And, since I am here, I thought, I might telephone Fräulein Dyer and ask if she's free. If she is, perhaps you and your lady friend—any one of your many extraordinarily lovely lady friends—might wish to have dinner with me?"

"I would be delighted," Peis said. "If you would permit me, Herr Standartenführer, I would be happy to telephone the lady and make the arrangements. And I presume you would like to stay at the Kurhotel again?"

"What I thought I would do, Wilhelm," Müller said, "is visit my mother this afternoon, and then we could meet for drinks at half past six at the Kurhotel?"

"Consider it done, Herr Standartenführer," Peis said. "And if I may make the suggestion, why don't I turn my car over to you this afternoon? Then I could have the Admiral serviced and fueled, awaiting you at the Kurhotel."

"I am really getting deeply into your debt, Wilhelm," Müller said.

"Not at all, Herr Standartenführer."

"I was thinking, Wilhelm, of giving the lady a little present," Müller said.

"Do you think there would be something, a small porcelain perhaps, or a painting, something like that, in protective custody?"

"I will pick it out myself," Peis said. "And have it delivered this afternoon."

"If it would be all right, I'd rather pick something out myself," Müller said. "Could that be arranged?"

"Of course, Herr Standartenführer," Peis replied. "We could go to the warehouse directly, if you wish."

"It's been a long drive from Berlin, Wilhelm," Müller said. "Why don't we go for a drink now to cut the dust, and then have a second to give me the courage to face my mother, and then go to the warehouse?"

[TWO]
21 Burgweg, Marburg an der Lahn
1715 Hours
15 January 1943

"*Guten Tag,* Wilhelm," Gisella Dyer said when she opened the door to Peis's impatient knock. "What can I do for you?"

There was an arrogance in her tone that he didn't like. He wondered if providing her to Müller had been such a good idea after all. Müller was obviously taken with her. That could become awkward, even dangerous.

"For one thing," he said coldly, reminding her of her position, "you can remember to call me by my rank when there are others around."

"Sorry," she said, but there was more amusement than concern in her voice. She looked over his shoulder down the stairway, her eyebrows raised in curiosity.

Two Kreis Marburg policemen, one of them an old man, were grunting under the load of a large object as they manhandled it up the stairs.

"What's this, Herr Hauptsturmführer?" Gisella asked.

He ignored the question.

"I have been looking for you for hours," he said.

"I was at the university," she said.

"Not in the library," he said.

"I was in Professor Abschidt's office, cataloguing," she said.

"You should leave word where you are," he said.

The two policemen now had the blanket-wrapped object on the landing. The old policeman, wheezing, supported himself on it.

"May I come in?" Peis asked.

Gisella stepped out of the way. He marched into the apartment and peered into each of the rooms as if making up his mind about something. He concluded that discretion dictated that the radio not be put in the sitting room, although that was the obvious place for it, but in Gisella's bedroom.

In the warehouse, Standartenführer Müller had been like an old maid. He had spent thirty minutes rejecting one thing after another as "not being quite right for Gisella." Peis had no idea what Gisella had done to the old fart, but whatever it was, he liked it. Müller was behaving like a schoolboy in love.

Müller had finally settled on an enormous, floor-model, Fulmar Elektrische Gesellschaft (FEG) combination radio, phonograph, and bar.

It had been the personal household property of the Jew who before his relocation had been the FEG dealer for Marburg. It came with two cardboard cartons of phonograph records, and a smaller cardboard carton that held the glasses and bottles—genuine Bohemian crystal—for the concealed bar.

Peis was not at all pleased with Müller's final choice. For one thing, he had had to go to the trouble of getting a truck and two policemen from the Kreis police station to bring it to Burgweg. For another, something was wrong with the phonograph, and he had to assure Müller that it would be his pleasure to have that repaired. And the radio was capable of listening to the BBC.

Once she learned that the radio had come from Müller, Gisella would feel free to listen to the BBC, which meant that she would be reported for listening to the BBC, which meant that he would have to have a word with Hauptscharführer (Sergeant Major) Ullberg, who handled such things, to stop him from going further with it.

There was a straight-backed chair and a small table against the wall of Gisella's bedroom.

"Find some other place for the chair and the table," he ordered. "Put them in another room."

"Are you going to tell me why?" she asked.

"Do what I tell you, if you don't mind," he said, but tempered the curtness with a smile. The thought had just flashed through him that Gisella might tell Müller how he was treating her. As smitten with the bitch as Müller was, that could mean trouble for him.

When she carried the chair from her bedroom, Peis picked up the table and followed her.

"Just put it down anywhere," Gisella said. "I'll decide where to put it later."

He set the table down, went to the door, and motioned for the policemen to pick up the FEG combination bar, phonograph, and radio. It just barely cleared the door, and it was necessary to move Gisella's bed out of the way before they could get the radio up against the wall.

"That will be all, thank you," Peis said to the policemen. "Don't forget to take the blanket with you."

"And the boxes in the truck, Herr Hauptsturmführer? What do we do with those?"

"You bring them up here, of course," he snapped.

When they had gone, Gisella said, "Very nice. Whose is it?"

"It is a small gift, a token of respect from Standartenführer Müller," Peis said. "He hopes you are free to spend the evening with him."

"Just the evening? Or dinner, too?" Gisella asked, artificially innocent.

"Listen to me, you dumb bitch," Peis snapped. "The Standartenführer is a very important man. He can be very useful as a friend."

"To both of us," she said.

"And very dangerous if displeased. And if he is displeased, I will be displeased."

"What time?" Gisella asked.

"I will be back here at quarter after six," he said. "We are to join the Standartenführer at half past six."

"We?"

"It will be a small party," he said. And then he added: "I want you to think it over, and consider why it is important for the Standartenführer to have a good time."

"I will," she said.

"Be outside at six-fifteen," he said. "I will be driving the Standartenführer's personal car." He paused, and then added, to prove how important that Standartenführer was, "An Opel Admiral."

"An Admiral?" Gisella asked. "The Standartenführer must be an important man. The only other Admiral I've seen in Marburg is the Gauleiter's."

"You should consider yourself fortunate, *Liebchen,*" Peis said, "to have attracted such a man."

"I attracted you," she said, smiling sweetly. "Why not a Standartenführer?"

[THREE]
Headquarters, Eighth United States Air Force
High Wycombe
15 January 1943

Lt. Colonel Edmund T. Stevens was waiting for Canidy just inside the front door of the former girls' school.

"You and I are being honored," Stevens said dryly. "We are to share a VIP suite."

"I hadn't planned to stay over," Canidy said. "I *can't* stay over. I have things to do."

"Neither had I," Stevens said. "That wasn't mentioned. I'll have to buy underwear and a shirt and shaving things in the PX."

"Fuck 'em," Canidy said. "Let's just claim the 'press of other duties.'"

"We can't do that, Dick," Stevens said. "We can't let them win this one by default. If we don't 'nonconcur,' then, by default, we'll 'concur.' You know how the system works."

"Oh, goddamn the Air Corps!" Canidy fumed. It earned him a strange look from an Air Corps major across the foyer.

What Canidy had thought would be a meeting lasting no more than three or four hours had turned out to be a full day (a twelve-hour full day), plus five hours of the following day, sitting on a hard-bottomed uncomfortable chair.

By then, there was a foul taste in his mouth from all the coffee, and his ass was sore not only from all the sitting but also from a rash on the soft skin of his inner thighs. There was apparently something in his new PX shorts that his skin didn't like. His upper thighs felt like they were on fire. And when the fire let up, they itched.

He hadn't wanted to participate in the meeting at all, correctly suspecting the worst, and had argued futilely when Stevens had "asked" him to meet him at High Wycombe at 0800:

"Bedell Smith told David Bruce," Stevens said, "that it was important for us to send 'someone senior'—by that he meant David—together with our 'best technical people.' "

"Doesn't that leave me out?" Canidy replied, even though he suspected that he was going to have to go, period.

"Richard," Stevens said patiently, "there is always a point beyond which resistance is futile. Eight-thirty at High Wycombe. What they call the properly appointed place, at the prescribed time, in the proper uniform. And with that in mind, wear your ribbons."

As Canidy had suspected, the purpose of the meeting was to "persuade" the OSS and Naval Intelligence to agree that "after evaluating new intelligence data," it had been concluded that earlier worries over the effect of German jet aircraft on the strategic bombing of the European landmass had been "overstated" and now posed little threat.

If there was little threat from the jets or the flying bombs, there was no point in keeping that sharp an eye on them. What the Air Corps called "reconnaissance assets," the P-38s and the B-26s fitted out as photographic reconnaissance aircraft, which were presently spending countless hours looking for jets and/or flying bombs, or facilities that might build or house them, could be diverted to "more productive" activity.

Eighth Air Force could not just assign their reconnaissance aircraft where they wanted to. They—and SHAEF—were operating under a mandate from the Chairman of the Joint Chiefs of Staff that gave OSS requests for intelligence gathering the highest priority.

Unless they could get the Joint Chiefs to revoke the mandate, which was very unlikely, the only option they had was to get the London station of OSS to agree that the reconnaissance was no longer necessary. They had pulled out all stops to do just that.

The Air Corps brass had a clear position: The Germans weren't close to fielding operational jet fighters. Even if sometime in the bye-and-bye they did actually manage to put a "handful of operational aircraft up," they would scarcely be effective against the wall of machine-gun fire a "block" of bombers could set up.

The Air Corps had made a concerted effort, at an enormous expenditure of matériel, to locate German jet-propelled aircraft and/or flying bombs and had been unsuccessful. It was therefore logical to presume that even if the Germans had such Buck Rogers experimental weaponry on their drawing boards, they were a long way from getting them into the air, much less operational.

It therefore followed that it was no longer necessary to continue the expenditure of reconnaissance assets at the present level. Reconnaissance would not be discontinued, of course. It would continue whenever assets could be spared from other, more pressing utilization.

The Air Corps paraded their experts, both professional airmen and commissioned civilians. All of them had decided—either professionally or because they knew which side their bread was buttered on—that the two-star generals were right.

The Navy didn't give much of a damn. Neither the jet fighters, because of their limited range, nor the flying bombs, because they could not be precisely aimed, posed any threat to ships at sea that they could see; the Navy quickly caved in.

That left in effect a hung jury. Against one wise and highly experienced major general and his experts stood one inexplicably difficult retreaded light colonel, and one ex–fighter pilot, still wet behind the ears.

Canidy believed, and Stevens trusted his judgment, that the current intelligence—actually the lack of it—proved that the Air Corps had not been able to find where the Germans were building or testing their jets and their flying bombs. It did not prove there were no jets.

Nothing the Air Corps had come up with disproved Donovan's—and now Canidy's—belief that there *were* jets and flying bombs. Unless something was done about them, the jets were going to shoot down B-17s and B-24s by the hundreds. And the flying bombs would certainly be sent against London, maybe even New York. In that case, more, not less, reconnaissance was necessary.

"General," Stevens said finally. "I'm afraid that the OSS must nonconcur with the conclusions drawn in your draft report."

"In other words, Colonel, you are putting your judgment, and that of your major, against everything we've shown you here?"

"General, with respect, the OSS has information that makes the existence of operational German jet aircraft seem far more likely than your people believe."

"But which considerations of security make it impossible for you to share with us, correct?" the general asked icily.

"Yes, sir, I'm afraid that's the situation," Stevens replied.

"Then there is not much point in going on with this meeting, is there?"

"Sir, I would suggest that everything has been covered," Stevens said.

The general nodded, and simply got up and walked out of the room.

If the meeting was to be considered a battle, Canidy thought, the Air Corps had lost. But the OSS's victory, if that's what it was, was worse than hollow. A large number of men, men like himself, men like Doug Douglass, were going to die because the OSS—which in fact meant Canidy, Richard—insisted on photographing every spot in Germany that looked likely to contain something interesting about jet airplanes and flying bombs.

Both Stevens and Canidy fell asleep in the backseat of the Princess on the way to London. There didn't seem to be anything to say, and the steady stream of expert opinion thrown at them, plus the growing acrimony, had left them exhausted.

They both knew that by the time they reached Berkeley Square, their reluctance to give in to the Air Corps would have preceded them. And they would have to justify it to David Bruce.

Two further annoyances awaited Canidy at Berkeley Square. The first came from Sergeant Major Davis: Ann Chambers had called to say she had gone to Nottingham, purpose unspecified, with Meachum Hope, and would be gone three days. The second came from Bruce himself, who announced that the CID (the Criminal Investigation Division of the Provost Marshal's Office) had caught one of the cooks at Whitbey House selling food rations on the black market. He would of course have to be court-martialed.

Since Canidy was not a bona-fide officer and could not legally convene a court-martial himself, the chief of station "suggested" the way to handle it was to transfer the thief to Richodan, where Major Berry, the Richodan commandant, "was equipped to handle this sort of thing."

For reasons Canidy had never understood, Major Berry had been taken into the OSS after proving himself an incompetent working for Bob Murphy in Casablanca. Canidy knew Berry to be the sort of sonofabitch who would joyously throw the book at the thief.

And Canidy was also more than a little aware that he himself had "diverted" from "the war effort" a Packard, a Ford, a B-25, and several tons of foodstuffs and liquor. Having set that example, he could not in good conscience send a corporal to the stockade for selling a couple of hams, or a couple of roasts, to get beer money.

"I'll handle it," he said. "I'll throw the fear of Christ into him. It won't happen again."

"Once is more than enough, Canidy," Bruce said.

"I don't want him, during a break from cracking rocks at Litchfield, telling the other prisoners all the interesting things he's seen at Whitbey House."

The chief of station's face tightened at that. His thinking had gone no further than "thieves must be punished."

"I'll leave it up to you, then," he said after a moment, and then went on to more serious matters: "About that meeting in High Wycombe, if you and Ed Stevens are in agreement, I'll back you to the hilt."

"The Air Corps has been heard from, I gather?"

"In the last forty-eight hours my phone has been ringing off the hook," Bruce said, smiling just a little. "As I was saying, since you and Colonel Stevens seem to be in agreement, I will, of course, stand behind you. But I want you to know that it's clear to me that you could have presented your case with a good deal more tact. Your position will prevail, but at a terrible price insofar as good relations among OSS and Eighth Air Force and SHAEF are concerned."

The truth was that Canidy had been as tactful as he knew how, and that the complaints had been an attempt by the Air Corps to have his objections overridden. But if he said so, he knew that the chief of station would take that reasoning as nothing but another manifestation of Canidy's "bad atti- tude."

"I'm sorry they took offense," he said.

"I really wish I could believe that, Dick," the chief of station said sadly. Bruce reminded Canidy of a master at St. Mark's School. Every time the boys had gotten in trouble, the master had been sorrowful, not angry.

"It's true, David," Canidy said with as much sincerity as he could muster.

"Well, it's water under the damn, I suppose," David Bruce said. "But I wanted to get that out of the way before the meeting."

"Oh, Christ, not another meeting! I'm meetinged out!"

"You may find this one interesting," Bruce said, gesturing for Canidy to precede him out of the office.

Outside, Bruce stepped ahead and climbed the narrow, squeaking flight of stairs to what had been the servants' quarters. Under the slant of the roof were now storerooms and small conference rooms.

Bruce stopped before one of the conference rooms and knocked at the door.

Colonel Wild Bill Donovan opened it.

[FOUR]

"Hello, Dick," Donovan said. "I have just been hearing in some detail about your war with the Air Corps."

Colonel Stevens, who was sitting at a small table with Stanley Fine, chuckled.

"That's not true," Stevens said. "I just told him that to my considerable astonishment you were the picture of tact and calm reason."

"We could have used you up there, Colonel," Canidy said as he shook Donovan's hand. "We were outnumbered."

"Ed told me it was tough," Donovan said. "It couldn't be helped. You understand, I suppose, that the meeting wasn't really about the reconnaissance missions you've been asking for."

"I don't understand," Canidy admitted.

"That's part of it, but only part. As long as we maintain there is a bonafide threat from jet-propelled aircraft, the whole Air Corps strategy for Europe is being questioned. The pressure on the people you and Ed were dealing with came right from the top. I'm sorry you had to stand up under it, but the alternative was David going, and I didn't want that."

"Or you," Canidy challenged.

"No way." Donovan laughed. "I was saying, I didn't want David to go. Which made you and Ed the sacrificial lambs. I just want you to know I know it must have been tough acting that small gemlike flame of reason, et cetera et cetera."

"I'm afraid there was antagonism, sir," Canidy said.

"They're going to be antagonized until we announce that we've been wrong all along," Donovan said. "And since we are not wrong—"

"Well, I'm glad to hear you say that, sir," Canidy said. "I was beginning to think I was on the shitlist."

"Don't be silly," Donovan said quickly, and then went on: "Before we get into this, Canidy—how important is Jimmy Whittaker to you?"

"Sir? I don't think I understand the question."

"There's an operation coming up in the Pacific where I think he'd be very useful. Barring a very strong objection from you—for example, if he's absolutely essential to your plans to get Professor Dyer out of Germany—I want to send him over there."

Canidy hesitated before replying: "Nothing specific at the moment, sir. I guess I think of him as my reserve. He has experience behind the lines. I'd really like to have him available in case I do need him."

"I need that behind-the-lines experience myself," Donovan said. "Or rephrasing that so I don't sound like God. Whittaker's experience in the Philippines is just what is needed right now in the Philippines."

"Sir, I don't follow you."

"Let me tell you what I have in mind," Donovan said. "There's an officer in the Philippines, a man named Wendell Fertig. Before the war, he was a civil engineer. He was a friend of Chesty Whittaker. He took a commission just before the war started, and then, refusing to surrender, took to the hills when Bataan fell. He made it to Mindanao and began guerrilla operations.

"He began by promoting himself to brigadier general—he was a major—apparently in the belief Filipinos wouldn't be impressed with anything less than a colonel. He also appointed himself 'Commander in Chief of U.S. Forces in the Philippines.' That allowed him to recruit guerrillas. But as you can imagine, it didn't endear him to Douglas MacArthur and his staff, who like to do things strictly by the book. . . ."

"I hadn't heard we had any guerrillas," Canidy said.

"As I was about to say," Donovan said sharply, annoyed at the interruption, "'General' Fertig and his guerrillas are being studiously ignored by Douglas MacArthur. MacArthur won't even reply to his radio messages. He says they're phony, controlled by the Japanese. MacArthur has a G-2 named Willoughby who says there is no way a useful guerrilla force can be organized or supplied.

"But Fertig made radio contact with the Navy in San Diego, it came to the attention of Navy Secretary Frank Knox—and the President—and Knox, who has his own private covert operation, called the Marine Corps Office of Management Analysis, has sent a team of Marines into Mindanao to see if they find Fertig.

"And if they find him, what?"

"There has been a suggestion from MacArthur's headquarters that Fertig is not playing with a full deck. The first thing Knox's people are supposed to do—presuming they can find him—is determine if he's sane, and then what his chances are of mounting a useful guerrilla operation."

"The Marines haven't found him yet?" Canidy asked.

Donovan shook his head "no."

"So far not a word," he said. "I rate their chances of their mission being successful as fifty-fifty. And if they don't make it, I rate the chances of the President—who is fascinated with the idea of American guerrillas in the Philippines—giving the mission of having another go at it to the OSS as one hundred to one."

He paused, waited until he decided Canidy had time to absorb what he had been told, and then asked:

"Are you beginning to get the picture?"

"Yeah," Canidy said thoughtfully.

"If I am ordered to send someone into the Philippines, I want it to be someone who won't antagonize MacArthur," Donovan said. "And Jimmy left the Philippines on the PT boat with MacArthur. Even Willoughby can't argue with that."

"And Jimmy, of course, knows the Philippines," Canidy said, "and speaks Spanish."

"It's even possible that he knows Fertig," Donovan said. "Before the islands fell, they were both blowing things up. So it would seem to me that Jimmy is the man to go. But it's your call. The Dyer mission, and the follow-ons, have the higher priority. If you think you really need him . . ."

It was a long moment before Canidy replied.

"The unpleasant truth seems to be," he said finally, "is that Jimmy falls into the 'Nice to Have' rather than 'Have to Have' category."

"The Philippines mission is important, Dick," Donovan said.

"It will screw up his love life, but what the hell, war is supposed to be hell anyway, isn't it?"

"It would be a volunteer mission. You think he'll be willing?" Donovan said.

Canidy nodded.

"And now, as they say," Donovan said, "to the business at hand. I understand that contact has been made with Helmut von Heurten-Mitnitz?"

"Three days ago," Canidy said.

"By whom?" Donovan pursued. "What was said?"

"The British have been helping us," Canidy said. "We don't have anyone in Berlin that we can use for this. Their help has been a little reluctant."

"That figures," Donovan said.

"Their story is that their men are involved in something 'rather more important, don't you know,'" Canidy said in a credible upper-class British accent. "They have told us that we are going to have to make our own arrangements and stop using their agents in both Berlin and Frankfurt. Specifically, they are going to give us one more contact. Probably, if we lean on them, we can make that two contacts. But after no more than two contacts with von Heurten-Mitnitz, we're on our own."

Donovan nodded.

"There's something else, Dick," he said, "that until now you didn't have to know, and which the British aren't going to be told about at this time. We have, we think, a pipeline in place. From Budapest out, I mean."

"Do I get to use it?" Canidy asked. "I've been going on the idea that we'll get Dyer and his daughter out by fishing boat from Holland. And why the long way around?"

"The Germans know that we, as well as the British, are bringing people out through Holland and Belgium. And they're getting better and better at finding those pipelines. We'll continue to use them, of course. And we'll set up others when they turn one off. But what we've done is set one up which will move people the other way, from Germany to Hungary, then through Yugoslavia. It won't be used much, just enough to keep it open. And it will be used only for those we *must* bring out. Do you follow the reasoning?"

Canidy nodded. "It's in reserve, so to speak."

"No," Donovan said. "Not the way I think you mean. It will not be used when one of the Dutch or Belgian routes is shut down. It will be used only when the people being run through are too valuable to run through the others."

"Dyer is that important to us?"

"Dyer can tell us about the metallurgy for the jet engines," Donovan said. "Do I have to tell you, of all people—you burr-under-the-Air-Corps-saddle-blanket—how important that is to us?"

It wasn't much of a joke, but everybody laughed.

"Why Yugoslavia?" Canidy asked.

"Your responsibility ends when Fulmar delivers the Dyers to Budapest," Donovan said. "So that's really none of your business, Dick."

"The only way to test a pipeline is to run something through it," Canidy said. "Is that what this is, another goddamned test? I send Fulmar in there, and he picks up the Dyers, and then we wait around to see if the pipeline works? Goddammit!"

"Just who do you think you're talking to?" David Bruce snapped.

Donovan raised his hand to shut him off.

"Fulmar is being sent in, Dick," Donovan said, "because Dyer is so important to us that Ed Stevens and I agreed it was worth the risk. Believe me, if I didn't think the pipeline would work, I would not send Dyer or Fulmar through it."

Canidy looked at Donovan and after a moment said, almost formally, "Thank you."

"We think it will take Fulmar's presence, his physical presence, to convince Dyer that it will be safe to leave," Stevens said. "I don't intend this as a criticism, but I thought I had made that point to you earlier."

Canidy nodded. "That was before this Yugoslav pipeline came up," Canidy said. "Yugoslavia worries me."

"Why?" Bruce asked.

"As I understand it," Canidy said, "there are two major guerrilla operations in Yugoslavia. One is run by an ex–Royal Yugoslav Army colonel named Dragoljub Mihajlovic, and the other by a Communist who calls himself Josef Tito. Presumably, we intend to use the colonel for the pipeline, for obvious reasons. But he and Tito are fighting each other. Tito's backed by the Russians, of course. So what happens if the Dyers and Fulmar get grabbed by Tito? Or is that what we're really doing here? Seeing if that's what's going to happen? Another goddamned Machiavellian test?"

"I am so interested in learning how you know so much about what's going on in Yugoslavia, Canidy," Donovan said, "that I am going to pretend I didn't hear the rest of what you said."

"I've been given 'disinformation' before around here," Canidy said. "Or not told things I should have been told."

"Now, see here, Canidy—" David Bruce spluttered.

"That has been unfortunately necessary in the past," Donovan said simply. "But I didn't do it, and that's not happening now."

"No, sir," Canidy said. "Not by you. My mouth ran away with me, and I'm sorry. I apologize."

"I should hope so," Bruce said.

Donovan shut him off as he had before, by holding his hand up.

"My question, Canidy," he said, "was the source of your expertise about Yugoslavia."

"I've talked to the people we're dropping in," Canidy said. "They naturally presumed that as the CO of Whitbey House, I had a need to know."

"And you pumped them!" Bruce accused.

"Very enterprising of you," Donovan said. "I should have guessed as much."

Canidy was really not sure whether it was a sarcastic reprimand or just what the words said.

Donovan looked at Stevens, then at Canidy.

"Obviously, Dick," Donovan said, "we are going to use Mihajlovic's forces to protect the Hungary–Yugoslav pipeline. For the moment at least, I'm confident that he can bring our people out safely. But aside from that, I'm afraid you're going to have to consider the question answered in all the detail you're going to get."

"Fulmar is going to ask me what will happen when he brings the Dyers to Budapest," Canidy said. " 'Trust me' is not going to be a satisfactory answer to that question."

"Tell him," Donovan said after a moment, "that they will be taken across the border into Croatia, pass into the hands of Mihajlovic's partisans, who will carry them through Bosnia-Herzegovina to the coast, where they will be carried by ship to the island of Vis. Once they get there, they will be picked up by aircraft."

"Whose aircraft?"

"The British have a fairly substantial force, more than a hundred men, on Vis," Donovan said. "Two of our people are with them. They have furnished us with the airfield dimensions. Have a look at them, then tell Stevens if you think your B-25 has the necessary range and can use the airfield on Vis. If it doesn't, we have been offered space on a British submarine."

Canidy's face registered surprise.

"We also have people with Mihajlovic and Tito," Donovan said. "It wasn't considered necessary that you know, Dick."

"I need one more piece of information," Canidy said. "Now that Fulmar has committed to memory a map of Leeuwarden, Holland, he's going to Budapest. *Where* in Budapest?"

Donovan chuckled.

"Stevens has that, too," he said. "Will you have any trouble getting it to von Heurten-Mitnitz?"

"It takes five days to put a piece of paper in his hand," Canidy said. "Overnight to Sweden, and then four days from Stockholm to Berlin."

"We don't want to cut it too close," Donovan said. "Better set that moving, Ed."

"Yes, sir," Stevens said.

"That's it," Donovan said, rising. "I've got a plane to catch. I can sense Chief Ellis growing nervous downstairs."

He went to each man to shake hands, and then he walked out of the sitting room. The chief of station and Colonel Stevens walked after him.

"I have just had an inspiration," Canidy said. "Let's find Jimmy and Fulmar, and go to some pub full of soldiers and get drunk. Maybe with a little bit of luck we can get in a fight."

"I'm going to surprise you," Fine said. "I'm going with you."

[FIVE]
The Dorchester Hotel Bar
London, England
2010 Hours
15 January 1943

Captain James M. B. Whittaker, Lieutenant Eric Fulmar, and Captain the Duchess Stanfield, WRAC, were sitting in the Dorchester bar where Canidy had expected to find them, at a table against the wall.

"We were wondering where you were," Whittaker said as Canidy sat down and inspected the bottles in paper bags. He was looking for Scotch.

"We were with the Boss," Canidy said.

"I thought he was with you at High Wycombe," Whittaker said.

"*The* Boss," Canidy said.

"There was a rumor he's in town," Whittaker said. "Got any interesting gossip?"

As a matter of fact, buddy, you're going to go back to the Philippines.

"Nothing important," Canidy said.

"And how was High Wycombe?" the Duchess asked.

"The less said about it the better, Your Gracefulness," Canidy said. "Even the Boss felt sorry for us."

"We ate," Whittaker said. "We didn't know when, or if, you were coming."

"No problem," Canidy said. "Stan and I came to take the third man here over to drink with the Air Corps anyway. Joe Kennedy's over there talking them out of aircraft parts. They have a pretty good kitchen in the O Club."

"The third man?" the Duchess asked.

"Another quaint Americanism, Your Gracefulness," Canidy said. "Two's company, three's a crowd."

She blushed, then quickly said: "We're not going back to Whitbey House tonight?"

"No," he said. "Both Jimmy and I have to see Stevens in the morning."

And Stevens will tell him to pack his things; his services are needed in the Philippines. The Great Romance will be put on hold.

Canidy sipped at his liquor. And wished that Ann were here. It would have been nice to spend what was certain to be Jimmy's last night on the town with the four of them together.

And then his eyebrows went up and he smiled mischievously.

"Stanley," he said, "there is a damsel yonder trying desperately to attract your attention."

"I know," Fine said. "I'm doing my best to pretend I don't see her."

"You don't want to be nice to the damsel, Stan?" Canidy asked.

"For God's sake, ignore her," Fine said.

Canidy raised his hand over his head and waved.

The woman across the room was a tall, slender woman with silver-gray hair combed upward under her Red Cross uniform cap. She pointed, signifying she was trying to attract Fine's attention. Canidy nodded and beamed happily at her and pushed Fine's shoulder.

"I think she wants to say hello to you, Stan," Canidy said innocently.

"You sonofabitch," Fine said, and turned toward the woman. "Oh, my God," he said. "Here she comes."

Fulmar and Canidy laughed.

"You'll stop laughing, Eric," Fine said, "when she sinks her fangs into you."

It had been inevitable that Stanley S. Fine would become a regular at the Dorchester bar. He had been temporarily housed at the hotel on his arrival in London, and when quarters were found, they were shabby and a long Underground ride across London. With a good deal less embarrassment than he had expected, he took over the apartment Continental Motion Picture Studios maintained in London for traveling stars and executives. It was at Park Lane and Aldford Street, two blocks from the Dorchester.

He found that he missed the people he knew in the motion picture industry, and it was at the Dorchester that people in the industry were billeted when they came to London.

Another Dorchester bar regular was the woman now marching across the room. Fine privately thought of Eleanor Redmon as "the Scorpion." She was a Red Cross girl, although that description was not precise. Eleanor Redmon was some sort of executive within the Red Cross organization, holding a position too exalted to require her personally to pass out coffee and doughnuts to the boys. For another, the Scorpion was no longer a girl.

She was, in fact, forty. She was from Duluth, Minnesota, where she had been left widowed, childless, and well-off shortly after the war began. Volunteering for the Red Cross seemed to be just the thing.

Her position carried with it enough assimilated rank for her to have a room at the Dorchester, and she spread enough cash around so that the room became a suite. She quickly got in the habit of dropping into the bar at cocktail time or after dinner with one or more of the prettier young Red Cross girls. They naturally attracted the handsome and dashing young pilots.

Eleanor Redmon had decided to cultivate Stanley S. Fine when she noticed the warm affection people had for him—people whom she had only previously seen on the silver screen.

It wasn't difficult. All she had had to do was save a place for him at her table. And the results had been more than worth the effort: Soon, the Scorpion was able to write home that Major David Niven and Private Peter Ustinov had sat at "her" table in the Dorchester bar at the same time, and that her new friend, Captain Stanley S. Fine, who had been a vice president of Continental Studios, had had to lend them the money to pay their bill.

For his part, Stanley S. Fine watched with morbid fascination the Scorpion arrange her nightly intrigues in the bar. Young officers who came to the Scorpion's table wondering how they would separate the blonde from the old broad frequently woke up the next morning with the old broad beside them in the old broad's bed.

To Fine, whom she regarded as a decadent (and thus understanding) "movie person," she frankly admitted that she found boys who wore officer's uniforms and pilot's wings—boys who were not old enough to vote— irresistible

He saw, too, how skillfully she charmed the middle-aged senior officers who frequented the Dorchester bar. To a man, they stoutly defended her when it was hinted that her interest in peach-skinned young officers was more than motherliness.

As the Scorpion, smiling broadly, reached the table, Fine saw that she was on her fifth or sixth Scotch, and thus likely to be both horny and bitchy.

With a little bit of luck, he thought, *she might go after Canidy.*

"Hello, Stanley!" she cried. "Introduce me to your friends!"

By friends, Fine understood, she meant Fulmar. Whittaker was obviously taken; and Canidy, wearing the uniform of a field-grade officer assigned to SHAEF and looking very tired, did not appear boyish. Fulmar, on the other hand, with his parachutist's wings and shiny boots and Silver Star, did.

"Captain Stanfield, Major Canidy, Captain Whittaker, Lieutenant Fulmar, may I present Miss Redmon?"

"I'm very happy to meet you all," the Scorpion said.

"Are you really going to sink your fangs into him?" Canidy asked.

"Jesus Christ!" Fine said.

"I beg your pardon?" she asked.

"Stanley said you were going to sink your fangs into Eric," Canidy said. "I've been wondering what he meant."

"I can't believe Stanley would say anything like that," she said.

"That's what he said," Fulmar said.

The Scorpion's eyes flashed with rage, but she elected to stay and pretend everyone was being very clever.

She sat down.

"Are you stationed in London, Major?" she asked as she took a cigarette from her purse and indicated she wanted a light from Fulmar.

"No," Canidy said.

"And you must be with the Eighty-second Airborne," she said to Eric.

"No," Eric said.

"Then you must be involved in whatever Stanley is doing," she said, "that no one's supposed to talk about," she added significantly.

"I thought Stan was with the SHAEF movie branch," Canidy said.

"I am," Fine said quickly.

"All right, then," the Scorpion said. "We won't talk about that."

Her appetite, Fine saw, was whetted by her belief that the horny young hero was involved in intelligence.

"We're assigned to the 32nd Bomber Group," Canidy said. "I'm an engineering officer, and Eric has the parachute-rigging detachment."

"Oh," she said, more than a little disappointed. "Then you just met Stanley?"

"Oh, no," Canidy said, "we're old pals. From Hollywood."

The Scorpion brightened considerably.

"You're in the industry?" she asked. Canidy nodded. She smiled at Fulmar. "I should have guessed. You carry yourself like an actor."

"I'm not an actor, sorry," Fulmar said sharply.

"But you were in the industry?" she insisted.

"Stuntman," Canidy said. "He did all of Errol Flynn's stunts. Alan Ladd's, too."

"Really?" she asked. "How fascinating!"

She beamed at Fulmar and sat down next to him.

Fulmar rose to the occasion. He told her that Errol Flynn had a phobia about horses, and that in his stocking feet Alan Ladd was five feet one and had to stand on a platform beside his leading ladies.

And then a full colonel, wearing a SHAEF patch and Chemical Warfare Service insignia, came to the table and asked the Scorpion to dance. She hesitated, and then got to her feet.

"Let's get the hell out of here while she's gone," Canidy said, standing.

Fulmar and Fine quickly followed him into the lobby.

"You don't have to come with us, Eric," Canidy said. "You could pursue the Red Cross lady. She seemed fascinated with you."

"Don't laugh," Fulmar said. "As she stood up to dance with the colonel, that kindly old gray-haired lady grabbed me on the cock."

"Well, you can't say Stanley didn't warn you," Canidy said, laughing.

"I didn't believe him," Fulmar said.

The Packard was outside, but the driver was a tall, thin WRAC corporal. Which meant, Canidy thought, that Agnes was off somewhere with Bitter.

"We'll take the car," Canidy said. "I don't think that Jimmy and Her Gracefulness are going out anywhere."

On the way to meet Joe Kennedy and John Dolan at the Air Corps Officers' Club, Eric said, "Before we get schnockered, what should I do about my mother? See her or not?"

"That's up to you, pal," Canidy said. "She's not my mother."

"I've been thinking about it," he said. "What the hell, she *is* my mother."

"If you're asking if there is any reason you shouldn't see her, some OSS reason," Canidy said, "the answer is the OSS doesn't give a damn, one way or the other."

"I wonder where she is, how I could find her?"

"Take care of that little detail for the lieutenant, Stanley, will you?" Candy said.

"Sure," Fine said.

"Thanks," Eric Fulmar said, emotionally.

XII

[ONE]
The Kurhotel
Marburg an der Lahn, Germany
17 January 1943

After Peis brought Gisella and some trollop into the restaurant, it was a little awkward between Müller and Gisella. Stiff and formal. Which was understandable. Gisella was embarrassed. Everyone would think she, too, was a whore Peis was serving up to him.

Gisella is not a whore, Müller thought. *She did what she did because she had no control of it. A whore is a whore because she wants to be a whore, because it is easier. Gisella was forced to sleep with other men because Peis is an asshole.*

But what other people think about Gisella tonight can't be helped. Actually, it's useful: It will be safer for both of us if everyone thought she was what she looked like: a young woman being sweet to an older man because he was a Standartenführer who could provide nice things that younger, less important men could not.

Even when Müller and Gisella danced—despite what had happened between them on New Year's Eve—it was awkward. They danced like a father with his daughter. Which was also understandable, though he wasn't quite old enough to be her father.

But as they came off the dance floor, Gisella caught his hand in hers. She squeezed his hand, and he squeezed back. When they reached the table and had to let go, he knew she really wished she could continue holding his hand.

Right after dinner, Müller let Peis know it was time for him to go and take his whore with him. Peis predictably made it clear he was quite aware that Müller was anxious to take Gisella to bed. As she rose to leave, Peis's whore kissed Gisella.

"Liebling," she said, wearing her most ravishing smile, "I know we'll be seeing a lot of each other."

This upset Müller more than he wanted to admit.

Peis then came to attention, clicked his heels, threw a stiff Nazi salute, and bellowed loud enough for everybody in the room to hear him (which was clearly his intention), "Guten Abend, Herr Standartenführer. Heil Hitler!"

Müller returned the salute with a casual movement of his arm.

After Peis and his whore had left, Gisella started smiling. Müller looked at her quizzically.

"I have seen more formal salutes," Gisella said.

Gisella was looking at him. Into his face—his eyes. It was the first time she had done that.

"I think I am going to have a brandy," Müller said. "Can I order something for you?"

"I will have a brandy, too, please," Gisella said.

The proprietor personally delivered the brandy, displaying it like a treasure. It was one of his last two bottles, he said, as he placed a balloon glass in front of Gisella and then Müller.

"Before the war," Gisella said when the proprietor had stepped away, "this is what my father used to drink."

"Then we'll buy him a bottle," Müller said.

Her eyes were bright with pleasure.

"Could you?"

"Of course," he said. "You heard him, he has two."

That didn't please her. It seemed to frighten her.

"When you're finished," he said, "I will take you home, if you like."

"I would like, I think, to dance."

This time, they did not dance like father and daughter. He could feel the softness of her breasts against him, and then Gisella laid her head against his chest, and he could smell her hair.

"I have to talk to you," she said.

"All right."

Is she in some kind of trouble? If that swine Peis . . .

"Are you sending me home, Johnny?" Gisella asked.

"I thought you—"

For an answer, she squeezed his hand again.

It is entirely possible that Gisella would prefer to be the girlfriend of a Standartenführer—even an old, turning-to-fat, balding, peasant Standartenführer—to being at Peis's beck and call.

So what? What do you care why, just so you can get in her pants?

And then he discarded as beyond credibility that she might like him for himself.

"Why don't we take the cognac to your room?" Gisella asked softly.

She knows what will happen there; that isn't a riding crop pressing against her belly.

Gisella went straight into the bathroom when they reached his room. She came out in her slip, which was cotton, practical, and ill-fitting.

I should have bought her some nice underwear.

Then Müller took a quick shower, and, a little self-consciously, splashed 4711 cologne on his chest and under his arms and down there. He wrapped a towel around his middle and walked back to the bedroom.

Gisella lay in the bed, and she'd tossed her ugly slip on the back of a chair. *She's naked under the blankets!* She raised her arm and held the sheets and blanket open for him.

When he slipped in beside her, she moved so that she was half on top of him, her leg over his, her face against his chest. He marveled at the softness of her back.

"Johnny," Gisella said, her voice muffled, "I've been listening to the BBC."

"You can go to jail for that," he said tenderly, making it a joke.

"I wasn't surprised when Peis brought the radio," she said.

"What do you mean by that?"

"'Gisella thanks Eric for the radio,'" she quoted.

"Aren't you afraid your neighbors will report you?" he asked.

"Yes, of course," she said. "I'm careful."

"I think it will be all right now," he said. "Peis is afraid of me."

"I should be afraid of you," Gisella said. "Somehow I'm not. Quite the opposite."

He tightened his arm around her.

"That was a message to you, wasn't it?" Gisella asked.

"Yes, we think so," Müller said.

"We?"

"The less you know, the safer you are," he said. And immediately knew that was nonsense. If they were caught, it wouldn't matter how much or how little Gisella knew. They would both die, very slowly and very hard, at the hands of someone like Peis.

"I knew the other one was, I don't know, a confirmation of the first."

"What other one?" he asked.

"There were two messages."

He looked down at her, saw her scalp where she parted her hair, looked down to see her breast half flattened against his abdomen.

He didn't want to talk about messages. He just wanted to be where he was, with her naked against him, feeling her heart beat against his chest.

"Ach, Gott!" he said, and then: "I don't know about a second message. And I have to know."

"'Bübchen wants to paddle Gisella's canoe again,'" she quoted, so solemnly that he chuckled.

"What's it mean?" he asked. "How do you know it's for you? What does it mean, about a canoe? *'Bübchen'?"*

She was silent for a moment.

"Why did you have to laugh?" she asked.

"Sometimes I'm an asshole," he said.

"I was older than Eric," she said.

"And you called him 'Bübchen'?"

She nodded her head "yes" against his chest.

"And the canoe? What's that mean?"

She told him about the picnic on the bank of the Lahn River the day before Eric Fulmar had disappeared from Marburg.

Surprising himself, he lowered his head and kissed her hair.

"It's humiliating, having to tell you," Gisella said.

"Why?" he said. "You were forced to be with him."

"Not that much," Gisella said.

"You fell in love with him?" he asked.

"Something like that was impossible," she said.

"Are you still in love with him?" he asked, with a valiant effort to sound dispassionate.

Gisella pushed herself off him and looked down at him.

"Would you believe me if I told you 'no'?"

"Yes," he said.

"Then 'no.'"

"I'm glad," he said.

She threw herself into his arms again.

"What the hell is it all about?" she asked plaintively.

"It's one of two things, I think," he said. "He—they—either want some-thing from your father, or they want to get him, maybe both of you, out of Germany."

"I have been asking Father to come up with some connection with Eric," Gisella said. "But he simply doesn't remember him."

"I'll have to have a go at that," he said.

"With my father?"

"Yes."

"He pretends he doesn't know about Peis," Gisella said. "I don't know how he'd react if you showed up at the house."

"We're going to have to find out," he said.

"I suppose," she said.

They lapsed into silence.

Two minutes later, Müller said, "You are the most beautiful woman I have ever seen."

"That's an elaborate compliment," Gisella said. "When men pay elaborate compliments, they generally want something."

He felt his face flush.

"Does that mean you want to make love?" Gisella asked.

"It didn't," he said, taken back, hurt. "But yes, I do," he added defiantly.

"Good," she said, pushing herself erect and looking down at him again. "I was afraid you would go to sleep on me." She saw the look on his face. "Why are you so surprised?"

"I don't know," he said. "I am. I've never . . . been successful . . . with women."

"You are with this one," Gisella said, and took his hand. "See? Feel?"

[TWO]
12 Burgweg
Marburg an der Lahn, Germany
1000 Hours
18 January 1943

No one really knew how old Burgweg was. Presumably, it had been there before the fortress was built. The guidebooks said the fortress had been built "circa A.D. 900 (?) around an earlier watchtower."

The road itself, paved with cobblestones, was steep. And covered as it was now with a thin layer of snow over ice, it was slippery. The rear end of Müller's Opel Admiral slewed from side to side, frequently bouncing against the curb on the down side of the hill. Several times it almost scraped the buildings that were flush with the side of the road.

The numbering ran from the top downward. They were almost at the gate in the fortress itself when Müller carefully bounced the right wheels of the car over the granite curb and brought the Admiral to a stop. The big car was now half off the road, with its nose almost touching a large sign.

The sign carried the standard No Parking symbol: a *P* crossed by a diagonal red bar as well as (for special emphasis) the legend "Parking Absolutely Forbidden at Any Time."

Müller was unconcerned. Few policemen would even consider issuing a citation to an Opel Admiral. None would be foolhardy enough to even look twice at this Opel Admiral. Müller's vehicle carried not only Berlin license plates, but also, in the spot where common citizens and lesser officials carried the stamp signifying the payment of taxes, his plates bore a small, inconspicuous stamp signifying that taxes had been waived for this vehicle as it was in the service of the Schutzstaffel-Sicherheitsdienst.

He pulled the keys from the ignition, pulled on the parking brake, stepped out of the car, and moved quickly around the rear to open the door for Gisella. By the time he got there, she had her door open and was swinging her feet out, carefully, because the car was so close to the edge. Her coat had opened and her skirt was hiked up, and a flash of white flesh was visible above the silk stockings he had brought her from Berlin.

He felt his heart jump.

Goddammit, she's beautiful!

"I can make it," Gisella said. Standing up and supporting herself on the car, she made her way to where he stood. She held in her hand a tissue-wrapped bottle. The proprietor of the Kurhotel had been more than pleased to present Herr Standartenführer with one of his two bottles of Courvoisier.

"Wait," Müller said, "there's more."

Gisella raised her eyebrows and looked at him curiously.

He opened the trunk of the car and took from it a large cardboard box.

"What's that?" Gisella asked.

"A few little things I picked up for you in Berlin," he said.

She looked at him with a warm sparkle in her eyes. "Thank you, sir," she said, and her voice caught. "Thank you very much."

She likes *me!*

As they entered the foyer of the old house, a door opened a crack and an eye peered out.

Peis's resident snoop, Müller decided.

He followed Gisella up the stairs and waited for the answer to the knock at her door.

Although he had examined his dossier carefully, Professor Friedrich Dyer was not what Müller had imagined. He expected an academic type, an absentminded professor in mussed and baggy clothes. Dyer was tall and erect with a full head of curly hair. There was a Hungarian somewhere in the bloodline, Müller decided. Perhaps that explained his rebellion.

"Heil Hitler!" Professor Dyer said, raising his arm.

"Heil Hitler," Müller mumbled. He stepped inside the apartment, and Gisella closed the door after them.

"Father," Gisella said, "this is Standartenführer Müller."

"How do you do, Herr Standartenführer?" Dyer said formally, neither coldly nor warmly. But his eyes, Müller saw, showed both contempt and shame.

Because his daughter is with an SS-SD officer? Or because he's meeting the man in whose bed his daughter spent the night?

"I am pleased to make your acquaintance, Herr Professor Doktor," Müller said. "As soon as your charming daughter relieves me of this burden, I will offer my hand."

Gisella giggled. Her father nodded his head, just perceptibly, but did not smile.

"What's in there, Johnny?" Gisella asked.

"It should go, I think, in the refrigerator," he said.

Gisella stepped up to him and opened the flaps of the carton.

"My God!" she said. "Where did you find all that?"

"Is there a refrigerator?"

"There's an icebox," she said.

"I'll have Peis bring you a refrigerator," he said without thinking.

"No," Gisella said quickly.

"We manage quite nicely with our old icebox," Dyer said. "Thank you just the same," he added, clearly not meaning it.

"Professor, I am here as a friend," Müller said.

"I'm sure," Dyer said, very carefully. He smiled. But the smile was artificial, and his eyes were wary. And contemptuous.

Müller had a sudden insight: *I could work on Dyer for the next twelve hours without making a crack in his hostility.*

"Would you come here a moment, Herr Professor Doktor?" Müller asked, taking Dyer's arm and leading him into the kitchen. He went to the small FEG Volksradio and turned it on, raising the volume. Then he turned on the water in the sink.

Gisella looked at him with both concern and curiosity.

He took her arms in his hands and pulled her to him so that he could bring his lips to her ear.

"Peis may have this place wired," he said. "If you have to talk in here, make sure the radio is going and the water is running. It would be better if you talked in the woods, or a park. Not near a lake."

She nodded.

He motioned Professor Dyer over and put his mouth close to his ear.

"Your daughter is going to tell you what's going on," he said. "Pay attention. And keep your mouth shut, or we'll all wind up dead."

When he let go of Dyer, he saw the confusion in the man's eyes. He went back to Gisella.

"Tell him what you know. And make sure he understands how dangerous this is. Find out what you can. Anything. Wild guesses, anything."

Gisella nodded and then, as she spoke into his ear, he could feel her warm breath:

"You're going? Now? Why?"

"He's made up his mind not to like me," he said. "So he wouldn't trust me anyhow. You have to make him do that." He looked into her eyes until she nodded understanding and agreement. Then he added, "And I have to drive to Berlin, remember."

He resisted the temptation to kiss her ears, and let her go.

He shut the water off and turned the radio volume down.

"It has been a great pleasure to meet you, Herr Professor Doktor," he said. "I look forward to that pleasure soon again. And I shall be in touch with you, my dear Gisella, just as soon as duty permits." He paused and said loudly, *"Heil Hitler und auf Wiedersehen."*

Then he met Gisella's eyes a moment before turning and walking out of the apartment.

He was almost at the foyer door when Gisella caught up with him.

"Johnny!"

She put her arms around him.

"Be careful," she said.

The foyer door opened and the resident snoop's eye appeared.

Müller yielded to the temptation to give her something to report. He kissed Gisella on the mouth, then put his hands on her rear end and pressed her against him.

He kissed her longer than he had intended, and more tenderly. Then he went out to the Admiral.

He thought, as he drove past the house: *The truth is that I am acting like a schoolboy about that woman. I am going to have to watch myself. Not only is the affection mostly imaginary, but emotion is always dangerous.*

But then: *After I have lunch with von Heurten-Mitnitz tomorrow, I'll take a run over and get her some of the black silk French underwear. And some French perfume, too.*

[THREE]
The Foreign Ministry
Berlin, Germany
20 January 1943

The situation was surreal, Helmut von Heurten-Mitnitz thought, dreamlike. Yet very real.

When he walked into his office earlier, he had received word that Reichs-minister for Foreign Affairs Joachim von Ribbentrop would be pleased if von Heurten-Mitnitz would take luncheon with him in his private dining room.

"I took the liberty, Herr Minister," Fräulein Ingebord Schermann said, "of informing the Herr Reichsminister's adjutant that so far as I knew there was nothing on your schedule that would keep you from accepting his invitation."

"That was precisely the right thing to say, Fräulein Schermann," von Heurten-Mitnitz said. "Thank you. The time?"

"Half past one, Herr Minister," she said.

He had had a little over four hours to consider how he would handle this meeting with von Ribbentrop.

He and von Ribbentrop had much in common, or so it appeared on the surface. They were both aristocrats and career officers of the diplomatic service. Von Ribbentrop had once been a commercial attaché at the German embassy in Ottawa, as Helmut von Heurten-Mitnitz had been an attaché in New Orleans. And von Ribbentrop, like the Graf von Heurten-Mitnitz, had been an early convert to National Socialism and the Führer.

Beneath the surface, however, there were substantial differences: Joachim von Ribbentrop's Almanac de Gotha pedigree was nowhere near as distin-guished as von Ribbentrop liked people to think it was. Nor was he nearly as clever or as skilled a diplomat as he thought he was. Like Müller, he had been promoted over his ability because he was not only trustworthy but an old-time—and thus deserving—Party comrade. Even Helmut von Heurten-Mitnitz's brother held von Ribbentrop with a measure of scorn.

Since his return to Berlin, Helmut von Heurten-Mitnitz had avoided von Ribbentrop. As indeed von Ribbentrop had avoided von Heurten-Mitnitz un-til it became apparent that von Heurten-Mitnitz would not be blamed for the American invasion of Morocco.

When he was asked to lunch with von Ribbentrop, von Heurten-Mit-nitz's first thought had to do with the report of French perfidy in Morocco. That was not any closer to completion than it ever had been.

But that question could have been asked over the phone.

Helmut von Heurten-Mitnitz had no idea what would emerge when he presented himself to von Ribbentrop's receptionist at twenty minutes after one.

The receptionist told him that the Reichsminister was tied up and offered him a chair, coffee, and a magazine.

At 1:25, the door burst open and General Ernst Kaltenbrunner, head of the SS, trailed by an aide, marched into the reception room, nodded curtly at von Ribbentrop's receptionist, shoved open the ceiling-high doors to von Ribbentrop's office, and went inside.

Kaltenbrunner, physically, was an imposing man. He was six feet eight inches tall, with weight to match, and his cheek bore a prominent scar from a saber slash.

His aide set down beside von Heurten-Mitnitz, glanced at him curiously, and then picked up a magazine.

Two minutes later, an officer in black SS uniform appeared in von Ribbentrop's door.

"The Herr Reichsminister will receive you now, Herr von Heurten-Mitnitz," he said.

Neither von Ribbentrop nor Kaltenbrunner was in von Ribbentrop's office. The SS officer led von Heurten-Mitnitz to von Ribbentrop's private dining room, a long, narrow room overlooking the interior garden. Its view was not unlike the one from von Heurten-Mitnitz's office, two floors above and a hundred feet south.

"My dear Helmut," von Ribbentrop said, turning to von Heurten-Mitnitz. "I'm so glad you were free."

He walked to him and offered his hand. He was an average-size man, with most of his brown hair, but there was a pallor to his skin that did not look healthy. His grip was firm, but that seemed an affectation.

"It was very good of you to ask me," von Heurten-Mitnitz said.

"You know the General, of course."

In fact, von Heurten-Mitnitz had never been formally introduced to Kaltenbrunner.

"Good to see you again, General," von Heurten-Mitnitz said. Kaltenbrunner crushed von Heurten-Mitnitz's hand in his massive, scarred hand.

"I always come when invited," Kaltenbrunner said. "Ribbentrop has the best chef in Berlin."

The long, polished mahogany table would have accommodated twenty people, but only three places had been set. Crisp, starched white place mats had been laid at one end. And there were long-stemmed crystal glasses, an impressive battery of sterling silverware with a swastika embossed on the handles, and elaborately folded napkins stood up on large, white, gold-rimmed plates.

Five hundred yards from here, von Heurten-Mitnitz thought, *as well as all over Germany, people are going hungry.*

A tall, good-looking SS trooper, with starched white jacket replacing his uniform tunic, walked over and offered a tray holding three cut-crystal glasses.

"An aperitif is always in order, I think," von Ribbentrop said. "In this case, I asked for Slivovitz"—Hungarian pear brandy. "Under the circumstances, I thought it appropriate."

Well, that explains it. I am to be ordered to the embassy in Budapest. Because I've hinted I want to be assigned there? Or because my brother has suggested it? Or simply because I am a minister who has lost his portfolio and there is an appropriate vacancy in Budapest? But why the private luncheon? And what does Kaltenbrunner have to do with it?

They each took a glass.

"The Führer," Kaltenbrunner intoned solemnly, and von Heurten-Mitnitz and von Ribbentrop parroted the toast.

"I've been telling the general," von Ribbentrop said, "about the report you've been preparing for the Führer. Coming along with it, are you?"

Ah, the report. Is that just a loose end to be tied up before I go? Or is it the reason I am going?

"I'm beginning to see the end," von Heurten-Mitnitz said.

"Then we'll move you at a propitious moment," von Ribbentrop said, and then interrupted himself. "Why don't we sit down?"

"That report sounds like one of Goebbels's 'anger-events,'" Kaltenbrunner said. An "anger-event" was a German coinage of Kaltenbrunner's own devising.

"General?" von Heurten-Mitnitz asked.

"The general theorizes," von Ribbentrop said, "and he may well be right, that Dr. Goebbels believes that the Führer is at his best when he is angry. Consequently, the good doctor tries to schedule at least three events a week that are sure to anger our Führer."

"And that report of yours would be one of them," Kaltenbrunner said. "As far as I'm concerned, the less said to the Führer about either Africa or the French, the better."

Two good-looking, blond young SS troopers came into the room. One pushed an exquisite wheeled serving cart. He placed it beside Kaltenbrunner, so that the second could ladle mushroom soup from a silver tureen into Kaltenbrunner's plate. Then the cart was moved to von Heurten-Mitnitz, and he was served, and finally to von Ribbentrop. Afterward, one of the waiters poured wine, a '37 Bernkastler.

"So far as my report is concerned, General," von Heurten-Mitnitz said, "'Mine' as the British said as they rode into the valley at Balaklava."

Kaltenbrunner chuckled, and von Ribbentrop looked puzzled.

"'Theirs not to reason why, theirs but to do and die,'" Kaltenbrunner furnished.

"How droll," von Ribbentrop said, moving on to cover his failure to catch the wit. "Helmut, we're going to have, I fear, some trouble with our Hungarian friends. It has been suggested that you be sent down there to see what you can do about it. The general and I would like to hear how you feel about that."

"That would depend, Herr Reichsminister," von Heurten-Mitnitz said.

"Depend?" Kaltenbrunner interrupted.

"On the nature of the trouble and whether or not I could do some good. Or do you just want me out of the way so my report on the French won't reach the Führer?"

Kaltenbrunner snorted. Joachim von Ribbentrop looked at him to see whether he was amused or angry. When he saw him smiling, Ribbentrop laughed.

"The nature of the trouble is spelled Horthy," Kaltenbrunner said, referring to the regent of Hungary.

Helmut von Heurten-Mitnitz raised his eyebrows.

"I would spell it Hungarian," von Ribbentrop said, "rather than single the admiral out. The Hungarians are having second thoughts about their alliance with us."

"If the question is out of line, please forgive me," von Heurten-Mitnitz said. "But is there anything concrete?"

"Yes, there is," Kaltenbrunner said. He stopped and looked at von Ribbentrop. "Is there any reason I shouldn't discuss Voronezh[1]?"

Joachim von Ribbentrop shook his head.

"For hundreds of years, von Heurten-Mitnitz, the Hungarians have been

---

[1]In January 1943, a 200,000-man Hungarian force had been routed by the Russians at Voronezh. There had been relatively few casualties, and a successful withdrawal had been made, but the Hungarians had lost essentially all of the tanks, artillery, and other weapons.

splendid fighters. Under the Austro-Hungarian empire, of course. One would presume that equipped with the very latest German equipment, they would be able to at least hold their own against the Russians."

He then delivered, dispassionately, a rather detailed report of Hungarian reluctance to engage the Russians at Voronezh, down to the numbers of tanks and cannon lost to the enemy.

"And I am unable to believe," Kaltenbrunner concluded, "and Ribbentrop agrees with me, that their senior officers would have acted as they did, except on orders from Horthy. Or someone very close to Horthy. With his blessing, so to speak."

Helmut von Heurten-Mitnitz said what was expected of him: "Then the officers should be shot, and the men forced back into the line."

"The Führer believes that would be unwise," von Ribbentrop said. "He believes that when the Hungarians come to understand that the alternative to an alliance with Germany is not neutrality and peace but enslavement by the Bolsheviks, they will fight in keeping with their warriors' tradition."

"Perhaps he's right," von Heurten-Mitnitz said.

"And perhaps he isn't," Kaltenbrunner said. Helmut von Heurten-Mitnitz was surprised at Kaltenbrunner's bluntness. Only a few men would dare to suggest that Adolf Hitler erred. "That's where you would come in, von Heurten-Mitnitz."

"I don't quite understand," von Heurten-Mitnitz said.

"Reichsmarschall Göring, Dr. Goebbels, and some others are going to Budapest to reason with Admiral Horthy," von Ribbentrop said. "And there is no doubt that they will return with a renewed pledge of allegiance from Horthy. And a new ambassador will be appointed. Inasmuch as Göring and Goebbels will appoint him—and not from the ranks of professionals, Helmut, since we bumblers have obviously failed to do what we were supposed to do—I rather doubt that he will report that the Hungarians have resumed trying to save their skins the minute Göring and Goebbels turn their backs."

"Forgive me if I seem to be jumping ahead, but if I were there, I wouldn't be believed, either."

"Not by those two, of course not," von Ribbentrop said. "No more than you were believed when you raised the alarm about an American invasion of North Africa."

"But the Führer would," Kaltenbrunner said. "Once we remind him that you are the man that no one listened to about North Africa."

"I see," von Heurten-Mitnitz said. He understood their reasoning, and understood, too, that doing what they asked was a good way to get himself shot.

"What I'm going to do, Helmut," von Ribbentrop said, "is make you first secretary of the Embassy. You have the rank for the job, and the experience. There will be no objection from any quarter. And then you do exactly what you did in Morocco. Except that you send your thoughts directly to me. This time, they will not be ignored. I will share them with the general, and when the time is ripe, we will take them to the Führer."

"It would make my position vis-à-vis the ambassador difficult," von Heurten-Mitnitz protested.

"Germany's position, von Heurten-Mitnitz, is difficult," Kaltenbrunner said.

"Your man in Morocco, General," von Heurten-Mitnitz said, "Standartenführer Müller, was very valuable to me there. It would be helpful—"

"He's yours," Kaltenbrunner said.

"Then I can only say I am flattered and humbled by the responsibility you are giving me."

"People like ourselves," von Ribbentrop said slowly, as if to emphasize the inarguable truth of his words, "for centuries have been called upon to assume greater responsibility for Germany."

And then von Ribbentrop stepped on von Heurten-Mitnitz's toe.

Startled, he looked at him.

"Sorry, my dear fellow," von Ribbentrop said. "I was reaching for the damned call button. I didn't want anyone in the room during that part of the conversation."

And immediately the two handsome young SS troopers appeared, this time bearing medallions of veal in a lemon butter sauce, and potatoes Anna, and *haricots verts*.

When he returned to his office, he told Fräulein Schermann that he did not wish to be disturbed by anyone less important than the Reichsminister himself. Now he really needed time to think, to come out of the surreal dream.

It wasn't only his new assignment, or the elegant meal, or the realization that as an American agent he had just been assured of the trust of the Reichsminister for Foreign Affairs and the head of the SS:

He had attended a reception at the Argentine Embassy the night before.

When he had retrieved his hat and coat from the checkroom and put his hand in the pocket, there was a postcard there that hadn't been there before he went into the embassy.

He had to wait until he reached home to have a good look at it.

It was a black-and-white drawing of a church in Budapest, specifically of St. Ann's Church on the Vizivaros, the flatland between the river and Castle Hill in Buda.

The address was smudged and illegible, but the message was clear, even under the purple censor's stamp:

"Hope to see you and F. and G. Here very soon. Will call. Fondly, Eric."

It had taken a moment before he was sure what it meant. But it was really very clear. He was expected to somehow get Friedrich Dyer and his daughter Gisella from Marburg to St. Ann's Church in Budapest. Someone would call and tell him when.

Fulmar himself? Or was "Eric" just identification?

And why did the Americans want Dyer? What did he know that justified all this effort and risk? And where would he—or Müller—find travel documents for these people?

Now, what had seemed almost impossible seemed to be impossibly easy. Both he and Müller could simply load the Dyers into Müller's car. No one was going to stop a car carrying an SS-SD Standartenführer and the newly appointed First Secretary of the German Embassy.

He seriously considered that he was indeed dreaming, and bit his knuckle to see if he could wake himself up.

His interoffice telephone buzzed.

"Forgive me, Herr Minister," Fräulein Schermann said, "but Herr Standartenführer Müller is here and insists on seeing you."

"Ask the Standartenführer to please come in, Fräulein Schermann," von Heurten-Mitnitz said.

As Müller came through the door, the air raid sirens began to wail.

[FOUR]
MATS Departing Passenger Terminal
Croydon Field, London
21 January 1943

When Captain the Duchess Stanfield tried to follow Captain James M. B. Whittaker past the clerk who was checking orders and travel authority, an Air Corps military police sergeant stepped in front of her.

"Sorry, ma'am," he said, "passengers only beyond the checkpoint."

Captain the Duchess Stanfield, her face stricken, stared at the back of Captain Whittaker as he turned a corner and disappeared from sight, then glanced over her shoulder at Dick Canidy, who stood with Ann Chambers and Agnes Draper just outside the building. They had said their good-byes to Whittaker in the car so that Jim and the Duchess could have a couple of minutes alone inside the building.

Canidy walked quickly to her. When he saw Whittaker disappear from sight, his eyes teared and a painful tightness caught his throat.

"What's the trouble, Sergeant?" Canidy said, his voice unnaturally high-pitched.

"Passengers only in the waiting room, sir," the MP said.

Canidy reached into the pocket of his tunic and came out with a small leather wallet. He showed it to the sergeant.

"It'll be all right for the captain to go into the waiting room," he said.

The MP sergeant had been shown samples of OSS credentials, but he had never actually seen the real thing. He was impressed, but not enough.

"I'm sorry, Major," he said, "but that won't pass you or the captain past here."

"Well, then, goddammit, Sergeant, you just take your pistol out and shoot us in the back. We're going in there," Canidy said, taking the Duchess's arm and pushing past the sergeant.

The sergeant's face flushed with anger. He didn't draw his pistol, nor try to physically restrain either the major with the OSS credentials or the English woman captain. He trotted across the room to find the terminal officer to tell him what had happened.

The two of them walked quickly into the room where the departing passengers milled around while the passenger manifest was typed. That was the last step before the aircraft would be loaded, the final sorting of priorities to determine who would go and who would have to wait for the next flight.

When the terminal officer found them, the OSS major and the English woman captain were standing with an Air Corps captain and two RAF officers, one of them an air vice marshal, and a group commander. The terminal officer laid a hand on the MP sergeant's arm. An air vice marshal was the British equivalent of a lieutenant general. It was better not to make waves when three stars were involved.

"Forgive me, Your Grace," the air vice marshal said, "but I flatter myself to think of the Duke as an old friend. Has there been word?"

"No," Captain the Duchess Stanfield said, "not a thing, I'm sorry to say."

"He'll turn up," the air vice marshal said. "You'll see. Stout fellow, the Duke. Resourceful."

"Yes," Captain the Duchess Stanfield said, looking at Captain James M. B. Whittaker.

The subject of a husband missing in action was a bit awkward. The air vice marshal changed the subject.

"I gather you're not going with us, Major?" he said to Canidy.

"No," Canidy said, somewhat curtly.

"And how far are you going, Captain—Whittaker, was it?"

"All the way to Brisbane," Whittaker said.

"Well, we'll be with you as far as New Delhi," the air vice marshal said.

"That'll be nice," Whittaker said, looking into the Duchess's eyes. "Maybe we can play cards or something."

"Let me have your attention, please," the clerk at the manifest desk said into a public address system microphone. "We are about to load the aircraft. The way the manifest is made up is by priority, not by rank, so pay attention, please. When I call your name, call out, pick up your hand luggage, go to the door, check the manifest to see that we've got the name, rank, and serial number right, and then go get on the aircraft."

"It would seem," the air vice marshal said, "that we are, in that charming American phrase, about to 'get the show on the road.'"

"Whittaker, James M. B., Captain, Army Air Corps," the public address speaker boomed.

"Yo!" Whittaker called out.

He looked at Canidy and then at Captain the Duchess Stanfield.

"God go with you, Captain Whittaker," Captain the Duchess Stanfield said, offering her hand.

"Thank you for seeing me off," Captain Whittaker said as he shook her hand.

"Don't be silly, Captain," the Duchess Stanfield said. "And let us hear from you."

"Of course," Whittaker said, and finally let her hand go. Captain the Duchess Stanfield came to almost a position of attention, her face rigid.

"Well, Dick—" Whittaker said. His voice sounded very strained.

Canidy said, "Try not to fly into a rock-filled cloud," and then he put his arms around Whittaker and hugged him, and whispered, "If anyone even looks cockeyed at her, I'll slice his balls off."

Whittaker broke the embrace.

"You do that, Major, sir," he said. And then he picked up his bags and proceeded to board the aircraft.

Canidy took Captain the Duchess Stanfield's arm, and they marched in almost a military manner out of the passenger terminal.

Sergeant Agnes Draper, WRAC, when she saw them coming, opened the rear door of the Packard.

"I'll drive, Agnes," Canidy said, motioning with his head for her to move to the back with the Duchess. He got behind the wheel and threw the lever that raised the glass divider. Ann Chambers slipped in beside him.

"Rough?" she asked.

"There was an old buddy of the Duke's in there," Canidy said. "What they got to do was shake hands."

"Oh, *God!*" Ann said.

"Stiff upper lip and all that crap," Canidy said.

"Why don't we take her someplace? Would that help?"

"I have other plans," Canidy said.

"Oh, really?" Ann snapped.

Canidy looked over at her.

"I'm now going to find Fulmar," he said, "and tell him what interesting things we have planned to keep him from getting bored."

"Like what?" Ann asked. And then she understood. She reached over and took his hand. "I guess I'm a selfish bitch, after all," she said. "I was just thinking, better him than you."

XIII

David Bruce was forced to admit that Dick Canidy's grasp of problems and his imaginative solutions to them were on a par with his own. Yet Canidy allowed emotion to enter into decisions, and he was prone to make them on his own authority, almost impulsively.

Canidy, for instance, had just now told Bruce that he had taken it upon himself to tell Fulmar *all* the details of the Dyer operation.

Fulmar should have been told no more than he had to know. What he needed to know was that he was about to be put inside Germany. What he was to do there was to be explained later.

Bruce could only guess what Canidy had actually said to Fulmar, but according to Canidy himself, he had told Fulmar that for reasons he himself did not know, it was important to bring Professor Friedrich Dyer out of Germany, via Hungary and Yugoslavia, that Helmut von Heurten-Mitnitz and Müller were involved, and that when they reached the island of Vis, he would be there with the B-25 to pick them all up.

In an operational sense, the worst thing Canidy had done was tell Fulmar that he would be given a Q pill in case things went wrong. The Q pill was actually a tiny glass vial containing cyanide. It caused almost instant death when crushed between the teeth.

The Q pill was absolutely the last thing on an agent's checklist. Agents wondered enough about getting caught without being reminded that the OSS was obligingly providing a Q pill just in case. Fulmar would now have a full ten days to dwell on the subject.

And until he actually crossed the German border, Fulmar had the unspoken right to change his mind. Someone else would be sent in, of course, but it would take at least two weeks—and very probably much longer—to recruit and train him. And he would not be as qualified as Fulmar, obviously; and besides, the schedule of events in Germany, Budapest, and Yugoslavia could not be put on hold.

"For God's sake, Dick," Bruce asked, trying to keep his temper under control, "why did you get into the Q pill with him?"

"Maybe, David," Canidy said, unrepentant, "I was hoping he would tell us to go fuck ourselves," Canidy said.

"He still may," Bruce said. "Presumably you've thought of that?"

"He'll go," Canidy said. "Ol' Wild Bill is very good at recruiting people who will put their head in the lion's mouth for God, Mother, and Apple Pie."

Bruce stilled his reply at the last moment. Canidy was one of those who'd had his head in the lion's mouth.

"Where is he now?" Bruce asked.

"He went to see his mother," Canidy said.

"He did what?" Bruce asked, incredulously.

"He went to see his mother," Canidy repeated.

"I don't think that was a very good idea," Bruce said, aware that it was a marvel of understatement.

"Neither do I," Canidy said. "But he decided that he wanted to see her, and I decided that it wasn't any of my business, our business."

"From his dossier," David Bruce said, "I would have thought—God, she has treated him like dirt from the moment he was born—I would have thought he would never want to see her."

"You can kick dogs, David," Canidy said, "and a lot of the time they keep coming back, hoping maybe this time you'll scratch their ears."

"Where is this touching reunion to take place?" Bruce asked after a moment.

"Her troupe is doing a show at Wincanton. I sent him up there—with Fine—in the Packard. Fine knows her. He'll be able to handle anything that might come up."

"You hope," Bruce said.

"'Hope springs eternal in the human breast,'" Canidy quoted. "You ever hear that, David?"

"I think that will be all, Dick," David Bruce said. "If anything unusual comes up, I'll expect you to let me know."

[TWO]
Wincanton Air Corps Base
Kent, England
2330 Hours
21 January 1943

Captain Stanley S. Fine and Lieutenant Eric Fulmar got lost on the way to Wincanton, despite a map Fine had the OSS Motor Officer make up for him.

So it was late, nearly half past eleven, when they finally made it to the Wincanton Air Base Officers' Club, an old stone barn jammed full of the drunken aviators who had come to be entertained by the fifteen or twenty young women in Monica Sinclair's USO troupe.

As they made their way to where Monica was whooping it up with a handful of the base's brass, Eric attracted her attention. His pink and green uniform, with the paratrooper patch sewn on his overseas cap, stood out from the way most of the Air Corps men were dressed, in leather flight jackets.

And then Fine saw in her eyes and in her smile that she was more than a little drunk, and knew there was going to be trouble.

Stanley S. Fine had never liked Monica Sinclair. Some of the dislike sprang from the way she had treated Eric—storing him out of sight like a piece of furniture that didn't fit in with her present décor but couldn't be thrown out with the trash because it was a gift from someone important.

But as Fine gazed at her now, and she looked at him with recognition dawning in her eyes, he realized that his dislike wasn't based just on principle: He despised her personally. The phrase in the industry was that she believed her own press releases. But that was too simple. She wasn't the only one guilty of that, certainly. But Monica Sinclair not only believed she was truly "America's Sweetheart," she was convinced that anyone who didn't believe it was her enemy.

That belief meant that "America's Sweetheart" deserved to have her every wish indulged. Shooting schedules never called for her to appear before half past nine in the morning. She was not at her best before that. Her dressing-room trailer was a Taj Mahal on wheels. And she checked other dressing-room trailers to make sure no lesser star had a better one than she did.

Max Liebermann had not officially given her cast control, but everyone knew she could be counted on to come down with an incapacitating migraine if she found on the set another actress who did not look at least five years older than she did.

When neither fans nor motion picture columnists were around, "America's Sweetheart" had a mouth like a sewer. That, too, was not unusual. Max Liebermann theorized that actresses used foul language the way infants used crying. But Monica Sinclair's foul tongue was legendary.

"Look who the fucking cat drug in!" Monica Sinclair exclaimed when she was sure it was indeed Stanley S. Fine swimming across the room in her direction.

She shrugged free of some arm that was around her shoulder and took two steps toward Fine.

"You were supposed to meet me in London, you asshole!" she said.

Some officer who had been looking down the front of her USO uniform now directed his somewhat drunken attention to Fine.

"Duty called, Monica," Fine said. "I came as soon as I could get away."

"Bet your sweet ass you did," Monica said. Then she put her hands on his neck, pulled his face down to hers, and kissed him wetly, loudly, and with a tongue probing in his mouth.

Her eyes then fell on Eric. And they lit up. For a moment, Fine thought there was recognition. But then, with a sinking feeling in his stomach, he knew that what had made her eyes bright was not maternal affection.

"And did Stanley bring you for me?" she asked.

Eric nodded.

"Fine, you prick," Monica Sinclair said, "all is forgiven." She snaked her arms around Eric's neck, pulled his face to hers, and kissed him open-mouthed. Then she rubbed her body lasciviously against him. It took a moment before Eric was able to push her away, his face showing shock and revulsion.

She stared at him, then turned to Fine.

"Stanley, who is this fucking fairy, anyway?"

Fine had seen the horror on Eric's face.

"Why, this is Lieutenant Eric Fulmar, Monica," he said. "Remember him?"

That set off a violent gust of obscenity: If this is your fucking kike idea of a fucking joke, and so on. Screams followed: When she told Max what he had done to her, he had fucking well better pray he got killed in the war, because he was through in the fucking industry.

At that point, an officious Special Services officer appeared, demanding to know just who they were and what in the name of Christ they had said to Miss Sinclair.

"This officer, Major," Fine said, "is Miss Sinclair's son."

The Special Services officer looked at Fine with dismay and loathing in his eyes.

"I can't even imagine why you would wish to embarrass Miss Sinclair this way, Captain," he said. "But that is the sickest joke I have ever heard."

"What's sick about it is that it's not a joke," Fine said.

"You two will leave the club immediately!"

Eric spoke for the first time.

"Piss off," he said contemptuously. Then he looked directly at his mother. "Hi, Mommy!" he said cheerfully. "Long time no see!"

"You ungrateful shit!" she hissed.

"Mommy!" Eric said, as if he were a little boy crushed by an unjust accusation.

Monica put her hands over her ears and howled.

The piercing shriek silenced the room.

Still holding her hands over her ears, Monica Sinclair screamed, "Get him the fuck out of here!"

The Special Services officer, carried away with righteousness, put his hand on Eric's arm and tried to pull him away. Fine called out a warning. He knew that trying such a move with Eric was foolish under any circumstances, but under these it was suicidal. Eric Fulmar's jaws were working, and there were tears in his eyes.

With blinding speed, Fulmar struck the Special Services officer on the bridge of his nose with the heel of his hand. Fine was familiar with the blow. He had learned it from the Berbers in Morocco and had taught it to Jim Whittaker, who, as a result of his own Philippine experience, was the OSS's acknowledged master of lethal hand-to-hand combat. Whittaker, in turn, had taught it to the English experts at Station X. Its effectiveness had awed even the highly skilled assassins of the SOE.

Blood gushed from the flack's eye sockets and his nostrils, and he fell screaming to the floor.

The other Air Corps officers in the room, as if in slow motion, slowly realized what was happening and came to the defense of the man screaming on the floor.

A large captain, with the massive neck and shoulders of a football player, advanced warily on Fulmar. And Eric, his eyes narrow, seemed to be matter-of-factly considering the best way to put him down.

"Eric," Fine shouted, "for Christ's sake, no!"

For a moment there was no response, but then, as if he were waking up, Fulmar looked over his shoulder at Fine, and then at the man on the floor, and then back at Fine. Sadness was now in his eyes.

"Shit," he said.

[THREE]

"I don't give a damn what this says, frankly, Colonel," the Air Corps colonel commanding Wincanton Air Corps Base said as he handed Lt. Colonel Edmund T. Stevens's OSS identity card back to him, "my flight surgeon tells me the officer your man struck is liable to lose an eye, and I'm not about to sweep this under the rug."

"Colonel," Stevens said, "if you question my authority, please call General Smith at SHAEF."

"Bedell Smith?" the Air Corps colonel asked. Stevens nodded. "I'm not going to call anyone, Colonel. I'm the base commander. This is my responsibility."

"Then I will call him," Stevens said.

Somewhat contemptuously, the Air Corps colonel waved at his telephone.

"Thank you," Stevens said politely. He picked up the telephone. "Get me London military two zero zero five, please," he said, glancing as he spoke toward Stanley Fine, who was sitting next to a wall trying to be invisible.

A direct order from Eisenhower's deputy, the second-ranking American officer in England, was enough for the Air Corps colonel to release Lieutenant Fulmar into the custody of Colonel Stevens, but it did nothing to assuage his anger.

"Just for the record, Colonel," he said to Stevens, "this isn't the end of this. I'm going to bring charges—it's assault upon a superior commissioned officer—and if this lieutenant of yours isn't tried, I'm damned sure going to find out why."

"I deeply regret this incident, Colonel," Stevens said.

"You damned well should, Colonel," the Air Corps colonel said.

And then he left them in order to order Fulmar released from the base stockade.

"I deeply regret this incident, Colonel," Fine said when they were alone. "I feel responsible for it."

Stevens looked at him.

"You know what I was just thinking, Stan?" he asked, and went on without waiting for a reply. "We're training people, by the hundreds, to . . . use their hands the way Fulmar did. What's going to happen five, ten years from now? When the war is over? In barrooms when they get drunk? In bedrooms when they are provoked?"

"I said, sir, that I feel responsible," Fine said.

"No more than I am," Stevens said. "Canidy told me you were going to bring him here. I didn't stop him. And there's something else. Maybe I'm being perverted by all this. I would like to think it's out of character for me to think this way, but the unpleasant truth is that when I called Bedell Smith, I was angry. Not at Fulmar, but at the damned fool who laid his hands on him and caused all this inconvenience."

"What am I to do with him when we get him back?" Fine asked.

Stevens's eyebrows rose as he considered the question.

"Under the circumstances, I think you should do with him what Dick would do with him," he said finally. "Go out and get drunk with him."

The Air Corps colonel appeared with Fulmar a few minutes later.

"I'm sorry about this, Colonel," Fulmar said.

"So am I, Eric," Colonel Stevens said.

"How's the guy I hit?" Fulmar asked.

"He's probably going to lose an eye," the Air Corps colonel said, "and I, Lieutenant, intend to see that you are brought before a court-martial."

"I'm sorry," Eric said. "I'm really sorry."

"Sorry won't wash, Lieutenant," the colonel said. "I'm going to do whatever is necessary to take that bar off your collar and put you in the stockade."

Colonel Stevens gestured for Fine and Fulmar to precede him out of the room.

When Fine and Fulmar reached the Dorchester, where Canidy, at Stevens's order, was waiting for them, it was long after hours and the bar was closed.

There was nevertheless the sound of voices and feminine laughter behind the door. Fine knocked, and a bartender quickly let them in.

Canidy was inside, by himself. Fine wondered where Ann Chambers was.

The Scorpion was there with the usual crowd of young officers hovering close to her. Her eyes lit up at the sight of Fulmar.

"What happened?" Canidy asked when they sat down beside him.

"The colonel had to call Bedell Smith to get him turned loose," Fine said. Canidy shook his head.

"They're going to court-martial me. I put a guy's eye out," Fulmar said.

They're not going to court-martial you. You could have put Bedell Smith's eye out, and they wouldn't court-martial you. Not now.

"You're leaving town just in time, then, aren't you?" Canidy said.

The Scorpion came over.

"And where have you two been all night?" she asked. She slipped into a chair facing Eric.

"As a matter of fact, they've been out carousing," Canidy said. "Whiskey, wild women, brawling. That sort of thing."

"That sounds terribly *naughty*," the Scorpion said.

"If I asked you a question," Fulmar said to her, "could I get an honest answer?"

She leaned forward across the table and ran her fingernails across the back of his hand.

"You can ask me anything you want, darling," she said. "Whether you get an—"

"Have you got someplace we could go?" Eric interrupted. "Or would you rather we stayed here and groped each other?"

"Don't be a bastard, darling," she said, stiffening. "I've never done anything to you."

"The question, then, is do you want to? And if so, where?" Canidy said.

The Scorpion angrily flashed her eyes at Canidy and then moved them to Fulmar.

He stood up and walked to the door, then turned and looked back at the table.

"Opportunity knocks but once," Canidy said.

"Fuck you, Canidy," the Scorpion said. He laughed, and she glowered at him. Then she got up and went to Fulmar.

She put her hand on his arm and turned.

"Good night, everybody!" she cried.

It pleased her, Fine saw, to have the world know that she had sunk her stinger into the plumpest baby rabbit of them all.

"Do you think there will be anything left?" Canidy asked. "By that, I mean, when she has sucked him dry, will she also eat the empty shell?"

"It was pretty bad with his mother, Dick," Fine said.

"I was afraid it would be," Canidy said. "Going to see her was not a good idea."

"I'm not sure his going with the Scorpion is such a good idea, either," Fine said.

"Well, you know what Benjamin Franklin said about older women," Canidy said. " 'They don't yell, they don't swell, and they're grateful as hell.' "

Fine laughed. "Franklin didn't say that."

"What is it you ambulance-chasers say? 'Or words to that effect'?"

Fine chuckled again.

"I was going to run her off," Canidy said. "But then I had a sudden insight. I think she's just what he needs tonight. Now, what can I do for you?"

"What?"

"I hate to send any of my loyal legion into the mouth of death without getting them a farewell live-today-for-tomorrow-we-die piece of ass. How does yonder redhead strike your fancy?"

Fine laughed. "I'm going to the U.S. Embassy in Bern," he said.

"First," Canidy said.

Fine smiled.

"Thank you, sir, but no thank you, sir. I am one of the few surviving members of that rara avis, 'faithful husband.' "

Canidy chuckled. "Is that what love is, Stanley, not wanting to fuck anybody else?"

Fine sensed that it was a serious question.

"You can look, but not touch," he said. "They call it fidelity."

"Then I must have caught it," Canidy said.

"Maybe you're coming down with a cold," Fine said.

"Screw you," Canidy said fondly.

[FOUR]
Fersfield Army Air Corps Station
Bedfordshire, England
29 January 1943

Lt. Commander Edwin W. Bitter was torn between annoyance and pleasure when he saw the Packard limousine bouncing directly across the airfield—rather than taking the access road or even the taxiway—toward the ancient B-17. He could see Sergeant Agnes Draper behind the wheel. That was fine. But there were two others in the backseat, two officers with the golden United States eagle on their caps. One of them was almost certainly Canidy, and the other more than likely Stanley S. Fine.

He'd suspected Canidy would show up, and that he would probably bring Fine with him. Fine was, after all, a former B-17 squadron commander with far more time in seventeens than either Joe Kennedy or Dolan. He was even, Bitter recalled now, a rated Instructor Pilot.

But when Agnes parked beside the sandbag revetment where the B-17 sat, Pete Douglass, not Fine, emerged from the Packard.

"Anchors aweigh, you-all," Douglass called out. Then Dolan and Joe Kennedy also appeared from inside the B-17. "And who is this booze-nosed old salt all dressed up to go flying?" Douglass asked.

"Why," Dolan said, chuckling, "I thought the major knew Lieutenant Kennedy." And then he corrected himself. "'The colonel,' that is. When did that happen?"

"Yesterday," Douglass said. "It will not be necessary for you to prostrate yourself. Kissing my hand will suffice."

"Congratulations, Pete," Bitter said. "Well deserved."

"Don't get carried away," Douglass said, suddenly bitter. "Eighth Air Force has a regulation. Lose half your command on a dumb mission, but come back yourself, and you get promoted."

"You were promoted because you deserved it," Bitter insisted loyally.

"Good morning," Agnes Draper said as she walked up to them.

"Good morning, Sergeant," Bitter said.

"Oh, what a tangled web we weave," Canidy quoted as he shook Dolan's and Kennedy's hand, "whene'er we try to deceive."

Bitter glowered at him. Agnes Draper showed no reaction at all.

"The radio types aren't here?" Canidy asked.

"Inside," Dolan said, jerking his thumb up at the B-17. "You want to have a look?"

"Yeah," Canidy said. "And so does the colonel. I figured maybe he'd see something we don't."

"Christ," Douglass said, looking up at the B-17. "Will this fugitive from the boneyard actually fly?"

It was less a flippant remark than a statement of fact. The B-17 had been reclaimed from the salvage yard. There were crude patches riveted to the fuselage and wings where it had been struck by antiaircraft and machine-gun fire. Just below the pilot's side window, a shiny new duralumin patch covered about half of the representation of a large-bosomed, scantily dressed female. It cut off her head, one breast, most of the legend—"Miss Twen" was all that was left—and what looked like half of a row of small bombs representing missions.

There were other crude patches fairing over what had been the Plexiglas in the nose and the gun positions in the fuselage. The fuselage and the wings had been painted white. But there had not been enough paint to do the job properly, and what paint there was had been more solvent than pigment.

"This is one of our better ones, Colonel," Joe Kennedy said to Douglass.

"I'd hate to see one of the worst ones," Douglass said.

Kennedy took his arm and led him out to a position on the taxiway that would let them see into the two adjacent revetments. One of them held an even more battered B-17. The other held Canidy's—technically, the OSS's—B-25.

"All we want from them is six hours," Kennedy said. "Just six more hours."

Douglass shook his head and walked back into the revetment. Canidy was no longer in sight. Sergeant Draper pointed up at the battered B-17, and Douglass climbed the aluminum ladder hanging from the fuselage under the nose.

There was barely room for him once he got inside. Four people were crowded into the cockpit area. And the flight engineer's station was packed with mattress covers. Figures, obviously representing weight, were crudely painted on these. Douglass wondered what they were using to duplicate the weight and bulk of the Torpex explosive that would be loaded into the operational aircraft.

He looked back into the fuselage. With its openings faired over, it was dark, except where the sun made beams of light through open rivet holes and unrepaired bullet and shrapnel holes. The fuselage was packed nearly shoulder high with more mattress covers stuffed with whatever they were using to duplicate Torpex.

A tiny Air Corps captain with horn-rimmed glasses was explaining to Canidy the function of the radio-controlled servomechanisms. These, it was hoped, would let the chase plane fly the B-17 by remote control.

"Take a look at this, Doug," Canidy said, and the two sergeants with the captain made room for him the only way they could, by climbing down out of the B-17.

The servomechanisms were simpler than Douglass expected them to be. They were in effect just electric motors whose direction of revolution could be reversed.

"And now let's go see how Captain Allen and his stalwart troops have fucked up my pretty B-25," Canidy said.

The tiny Air Corps captain smiled.

"I told you, Major," he said, "hardly at all. All I had to do was install one long wire antenna to each of the vertical stabilizers. They use the same mount on the fuselage. Unless you look for it, you'd never know it was there."

The three of them examined the B-25 from the outside.

"Okay," Canidy said. "So I won't have to castrate you."

The captain beamed in Canidy's approval. He had been a ham radio operator in civilian life, and the Air Corps had put him in charge of a radio overhaul facility. What he was doing now was right down his alley, and it gave him a feeling of making a real contribution to the war effort.

"Dick," Bitter said, a little uncomfortably, "I had planned to ride with Joe."

"Had you now?" Canidy asked dryly.

"I want to take notes," Bitter said, more than a little lamely. "Joe will have his hands full flying it."

"And who was going to fly the remote control?" Canidy said.

"Dolan," Bitter said.

"And who was going to fly my B-25?"

"There's half a dozen people checked out in it," Bitter said.

"And if something goes wrong, how do you plan to get out of the seventeen with your stiff knee?" Canidy asked.

"I can get out of it," Bitter said.

"What we'll do is send the colonel to take notes," Canidy said.

"In a pig's ass you will," Douglass said. "I'm not going up in that flying junk heap."

"In that case, Eddie, okay," Canidy said. "We about ready to go?"

"Anytime," Bitter said.

"Captain Allen, would you like to ride in the B-25?" Canidy asked.

"It might be a good idea if I did, sir," the tiny captain said, visibly thrilled at the prospect.

"Maybe we better get you on flight pay," Canidy said. "You're the only one around here who seems to know what he's doing."

Canidy's good at that, Douglass thought. *He's made this pint-size radio genius feel ten feet tall.*

Douglass followed Canidy and Dolan in their walk-around preflight of the B-25, and then motioned Captain Allen ahead of him into the B-25. He strapped himself into one of the four airline passenger chairs Canidy had had installed in the back, telling himself that's what he was on this flight, a passenger. But then curiosity got the better of him, and he went forward to the cockpit as the engines were started.

Dolan, in the pilot's seat, held an aluminum box with a Bakelite cover in his lap. The box was connected to the radio panel by a thick cable running along the deck. The box was obviously the remote control system controls. But there were only toggle switches. Douglass had expected a joystick.

It seemed impossible to believe that an airplane as large as the B-17 could be controlled by something so simple.

Captain Allen handed Douglass a set of earphones. He put them on in time to hear Canidy call the tower and request taxi and takeoff permission.

[FIVE]
The Swiss-German Border
0905 Hours
29 January 1943

The train that rolled slowly to a stop in Lörrach, just across the border from Basel, was the first train that Unterinspektor Lorin Wahl of the Geheime

Staatspolizei had been directed to examine on his own, without supervision.

Wahl was tall, slender, and blond-haired. His face was scarred with acne and his skin was pale. And his prominent eyes were pale blue. Lorin Wahl had been born in Munich in 1918 to a working-class family. He had joined the National Socialist Transportation Corps at sixteen, anticipating a career in either truck or rail transportation. Later, his father, who had early on joined the National Socialist German Workers' Party and was then employed in the administrative offices of the Gauleiter for Schwabing, had enough influence with the Gauleiter himself to arrange that his son be taken on by the Bavarian State Police.

It was not anticipated by either of them that he would actually become a policeman, but Lorin Wahl did extraordinarily well in the basic police school; and when an administrative bulletin came down from Berlin directing the recruitment into the Gestapo of promising young police cadets, he was immediately thought of. He was not only undeniably Aryan, but his father was in that now-esteemed group of National Socialist Party members known as the *"Unterfünftausender."* His Party card carried a number below five thousand.

At nineteen, Lorin had become a Railway Police Cadet, his records indicating that he was a candidate for the Gestapo. He took a number of courses designed both to train him as an investigator and to convince him that the entire fate of the Third Reich depended on the vigilance of the Gestapo.

At the age of twenty-two, he was assigned as a probationer to the Gestapo office in Dresden, where he worked for twelve months under the close supervision of experienced inspectors, met their approval, and took a final examination.

A week after his twenty-third birthday, he was notified of his appointment (subject to a year's satisfactory performance) as an Unterinspektor of the Gestapo and issued a Walther PPk .32 ACP semiautomatic pistol and the credentials of his profession. These consisted of an identification card (bearing his photograph and the signature of Heinrich Himmler himself) and the Gestapo identity disk, an elliptical piece of cast aluminum bearing the Seal of State and his serial number.

The disk announced that the bearer possessed: authority to arrest anyone without specification of charges, immunity from arrest (except by other officers of the Gestapo), and superior police powers over all other law-enforcement agencies. Illegal possession of the Gestapo identity disk was a capital offense, and loss of his disk by a member of the Gestapo was punishable by immediate dismissal.

On his appointment, Lorin Wahl was transferred from Dresden to the Stuttgart Regional Office in Württemberg-Baden, with further detail to Freiburg, twenty-four kilometers from the French border and three times that far by road from Lörrach, the first stop inside Germany for trains inbound from Basel.

He took a small furnished apartment in a pension owned by the mother of one of the other Gestapo officers. It was the first time in his life that he did not have to share a bathroom.

The Kreditanstalt branch bank in Freiburg advanced him the money to purchase an Autounion closed coupé, a nice car, formerly the property of a Jew who had been relocated and had died, according to the records, of complications resulting from an appendectomy at a place called Dachau in Bavaria. Wahl had been told Dachau was a sort of reception center where the Jews were taken for classification before being relocated in the Eastern Territories.

Lorin Wahl was permitted to bill the Freiburg Suboffice of the Gestapo for the expenses involved in the official use of his personal car. The officer-in-charge had informed him that since Gestapo officers were never off duty, anywhere they drove their personal automobiles was on official duty. The payments he received for the use of his car would be more than enough to meet his loan payments.

He was first started out under supervision examining trains crossing the German-Swiss border just the other side of Lörrach. Later, he would be allowed on his own. While most of the travelers in and out would be perfectly respectable Swiss with business in Germany, he was told, there would be people illegally attempting to leave—"and not all of them Jews, Wahl, keep that in mind!"—or to enter Germany. In the latter category would be spies, French, English, and others.

He was instructed to examine identity documents and entrance and exit visas with extraordinary care, and to detain anyone whose documents, or behavior, was not absolutely beyond question.

"It is better, Wahl, to temporarily inconvenience some perfectly respectable businessman than to let an illegal, an enemy of the state, slip through."

After a month of supervised duty, he was finally judged competent to work by himself, as of 28 January.

On the next day, he left his apartment an hour before he really had to, just to make sure that a flat tire or some other mishap would not keep him from meeting the Basel train.

The nominal inspection of the train was a responsibility shared by the Border Police and the Railway Police. The Gestapo was present as much to see that the others did their jobs properly as it was to personally inspect the train and its passengers.

Regulations required that the conductor of every train prepare and furnish a passenger manifest, identifying each passenger by name and listing his or her seat or compartment. Wahl's first duty was to take the manifest and compare it with a list of persons furnished, via Stuttgart, by Berlin. These were people believed by headquarters to be likely to try to leave or enter Germany illegally. He was of course expected to make sure the Border Police searched the passenger manifest for names of people who were fugitive from German law, and whose names were provided by Berlin on a separate list, through regular—as opposed to Gestapo—channels.

But it had been explained to him that he was really looking for people whose names would not be on any list. Spies do not identify themselves.

In the first of the three first-class wagons-lits on the train, something caught Wahl's eye.

There was nothing that he could put his finger on. It was a gut feeling. He had learned in school that gut feelings were not to be dismissed as unprofessional. There was even a proper word for them: intuitive. He had been told that over time he would be able to "intuit" something illegal, to "sense it intuitively."

Something didn't ring true about the young Swiss who was alone in the first-class compartment.

In Wahl's professional judgment, it was unlikely that the young Swiss was a spy, or any other kind of an enemy of the state. He was too young for that; he didn't *look* like a spy. What he was, Wahl thought, was a healthy young man of German blood who because of a line drawn on a map was able to sit safely on the sidelines while his brothers were dying in Russia to protect European culture. And it was entirely likely that in his luggage there would be a dozen or so twenty-one-jewel Swiss watches.

Wahl decided to have a look at the young Swiss's luggage. He would examine it politely, of course, but with more care than the Border Police had examined it. And perhaps ask a few polite questions.

It would be nice, he thought, if he could make an arrest on his very first day of unsupervised duty. And especially nice if it was this "neutral" German-Swiss for smuggling contraband.

He made his way to the first car of the three first-class wagons-lits and, without knocking, slid open the door to the compartment.

The young Swiss was standing up, in the act of putting one of his suitcases on the luggage rack. Or taking one of them down. He looked just a little nervous.

"Guten Tag, mein Herr," Wahl said, correctly. "Passport, please."

"It's already been examined," the young Swiss said, "by the Border Police."

"Passport, please," Wahl said impatiently.

The young Swiss shrugged and took the document from the breast pocket of his suit jacket and handed it over.

Wahl carefully compared the photograph in the passport with the young Swiss's face. It was without question him. He asked the ritual questions, date and place of birth, address, and occupation, and the young Swiss without hesitation replied with answers that matched the information on the passport.

"You're going to Sweden?" Wahl asked.

"That's right."

"What is the nature of your business in Sweden?"

"I can't really see where that's any of your business," the young Swiss replied.

Wahl took his Gestapo identity disk from his pocket and displayed it in the palm of his hand.

"Gestapo, *mein Herr,*" he said. "I decide what is my business."

"I'm an electrical engineer," the young Swiss said. "In the employ of Carl Färber und Söhne. I'm going to our Stockholm office."

Wahl nodded curtly.

"Take your luggage from the rack, please," he said.

"That's been examined, too," the young Swiss said.

"I wish to examine it again," Wahl said.

The young Swiss shrugged. Annoyance was all over his face.

There were three pieces of luggage on the rack.

The young Swiss took them down, one by one, and laid them on the seat. Then, he gestured at them.

"Help yourself," he said.

Wahl opened the first suitcase and felt through its contents carefully. It was thin-sided, so there was no possibility of a hidden compartment. He found nothing in the first suitcase of a suspicious nature.

In the second, he thought he was onto something. In feeling the rolled-up socks, he touched what appeared to be a hard object concealed inside them. He unrolled the socks. It was a small bottle of aftershave lotion.

"You can put those back," Wahl said, and opened the third case.

Lorin Wahl had perhaps two seconds to see that the third case held the uniform of an Obersturmführer SS-SD.

He felt a hand over his eyes, pulling his head back, and then for a brief moment, there was a sharp pain at the base of his neck.

And then he felt nothing at all.

Eric Fulmar and Stanley Fine, equipped with diplomatic passports and in civilian clothing, had traveled to Switzerland by air via Dublin and Lisbon. In Fine's luggage, exempt from customs examination, there had been the equivalent of $10,000 in Reichsmarks; a Swiss passport in the name of Martin Reber; the identification card and travel authorization for SS Obersturmführer Erich von Fulmar, temporarily attached to the staff of the Reichsführer SS in Berlin; and identity cards and travel authority in fictitious names for travel to Budapest for Professor Dyer, Gisella, and Fulmar.

The Reichsmarks and the American passports were genuine. The Swiss passport and the SS-SD identification and travel authority were forgeries. The counterfeit German identity and travel documents were to be used in case von Heurten-Mitnitz could not produce similar documents on his own. Or in case he changed his mind at the last minute and refused to help.

The basic cover story was that Fine and Fulmar were employees of the Department of State who were being sent to the United States Embassy in Bern for duty as consular officers. There was a three-week period (fifteen working days) before newly arrived diplomatic personnel had to present themselves to the Swiss Foreign Ministry.

Subtleties of international law and diplomatic custom were involved: Until they actually presented themselves to the Swiss Foreign Ministry and were issued the identification cards issued to accredited diplomatic personnel, so far as the Swiss were concerned—and even though they would be traveling on diplomatic passports—they would not in fact be accredited diplomatic personnel.

Under the ground rules laid down by the Swiss, who knew full well that there were as many spies and agents in Switzerland as there were in Lisbon or Madrid, Switzerland was not to be used as a transit point by Allied agents with diplomatic status to enter or leave France, Germany, or Italy.

If two Americans with diplomatic status were caught in such activity, they were expelled from Switzerland, and the U.S. Ambassador or chargé d'affaires was handed a note informing him of the Swiss government's regret that owing to the shortages caused by the war, the United States must reduce its diplomatic staff by two individuals.

If there was a reduction in the authorized staff of a Western embassy, there was an equal increase in the staff of an Axis embassy. Or vice versa.

Individuals who were not officially accredited as diplomats were of course liable to prosecution by Swiss authorities if they violated Swiss laws regarding espionage or immigration; but the various ambassadors could not, of course, be held responsible for the actions of their countrymen who were not officially accredited to their embassies.

Upon arrival in Bern aboard a Swiss Air transport, Fine and Fulmar had boarded a railroad train for Zürich. Fine left the train there, taking with him Fulmar's luggage and U.S. diplomatic passport.

Fulmar continued on to Basel, traveling now on the forged Swiss passport with a forged German "traverse only" visa. It had ostensibly been issued to Martin Reber, an electrical engineer in the employ of Carl Färber und Söhne, Zurich, and stated that Reber's purpose was to traverse Germany— meaning without permission to leave the train—en route to Stockholm, where Carl Färber und Söhne, who were manufacturers of electrical timing equipment, maintained an office.

When the train had stopped at Lorrach, just inside the German border, for German customs examination, he found the suitcase that had been placed in his compartment. It held a Freiburg-Kassel railway ticket and the uniform of an SS Obersturmführer.

He would change into the uniform and then dispose of the civilian clothes and Martin Reber's suitcases. Reber's Basel-Stockholm ticket would be burned.

All that would then be necessary would be for Fulmar to leave the train at Marburg an der Lahn and establish contact with Gisella Dyer. From there, Helmut von Heurten-Mitnitz and/or Standartenführer Johann Müller would take over and arrange transportation for Fulmar and the Dyers to Budapest, where they would enter the pipeline.

The best-laid plans of the OSS began falling apart when Unterinspektor Lorin Wahl of the Gestapo decided to see if he could catch the goddamned Swiss doing something, anything, wrong.

XIV

[ONE]
Little Ross Bay
County Kirkcudbright, Scotland
1105 Hours
29 January 1943

Little Ross Bay was near the mouth of the Solway Firth, not far from the English-Scottish border. There wasn't very much on its western shore. No towns, no villages, just one narrow road, and the cliffs. And the cliffs weren't much either, not compared to the White Cliffs of Dover. They rose no more than a hundred feet from the rocky beach at the shore of the choppy Little Ross Bay.

But it was just what Richard Canidy wanted—a place with nobody around, with cliffs that could be made to look from the air like the mouths of the sub pens at Saint-Lazare.

H.M.'s Government made the site available to their American allies for a nominal cost, and the Kirkcudbright Constabulary was ordered to evacuate a specified area of the site for a twenty-four-hour period beginning at 1700 28 January.

On 25 January, a platoon of U.S. Army Engineers had gone to Little Ross Bay in an eight-truck-and-two-jeep convoy and spent three days in the blowing rain and icy winds doing what none of them could see any purpose for. But according to a rather passionate speech from the battalion commander himself, whatever it was, it was vital to the war effort, and was consequently to be regarded as a secret that absolutely could not be allowed to become known to the enemy.

What the Second Platoon of "Baker" Company, 4109th Engineer Light Equipment Battalion, did was erect from the base of the cliff a framework of four-by-eights 60 feet high and 155 feet wide. Then they nailed four-by-eight-foot sheets of plywood, lengthwise, to the framework. Then they painted the plywood in diagonal black and yellow two-foot-wide stripes to make it visible, and then draped camouflage netting over whatever the hell it was to make it invisible.

Then, leaving behind an officer and eight men in a truck to make sure whatever the hell it was didn't get blown down by the wind, the platoon returned to its base in England, where they were again admonished not to discuss with anyone what they had done in Scotland.

Canidy's delight with the western shore of Little Ross Bay had also caused the U.S. Navy Auxiliary Vessel *Atmore* [YD-1823] to steam the previous evening across the very unpleasant Irish Sea from Liverpool to Little Ross Bay, where it now rode at anchor. Everyone from the skipper down was either seasick or saying unkind things about the idiocy of the Naval Service in general and whichever fucking idiot had dreamed this up. Or both.

"This" was their orders, classified Secret. These, in addition to giving the location of Little Ross Bay and telling them where precisely they were to drop anchor in Little Ross Bay, informed them that they were to be "prepared to take aboard certain U.S. Military personnel who may be parachuted into the bay, or onto the western shore thereof."

Since the engineers had done a good job with the camouflage netting, the structure the engineers had built was not visible to the skipper or the lookouts of the *Atmore,* who consequently believed themselves to be sitting all by their lonesomes in the middle of fucking nowhere.

And then, suddenly, a B-17 appeared.

"Battle stations, battle stations," the loudspeakers boomed. "Boat crews, man your boats. Davit crews, stand by to launch rescue boats."

The B-17 came right over the *Atmore,* so low they could see the engine exhausts, and so close that some of the crew swore that there had been no machine-gun turrets on it, or gun positions in the fuselage.

The B-17 flew right into the cliffs on the west shore of Little Ross Bay and exploded.

When the rescue-boat crews finally made their way to the crash site, they found they had been preceded by an Army Engineer lieutenant and eight men, and by a first lieutenant wearing a SHAEF Patch.

Both the lieutenant (j.g.) commanding the rescue boat landing party and the lieutenant from the Engineer platoon were immensely relieved when the officer from SHAEF, a Lieutenant Jamison, told them that the crew of the B-17 had parachuted to safety about an hour before, so it would not be necessary to search the crash site for bodies.

Both junior officers had questions:

The Engineer lieutenant wondered, *If there was no crew in that thing, how come it hit that whatever-the-fuck-it-was we built right in the middle?*

The Lieutenant (j.g.) wondered, *If that was an accident during a routine training flight, how come they sent us up here maybe twelve hours before that plane took off?*

And both of them were very curious about Lieutenant Jamison: *How come a SHAEF officer, not even Army Air Corps, just happened to be on the western shore of Little Ross Bay when the B-17 crashed?*

And how did he know the crew had parachuted to safety?

But Jamison hadn't wanted to talk to them, and there was no one else they could think of who would have the answers, and the brass seemed hysterical about secrecy, so they kept their mouths shut.

[TWO]
Batthyany Palace
Holy Trinity Square
Budapest, Hungary
1115 Hours
29 January 1943

Beatrice, Countess Batthyany and Baroness von Steighofen, was wearing a sable coat that reached nearly to her ankles when she walked across the parquet floor to take the telephone call.

Under the coat, she wore a tweed skirt and two sweaters. Her feet were in a pair of sheepskin-lined over-the-ankle boots that had once belonged to her late husband, and her legs were encased in knitted woolen stockings reaching over her knees. Her red hair was somewhat sloppily done up in a loose bun, into which she had just stuck the side pieces of a rather ugly pair of tortoiseshell spectacles.

The Countess had been reading when informed of the telephone call, and Batthyany Palace was as cold as a witch's teat. The palace, directly across

Holy Trinity Square from St. Matthias' Church, had been built at approximately the same time (1775–77) as the royal castle (1715–70) atop Castle Hill, and it had always been difficult to heat. Without adequate supplies of coal, it was now damned near impossible.

The irony was, she had coal, lots of it. There were half a dozen coal mines running around the clock on Batthyany property. The problem was in getting the coal from the mines to Batthyany Palace. That required trucks. She had been allocated one truckload per month, and she didn't always get that. Even when she did, one truckload was nowhere near enough to heat the palace.

She didn't bother trying to heat the lower floor, nor the upper two floors. They had been shut off with ugly, and really not very effective, wooden barriers over the stairwells. Only the first floor was occupied.

The Countess was living in a five-room apartment overlooking Holy Trinity Square, but she often thought she might as well be living in the basement for all she saw of the square. Most of the floor-to-ceiling windows had been timbered over to hold in the heat from the tall, porcelain-covered stoves in the corners of the rooms. The two windows leading to the balconies over the square, and, in the rear, the garden that were not timbered over were covered with seldom-opened drapes.

The telephone beside the Countess's bed had stopped working two months before. When she had—personally, after her butler had gotten nowhere with them—called the Post Office people to complain, she had been rudely informed that there was a war on, and that they couldn't tell her when there would be someone available to come fix it.

"I regret, my dear Countess," the man had said, "that you will be forced to use one of the other eleven telephones my records show you have available to you in the palace."

He was unmoved when she told him that eight of the twelve telephones in the palace were in the shut-off portions.

The nearest working telephone to the Countess's bedroom was in the corridor leading to her apartment from the first-floor sitting room. It was—like the porcelain stoves—American. The Countess was convinced that it was faults in the Hungarian Post Office wiring rather than in the American telephone that forced her into the corridor.

She picked up the telephone, and as she did, she glanced at herself in the gilt-framed mirror on the wall. She shook her head at the way she looked.

"My dear von Heurten-Mitnitz," the Countess said. "How nice to hear from you! Are you in Budapest?"

"I have been appointed First Secretary of the Embassy," von Heurten-Mitnitz said.

"May I offer my congratulations?" the Countess said.

"That's very kind of you, Countess," von Heurten-Mitnitz said.

"How long have you been here?" she asked.

"I arrived last night," he said.

"Beastly train ride, isn't it?" she said. "You must be exhausted."

"Actually, I drove," von Heurten-Mitnitz said. "Standartenführer Müller has also been assigned here, and I brought his car down for him."

"That's your friend? That plump little Hessian, the one who looks like a pickle barrel?" the Countess asked.

Helmut von Heurten-Mitnitz laughed.

"Indeed," he said.

"The situation—I won't say 'politics'—" the Countess said, "makes for strange bedfellows, doesn't it?"

It was a rather snobbish thing for her to say, von Heurten-Mitnitz thought.

But she is a countess, and my brother is no less a snob.

And then he thought of something else, and said it.

"That's an Americanism."

"Is it really?" the Countess said.

"I realize this may well be an imposition," von Heurten-Mitnitz said, "and I will certainly understand if you have other plans—"

"But?" she interrupted.

"What I had hoped to do, on this very short notice," he said, "was to ask you to take lunch with me—"

"I accept," the Countess interrupted again.

"—following which," von Heurten-Mitnitz went on, "would you be good enough to serve as my guide around town? I've been given the addresses of several available flats, and I—"

"But of course," she said. "Offer me a good meal, and I am yours."

Helmut von Heurten-Mitnitz laughed, just a little uneasily.

"I'm at the Imperial," he said. "To judge by dinner last night—"

"Not what it once was," she interrupted once again, "but passable."

"Precisely," he said. "What time would be convenient for you?"

"Come by at quarter to one," she said. "You know how to find it?"

"Holy Trinity Square," he said.

"Quarter to one, then, my dear Helmut," the Countess said.

She hung up the telephone and went back into her apartment.

She opened one of three ceiling-high wardrobes and selected from it a dress meeting two criteria, warmth and style, in that order. She settled on a black wool dress and laid it on her bed. Then she went to a chest of drawers and searched through her alarmingly dwindling selection of lingerie. She chose in the end to go all black, although there was a temptation to go all red. There was still a rather nice red silk chemise and slip.

She considered a bath and decided against it. For one thing, there was barely time. There was no longer hot water on demand. The hot-water heater in the bathroom was fired up only when a bath was planned. And, she thought, there were some men, and she suspected Helmut von Heurten-Mitnitz was among them, who preferred the smell of woman to the smell of soap. Or, she corrected herself, the smell of a *perfumed* woman. Besides, she still had adequate supplies of scent. When Manny had gone to Paris, he'd bought everything he could lay his hands on for her.

She laid on the bed one of her remaining half-dozen pairs of silk stockings beside the black dress and the black underwear. Then, taking a deep breath as if facing an ordeal, she very quickly slipped out of the sable coat and the sweaters and the skirt. Then, naked save for the knitted stockings, she ran to her dressing table and liberally anointed herself with Chanel #5. Her skin was covered with goose bumps, and her nipples grew erect.

She ran back to the bed and quickly put on the underwear, the dress, and the sable coat. Then she returned to her dressing table and did her hair and her face. When that was done, she spun around on the stool, removed the boots and the knit stockings, and pulled on the silk stockings. Finally, she hoisted the skirt of her dress out of the way and hooked the stockings to the garter belt. Then, on the balls of her feet, she walked to one of the wardrobes, selected a pair of pumps, and slipped them on.

Then she rang for her maid

"I'm going out for lunch," she said. "When I return, I'd like these rooms warm. I will more than likely have a guest with me, so clean the place up. Put some decent sheets on the bed."

"Countess," the maid, a gray-haired woman in her sixties, said, "we don't have all that much coal—"

"I have an idea my guest may be able to remedy that," the Countess said. "Just do what I tell you."

The maid nodded.

"And bring me the silver fox, the knee-length one," the Countess said. "And the matching hat. I look like Catherine the Great, at seventy, in the sable."

"Yes, Countess," the maid said.

Helmut von Heurten-Mitnitz was five minutes early, but the Countess was waiting for him. When the Opel Admiral pulled to the curb, she rushed out and stepped in before he could get out.

"I suppose that makes me look dreadfully eager," she said.

"Not at all," von Heurten-Mitnitz said.

"But I didn't have breakfast, and I'm famished."

She smiled at him. He was discomfited, but not much. He was a man of the world, and God knew, there were damned few of them left. She was pleased that she had chosen the black underwear; she suspected he would like that.

They had a very nice luncheon in the Hotel Imperial dining room. The Countess ate delicately but heartily as von Heurten-Mitnitz told her the latest gossip from Berlin.

He did not seem surprised at her curiosity about Standartenführer Müller. He told her that Müller had just been summoned to the Wolf's Lair, Hitler's secret command post, in Rastenburg, where General Kaltenbrunner thought it might be a good idea, if it could be arranged, that he meet the Führer personally.

"There seems to be some question, Countess," he said, "of Hungarian devotion to the alliance. I suppose the real purpose for Müller and I coming here is to reassure von Ribbentrop and others that these fears are groundless."

"I am sure you will find, Helmut," the Countess said, "that there has been no change in Hungarian opinion."

If he detected a double entendre in her reply, he gave no sign.

He's really quite good-looking, the Countess thought. *And although he's doing his very best to be a Pomeranian gentleman, he has not been able to keep his eyes off my bosom.*

When they left the hotel, the Countess suggested that she drive.

"Splendid idea, if you don't mind," von Heurten-Mitnitz said. "One gets to see so little when in an unfamiliar city."

"Where are we going?" she asked when they had moved away from the hotel.

"Could we start at St. Ann's Church?" von Heurten-Mitnitz asked. "Then I could use that as a base point until I find my bearings."

When they reached the Vizivaros and St. Ann's Church, the Countess circled the church and pulled the Opel Admiral in to the curb, nose first, in front of it.

He looked at her curiously.

"Might I have a cigarette?" she asked. He produced his case, took one out, and then lit it for her. She held his wrist in her gloved fingers as he did.

"I don't know him, you know," the Countess said.

"I beg your pardon?" von Heurten-Mitnitz asked, confused.

"I don't even know what he looks like," the Countess said. "Eric Fulmar is Manny's first cousin, or second cousin, or whatever. But when he was at Marburg, we weren't at Schloss Steighofen. Or vice versa. I never laid eyes on him, and they haven't given me a description. Until you showed up, I was afraid I was going to have to just hang around here looking for a young SS officer with a familial resemblance to my late husband, and a middle-aged man who looked both professorial and just a little nervous."

"You are a truly remarkable woman!" Helmut von Heurten-Mitnitz said.

The Countess Batthyany and Baroness Steighofen smiled at Helmut von Heurten-Mitnitz's discomfiture.

"Tell me, Helmut," she asked, "do you think you'll be given a heating coal allowance, or can you get one?"

The question made no sense to him, but he answered it.

"As a matter of fact, I was told I would be. They said it would make a difference to landlords."

"Yes, it does," she said. "There are two apartments on the first floor of my place. Providing you have a coal allowance, I'd be willing to make you an attractive price."

He hesitated a moment.

"Questions *could* be asked," the Countess said. "But you do know me— you were even at Manny's funeral—and the Housing Office has been after me to make the other apartment available for use."

"You're a remarkable woman, Countess," von Heurten-Mitnitz repeated.

She put the Admiral in gear and backed away from the curb.

"If you don't mind my asking," she said, "how is it you never married?"

Helmut von Heurten-Mitnitz was now growing used to her rapid changes of subject and odd, probing questions.

"There has never been time, I suppose," he said.

"But you're not queer?"

"No," he said, then: "Did you think I was?"

"I thought I should ask," she said. "Unless your heating coal ration will be much larger than I think it will be, we will have the option, now that we'll be living together, of keeping two apartments just above freezing, or one apartment as warm as toast. Or am I shocking you?"

"I am afraid, my dear Countess," von Heurten-Mitnitz said, "of believing my incredible good fortune."

He reached over and caught her gloved hand and kissed it.

"How gallant!" she said, pleased. "And since it will not be necessary for you to spend the afternoon looking for an apartment, may I assume that you're free?"

"Yes," he said, "I'm free. What did you have in mind?"

The Countess Batthyany laughed deep in her throat.

[THREE]
The Baseler-Frankfurter Express

Eric Fulmar lowered the Gestapo agent's body to the floor. He was breathing heavily, and his heart was beating rapidly.

He looked at the body for a moment, then stepped over it and fastened the latch on the compartment door.

"Shit!" he said, in German.

He stepped over the body again, then turned and bent over it and, grasping the back of the head with one hand, tried to draw the thin-bladed knife out of the head. It wouldn't come. Either when he had twisted it—to scramble the brains—or when he'd lowered the Gestapo agent to the floor, the bones, or the muscles, or the sinews, or all three, had shifted, locking the blade in place.

For a moment, he considered just leaving the fucking knife where it was.

This hadn't been "projected" as a "possible difficulty."

Neither was the knife included in the planning. They hadn't brought the subject up. And, since he had already made up his mind to bring the knife with him, he hadn't brought it up either. If he had, they might have kept him from taking it.

He had bought the knife from an English sergeant at SOE's Station X. All

British commandos had one, the sergeant had told him. It had a blade about six inches long, and a handle just big enough to be wrapped in the fingers. The knife, which had been invented by an Englishman, then running the Shanghai police force, a man named Fairbairn, came in two versions. The "regular" one was larger and was intended for use in combat. Its scabbard was sewn either to the trouser leg or the boot.

The one sunk to its hilt behind and under the Gestapo agent's ear was the "baby Fairbairn." It was small enough to be carried hilt downward, hidden between the wrist and the bend of the elbow.

It had performed as promised, and it was possible that he would need it again.

Grunting with the effort, he rolled the body of the Gestapo agent on its side, took a good grip on the handle, put his foot against the Gestapo agent's ear, and gave a mighty tug. Moving the body removed whatever had obstructed the blade, and it now came out easily. So easily that he sat down heavily on the suitcase on the seat.

There was not much blood on the blackened blade. Fulmar leaned forward and wiped it several times against the Gestapo agent's trousers. Then he replaced it in the sheath on his left arm.

He became aware of his heavy breathing and the beating of his heart. He was excited. Excited people don't think clearly.

The first thing to do is get rid of the body, then change into the uniform and get rid of the civilian clothing and the luggage.

But that means opening the window twice.

Will that fucking window even open? If it doesn't, then what?

What if someone sees me putting him out the window?

Would it be better to throw him and the luggage out all at once, or to wait a little, so the body will be a couple of kilometers from the luggage when it's found?

The first thing to do is the first thing: See if the fucking window will open.

For a moment the window seemed frozen in place, but then he saw that there was a track for it to move upward. He gave a mighty heave, and the window opened.

Now that he had taken one action, everything seemed to fall into place.

The thing to do first is get rid of the body.

He looked out the window, then up the track. He could see nothing up ahead but the roadbed.

He grabbed the body under the armpits, heaved, and got the head into the open window.

The sonofabitch weighs five hundred pounds!

He wrapped his arms around the waist and heaved and shoved at once. Fulmar's face was right next to the entrance wound. A glob of blood oozed from it. When he let go, the body was halfway through the window, bent double at the stomach.

He wrapped his arms around the knees and heaved and shoved again. For a moment it seemed caught on something, but all of a sudden the body let loose and was gone.

Without thinking why, he closed the window and sat down on the seat. He was sweat-soaked and exhausted.

After a while, he hoisted himself to his feet and turned and opened the suitcase. He took out a brimmed cap with the Nazi eagle on the crown and the SS skull and crossbones on the band, and tossed it on the opposite seat.

Sure as Christ made little apples, that hat is either going to slide down over my ears, or be so small it will sit on my head like a pimple.

There was a shirt and a tie in the suitcase, a tunic with Sturmbann-führer's insignia on the collar and epaulets and the SD triangle sewn to the left sleeve above the cuff, a black leather belt for the outside of the tunic, a pair of breeches, a pair of calf-high black leather boots, and finally, on the bottom, a black overcoat.

Fulmar wondered where the uniform had come from. Probably stolen, he decided. The next thing he noticed was that the SS uniform was cheap and shoddy compared to the U.S. Army wool gabardine pinks-and-greens he had left at Whitbey House. He was surprised. He had been told the SS had the best uniforms and equipment.

He dumped the contents of the suitcase onto the seat, then quickly stripped to his underwear. After that, he put the discarded civilian clothing into one of "Reber"'s suitcases. At first he just threw it in, but then he reconsidered. Presuming it did not burst open when it hit the railroad right-of-way, it would be best if the suitcase were found neatly folded. He therefore carefully folded "Reber"'s clothing and placed it in the suitcase.

Then he dressed. It had been "projected as a possible difficulty" that the uniform would not fit him. But it had been decided that nothing could be done about that. As it turned out, the shirt fit, but the breeches were too large and the tunic was tight. The hat that he had worried about fit perfectly, but the boots were so tight that he had difficulty getting them on.

The likelihood that the boots would not fit had been another "possible difficulty," but for this problem there had been a "possible solution": Soak the boots in water and keep them on until they dried. That *might* permit them to stretch.

He found a match and burned the Reber passport and tickets one page at a time, catching the ashes on a sheet of newspaper. Then he opened the window and quickly closed it again. Up ahead the track was curving, and there were buildings in sight that suggested they were approaching a town.

The town flashed by the window a minute or two later. When there were no more buildings in sight, he opened it again. He got rid of the ashes by letting the wind catch them. But the track ahead was curved, and he could see six or seven cars and the locomotive. If he could see those cars, someone in those cars could see his. And might see him throwing the suitcases out.

After what seemed like a very long time, the track straightened out.

He seemed to be thinking more calmly now. There was no reason to throw the suitcases out the window at all.

If someone came into the compartment, he could say the suitcases had been here when he came into the compartment and he had no idea whom they belonged to. It would be much safer to wait until they got to the next stop and see if there would be an opportunity to safely dispose of them then.

He put Reber's suitcases in the rack and carefully checked to see if there was anything he had missed in the compartment. He stepped to the compartment door and unlatched it, then sat down and picked up the newspaper.

The excitement of a few minutes before was gone, replaced now by a terrible feeling of depression.

He allowed himself to dwell on the feeling that he was being used. He wondered what Dick Canidy would have done if he had told him to go fuck himself, that he had no intention of putting his head on the block under the guillotine by going inside Germany.

Shit! The fucking Q pill is in the change pocket of Reber's jacket. I forgot about it. I almost threw it out the fucking window!

He took the suitcase from the rack, found the jacket and the glass vial, and—taking a perverse pleasure from doing so—put it between his teeth as he closed the suitcase and replaced it on the rack.

I am the squeeze of my jaws away from whatever happens next.

Canidy had told him that, while he couldn't of course speak from personal experience, he had been reliably informed that once you bit the vial, that was it; you never knew what hit you. Then he said there was another theory, that after you bit the vial, first your balls fell off, *then* you dropped dead.

Fulmar reached into his mouth, took the Q pill in the palm of his hand, and looked down at it. It was three-quarters full of what looked like watery milk. He wondered how much of it was actually necessary to take you out.

What if I bit it and sneezed and three-fourths of it got blown away? Would what was left do anything to me?

Then he looked in vain in the SS tunic for a counterpart to the change pocket in "Reber" 's jacket. Finally, he took the brimmed cap and found a place for the vial between the headband and the stiff whatever-it-was that held the front of the crown up.

His feet were hurting him, and he remembered about soaking the boots so they would stretch.

There was a water faucet, and a small, well-worn glass. He had to push the button that opened the faucet so hard and so long to fill the glass that his thumb hurt. And when he poured the water on the boot, it beaded and ran off.

He filled the glass again, took off the left boot, poured the water into it, and with great effort managed to get the boot back on. He stood and looked down at the foot of the boot. A little water was oozing out. When he pressed downward, there was a squishing noise. He wondered if it was as loud as it sounded or whether he was "hearing" the sensation.

He filled the glass and repeated the operation with the other boot.

Then he walked back and forth between the compartment door and the window until he could detect no more "loose" water slopping around. His socks and feet were still wet, and now they seemed to grow cold.

The train began to slow. It was the scheduled stop at Offenburg.

He opened the window. People were streaming from the train for the station.

It's piss-call time!

He took Reber's suitcases from the rack, adjusted the brimmed cap on his head at an angle appropriate for a young lieutenant of the SS-SD, and picked up the suitcases and left the train.

He was disappointed when he got inside the station. There were long lines before the rest rooms, and there didn't seem to be any other place he could "forget" the suitcases. He made a circle of the crowded waiting room and started for the train.

"Watch it, please, Herr Sturmbannführer!" a voice called, and Fulmar looked over his shoulder and saw two workmen pulling a station cart loaded with luggage and packages. Fulmar stepped out of the way and then, taking the chance, added Reber's suitcases to their load.

Wherever they were going, it would take them some hours to find they had two suitcases more than they were supposed to, and several hours more before they did anything about them. He followed the baggage cart onto the platform and stood watching it for a moment. The handlers pulled it all the way down the platform past his train, then crossed the tracks behind it.

Feeling very pleased with himself, he boarded the train again. From the aisle, he could see what had happened to the luggage cart. It was standing under a sign, "Tuttlingen/Mengen/Neu-Ulm." It would be at least a day before someone asked questions about it there. By then, for sure, they would have discovered the Gestapo agent's body anyway, and the shit would begin to hit the fan.

When the train was moving again, he went into the compartment. There were two people in it, two middle-aged men who looked like bureaucrats.

"Heil Hitler!" they said, almost in unison.

Fulmar raised his hand from the elbow, answering the salute, but did not speak.

He had a choice now. The remaining suitcase was empty and could not be tied to him. He could leave it, claim it, or leave and come back later and claim it.

It was time to eat. There were ration cards with his identification, but Baker had told him to avoid using them if at all possible because they could not positively guarantee they would be accepted.

The "suggested solution" was to offer money in lieu of the coupons.

He would order something to drink. If there were ration coupons required for that, a young officer could credibly be expected to ask for them without coupons. All they could say was no. Then he could watch the others in the dining car and see how they handled the ration coupons for food. He would tip generously for the drink, or drinks, make it clear to the waiter that he had plenty of money.

Both alcohol and food proved to be simple. They had only wine, and he had two glasses, tipping generously each time. He saw that there was food, but that ration coupons were necessary in advance.

When he ordered the third glass of wine, he looked up at the waiter and smiled.

"What is a hungry man to do?"

"If he has coupons, he eats," the waiter said.

"Will these coupons be all right?" Fulmar asked, holding up a couple of bills folded tightly.

The waiter looked at him for a moment, then took the money in a smooth movement.

"I believe we can take care of the Herr Sturmbannführer," he said.

What he got a few minutes later was two slices of dark bread, between them a slice of salami.

Six days before, Fulmar thought, he had been disappointed because there was only ham and roast beef for sandwiches at Whitbey House; some sonofabitch had eaten all the turkey.

[FOUR]

Fulmar stayed in the dining car for an hour, until the train had stopped at and left Strassburg.

The waiter had not seated anyone else at his table, and that eliminated the necessity (and the risk) of carrying on a conversation. Canidy had been blunt about that: He was not to get overcocky because his German was flawless. The minute he opened his mouth he would risk saying something he should not say, or of being asked a question he could not credibly answer. Consequently, he was to avoid conversation wherever possible. The whole idea was to be inconspicuous. And if he stayed in the dining car any longer, he was likely to become conspicuous.

And the wine had "calmed him down." Which meant that it had dulled his senses. And that he couldn't afford.

The waiter nodded at him as he left the dining car.

"Heil Hitler!" Fulmar said, raising his hand from his elbow in a casual salute.

The dining car was behind the three first-class wagons-lits coaches. In the first, the conductor was taking tickets and two border policemen were checking identification and travel authorization. One of the border policemen looked at him without suspicion and flattened himself against the window as he went past.

The train, he noticed, was now almost full. Until now, it had been two-thirds empty.

He was almost through the second first-class car when he heard a female voice call out his name.

He hesitated momentarily, in the blink of an eye deciding that some other Eric was being called.

"Eric von Fulmar!" the voice called again, louder this time.

Christ, now what?

He stopped and turned.

A young woman, round-faced, dark-eyed, was walking quickly down the aisle to him. It took him a moment to recognize her. She was in a blue uniform, without makeup, with her dark brown hair done up in a bun. He identified the uniform by the armband. She was in Organization Todt, which Hitler had set up under Dr. Fritz Todt, the man who had built the Autobahn, to control all German construction and industry for the war effort.

Her name was Elizabeth von Handleman-Bitburg, and the last time Fulmar had seen her was in Paris. They had had dinner, she and Sidi Hassan el Ferruch and some other German girl whose name he could not now recall, in Fouquet's restaurant on the Champs Élysées.

After dinner, in the backseat of el Ferruch's Delahaye, she had slapped his face just after he had put his tongue in her mouth and his hand up her dress. And then she had made things worse by sobbing.

Her father was Generalmajor Kurt von Handleman-Bitburg. No. He corrected himself. Eldon Baker—*the first contact I had with that sonofabitch*—had been in Fouquet's that night, checking on Fulmar, and Eldon Baker never forgot anything.

At Deal, on the Jersey shore, Baker told me that "your girlfriend's father got himself promoted."

Elizabeth was the daughter of Generaloberst von Handleman-Bitburg.

"I thought that was you!" she said happily, offering her hand.

"Doing your bit for the fatherland, I see," Fulmar replied.

"Isn't this uniform dreadful?" she asked.

"I didn't recognize you at first," Fulmar said.

"When did you go into the SS?"

"March 12, 1942," he said without thinking. That date had been drilled into his memory, as had the particulars of his service since then—until his detail to the staff of the Reichsführer SS—with Waffen-SS units that had been conveniently wiped out in Russia or captured in North Africa.

"You look very nice in your uniform," she said. "And please don't say 'so do you.'"

"All right," he said. "I won't."

"I always wondered what happened to you," Elizabeth said. "I didn't have an address, so I couldn't write."

"The last time I saw you, you slapped my face," he said, and was a little proud of himself. The way to handle this situation was not to stick the baby Fairbairn into her skull and scramble her brains, but to get her mad.

She flushed, but she met his eyes.

"I was young, Eric," she said, "and you had no right to expect from me what you did."

When he did not respond, she smiled and cocked her head, a gesture he found very attractive.

"I'm working for your father," she said. "What about that?"

"Working for my father?"

"At the FEG office in Hoescht," she said. "I'm a secretary."

"Oh," he said.

"Where are you going?" she asked.

"Berlin," he said.

"Oh, good," she said. "There's a two-hour wait for the Berlin train. We can have a nice visit."

He nodded.

She cocked her head again and looked at him intently. And then she took his arm and led him out of the aisle onto the connecting platform between cars.

"What's this?" he asked.

"I don't know how to begin. . . . There's an interesting story going around about you, Eric," she said evenly.

"Is that so?"

"My father told my mother," she said. "I overheard them. I didn't hear it all. And when I asked him, he wouldn't tell me."

"Wouldn't tell you what?"

"What I did hear was that a friend of his, a Minister in the Foreign Ministry, had told him that you were seen in Casablanca."

"I was in Morocco, of course," he said. "You remember el Ferruch?"

"In the uniform of an American officer," Elizabeth von Handleman-Bitburg said.

She was looking into his eyes now. As he was trying to frame a reply, she said: "Oh, my God, it's true!"

"What I'm supposed to do now," Eric said, almost conversationally, "is kill you."

Her face went white, and her tongue came out and licked nervously at her lips.

"And I suppose what I'm supposed to do is scream," she said, very softly. Then she met his eyes again. "Are you going to kill me?"

"Shit!" Fulmar groaned.

The door to the car started to open.

He quickly put his arms around her. There was a moment's resistance, and then she understood what he was doing. Whoever was passing between cars would see a young officer kissing a young woman.

She raised her face to his.

It was the two border policemen passing between cars with the conductor. *"Guten Tag, Herr Sturmbannführer,"* one of them said. One of the others chuckled.

They remained in an embrace until the three had entered the next car. Fulmar was aware of two physical sensations: the hilt of the baby Fairbairn under the balls of fingers and the pressure of Elizabeth von Handleman-Bitburg's breasts and legs against his body. And then there was a third sensation. Her tongue came out, and for the briefest moment went between his lips and found his.

Then she pushed him away.

"Now they've seen you with me," she said. "Now you can't kill me."

"You should have called for help," he said.

"Why? I knew you weren't going to kill me."

"You seem pretty goddamned sure," he said.

"If you were going to kill me," she said reasonably, "you wouldn't have talked about it first. And then I looked in your eyes."

"Jesus H. Christ!"

"Wasn't it nice to be given a kiss, instead of the other way?"

"You're out of your goddamned mind, you know that?"

"My father told my mother that when the Russians come, life won't be worth living," she said. "I've changed since the last time I saw you. If you're going to die, you might as well take as much of life as you can before that happens."

"He could be shot for saying things like that," Fulmar said.

"No," she said calmly. "That is now the official position of the Propaganda Ministry." She quoted, "'The German people must come to understand that if the war is lost, Germany as we know it will disappear from the face of the earth.' That came straight from Dr. Goebbels."

"The operative words are 'if' and 'when,'" he heard himself say. "'If' is not defeatism. 'When' is."

She shrugged.

"Where are you really going?" she asked.

"I can't tell you that," he said.

"I'm not going to turn you in, Eric," she said.

"If those border policemen remember the Sturmbannführer kissing the girl, and if they remember your face, the Gestapo will come after you and question you. And if you knew, you would tell them."

"Are they looking for you now?" she asked.

"Yes, but don't ask why."

"Maybe I can help," she said.

"The best thing you can do is go back to your compartment and forget you ever saw me," he said.

"That in itself would be suspicious," she said. "And maybe I can help you. When they ask for my identification, which says that my father is a General-oberst, they generally stop right there."

He looked at her.

"And besides, if we went to the Bahnhof Hotel in Frankfurt and took a room while you're waiting for the Berlin train, there would be less chance of you being asked questions than if you stood around the Bahnhof waiting."

"I'm not going to Berlin," Fulmar blurted. "I'm going to Marburg."

"Not on this train, you're not," she said. "The first stop after Frankfurt is Kassel."

"How do you know that?"

"I go to Marburg all the time," she said. "I know the schedule. The first train you can catch to Marburg will put you in there at half past three in the morning. Do you want to arrive at half past three in the morning?"

"And the one after that?"

"Arrives in Marburg a little after nine," she said.

"Maybe the thing to do is get a hotel room," he thought aloud. "Then you could go."

"What have you done," she asked, "changed your mind? Lost interest?" He looked down at her.

She raised her hand and put it on his cheek.

"I told you," she said, "I've changed. I want what I can get now before it's too late."

Then she pulled his face down to hers. And she did to him what she would not let him do to her in the backseat of el Ferruch's Delahaye in Paris.

[ONE]
Hauptbahnhof
Marburg an der Lahn, Germany
0920 Hours
30 January 1943

The train from Frankfurt am Main to Kassel, with stops at Bad Homburg, Bad Nauheim, Giessen, and Marburg, did not run on Saturday. It was necessary for Fulmar to take the Kassel express, and to change at Giessen.

He absolutely forbade Elizabeth to return to the Hauptbahnhof in Frankfurt with him. She was hurt. She was crazy, was what she was. The way she'd talked, he had naturally decided that she had been fucking all comers, since she was convinced she was going to die.

That had not turned out to be the case. In the Bahnhof hotel, after the first time—which did not turn out to be terrific for either of them—she had come out and admitted that she had tried "it" three times before, because everybody seemed to make so much of it, and those times, too, had been disappointing.

But something happened when they tried it again in the morning. He did it then more or less because he thought she expected him to, and he imagined it would turn out no better than it had the night before. But it really turned out to be not only better, but different. He had no explanation why. It had just happened. It had, as a matter of fact, happened twice. And it would have happened a third time if he hadn't had to catch the goddamned train.

And she said something else crazy just before he put her on the bus to Hoescht.

"Take care of yourself, Eric," she said.

"You, too," he replied.

"Ich liebe dich," she said.

"You're crazy," he said.

"And you, too," she said, still shaking his hand. "Why else?"

And then she blew him a kiss and stepped on the bus. He stood there on the curb, looking for her in the window. When he found her, just before the bus pulled away, she blew him another kiss.

He thought about—even mentioned—taking her out with him. She'd laughed at him, said he wasn't very smart. Didn't he know what they did to the families of people who just disappeared?

"Let 'em think you got killed in a bombing raid," he had argued. "Blown away."

"Have you got a passport for me? Travel authority?" she asked, and made him feel like a damned fool.

She hadn't gotten into that *"ich liebe dich"* crap, however, until the last minute.

By the time he got off the train in Giessen, he'd thought some more about her. Maybe there *was* something special between them. He had certainly never felt better screwing than the last couple of times. There had to be an explanation for that. He had done a lot of plain and fancy fucking in his time, and it had never been like that.

He had a couple of really wild, childish thoughts. When this fucking war was over, he would look her up. Maybe he could even get her out before it was over.

Giessen brought him to his senses. The place was in ruins. The moment they opened the doors of the train, he could smell burned wood, and the more pervasive smell of decaying human flesh.

Giessen had been hit and hit hard. He wondered why. As far as he could remember, there were no factories of any importance here, certainly nothing worth all the effort it had taken to bomb the shit out of the place. Could it have been bombed by mistake? He had heard Canidy and Whittaker joking about their astonishment that B-17 pilots with 200 hours total flying experience could find Germany, much less a particular city in Germany.

But the bomb destruction reminded him that there was a war, and that neither he nor Elizabeth von Handleman-Bitburg were liable to make it through that war. He certainly wouldn't, if he kept acting like some high-school kid with a bad case of puppy love.

The train from Giessen to Marburg, which stopped at every other crossing, was ancient. It looked as if it belonged under a Christmas tree. There was only one class, un-upholstered benches in unheated coaches, and he rode most of the way beside a fat peasant woman with a potato bag full of cabbages. She told him that her son had been captured by the Americans in North Africa, and asked if he had been stationed there. He told her he had and that he'd almost been captured himself.

He had a mental picture of her son sitting at Fort Dix or someplace, wearing American fatigues with a big *P* painted on the back, eating three meals a day, and congratulating himself on being alive and out of the war.

When the train approached the outskirts of Marburg, he stood up, squeezed past the people in his row of seats, left the car, and stood on the platform, turning the collar of the black overcoat up against the cold wind.

He wanted to see how much damage had been done to Marburg. Aside from what looked like filled-in bomb craters along the roadbed, he could see no evidence of damage. The roadbed reminded him, however, of the Gestapo agent. By now, they must have found the body and started doing whatever they did when somebody stuck a knife in a Gestapo agent.

In just a couple of hours, if they hadn't found out already, they would learn that Reber was no longer on the train. And they would, if they hadn't already, start looking for him.

He told himself that if the train stopped at the Südbahnhof, he would get off there and ride into the center of town on the Strassenbahn.

The train slowed as it went through the Südbahnhof, but not enough for him to jump off.

Five minutes later, it jerked to a halt in the Hauptbahnhof. The station here was intact, too, just as he remembered it. The one in Frankfurt had some damage, and most of the glass in the arches over the platforms had been blown out. There was no glass roof over tracks in Marburg. There were just platforms on both sides of both tracks. Steps down from them led to a tunnel under the tracks to the station building itself.

Railroad police were on the platform, but they were just keeping an eye on things, not asking for identification and travel authority. But there would be a checkpoint somewhere. As soon as he went down the stairs to the tunnel, he found it. It had been set up in the tunnel under the tracks, out of the cold wind. What the railroad police were doing on the platform was making sure everybody went through the tunnel and didn't take off across the tracks to avoid the checkpoint.

The line moved quickly. It looked as if it were a routine checkpoint, not one set up to catch somebody special. Like whoever had scrambled a Gestapo agent's brains.

He had almost reached the head of the line when an SS-Unterscharführer (Sergeant) standing behind the table the railroad police had set up spotted him and shouldered his way through the crowd to him.

"Heil Hitler!" he barked, giving a straight-armed salute.

Fulmar returned the salute casually, smiled, and without being asked, produced his identification.

The document was studied casually, and handed back, with another salute.

"Pass the Sturmbannführer!" the sergeant called loudly.

"Danke schön," Fulmar said.

He was almost at the table when the sergeant ran after him, caught up, and touched his arm.

Fulmar, his heart jumping, turned to look at him, wearing what he hoped the SS noncom would consider a look of polite curiosity. He was relieved to see that the sergeant was smiling, but he still felt clammy sweat.

"The taxis are out of gas again, Herr Sturmbannführer," the sergeant said. "May I offer the Herr Sturmbannführer a ride?"

"That's very kind of you, Scharführer," Fulmar said. He would, he decided instantly, have himself driven to the Café Weitz and announce that he was meeting friends there.

"It would be a long cold walk up the Burgweg today," the sergeant said.

How does this sonofabitch know I'm going to Burgweg?

"I beg your pardon?" Fulmar asked coldly.

"It was an attempt at humor, Herr Sturmbannführer," the sergeant said. "No offense was intended."

"None so far has been taken," Fulmar said. "I don't know what the hell you're talking about."

"I simply presumed that since the Herr Sturmbannführer is on the staff of Reichsführer-SS, he might be looking for a certain very senior officer, also stationed in Berlin. I repeat, Herr Sturmbannführer, that no offense was intended."

"I took none," Fulmar said, and smiled, "but I know a certain Standartenführer who might."

"If we are talking about the same Standartenführer, Herr Sturmbannführer, I would be grateful if you would not—"

"Of course not," Fulmar said. "He's here in Marburg already?"

"Oh, no, sir," the sergeant said. "There was a teletype message, unofficial, of course, that the unexpected duty would preclude his visiting Hauptsturmführer Peis this weekend."

Fulmar took the news that Müller was not going to show with a calm that surprised him. That "possibility" had been planned for. The only question was why he wasn't coming. Had he really been given some duty that kept him from coming here? Or had he backed out at the last moment? Or had the entire operation been compromised?

"I guess that happened after I left Berlin," Fulmar said. "I hadn't heard about that. I was just told . . ." He stopped and smiled. "Oh, I see! You thought I was delivering a little gift, to make the lady's disappointment a little less?" Fulmar asked.

The sergeant shrugged.

"I must say that you are both alert and perceptive," Fulmar said. "But that's not it." He paused thoughtfully. "Maybe there's a message for me at Burgweg. I gratefully accept your kind offer of a ride."

"It is my pleasure. Herr Sturmbannführer," the sergeant said.

When they reached the Dyer house, the sergeant said that he could wait if he wasn't going to be long.

"The very least I'll have to do is call Berlin," Fulmar said. "And I wouldn't be a bit surprised if there was an errand or two for me to run."

The Unterscharführer didn't seem suspicious. He replied that he would be on duty all weekend, and if the Herr Sturmbannführer needed a ride, all he had to do was call.

Fulmar thanked him and went to the door.

He knew the building, but he had never been inside before. Gisella had never wanted him to come to her house.

When he rang the bell, a small, hunched-over middle-aged woman, with a blanket wrapped around her shoulders, came to the door. She looked at him suspiciously.

"Fräulein Gisella Dyer, please," Fulmar said.

"Top of the stairs and to the right," the middle-aged woman said.

Gisella opened the upstairs door. She recognized him immediately, and there was fear in her eyes.

"Heil Hitler!" Fulmar barked, for the benefit of the woman who he was sure was listening at the foot of the stairs.

"Heil Hitler," Gisella replied. "How may I help you, Herr Sturmbannführer?"

"I have a message from a mutual friend," Fulmar said.

"Please come in," she said.

When he had gone past her, she closed the door and leaned against it.

"My God, what are you doing here?" she asked. "Where did you get that uniform? Are you crazy?"

"Where the hell is Müller?" Fulmar countered. "He was supposed to be here. Or send word when he would be."

Instead of replying, she put her finger in front of her lips and pulled him into the kitchen and turned the water faucets on.

"Where the hell is Müller?" Fulmar repeated.

"He sent a message through Peis that he couldn't make it," Gisella said.

"That's not what I asked," Fulmar snapped.

She shrugged her shoulders helplessly.

Fulmar decided that she really didn't know. The decision had to be made, and he made it.

"We'll have to go without him," he said.

"We can't do that," she said. "He'll be here next weekend, if not before."

"Right about now, there's going to be a lot of people looking for me," Fulmar said. "We go now."

"What about papers? Passports? Travel authority? How do you plan to get us across the Dutch border? We'll need a car."

"We don't need a car. We'll go by train, and we're going to Vienna, not Holland. I have documents," he said.

"Vienna?" she asked. "What happened to Holland?"

"The plans have been changed," Fulmar said. "Müller knew that. Maybe the reason he's not here is because he'll meet us in Vienna."

And maybe he's changed his mind. And maybe he's been arrested.

"He sent word that he had documents," Gisella said. "Travel documents, I mean. Johnny said 'theater tickets,' but I'm sure he meant documents. But he didn't say anything about Vienna."

"'Johnny'?" Fulmar parroted accusingly. "Well, it was 'projected' that 'Johnny' might not be able to make it. And an alternative plan was set up. How long will it take you to get ready?"

"I'm not sure my father will go with you," Gisella said. "I'm not sure I want to. You're no longer a little boy, but *Vienna?*"

"Your father doesn't have any choice," Fulmar said. He waited until she looked at him, then finished: "I was driven here by an SS-SD sergeant from the local office. He knows I'm here, and so does your concierge. They will know I've been here."

"So what?" she said. "I'll worry about that. I'll think of something to tell them, if they ask."

Another decision had to be made, and he made it without very much thought.

"Gisella, my orders are that neither you nor your father are to be available for interrogation," he said.

"Meaning what?" she asked, nastily sarcastic.

"The reason they will be looking for me is that it was necessary to eliminate a Gestapo agent on the train on the way here," Fulmar said. "If necessary, I will eliminate you and your father."

"Are you serious?"

He ignored that. "Where's your father?"

"At the doctor's," she said. She looked at her wristwatch. "He should be here within the half hour."

"What's wrong with him?" Fulmar demanded.

"He had a cough, a bad one," she said.

"Use the half hour to pack," he said. "Nothing of value. Just what you would take in the way of clothing for a couple of days."

"I think I'm going to be sick to my stomach," she said.

"Well, then, go ahead and throw up," Fulmar said. "Just do it where I can see you."

She looked at him with horror and loathing, but she did not throw up.

There was a knock five minutes later at the door.

"Is that your father?" Fulmar whispered.

She shook her head.

"He would have a key," she whispered, and then raised her voice. "Who is there?"

"Hauptsturmführer Peis, Fräulein Dyer," Peis called.

Gisella looked at Fulmar to see what to do.

Fulmar walked on the balls of his feet to the door, then gestured for Gisella to open it.

She walked to the door and opened it.

"Guten Tag," she said politely.

"I understand we have a visitor from Berlin," Peis said. "I thought I would ask if I could be of any—"

Fulmar killed him as he had killed the Gestapo agent on the train, quickly, soundlessly, by inserting the narrow, very sharp Fairbairn blade into his skull so quickly that brain death was virtually instantaneous. Peis's body, as Lorin Wahl's had, flopped around in his arms for a moment before the nerve reflexes died. Then Fulmar let Peis's body slide to the floor.

He bent over him, put his boot on his face, and pulled the baby Fairbairn from Peis's skull. He wiped the blade on Peis's jacket and sheathed the knife. He looked at Gisella. She met his eyes for a moment, then turned her head.

Fulmar dragged the body into the living room, putting it where it would be out of sight of someone standing at the door, but making no other effort to conceal it. Then he straightened the rugs he'd put into disarray dragging the body.

"Did you have to kill him?" Gisella asked, very low.

"It was necessary," he said, then thought that sounded a little too harsh. He wanted her afraid of him, not hysterical.

"I knew him, you remember. He would have remembered me. I haven't changed that much."

She laughed nastily at that.

"My God," she said, "if they catch us, they'll kill us."

Fulmar didn't reply. He went to the window and looked down at Burgweg. There was a small, diesel-engined Mercedes parked by a No Parking sign.

"Does Peis have a driver?" he asked.

"No," she said.

"Then as soon as your father gets here, we'll take his car to Frankfurt and catch the Vienna train."

"Why are we going to Vienna?" she asked. "It's in the opposite direction."

"Because it's safer," he told her.

They were going to Budapest, but if they were caught on the way, it was better that neither she nor her father knew their ultimate destination.

"My father's liable to have a heart attack when he sees Peis," Gisella said. It was not a cliché; she meant it.

Fulmar shrugged.

"When you . . . left Marburg, the last time," she said, "and he questioned me, he burned my breasts with lighted cigarettes. The pain . . . I should feel something now that you've killed him. But I don't. I just can't believe any of this is happening."

There was the sound of footsteps on the stairs, and a moment later, the sound of a key in the lock.

Professor Friedrich Dyer stepped into the room.

"The door was not locked," he said, and then he saw Fulmar. "You have a guest, I see."

Fulmar motioned for him to close the door.

"Don't go in the living room, Daddy," Gisella said.

"Why not?" he asked, and walked across to the living room.

"Did you do that?" he asked Fulmar matter-of-factly.

"It was necessary," Fulmar said.

Professor Friedrich Dyer leaned over Peis's body and spat. Then he turned to Fulmar.

"Who are you?" he asked.

"I'm Erich von Fulmar."

Dyer nodded, as if that too came as no surprise.

"What do you plan to do with that swine's carcass?" Dyer asked.

"As soon as you throw a couple of things in a bag," Fulmar said, "we are going to take Peis's car and drive to Frankfurt. We will leave the body here. It should be a day or two before it's discovered."

Dyer looked at his daughter.

"Are you all right, *Liebchen?*"

She nodded.

He turned to Fulmar.

"And what if we are stopped at a roadblock?"

"I have passports and travel authority for you," Fulmar said. "And my SS-SD identity card."

"Do we have time to go by my office?" Dyer said.

"No," Fulmar said immediately.

"Don't answer that so quickly," the old man snapped. "I have given a good deal of thought to why all this effort is being made on my behalf, and I have concluded it is my work that makes it worthwhile, not an old man."

"Work?" Fulmar asked. "What kind of work?"

"You wouldn't understand," Dyer said impatiently. "Work on the molecular structure of metals."

"Nothing was said to me about papers," Fulmar said.

"I would like to either take them—some of the more important papers, not everything—or destroy them."

"We are not going to the university," Fulmar said. "Discussion closed. Put a couple of shirts in a bag, Herr Professor."

[TWO]
Organization Todt Bureau Hoeschtwerk, FEG
Hoescht am Main, Germany
1540 Hours
30 January 1943

"Guten Tag," the caller said. "Would you put me through to Fräulein von Handleman-Bitburg, please?"

"Fräulein von Handleman-Bitburg does not work in this office, and she cannot be called to the telephone."

"I am calling for Generaloberst von Handleman-Bitburg," the caller said coldly. "Please get Fräulein von Handleman-Bitburg on the line, or let me speak with your superior."

"One moment, please, *mein Herr,*" the woman said.

Precisely two minutes and forty-one seconds later—the caller was looking at his watch—Fräulein von Handleman-Bitburg came on the line.

"Hello?"

"Ich liebe dich," the caller said.

"How are you?" Fräulein von Handleman-Bitburg said.

"Did you hear what I said?"

"I think I already knew," Fräulein von Handleman-Bitburg said. "But thank you for telling me."

The caller hung up.

Then he ran across the Frankfurt Hauptbahnhof and boarded the Danube Express for Vienna.

[THREE]
Leitha, Ostmark
31 January 1943

There was a customs house just beside the station at Leitha. It was sturdily constructed of brick, and above the door there was, carved in sandstone, the double-headed eagle of the Austro-Hungarian Empire. A stark sign, black on white, had been fixed to the building, "GRENZPOLIZEI" (Border Police), but it did not quite cover the sandstone crest. The two eagle heads were visible, for all the world as if they were looking over the sign.

The border divided what had been the two major divisions of the Austro-Hungarian Empire. Hungary was now an independent state. And Austria too had been independent, but it had been taken into Greater Germany and was now officially the State of Ostmark, on a par with Bavaria, or Prussia, or Hesse.

Twenty miles north of Leitha was the border between Ostmark and what had been another two parts of what had been the Austro-Hungarian Empire. These were the former Provinces of Bohemia and Moravia, which for a few years had been the Republic of Czechoslovakia.

The Prime Minister of Great Britain, Neville Chamberlain, in exchange for "peace in our time," had allowed Hitler to take over that country. But it hadn't fared as well as Hungary and Austria. It was now a "Protectorate," which meant that the Bohemians and Moravians were not considered quite as good as Germans, and were not permitted to send representatives to the Central Government in Berlin.

Richard Canidy had given this snippet of history a good deal of thought before deciding that the safest place to cross the border between Germany and Hungary was at Leitha. Hungarians and Germans were allies.

Residents of the Protectorates of Bohemia and Moravia seemed not to understand the privilege of their association with Germany, as nearly equal citizens. Not only had they assassinated Reinhard Heydrich, the Protector himself, but they seemed to be always trying to get out of Bohemia and Moravia into either Hungary or Ostmark.

Consequently, the borders between the Protectorates and Ostmark or the Protectorates and Hungary were more closely guarded than the border between Ostmark and Hungary.

At Leitha there would be only one inspection of documents, and that one inspection would probably be more or less perfunctory.

But an inspection was conducted, and it was not pro forma. The primary concern of the authorities was the disparity between food supplies in Germany and Hungary. Hungary, which had been the breadbasket of the Austro-Hungarian Empire, still had surplus supplies of food that farmers or their agents were perfectly willing to sell to anyone with the money.

On the way from Hungary to Germany, travelers were searched for contraband sausage, salami, and smoked pork. That was considerably easier to find than excess-of-the-limit money, which was usually the contraband carried in the other direction.

The inspection of documents and the searching of luggage began almost as soon as the train left Vienna's Hauptbahnhof on Mariahilferstrasse. It was only fifty kilometers from Vienna to Leitha, and the train covered this in about forty-five minutes. Forty-five minutes was not sufficient time for the border police to search all luggage and to inspect all documents.

The Budapest Express had been stopped at Leitha for thirty minutes as the inspection continued, when the inspecting quartet—the conductor, two border policemen, and a Gestapo agent—slid open the door to a compartment that held an Obersturmführer SS-SD, an attractive young woman, and a tall, erect man whose documents identified him as both the young woman's father and as an engineer employed by Siemens.

Their documents seemed to be in order. The young Sturmbannführer had even naively confessed to have in his possession far more Reichsmarks than the law permitted. He had not, in other words, tried to conceal them, which would have been suspicious. But, as everyone knew, anyone attached to the personal staff of the Reichsführer-SS, even a lowly Sturmbannführer, tended to be a little loose as far as any regulation was concerned.

In ordinary circumstances, after satisfying himself of the bona fides of the Sturmbannführer's identification, the Gestapo agent would have turned a blind eye to the extra currency he had in his possession.

But there had been an urgent teletype message from Berlin that morning. The body of a Gestapo agent had been found near the Swiss border the previous evening.

He had been brutally stabbed to death before being thrown from the Baseler-Frankfurter Express. The murderer was believed to be a Swiss national, or at least someone equipped with a Swiss passport, in the name of Reber. "Reber" had disappeared from the train, and there was not much of a description available of him, but what there was fitted the Sturmbannführer.

It was a delicate situation for the Gestapo agent. If this young officer was on the personal staff of the Reichsführer-SS, then clearly he had friends in high places, friends who were going to raise all kinds of hell if he was dragged off the train and accused of being either a Swiss black marketeer or an enemy agent. But on the other hand, duty was duty. It simply called for a little tact.

"I am sure the Herr Sturmbannführer will understand the situation," the Gestapo agent said.

"What situation?"

"There is a certain situation which I do not wish to discuss in public," the Gestapo agent said.

"You would like to talk to me in private," Fulmar said, and stood up.

"If you would be so kind," the Gestapo agent said.

"Very well," Fulmar said, and stepped out of the compartment.

The Gestapo agent led him to the vestibule at the end of the car.

I'm going to get bagged five kilometers from the fucking border!

"Would it terribly inconvenience the Herr Sturmbannführer to give me a number we could call of someone who could vouch for the Herr Sturmbannführer?"

"What's this all about?" Fulmar demanded impatiently. "What is it you did not want to discuss before the others?"

"There was an incident, Herr Sturmbannführer, in which a Gestapo agent lost his life. There was a teletype this morning, giving a description of the man who is the prime suspect."

"And you think I'm the man you're looking for?" Fulmar asked. "Incredible!"

"The Herr Sturmbannführer will, I am sure, understand my position."

"Well, let's get it over with," Fulmar said. "Can we get through to Berlin from here? Standartenführer Müller will vouch for me. Would that suffice? Or will it take the Reichsführer-SS himself?"

"Herr Sturmbannführer," the Gestapo agent said, "the Gestapo agent was brutally murdered. He was stabbed to death. It is believed that his murderer is an enemy agent. The situation, as I'm sure you will understand, calls for extraordinary measures, even to the point of checking out someone like the Herr Sturmbannführer."

"Well," Fulmar said, "you should have told me the situation right off. No apologies are required. To the contrary, I should offer, and do, my apologies for my resentment. You say there is a phone here?"

"In the Grenzpolizei office, Herr Sturmbannführer."

Müller, obviously, has changed his mind about this whole thing. When he comes on the phone, he is either going to say he never heard of me, or tell this guy to arrest me, that I'm an agent. In either case, I have between now and the time Müller answers his phone to do something.

The only chance I have now is to get alone with him, before he gets on the phone, and kill him, and hide the body, and get back on the train, and hope the body isn't discovered until we're across the border.

I'm bagged, and that's it. Shit, and so close!

Well, if the Gestapo doesn't go apeshit when they find they've bagged me, and the Dyers don't go apeshit when they find out I've been arrested, they may make it.

The obvious solution to this situation is for me to check out now. If they interrogate me, Elizabeth's name will come out.

Fulmar swiped at his face as if at an insect, and knocked his hat off.

The Gestapo agent quickly bent and retrieved it, and handed it to him.

"Danke schön," Fulmar said, and brushed the front of the crown. He looked at it and straightened it, and when he took his hand from the inside, he had the Q pill. He put the hat on his head and coughed, and the Q pill was between his teeth.

Here? he wondered, surprisingly calm. *Or should I wait to see what happens?*

"The call will go from here to Vienna, which is sometimes difficult," the Gestapo agent said. "But from Vienna, we have a direct line to Berlin."

"Fine," Fulmar said, not moving his jaws. He ran his tongue against the slippery vial between his teeth.

"Eric!" a male voice called. "Eric von Fulmar!"

Fulmar and the Gestapo agent turned to see who was calling.

A tall, thin, aristocratic man wearing a Homburg was standing on the platform of one of the cars.

"Heil Hitler!" Eric said. The Q pill was now loose in his mouth. He was afraid he would either swallow it, or cough and spit it out. He coughed again, aware that it must sound artificial, and had the Q pill in his hand again.

"Where in the world are you going?" the man said.

"Tell him," the Gestapo agent said, "that you'll be back in just a moment." *The sonofabitch is suspicious.*

"I'll be right back," Fulmar called out. "We have to call Berlin."

The man jumped off the train and walked quickly to them.

Now the Gestapo agent was annoyed.

He dug into the pocket of his ankle-length leather overcoat and came out with his aluminum Gestapo identity disk, holding it out for the man to see.

"Gestapo," he announced.

"I surmised as much," the man said. "Be good enough to explain this."

"This is none of your business, mein Herr!"

"Oh, but my dear sir," the man said icily, "it is my business."

The man then reached into the breast pocket of his suit and took out a pigskin folder, something like a thin wallet. He held it in front of the Gestapo agent's face.

"Be so good as to examine this," he said softly.

The Gestapo agent took a good look. He had never actually seen one before in the hands of the person it had been issued to. He had seen examples of them, of course, in school.

It was an identity card issued by the Minister for State Security, signed by Heinrich Himmler himself. In the name of the Führer, it commanded all German law-enforcement authorities to place themselves at the orders of the bearer, Brigadeführer SS-SD Helmut von Heurten-Mitnitz.

"I am at your orders, Herr Brigadeführer," the Gestapo agent said.

"Then you will be so kind as to explain what you're doing?"

"If I may be so bold, Herr Brigadeführer," Fulmar said. "This officer was simply doing his duty."

"Indeed? How is that?" von Heurten-Mitnitz said.

"There is a call out for someone meeting my description. What this gentleman was doing was making sure I am who I say I am."

"Obviously, Herr Brigadeführer," the Gestapo agent said, "that will no longer be necessary."

Von Heurten-Mitnitz ignored him.

"Your aunt Beatrice told me you were probably going to be on this train," he said. "I looked for you in Vienna but couldn't find you."

"I almost missed the train," Eric said.

"With your permission, Herr Brigadeführer," the Gestapo agent said, "I will return to my duties."

Von Heurten-Mitnitz dismissed him with a casual wave of his arm, in a sloppy Nazi salute.

"Heil Hitler," he mumbled.

The Gestapo agent started back to the train.

"You, there!" von Heurten-Mitnitz called after him, and when the Gestapo agent turned, added: "Your zeal is to be commended."

"Thank you, Herr Brigadeführer," the Gestapo agent said, pleased.

"That was rather close, wasn't it?" von Heurten-Mitnitz said. "How was he going to check you out?"

"I was going to call Müller," Fulmar said.

"He wouldn't have been there," von Heurten-Mitnitz said. "The moment I heard about what happened on the train from Switzerland, I tried to call him. He's still at Rastenburg with Kaltenbrunner."

"I thought he'd changed his mind," Fulmar said, "or been bagged. I was about to bite that fucking pill."

Helmut von Heurten-Mitnitz looked at him intently for a moment but didn't reply.

"Is there anything else I should know? Was there any trouble in Marburg?"

"I had to take out the local SS-SD man," Fulmar said.

"Take out?"

"I killed him," Fulmar said. "The body is in the Dyer apartment. We drove to Frankfurt in his car."

Von Heurten-Mitnitz thought that over a moment.

"Well, it's a good thing, then, that Müller is at the Wolf's Lair, isn't it? Anything else?"

"Dyer wanted to bring some papers with him, or to destroy them before we left. I told him there wasn't time. Do you know anything about that?"

Von Heurten-Mitnitz thought that over a moment, then shook his head.

"I have no idea," he said.

He would tell Müller to get his hands on Professor Dyer's papers, if he could do so without causing much suspicion. If Dyer thought they were important, it probably explained why the Americans had gone to all this trouble to get him out.

"I have a bit of news for you," von Heurten-Mitnitz said. "On my arrival in Budapest, I learned that your contact there is your cousin by marriage, the Countess Batthyany."

Fulmar's eyebrows rose. "All I had was St. Ann's Church, and the date and time," he said.

"Why don't we get back on the train, my dear Eric?" Helmut von Heurten-Mitnitz said.

"What happens next?" Fulmar asked.

"Tomorrow, or the day after, you will be taken to Yugoslavia. Once you're in Mihajlovic's hands, I am assured the risky part of the journey will be over."

Fulmar snorted. " 'Assured'? Assured by whom?"

"Someone very close to the top of the Hungarian resistance," von Heurten-Mitnitz said. "Someone in whom I am acquiring a certain faith."

"But you're not going to tell me who?"

"I did," von Heurten-Mitnitz said. "The Countess Batthyany."

Fulmar's eyebrows rose again.

"I think you will find her to be a rather remarkable woman," von Heurten-Mitnitz said. "That has been my reaction to her, at least."

Fifteen minutes later, when the train had left, the Gestapo agent telephoned his chief in Vienna and reported the presence of a Brigadeführer-SS from Berlin on board the train.

"I trust everything went smoothly?"

"Yes, of course."

"They sometimes show up, you never know when or where."

"Yes, sir."

"Don't be so impressed, Franz. They piss and shit like the rest of us."

[FOUR]
East Railway Station
Budapest, Hungary
1145 Hours
31 January 1943

When the Opel Admiral was found in the Official Cars Only parking area of the East Railway Station, it quite naturally caused a certain curiosity among the Gestapo agents assigned to the station.

For one thing, there were few Admirals around anywhere, and possession of one was a symbol of power and authority. This one, moreover, bore Berlin license plates, a CD (Corps Diplomatique) plate, and, affixed to the Berlin license tag where the tax sticker was supposed to go, a sticker signifying that taxes had been waived because the automobile was in the service of the German Reich, and specifically in the service of the SS-SD.

Obviously, whoever had parked the car was someone of high importance. The question was just who he was.

First things first. Josef Hamm, the raking Gestapo agent, ordered that the Hungarian railway police be "requested" to station a railway policeman to watch the car. If there was one thing known for sure, it was that, whoever the high official was, he would not be at all pleased to return to his car and find that someone had taken a key or a coin and run it along the fenders and doors.

There had been a good deal of that lately. A number of Hungarians took offense at the Hungarian-German alliance generally, and at the large—and growing—presence of German troops and SS in Budapest specifically, and expressed their displeasure in small, nasty ways.

Then Hamm called the security officer at the German embassy and asked who the car belonged to.

"It probably belongs to von Heurten-Mitnitz," the security officer said. "That would explain the SD sticker, and he's the type to have an Admiral."

"Who's von Heurten-Mitnitz?"

"Helmut von Heurten-Mitnitz," the security officer said. "He's the new first secretary."

"How does he rate an SD sticker?"

"Because when he's bored with wearing striped pants, he can wear the uniform of a Brigadeführer SS-SD," the security officer said. "You could say that von Heurten-Mitnitz is a very influential man. His brother is a great friend of the Führer. If you'd like, I can check the license-plate number of the teletype with Berlin."

"How long would that take?"

"Thirty, forty minutes," the security officer said.

"I'll call you back in an hour," Josef Hamm said. "Thank you, Karl."

When he called back, Hamm was told that von Heurten-Mitnitz did not own the Admiral. It was owned by Standartenführer Johann Müller, of the SS-SD.

"Do you think he knows von Heurten-Mitnitz is driving it?"

"I think if it was stolen, Josef," the security officer said sarcastically, "they probably would have said something. Müller is with the Führer at Wolf's Lair. Nobody takes a personal car there. So maybe he loaned it to von Heurten-Mitnitz."

"Have you seen this von Heurten-Mitnitz? What's he look like?"

"Tall, thin, sharp-featured. Classy dresser. If you're thinking, Josef, of asking von Heurten-Mitnitz what he's doing with Müller's car, I wouldn't."

"I'm thinking of finding the new First Secretary when he comes back and telling him that if he will be so good, when he leaves his car at the station, as to tell us, we will do our very best to make sure some Hungarian doesn't piss on his engine or write a dirty word on the hood with a pocket-knife."

The security officer chuckled. "You're learning, Josef," he said, and then hung up.

Josef Hamm and two of his men were waiting at the end of the platform when the train from Vienna pulled in. The two men positioned themselves at opposite ends of the three first-class cars, and, when one of them spotted a "tall, sharp-featured, classy dresser" getting off, he signaled to Josef Hamm by taking off his hat and waving it over his head, as if waving at someone who had come to meet him at the train.

Hamm saw that Helmut von Heurten-Mitnitz was indeed a classy dresser. He wore a gray homburg and an overcoat with a fur collar. With him were three people, an Obersturmführer-SS and a man and woman who looked like father and daughter.

When they had almost reached the police checkpoint at the end of the platform, Hamm walked around it and up to von Heurten-Mitnitz.

"Heil Hitler!" Hamm said, giving a quick, straight-armed salute. Von Heurten-Mitnitz made a casual wave in return.

"Herr Brigadeführer von Heurten-Mitnitz?" Hamm asked.

"Yes," von Heurten-Mitnitz said, but he did not smile.

"Josef Hamm at your service, Herr Brigadeführer," he said. "I have the honor to command the Railway Detachment, Gestapo District Budapest."

"What can I do for you, Herr Hamm?" von Heurten-Mitnitz asked, obviously annoyed to be detained.

"First, let me get you past the checkpoint," Hamm said.

"This officer and these people are with me," von Heurten-Mitnitz said.

The young SS officer raised his hand in a sloppy salute.

"Make way for the Brigadeführer and his party!" Hamm called out as he led them to and past the checkpoint.

"Very kind of you," von Heurten-Mitnitz mumbled. "Now, what's on your mind?"

"Herr Brigadeführer," Hamm began, "If you would be so kind as to notify one of my men whenever you park your car here at the station—"

"Why would I want to do that?" von Heurten-Mitnitz interrupted.

"—I can make sure that no one bothers it while you are gone."

Helmut von Heurten-Mitnitz looked at Hamm without speaking, but a raised eyebrow asked, *What the hell are you talking about?*

"There have been unfortunate incidents, Herr Brigadeführer," Hamm explained, "where cars have been . . . *defiled* . . . by unsavory elements among the Budapest population. Paint scratched. Worse."

Von Heurten-Mitnitz seemed to consider this a moment, and then he smiled.

"I believe I am beginning to understand," he said. "You saw my car parked, and took the trouble to find out whose it was, and then to meet me. How very obliging of you, Herr Hamm! I am most grateful."

"It was my pleasure, Herr Brigadeführer," Hamm said.

"You can do me one other courtesy," von Heurten-Mitnitz said. "Please do not use my SS rank when addressing me. The less well known it is in Budapest the better, if you take my meaning. I also hold the rank of Minister."

"That was thoughtless of me, Herr Minister," Hamm said. "I beg the Herr Minister's pardon."

"Don't be silly, my dear Hamm," von Heurten-Mitnitz said. "How could you have known?"

"Is there any other way in which I can help the Herr Minister?" Hamm said.

"I can't think of one," von Heurten-Mitnitz said after a moment's hesitation. He offered his hand. "I am touched by your courtesy, Herr Hamm, and impressed with your thoroughness. I shall tell the ambassador what you've done for me."

They were by then standing beside the Admiral. Hamm opened both doors and, after the father-and-daughter had gotten into the backseat, closed them. The young SS officer walked around the rear of the car and slipped in beside von Heurten-Mitnitz. Hamm gave another salute, which von Heurten-Mitnitz returned casually, and with a smile, and then Hamm stood back as von Heurten-Mitnitz backed the Admiral out of its parking space.

All things considered, Hamm thought, *I handled that rather well.*

When they were a few yards from the station, the tall, gray-haired man in the backseat spoke. "My God, when he stopped you, I thought I was going to faint."

"You really don't faint when you're frightened, Professor," Eric Fulmar said. "Fear causes adrenaline to flow, and that increases, not decreases, the flow of blood to the brain. Shutting off blood to the brain is what makes you faint."

"Oh, my God!" the young woman in the backseat said with infinite disgust.

Helmut von Heurten-Mitnitz chuckled.

"How very American," he said.

"Where are we going?" Professor Doktor Friedrich Dyer asked.

"To Batthyany Palace," von Heurten-Mitnitz said. "It's on Holy Trinity Square. Not far from here."

"And what happens there?" Professor Dyer asked.

"I don't know about anybody else," Fulmar said. "but I intend to go to work on a bottle of brandy."

"That's not what I meant," Professor Dyer snapped.

"You'll be told what you have to know, Professor," Fulmar said, "when you have to know it. The less you know, the better. I thought I'd made that plain."

Professor Dyer exhaled audibly and slumped against his seat. His daughter flashed a look of contempt at the back of Fulmar's head, and shook her own head in resignation.

Von Heurten-Mitnitz turned off the square, stopped the Admiral with its nose against the right door of Batthyany Palace, and blew the horn. A moment later, one by one, the double doors opened. He drove through, and the doors closed after him.

Beatrice, Countess Batthyany and Baroness von Steighofen, was standing in a vestibule waiting for them. She was wearing a sable coat that reached nearly to her ankles and a matching sable hat under which a good deal of dark red hair was visible. Von Heurten-Mitnitz drove past her into a courtyard, turned around, and returned to the vestibule, where he stopped.

The Countess went to the rear door and pulled it open.

"I'm the Countess Batthyany," she said. "Won't you please come in?"

Professor Dyer and Gisella got out of the car and, following the direction indicated by the Countess's outstretched hand, walked into the building. The Countess turned to smile at Fulmar. "And you must be my dear cousin Eric," she said dryly. "How nice to finally meet you."

Fulmar laughed. "Hello," he said.

She turned to von Heurten-Mitnitz, who had walked around the front of the car.

"I see everything turned out all right," she said.

"The Gestapo man at the station personally led us past the checkpoint," he said.

"Oooh," she said. "I suppose you could use a drink."

"I could," Fulmar said.

She turned to look at him again.

"You look like Manny," she said. "You even sound like him. That terrible Hessian dialect."

He chuckled.

"Let's hope you are luckier," the Countess said as she started into the house.

"Let's hope there's some of his clothing here, and that it fits," Fulmar said. "Particularly shoes."

She turned and looked at him again, this time appraisingly.

"You're a little larger than Manny was," she said. "But there should be something. I gather you want to get out of that uniform?"

"They're looking for an Obersturmführer who looks like me," Fulmar said. "There was a Gestapo agent at the border who thought he had found him."

"That close?" she asked.

"I think it's been smoothed over," von Heurten-Mitnitz said. "It was close, but I think it . . . is smoothed over."

The Countess considered what he had said and nodded her head.

The Dyers, not knowing where to go and looking uncomfortable, waited for the others to catch up with them at the foot of what had been the servants' stairway to the first floor. The Countess went up ahead of them. They came out in the large, elegantly furnished sitting room overlooking the square.

Fulmar immediately sat down on a fragile-looking gilded wood Louis XIV sofa and began to pull his black leather boots off.

The Countess looked askance at him, but von Heurten-Mitnitz sensed there was something wrong.

"Something wrong with your feet?" he asked.

"The goddamned boots are four sizes too small," Fulmar said. "I soaked them with water, but it didn't help a whole hell of a lot."

When he had the boot off, he pulled a stocking off and, holding his foot in his lap, examined it carefully.

"Goddamn, look at that!" he said. The skin was rubbed raw and was bleeding in several places.

The Countess walked to the sofa, dropped to her knees, and took the foot in her hand.

"How did you manage to walk?" she asked.

"Why, cousin," Fulmar said, "I simply considered the alternative."

"You'll have to soak that in brine," she said. "It's the only thing that will help."

"By brine, you mean salt in water?" he asked, and she nodded.

"Before we do that, I would like a very large cognac," he said, and pulled off the other sock. The other foot was worse. The blood from the sore spots had flowed more copiously, and when it had dried, it had glued the sock to the wounds. He swore as he pulled the stocking off.

The Countess walked to a cabinet and returned with a large crystal brandy snifter.

"I'll heat some water," she said. "And make a brine."

"And pickle my feet," Fulmar said dryly. "Thank you, cousin, ever so much."

"Why do you call her 'cousin'?" Professor Dyer asked.

"We are, by marriage," the Countess said. "My late husband and Eric are, or were, cousins."

"Your late husband?" the professor asked.

"The professor tends to ask a lot of questions," Fulmar said mockingly.

"My late husband, Oberstleutnant Baron Manfried von Steighofen, fell for his fatherland on the eastern front," the Countess said dryly.

"And you're doing this?" the professor asked.

"It's one of the reasons I'm doing 'this,' my dear Herr Professor," the Countess said.

"And the other?" Fulmar asked.

"Is it important?"

"I'm curious," Fulmar said. "If I were in your shoes, I would be rooting for the Germans."

"If I thought they had a chance to win, I probably would be," she said matter-of-factly. "But they won't win. Which means that the Communists will come to Budapest. If they don't shoot me, I'll find myself walking the square outside asking strangers if they're looking for a good time."

"Beatrice!" von Heurten-Mitnitz exclaimed.

"Face facts, my dear Helmut," the Countess said.

"The flaw in your logic," Fulmar said, "is that you are helping the Russians to come here."

"In which case, I can only hope that you and Helmut will still be alive and in a position to tell the Commissar what a fearless anti-Fascist I was," she said. "There's a small chance that would keep them from shooting me out of hand." There was a moment's silence, and then she went on. "What I'm really hoping for is that there will be a coup d'état by people like Helmut against the Bavarian corporal, and in time for whoever takes over to sue for an armistice. If there's an armistice, perhaps I won't lose everything."

"Huh," Fulmar grunted.

"And what has motivated you, my dear Eric," the Countess said, "to do what you're doing?"

It was a moment before he replied. "Sometimes I really wonder," he said.

The Countess nodded, then turned to Gisella Dyer.

"Would you help me, please?" she said. "I made a gulyás, and if you would help serve it, I'll heat some water to 'pickle' Eric's feet."

The sting of the warm salt water on his feet was not as painful as Eric

Fulmar had expected, and he wondered if this was because he was partially anesthetized by the Countess's brandy, or whether his feet were beyond hurting.

The gulyás was delicious, and he decided that was because it was delicious and not because of the cognac—or because they'd had little to eat save lard and dark bread sandwiches since leaving Marburg an der Lahn.

Von Heurten-Mitnitz waited until they were finished and Fulmar was pouring a little brandy to improve his small, strong cup of coffee, and then he said:

"I think it would be best if I knew precisely what has happened since you entered Germany, Eric."

"A synopsis would be that everything that could go wrong, did," Fulmar said.

"What about the Gestapo agent? Did you have to kill him?"

"I killed him when he opened the luggage that had been left on the train for me," Fulmar said matter-of-factly, "and found the Obersturmführer's uniform. And then the boots didn't fit."

Von Heurten-Mitnitz nodded. "And in Marburg, was what happened there necessary?"

"Yes, of course it was," Fulmar said impatiently. "I don't like scrambling people's brains."

"You could learn some delicacy," the Countess said.

"We are not in a delicate business, cousin," Fulmar said.

"But that's it? There's nothing else I don't know about?" von Heurten-Mitnitz asked.

Fulmar's hesitation was obvious.

"What else?" von Heurten-Mitnitz persisted.

"I was recognized on the train," he said. "Before I got to Frankfurt. On the way to Marburg."

"By whom?"

There was another perceptible hesitation.

"Christ, I really hate to tell you," he said. "I don't want you playing games with her."

"I think I have to know," von Heurten-Mitnitz said.

"Fuck you," Fulmar said. "You have to know what I goddamn well decide to tell you."

Von Heurten-Mitnitz stiffened. He was not used to being talked to like that. But he kept control of himself.

"Someone you knew when you were at Marburg?" he asked reasonably. And then, when Fulmar remained silent, he added, "I don't want to sound melodramatic, but I will be here when you are safe in England."

"Tell him, Eric," the Countess said. "As you pointed out, we are not in a delicate business."

"I don't want you trying to use her, you understand me? Her, or her father."

"Who recognized you?" von Heurten-Mitnitz persisted, gently.

"Elizabeth von Handleman-Bitburg," Fulmar said.

Von Heurten-Mitnitz's eyebrows went up. The Countess looked at him with a question in her eyes.

"Generaloberst von Handleman-Bitburg's daughter?" von Heurten-Mitnitz asked.

Fulmar nodded.

"Possibly it's meaningless," von Heurten-Mitnitz said. "She met a young Obersturmführer whom she had once known. Was there any reason you think she was suspicious?"

"Her father had told her that I was seen in Morocco in an American uniform," Fulmar said. "She knew."

"And what do you think she will tell her father?" von Heurten-Mitnitz asked.

"Nothing," Fulmar said. "She won't tell him a thing."

"I wish I shared your confidence," von Heurten-Mitnitz said

"The only reason I'm telling you this," Fulmar said, "is that I don't want you to protect your ass by taking her out."

"Telling me what?"

"We spent the night together," Fulmar said. "Okay? Get the picture?"

"Yes, I think I do," von Heurten-Mitnitz said.

"If anything happens to her," Fulmar said, "I will—"

"Don't be childish," von Heurten-Mitnitz said.

"I was about to say something childish," Fulmar said. "Like I will come back here and kill you myself. But I won't have to do that. All I'll have to do is make sure the Sicherheitsdienst finds out about you."

"My God!" von Heurten-Mitnitz said.

"I made a mistake in telling you," Fulmar said.

"No, you didn't, Eric," the Countess said. She walked to von Heurten-Mitnitz and put her arm in his, then stood on her tiptoes and kissed his cheek. "Helmut understands that even in the midst of this insanity, people fall in love."

Fulmar looked through them, then chuckled.

"Well, I'll be goddamned," he said. "The Merry Widow in the flesh."